"Jane Kirkpatrick's riveting history of Emma Wagner Giesy holds up an antique mirror whereby we may regard ourselves today. Kirkpatrick's intuitive, effulgent prose leads us from our self-possessed age to the nineteenth century, where we participate through Emma in an emerging civilization. Kirkpatrick tears away the proscenium, allowing us to experience Emma's firm opinions, ravaging losses, fathomless grief. Emma's life teaches us that without community we lose synergy, love, protection—and perhaps even God. Yet without a strong sense of self, we have no convictions, no dreams—no *Sehnsucht* (to borrow Emma's word), and therefore, nothing to contribute. In seeing ourselves through this true, fictional rendering of a real life, perhaps we can find the courage to grow and the wisdom to learn."

—DOROTHY ALLRED SOLOMON, author of *In My Father's House;*
    Predators, Prey, and Other Kinfolk: Growing Up in Polygamy;
    Daughter of the Saints; and *Sisterhood*

"Once again Jane Kirkpatrick's attention to historic detail brings the hardscrabble existence of the Willapa Bay pioneers to life. In *A Tendering in the Storm,* Emma Wagner Giesy struggles with choices she makes in response to great tragedy. With rigid honesty, Kirkpatrick shows the consequences of these choices and how Emma regains her strength through love, trust, and sacrifice."

—KARLA K. NELSON, owner of Time Enough Books in Ilwaco,
    Washington

"The title *A Tendering in the Storm* keenly expresses the continuing story of the intrepid Emma Wagner Giesy as she struggles between the comfort and security of her religious community and self-reliance in the midst of tumult. Jane Kirkpatrick's impressive research on this true character reveals many realities of one woman's efforts to carve out a life for herself and her children on the burgeoning frontier of Washington Territory. In her engaging style rich with metaphor and imagery, the author explores issues still relevant in today's world: women's rights, child custody, property rights, domestic violence, and religious freedom. Bravo!"

—SUSAN G. BUTRUILLE, author of *Women's Voices from the Oregon Trail*
    and *Women's Voices from the Western Frontier*

A Tendering *in the* Storm

Books by Jane Kirkpatrick

Novels

A Land of Sheltered Promise

Change and Cherish Historical Series
A Clearing in the Wild
A Tendering in the Storm

Tender Ties Historical Series
A Name of Her Own
Every Fixed Star
Hold Tight the Thread

Kinship and Courage Historical Series
All Together in One Place
No Eye Can See
What Once We Loved

Dreamcatcher Collection
A Sweetness to the Soul
(winner of the Western Heritage Wrangler Award
for Outstanding Western Novel of 1995)
Love to Water My Soul
A Gathering of Finches
Mystic Sweet Communion

Nonfiction

Homestead: A Memoir of Modern Pioneers Pursuing the Edge of Possibility
A Simple Gift of Comfort (formerly *A Burden Shared*)

Anthologies

Daily Guideposts 1992
Storyteller Collection, Book 2
Crazy Woman Creek, "Women Rewrite the American West"

A Tendering in the Storm

a novel

JANE KIRKPATRICK

WaterBrook
PRESS

A Tendering in the Storm
Published by WaterBrook Press
12265 Oracle Boulevard, Suite 200
Colorado Springs, Colorado 80921
A division of Random House Inc.

Scripture quotations are taken from The Holy Bible, containing the Old and New
Testaments, translated out of The Original Tongues, and with the former translations
diligently compared and revised. New York: American Bible Society, 1858.

This book is a work of historical fiction based closely on real people and real events.
Details that cannot be historically verified are purely products of the author's imagination.

Grateful acknowledgment is made for the use of the Paul Johannes Tillich quote on page xiii.

ISBN 978-0-7394-8321-3

Printed in the United States of America

———

*To the descendants
of Emma Wagner Giesy.*

CAST OF CHARACTERS

AT WILLAPA BAY

Emma Wagner Giesy	German American living in Willapa Bay area of Washington Territory
Christian Giesy	Emma's husband and former leader of scouts
Andrew "Andy" *Catherina "Kate"* *Christian* *Ida*	Emma's children
Sebastian "Boshie" and Mary Giesy	one of Christian's brothers and his wife
Louisa Giesy	youngest sister of Christian, sixteen years old
Martin Giesy	a future pharmacist and one of Christian's brothers
John and Barbara Giesy	one of Christian's brothers and sister-in-law
Rudy, Henry, and Frederick Giesy	Christian's brothers
Andreas and Barbara Giesy	Christian's parents
Karl Ruge	German teacher, remained a Lutheran
Joe Knight	oysterman and former scout
Sam and Sarah Woodard	settlers at Woodard's landing
Jacob "Jack" or "Big Jack" Giesy	a distant cousin of Christian's
Wagonblast family	German Americans traveling to the Bay with Keil, not members of the colony

At Bethel

David and Catherina Zundel Wagner   Emma's parents

David Jr.   Emma's siblings
Catherine "Kitty"
Johanna
Louisa "Lou"
William

Andreas "Andrew" Giesy Jr.   one of Christian's brothers; physician and codirector of Bethel Colony in Keil's absence

August Keil   one of Wilhelm and Louisa Keil's sons, sent to assist with colony business

At Aurora Mills

Wilhelm Keil   leader of Aurora Mills, Oregon, Colony

Louisa Keil   Wilhelm's wife
Willie   their deceased son, buried in Willapa
Gloriunda   their daughter
Aurora   their daughter
Amelia   their daughter
five other Keil children

Jonathan Wagner   one of Emma's brothers
Helena Giesy   one of Christian's sisters
*Margaret   a woman of the colony
Nancy Thornton   painter in the Oregon City area

* not based on a historical character

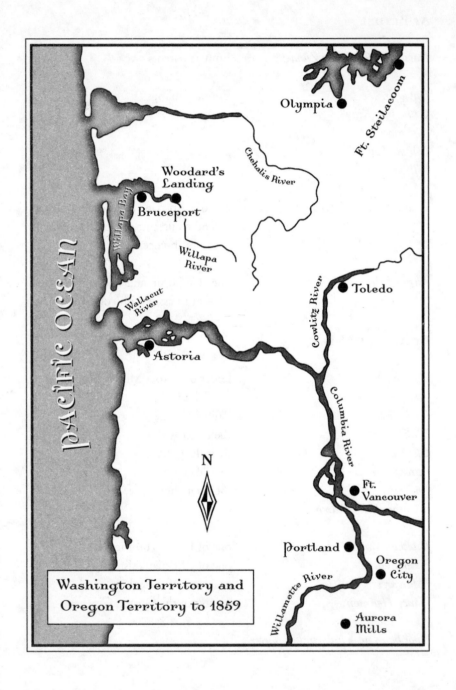

Pacific Ocean

Willapa Bay

Olympia

Ft. Steilacoom

Chehalis River

Woodard's Landing

Bruceport

Willapa River

Wallacut River

Cowlitz River

Toledo

Astoria

Columbia River

Ft. Vancouver

N

Portland

Oregon City

Willamette River

Aurora Mills

Washington Territory and
Oregon Territory to 1859

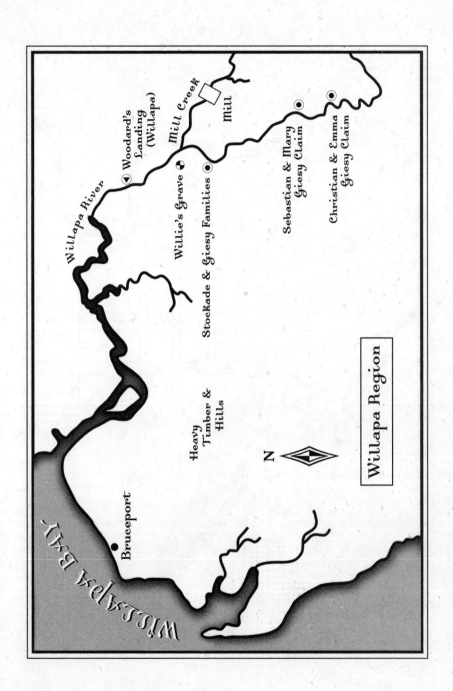

Willapa Bay

Willapa Region

N

Woodard's Landing (Willapa)

Willapa River

Mill Creek

Mill

Willie's Grave

Stockade & Giesy Families

Sebastian & Mary Giesy Claim

Christian & Emma Giesy Claim

Heavy Timber & Hills

Bruceport

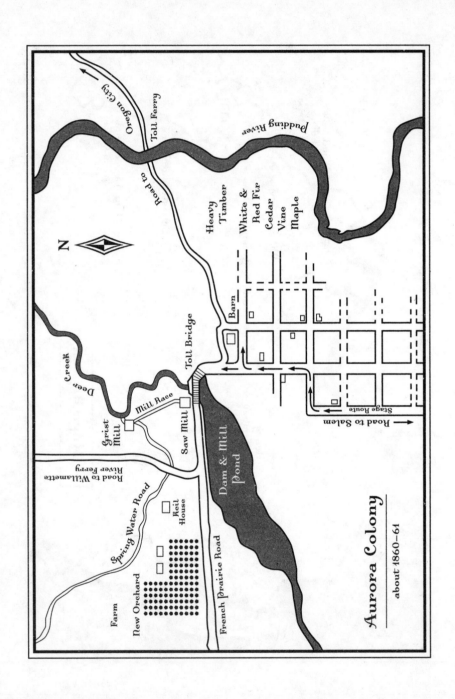

Aurora Colony

about 1860–61

We cannot kindle when we will
The fire that in the heart resides,
The spirit bloweth and is still,
In mystery our soul abides.
MATTHEW ARNOLD

Who is among you that feareth the LORD, that
obeyeth the voice of his servant, that walketh in
darkness, and hath no light? let him trust in the
name of the LORD.... Behold, all ye that kindle a
fire, that compass yourselves about with sparks:
walk in the light of your fire, and in the sparks
that ye have kindled. This shall ye have of mine
hand; ye shall lie down in sorrow.
ISAIAH 50:10–11

But if we walk in the light, as he is in the light,
we have fellowship one with another.
1 JOHN 1:7

Grace strikes us when we are in great pain and
restlessness. It strikes us when we walk through
the dark valley of a meaningless and empty life.
It strikes us when we feel that our separation is
deeper than usual.... Sometimes at that moment
a wave of light breaks into our darkness, and it is
as though a voice were saying: "You are accepted."
PAUL JOHANNES TILLICH
in *The Shaking of the Foundations*

Prologue

The light of the whale-oil lantern I hold above my head fans out across the darkened beach like the tail fins of a dog salmon. I can only see what the arc of light unveils; beyond, all is black. A tiny crab startles at my feet. Tree roots of once noble firs have fallen and been tossed against the shore like the sticks my Andy uses for his sword play. Their roots, like knurled knuckles, reach out to me, then disappear as I pass by them in the night. It's as though they seek me out of darkness. That's an illusion, for I move toward them carrying the lantern Christian made for me, and they lie there still but for the brush of salty breeze lifting sand against their barren roots. It's me who advances and then passes on by, darkness closing in behind me on the scent of loam and sea.

Though I cannot see the gentle waves pushing across the shoals on Willapa Bay, I know the tide line by the sound. I hear the lap of water and watch as some small bird flies through my arc of light. I know the sea is there and in the daylight I will find it once again, but it will look so different. This is the promise of a night walk on the beach, this, and that my light might shine upon some treasure, glass jars blown by hands and mouths a thousand miles away, arrived here whole, despite a shipwreck, glowing green beneath my fleeting light. I look for that. Something to remind me of the treasures of my days. Something to remember that is a joy instead of the times I stumbled in the blackness with no hand to catch me while I fell.

"Let me hold the lantern higher for you," my husband says. "I'm taller, Emma. Let me be Luke, Bearer of Light."

"*Ach,* no," I tell him. "I want to do it by myself, see what my light uncovers from the darkness."

"*Ja,* it's what you do, Emma." He spoke from the blackness behind me. "One day, I pray you won't."

We return to the tent and our sleeping children.

I lie down beside my husband, find comfort in his brackish scent, a blend of oystering and mustache oil and sweat. In our closeness, he gives to me without regard for what I might give him back. He offers without obligation, without debt. That is perhaps the greatest gift of love. In it lies sweet shelter.

1

Emma

The Image of a Hinge

A quiet surf oozed around our wooden shoes as we inhaled the salt and sea of Washington's Willapa Bay. Beyond swirled the Pacific. I pulled my skirt up between my legs and tucked the hem into the waistline of my Sunday apron.

After months of having our days and nights and futures directed by *Herr* Keil, formerly of Bethel, Missouri, and now of…somewhere far away, I found that his departure from Willapa left a tear in our family's fabric. That surprised me. I suppose when one devotes outrage and anger toward a person and then they leave, well, then one has pent-up steam to let off. We must find new things to fill the space, or so I told my husband.

That's what we'd done this spring of 1856 in Washington Territory.

"What do we do first?" I asked our partner, Joe Knight. Joe, a former religious scout, had spent a year already in Bruceport on the Bay finding out about how one nurtured and protected oysters from starfish or drills or human thieves.

"Begin to see with new eyes. There," Joe said. He pointed with his finger. "Those red alder saplings I placed in the water. That marks our bed." He looked down at my clog-clad feet and shook his head. "You need boots," he said. "And you'll need to study the mud and sand. As the tide goes out, the mud can suck a grown man right in if he's not careful. Someone as little as you are, or the children...*ja*, well, they could sink to Beijing." He grinned, and might've been teasing, but I stepped back, putting my feet on solid wet sand.

"*Nein,*" my husband told him. "She has no need of boots. She's going up the Willapa River where she'll be safe."

"I could learn oystering," I defended.

"Emma, you agreed to remain with my parents until we build our house," my husband, Christian Giesy, said. I stared at piles of oysters in the distant sea. They reminded me of cobbled dirt in dark fields back in Missouri. "Indeed, *Liebchen,* that was a primary condition of my considering the possibilities in oystering, that you and the children will be safe."

I pouted, dug at the sand with my toes. I could see Indian women separating oysters in culling beds. The green crown of leaves topping their alder stakes fluttered in the breeze. It was May and no one was allowed to harvest again until September, but clumps of oysters still had to be broken apart so they could grow larger, stronger. "I just thought I could help," I said.

"You want to avoid living with my parents," he told me. *He knows me so well.*

Joe interjected then with oyster talk. The salty air brushed against my face as I listened, still holding my Kate. Our two-year-old Andy slapped at shoalwater pools with his hand and looked so sweet. "His hand is already tan as walnuts," Christian said, when I pointed with my chin toward our son. "Same color as your eyes and your hair. I'll miss seeing those every day."

"*Ja,* me too."

Joe cleared his throat. He spoke mostly English now, having learned it from his time in San Francisco. My husband bent his head to catch Joe's words over the loud calling of the seagulls fighting over clams or waiting for us to throw dried bread up to them.

"Charlie?" Andy pointed. I shook my head.

"During spawning," Joe continued, "the water'll be milky with the eggs and sperm of oyster beds. They're a saucy creature, they are." He looked at me, and I thought he blushed.

I surely didn't. These were necessary discussions of the natural way of things. Why was a woman expected to be protected from the lusts of life?

Herr Keil, our *former* religious leader, came to mind. In spite of his own prolific family-building—he had several children—he advised lives of celibacy for the rest of us. This complicated, I thought, his view that women are saved from damnation only when they bear children and have to endure the pain of Eve's sin. I doubted he'd thought of that contradiction as yet.

Ach, I must not let every thought come back to Keil!

I took a deep breath that pushed against my Kate. I rested my chin lightly on her bonneted head and watched an old woman scrub at the mud of an oyster in her lap. She wore a scarf around her full brown face that marked her as a Chinook or Shoalwater or even a Chehalis native. Something in the way she held herself promised strength if not wisdom too. Both were necessary to survive on this Bay.

Andy squatted at the tide pool, pulled at a starfish. He laughed as he plopped back onto the mud.

"There are four tides a day on this Pacific," Joe said. "Our work is dependent on being out there on the flats when the tide goes out and exposes the oysters. We break up the clusters. If there's an oyster ship awaiting, we pick the larger ones, toss them into baskets or bags and sail them out, and we've earned our wages. There are more oysters out farther, have to reach them by boat and bring them in closer to seed our beds. In the winter, you'll be working in darkness, so you best get that lantern of yours ready."

"Indeed," Christian said. "I've been meaning to make a tin cover for Emma's lamp, one where the wind can't ever blow out the light." He smiled at me, then brushed a wayward hair strand beneath my bonnet. Both the act and the look he gave me told me I was cherished.

I wanted to live with them in Bruceport, though it would mean close quarters along the beachfront, huddled in huts made of driftwood or maybe out on stilts built over the oyster beds. But I could cook for Joe and Christian and the children. Our family would be together. That's what I wanted.

But I had compromised. Anything to avoid going to Oregon with *Herr* Keil. I'd agreed to stay with the children miles away with the remainder of Christian's kin and the scouts. My in-laws would "look after me," as Christian put it. One day on the Willapa River, once we built it, I'd have a home to call our own. This was my desire, a home without a dozen other people in it. A dwelling, safe, filled with my family and only the things I treasured, safe from others telling us what to do or think.

"Best you ready yourself for the boat," Christian told us. Andy began dragging a very long, double fork–like tool, scraping it across the beach as though it were a boat in tow. Christian lifted it from him and the tongs stood on end at least two times the height of my husband, who was over six feet tall. The tool had a hinge to open the two forks.

"Works like a pincher, *ja?*" Joe said, as he reached with his thumb and middle finger to pretend to pinch at Andy's nose. My son giggled. "You'll get skilled enough using those tongs, Christian," Joe said. "As I steer our oyster boat, you'll stand on the bow and with the tongs feel the bottom like you were searching for treasure. When you feel a clump, you close the hinge and pull them up and drop them in the basket in the boat."

Christian tried to open and close the long oyster tongs. "Like fishing in the dark," Christian said. He was awkward on land, and both he and Joe laughed.

"It'll come to you in time," Joe said. "Worst part will be learning to stand on the bow without slipping yourself into the Bay, though a salty bath will wake you up."

"Perhaps I should learn how to swim," Christian said. Joe hesitated but then chuckled, clapping Christian on the back.

"That's a good one," Joe said. "*Ja,* that's a good one."

I'd remember that day later, hold it to me like a hug that time permits to bring one warmth. My husband and I began a new adventure, one not sanctioned by the infamous *Herr* Keil. The tools of our new trade were long tongs and sailboats. It was a new way of tendering through life's storms, and I was hopeful despite my disappointment.

———

"We've weathered the biggest storm of 1856," Christian told me as we walked back toward the shoreline. His arm wrapped around me while tidewater unveiled its treasures. Wet sand clung to our wooden shoes. Our son chased after quick-footed birds. A skiff of wind lifted our son's little flat hat, and Christian took two steps in his brogans to retrieve it. "I'm not a rich oysterman yet, *Junge*," he told Andy, tapping the hat onto his head. "So hold on to this."

My husband's reference to the storm referred not to the great western winds that blustered in off the Pacific Ocean and toppled trees, leaving them crisscrossed on the forest floor. My Swiss-born husband wasn't even talking about the martial law imposed in the Territory by Governor Stevens, meant to protect us from the Indians. No, my husband referred to the turbulence that brewed and bubbled then settled after it tore our colony of Christian believers in two and nearly splintered our marriage as well. It was the "bread of adversity" and "the water of affliction" as Scripture notes it that Christian and I, Emma Wagner Giesy, his wife, had weathered.

My husband, a tall man (I barely reached his chest) with a compassionate heart, once shared in the leadership of our colony of one thousand Missouri Bethelites who planned to move the settlement to the Washington Territory. Instead, earlier this spring we severed our relationship with the mostly German members of the Bethel colony who ventured west. The former scouts and many of my husband's fourteen brothers and sisters and their families stayed here. After our terrible winter when Keil refused us the use of ammunition to hunt, wanting it saved for "protection," Keil ordered many of the colonists not to come north from Portland. So I never even saw my brother, though he rode in Keil's wagon train. Keil barked his orders and the colony split. It was like chopping willows at the root base.

A few noncolonists chose to settle in our Willapa Hills and Valley. A family named Wagonblast had joined up with Keil at St. Joseph, Missouri, and remained at the Willapa, their young children right now probably playing jack stones, oblivious to the anxieties of their elders. Karl Ruge, an old teacher who'd been faithful to *Herr* Keil though he remained a Lutheran, stayed. I was glad for it. I found comfort watching Karl smoke his three-foot-long clay pipe with its wide bowl that curved up like an elbow. The smoke swirled around his stringy beard, lifting like mist to the cedars above. Karl loved words and read books without apologizing, so at the very least, our children would have an education beyond *Herr* Keil's Bible or teaching of practical things, "useful reading" Keil called it. Karl's presence gave me reason to hope such education would include my daughter Kate one day, and not only my son. Without the colony rules to shape us, everything would be new. Or so I hoped.

One other Giesy named Big Jack, a distant cousin of my husband's, traveled around the Isthmus of Panama to settle here too, where the timber towers and the blackberry brush tangles. Big Jack chose the Giesy name, I'm told, to start anew. His arrival in Willapa caused a storm. But that's a story better left for later.

I loaded the children onto the mail boat going upriver with the incoming tide. We'd been apart before in our marriage, when my husband recruited for new colony members. But I'd grown accustomed to his snores, his pushing-ups each morning, his mustache-covered kisses smelling of earth and onion every day, and I would miss him. *Keil is the fault of all this separation.* Ach! *My life must not always come back to Keil.*

But perhaps once one has given their all, foolishly even, as *Herr* Keil would put it, to a grand dream, then abandoning what we'd done here and turning back would be...a violation of that pioneering spirit. To "listen to reason," as our colony leader said, and follow him to Oregon would remind us always of the months and years we put into readying this place for others, believing we were in the palm of God's hand. To leave would make us ever regretful. Or so we told ourselves that spring.

It takes time for the mind to swing upon a different hinge.

We're a hopeful people, we Swiss and Germans, and faithful and perhaps dreamers too, or we never would have journeyed west at all. We heeded the *Sehnsucht,* that great yearning, rather than remain in the warmth of our brick Bethel houses with readied fireplaces and streets with sturdy names like King and Elm. We gave up living close to bustling cities like Hannibal and Independence. Instead, we live isolated—fifteen river miles from the vast Pacific Ocean.

It was my plan that convinced my husband to try oystering. It was a kind of farming, though of the sea instead of land. Farming was something we knew about. Christian had been a tinsmith and recruiter, but in the colony we all set aside our various tasks to help with planting or weeding or harvest. We knew that farming required focus and effort. Risk pervaded farming, too, but with many hands helping, we could bring in a good harvest if the locusts or hailstorms didn't get it first. But in Bethel, even if we lost the harvest or it was poor, we would still be fed. For whatever anyone earned making gloves or wagons or cloth or preserves went into a common fund. Then whatever we needed we were allowed to take out. We cared for others, served up the Diamond Rule, making others' lives better than our own. But we owned not a thing in our names. It was all in Keil's name. I think that's one of the things that turned Keil off of Willapa: he wanted all land to be his.

Here, because of donation land claims, Christian and I had land in our names, as did his parents and brothers. But we didn't have the security that if a crop failed we might still eat, unless we leaned on our neighbors or found some other way to live.

Our leader said we'd made him broke almost, buying up land claims when we could have gotten free land in a more forgiving landscape. Worse, he claimed we'd been unfaithful, hadn't listened to the calling of our God, and that was why we'd had such a trial here attempting to build our homes, clear ground, survive the wailing winters.

I think that hurt my husband most, the suggestion that his faith wasn't strong enough to stave off suffering and loss. I remembered once Keil saying Brother John Will back in Bethel lacked faith enough for Keil to heal his tailor's arm. In the church, Keil upbraided him for this weakness. That very day, Brother Will hanged himself for failing Keil, and our leader chastised him even then, saying his arm could not sew but it could work well enough to bring on his death. I feared such might happen to my husband if we had stayed in the shadow of Keil.

We'd been sent to find a place of isolation so that our children would not be influenced by the outside un-Christian world; to find timber and a place where one could sell our produce, our furniture, our milk and cheese, and our wagons to others as we had in Bethel. Our choices required a delicate balance, weighing safety and isolation with survival and success through commerce with the outside world.

I'd found my place in this Willapa country. I recognized wild celery now and knew how to prepare it. I located *wapato,* Indian potatoes, and knew how to cook them. While at the beach, I watched as the Shoalwater people collected clams, raking at the sandy dimples that signaled a clam's presence. They dug pits and heated stones until the rocks glowed, then laid the clams on top of the stones, covered them with mats of weeds and grass, and watched the steam as the clam juice filtered down onto the hot rocks, the sizzle offering up a scent like the blacksmith's cooling of hot iron.

My friend Sarah Woodard, who lived with her husband at the landing, showed me how to strip wild raspberry roots to find that center as tender and tasty as a cucumber. We learned much from those outsiders, if we listened, watched. Keil didn't see this. He let the light of insight illuminate few of his dark thoughts.

Perhaps that's why in the end my husband agreed to try oystering. We hoped to prove that challenges are not necessarily God's punishment for disobedience. They do not mean one has erred. If we forge ahead, we'll still find blessings and new paths. That's what I told myself as I waved good-bye to him that day.

———

As I write this, years later, my youngest daughter, Ida, works at her school books. She asks me to explain the word *hinge,* using English. I'm not sure when she decided to speak just English, but it pleases me as a mark of her independence. I press my hand upon the circle of braids she wears at the top of her head and inhale the sweetness of her. I tell her first that a hinge is the thing that keeps the two sides of the oyster shell together, so what is inside may stay alive. She frowns. "It's the little piece of flesh that opens and closes, allowing the two sides to be a whole." Then I show her the top of Christian's lantern, how the hinge lets it open and close. She nods, returns to her writing, leaving me to ponder still.

A hinge is so much more. It divides two sides of a story. It is what separates mourning from joy, belief from aimlessness, surrender from independence. It's what holds those halves together. "A hinge is a circumstance upon which later events depend," I add, more for me than for Ida. Who could have known that day on the river how I'd soon long for the hinge of faith, and with it the hope that I'd once again find home.

2

Louisa

Before my husband received the call to prepare him to sit at the right hand of Jesus, he was a tailor.

It's fitting he was such, for tailors create and re-create. They stitch and mend and realign, ever mindful of the cloth, the thread, and the person who will wear the mantle on the body God prepared. Oh, I know my husband, Wilhelm Keil, does not truly create as God does. But God works through him, and he comes as close to our brother Jesus as any man can and still have his feet upon this earth. He chose me as his wife, kissed the part in my dark hair, never mentioned the tiny mole at the side of my face that I saw as imperfection. He chose me to be the mother of his children, and I am blessed to be his handmaiden. Well, hand*matron* I suppose I should say, though not to Dr. Keil, who might object to such musings on my use of words. It's why I write in this private little book the thoughts I'd not share with him.

Dr. Keil must not be distracted. We need his wisdom and his visionary sight. Our journey west from Bethel was a quilt requiring many stitches to hold it all together, and we're still sewing. He'll use whatever he must to be successful and to carry out his belief in what he is called to do.

Some years back, when he dabbled in the mystical, he wrote his formulas for healing in a book. He used his blood for ink. I did not know of this when I met him. A wife is not privy to a saint's workings, nor should she be.

Emma Giesy might take note of that. She's one who wants to know her husband's thoughts, and while her husband is not the leader that mine is, she will be challenged in how to be a good wife to one who is a lieutenant in God's army. What such leaders share with their wives are gifts we cannot ask for, nor do we deserve them when they arrive. We're to treat such secrets as fragile porcelain easily crushed. But my husband told me of that blood-lined book when he burned it and found his true calling in gathering disciples to him to live communally, each according to his need, each according to his gifts so all are loved and served as the book of Acts advises.

I write these words not in blood but blackberry-juice ink.

He receives no pay, my husband. In Pennsylvania, he once led a group of followers away from the American Methodist Evangelical Church when he learned they intended to pay their pastor four hundred dollars in annual wages. "Four hundred dollars!" he raged, and rightly so. No one should receive a salary for doing the Lord's work. God provides, for heaven's sake. The products of our hands and fields will fill the common purse, but this is the outcome of doing the Lord's work, and pay enough.

That's why we sell whiskey.

Yet he works so hard, has such responsibility for this flock now spread across two thousand miles from that desolate Willapa Valley to here in Portland, Oregon, and back to Bethel. We still have friends in Pennsylvania—Phillipsburg and Harmony—though my husband is no longer considered the head of those colonies, just the one in Bethel. Nearly one thousand people rely on his leadership and guidance. Only a quarter of us headed west last year. This was wise in retrospect as what awaited us was troublesome indeed. Still, the lack of full compliment worried my husband, I could tell. He mentioned often those left behind. Everyone wanted to come, he told me, but some had to be left behind to run the businesses until we are established here in the West. Andrew Giesy, Christian's brother, is a trustworthy man. He stayed behind to lead at Dr. Keil's request.

Others have waited to leave Bethel only because they want to come to a settled place. "Such little faith," my husband says. But I tell him, "It is evidence that we have too long been influenced by the world." We do need to find an isolated place where we can live without so many worldly things to compare ourselves with. To some, even among the Bethelites, we appear to lack, and yet we had sturdy homes, food enough for all, help when needed, and opportunity to work at many tasks, all in service to each other and our Lord.

But I've spied magazines with drawings of women wearing huge hats, the cost of which could feed a family for a week. I see them now on women who ride past in primitive carriages on the muddy streets of Portland. I watched when men rode into our old Bethel to buy up wagons, smoking their cigars. I do not mind the smoking. Tobacco comes from the land, so it is a gift from God. But their vests were draped with gold chains and watches they look at just for show as they stayed overlong, bothering the workers with their many questions, filling their heads with thoughts of fine horses and money for themselves. They don't watch the time. They take our men and women from their labors, so they do not seem to need their watches.

Yes, going west was good. The discussions before leaving energized the old and encouraged the young. I only wished we had all come. I miss David and Catherina Wagner and others whom I've served meals with at the *gross Haus,* our Elim. Such a lovely house. The Wagners sent their oldest son, and this was good. And they sent their daughter Emma, though I suspect that was a relief. She has such a willful way about her. She never would wear her hair with the part down the middle as I do, as most matrons of the colony who understand their place do.

What happened there in Willapa did nothing to change my mind about that woman's passion to be different. Christian Giesy is a good man, though I worried about his possible distraction with a young and spirited wife so close. My worries were well founded. They remain at Willapa, for now, which presents new challenges for my husband, all because the scouts did not do proper work. Or perhaps were all distracted by that Emma.

We sold colony property to raise funds for the journey west. My Willie and Jonathan Wagner prattled on at length about this grand adventure. Eighteen our Willie was when he died, and we carried him across the continent to bury him in Willapa, kept inside our Golden Rule Whiskey and lead-lined coffin. Friends suggested we make a barrel to place him in, but my husband insisted on the proper coffin.

To lose a child, well, what can be said to help a grieving mother? Willie longed for newness and change and so he has it now. I do not think this is anti-scriptural. After all, we went west at my husband's insistence, so it must be scriptural to make change.

I suppose Dr. Keil is not really the Lord's true brother, or else he'd be able to read my thoughts and know that I worry for our children's safety as we huddle in this thin wooden house in Portland in the Oregon Territory. I worry for my own safety too, and most of all for my husband. It is what a wife should do.

I miss Bethel but this is something I would never tell my husband. He has enough to worry over. Each day consists of his tending. His secretary, Karl Ruge, decided to remain at Willapa, an ache in my husband's side, of this I'm certain. There'll be few letters going back east now, at least until we have something more hopeful to say.

I must not let him think I feel hopeless, but I do. My son is dead. I live in someone else's house in a strange city where the smell of horse dung overpowers that of spring flowers. My children are hungry and must wait until the end of the day to see if someone in this West Coast Portland will pay me for my washing of their clothes, and then pay me correctly since I speak no English and wouldn't know. Or we wait to see if an ill person will feel well enough to pay Dr. Keil in grain or rubbery vegetables for his herbal treatments. He is such a wise and loving man and feels great weight that he could not rescue our son Willie from malaria. Now, I have little hope of even visiting his grave since we have separated from those at Willapa. I can only hope that maybe Christian's mother or John's wife will keep the grave up. I doubt Emma would even think of such a kindness.

Oh, I mustn't malign her. That's un-Christian of me. She has her own cross to bear with that willfulness of hers.

While I scrub on the washboard, I remember Willie. He was to ride in an ambulance on a small cot for comfort, and thus we planned to walk beside him. That's what *comfort* means in Greek, my husband tells me, "to come along beside."

Willie begged us not to leave him behind. He could have stayed with the Wagners or a dozen other families and come with the group Dr. Keil hopes will come next year, when we are ready for them. Much depended on Christian's successes at Willapa and the returning scouts were all hopeful. So much timber, they said. We could have a mill in no time and sell the lumber easily.

I directed my daughter Amelia about which quilts to take, how to wrap some of our precious things like dishes in the flour barrels. They weren't fancy dishes. We kept a separate barrel for Dr. Keil's glass cups in which he mixes herbs. Gloriunda and Louisa, my namesake—well, a portion of my namesake—brought clothes to show me and I'd nod, leave or take. My parents named me Dorothea Elizabeth Louisa Ritter, but Dr. Keil preferred Louisa and so that's what I'm called, my daughter too, for the Prussian queen, our beloved queen.

There was so much to sort through. It's all still packed in barrels. We're still not home.

"God heals," Dr. Keil says. I know that is so. Didn't my husband heal me of a weak leg? I limp some, but the leg is healed. My faith was enough to heal. I didn't want to remember Brother Will's death.

One never knows how another will respond to such deep and separating grief even when one has lived with the other for more than twenty years. My husband believes that deaths of children are a mark of sinfulness of the par-

ent. My heart pounded at Willie's deathbed while I waited for Dr. Keil to
turn to me and ask, "What have you done?"

Those were God's very words to Eve.

I'd heard my husband ask a grieving mother this; listened while a father
wept in search of what sins he'd committed that had fallen onto his own flesh
and blood. My husband would take those parents in his wide arms, both
pulled into his woolen vest, and beg God's forgiveness for what neither of
them could name. And they would go away, those parents, adding guilt to
grief. They never heard a sermon letting them believe that God's lap was large
enough to take them in, sin and all, and give them rest. My husband never
failed those parents, exactly. He didn't continue to rail against their sinful
ways, but he did agitate them, I believe, especially when they could never
find the cause, or when they had trouble imagining a God who would pun-
ish an innocent over the foul acts of the innocent's elders.

I'd done nothing wrong, nothing I could remember. My husband was
perfect, called so by God to lead us all. So where did that leave us with this
gaping hole of pain that had once been a mother's heart meant to love a son?
Dr. Keil says there can be no pain without sin, no suffering without evil.

With Willie's death, I prayed that Dr. Keil would find another way to
hear the Word, some other understanding than that if a child dies it is because a parent sinned. I wanted my grief and Willie's death to lessen another
mother's pain, not add to it.

I waited for his charge, but none came. He shook his head as though he
couldn't understand it. I could. Life and death are tethered together. That I
understood didn't mean I wished it wasn't so.

All that was one year past. I spent the anniversary of my son's death scrubbing clothes of people I didn't know. I wanted someone to talk to, to share
my grieving with, but Dr. Keil did not speak of Willie once we buried him at

Willapa. It's not good for a mother to weigh her daughters down with her grief. And so I held it to myself, wondering if the time would come when we'd be living closely again with other colony members, close enough that we shared our meals, and expressions of grief could be shown in between the slicing of potatoes and the serving of our men.

"Ah, Emma," I said out loud, "I hope you're strong."

The thought surprised.

It is time I stopped my writing in this diary and look instead to the comfort of my children and their father. Tending to each other is how we'll all survive. Dr. Keil has found a site not far from Portland where he says we will eventually move, all of us, even those in Willapa. He calls it Aurora Mills, for our daughter. I want to celebrate my lovely, patient, faithful daughter's having a town named for her, such a sign of fatherly affection. But I feel a mother's regret for her too. There is much weight carried in a name. If things do not succeed, well, she will bear that weight.

Ah, these are unfaithful thoughts. Of course Aurora Mills will succeed. It is my husband's following of God's plan. It must succeed: my daughter's name is attached to it.

Still, if it does not, I'll tell my child that perhaps the town was named "Aurora" not so much for her but for the Latin word for *dawn*. There is always dawn even after the darkest nights.

3

Emma

No Sin to Stand Out

Christian's brothers, my brothers-in-law, were known to be good thinkers, hard workers, men who contributed well to the coffers of the common fund. Martin, with a penchant for healing herbs (not unlike our *Herr* Keil), lived with his parents along with Christian's sister, another Louisa, so my children and I got to know them best as that's where we boarded. The Wagonblasts without relatives here felt a bit lost. They left in the summer. I didn't know where they went.

Rudy and Henry came up from Portland next, staying with Mary and Sebastian (whom my son called Uncle Boshie) though the bachelors intended on building their own house. The brothers might have stayed with Christian's parents, but I was there. Associating with me, I suspected, was like spitting on the spider when it was still hot: people wanted to avoid the spray.

I hoped they'd work on our home but instead they began to build the mill along a little creek that flowed into the Willapa not far from the claim Christian and I had purchased.

Building the mill was quite an event. They split spruce for the walls and floors but ordered lumber for the second story and bins from a kind of tree called redwood that came all the way from California. John Giesy said the redwood formed ships' ballasts and would last forever and resist insects. My in-laws had brought the grist stones from Missouri and left them in San

Francisco, so a contingent sailed south in the summer to bring them north to install them in the mill. Boshie named the tributary Mill Creek, of course, though I was always partial to wondering what the natives might have called it. Names of places are important, I always thought, and *Mill Creek* lacks the particularity of a stream like the *Cowlitz*. Christian couldn't help much as he was busy oystering, but even Karl Ruge, the old teacher, augured holes for the pegs to keep the floor notched in place.

The mill rose up out of the blackberries and willows, topped the trees near the river, then formed a peaked roof with a window at the top. What a view there'd be from the mill. While I chomped at my bit so our house could be built, I knew that the community needed the mill, and I was pleased at least to be a part of the venture, offering my *Strudels* and *wapato* dishes to keep the men fed.

My brother Jonathan did not come to help with the mill, not even for a visit. Nor did Christian's distant relation Jack, who'd headed for Portland within days after his arrival. I'd have nothing to tell my sister Catherine about him the next time I wrote. I was not sure where her curiosity about this Giesy cousin grew from, but each letter from her asked if I had seen him. He was much too old for Catherine. The Giesy brothers said Jonathan and Big Jack were busy helping to build at Aurora and making cider vinegar. *Herr* Keil already had an industry going from those bushels of apples he'd purchased. He turned the skins into cider to sell back to the Willamette Valley settlers for twice what he'd paid them for the apples. *Shrewd* would be a word for him. Christian would say *inventive*.

Martin brought a comfort, though. My own supply of herbs had been used up the past two winters, and Martin shared his with me. I was grateful for the tansy that we hung near the food to keep the flies away. We spread some on the floor, too, and I think it kept out spiders, at least a bit. Martin didn't speak much to me, but he had Christian's gentle ways. He'd step aside if I came through the small room carrying Kate and even picked up the tin plates after a meal, washing them in the bucket—what they call pails here in the west—as though it wasn't a woman's task at all.

Karl Ruge and Mary Giesy and some of the others met on a clear Sunday morning at the stockade after the mill was finished. John Giesy said we'd use the stockade for a school too, but this day Karl read from Scripture mentioning the word *Andrew,* and my little Andy perked up at the sound of his name. It was a good gathering time of worship and expressions of gratitude. I missed Christian most during these times. I could always stare at him on the men's side if the messages bored. His absence made me impatient for his presence.

Afterward, we sat in the shade watching while the men took turns splitting cedar bark into shingles we'd use to roof our houses and replace those leaking canvas tarps.

"Keil's not building his house yet in Aurora," Rudy told us. "He sent a dozen men and one woman to cook for them out to Aurora Mills, but that *gross Haus* will be temporary. It'll be big and the bachelors and some of the families can come out and start laying up houses on the property. Get a store going so we can bring neighbors in to sell to them and meet our own needs too."

One woman. I wondered who she was and whether, like me, Keil had sent her out as punishment for being independent, though I turned that into triumph.

"Doesn't he fear people will want to stay in Portland, maybe not follow him to Aurora?" I asked.

"*Nein,*" Rudy said. He stopped to wipe his brow of sweat. Karl Ruge motioned for the frow, offering to give Rudy a break, but John Stauffer, one of the scouts, stepped in to spell him. I handed Rudy a tin of water. He drank his fill.

"*Ja,* he waits until he has his usual comforts, I suppose," I said under my breath. Then louder, "He wouldn't want to be there to encourage the flock or gain an understanding of the time and effort that such building of a community takes. It might change his mind about building a colony from scratch."

"*Ach,* don't talk so dumb," my father-in-law told me. His words stung. "He knows about building up colonies from Pennsylvania to Missouri and now here."

"Not here," I said.

"He went to Aurora Mills for the Fourth of July celebration," Rudy noted. "Most everyone from Bethel traveled out from Portland to see where one day soon they'd be living. Our band played." He said "our band" as though we were still a part of it. "They had good food and dancing. A hearty time."

I felt a pang of something. Regret?

"Next year we'll have such a celebration here," I said. "With steaming *wapato* mixed with herbs."

"There were speeches, too," Frederick told us, "about the candidates for the presidential election and the locals, too." I'd forgotten there was to be an election, even one in this Territory too, I supposed, though I didn't know who might challenge whom. I wondered what Christian thought about the candidates. Martin added that the group learned news of a man named John Brown and a war that people called "Bleeding Kansas" and the repeal of our Missouri Compromise, meaning slaves' lives were still in peril.

Martin spoke as though he didn't want to upstage his older brothers. "It was good we left Missouri. Things will get worse there."

"Not so sobering now, Martin. Talk about the good things," Rudy said.

"Like my John being named school superintendent," my sister-in-law cooed. I didn't even realize there'd been an election for that.

"*Ja, ja,*" Henry said. "Or that Christian has been named a territorial marshal. From all that fuss in the stockade, we hear."

"He earned top votes as the territorial representative, too," John said. "Twenty-two votes."

This was news to me too, that Christian had been given some sort of commission, an important job in the Territory, been elected a representative, and I'd known nothing about it. He'd been named a justice of the peace the first months after we were in Willapa and even made Sarah and Sam Woodard's common-law marriage official, but at least he'd told me about that.

"When did—"

"It was a festive time, that Fourth of July." Rudy said, taking the topic elsewhere. He laughed with a high-pitched giggle and began rocking back and forth on the balls of his feet in preparation for a story. "That Big Jack," he shook his head as though indulging a teasing toddler, "he gets himself some fireworks, *ja?* We don't any of us know where he got them, but he sets the fireworks up behind the privy and waits. He might have had a pint or two of our whiskey behind there with him, you know Jack. Well, he peeks around and sees one of the girls go inside. He lets her settle down like a hen on her nest, and then he counts and sets the flame. What an explosion! It nearly caught the grass on fire, and it sent all the blackbirds in the oak tree flying up in a squawking haunt. Such a laugh we got from that: the noise, the birds, the girl squealing." He shook his head, still smiling. "And then her charging like a bull through the door with her drawers lassoed around her ankles so tight she fell on her face." He slapped his knee with glee.

"That doesn't sound very funny to me," I said. I held a yarn ball for Kate to grab for as she sat on my lap.

"Big Jack didn't think it was funny neither, because he got tangled up in some blackberry vines trying to come out and watch what was happening. He ended up stuck behind the privy and never even saw the fuss. He just doesn't always think things through, that Jack. And she wasn't that hurt, Emma." Rudy chuckled, then took the frow back from John. I watched my mother-in-law shake her head with a smile on her face.

"Well I hope she was all right," Mary said.

"Martin gave her some bee balm tea to relieve her nausea—"

"And her flatulence," Rudy joked.

Henry ignored his brother's interruption. "And the borage compress Dr. Kiel made for her relieved the swelling on her chin."

"Lucky she didn't have her tongue between her teeth when she fell," Rudy said. "She'd have ended up as the silent Schwader girl!"

"At least she has teeth. Those apples Keil bought helps with that." Henry wiggled what looked like a loose tooth.

"And Dr. Keil was there to fix things," Martin said. "He's a great, good man whose timing is divinely apportioned."

Divinely apportioned? Martin's declaration of adoration of Keil made me look twice at him. Maybe Big Jack wasn't the only Giesy who just didn't always think things through.

———

That autumn, we harvested the oats we'd planted. We winnowed the grain, then took the heads by mule to the mill, where Boshie ground it. Our first. Our own. We'd have to buy our wheat, though. The climate proved too cool too long to place our hope in raising wheat. Sarah said it rained ninety inches a year here. I couldn't imagine that was true. Still, it was strange to have grown our own sustaining food in Missouri. Not here. Oats might do. Maybe millet.

The men hunted together and we smoked venison and bear meat and salmon filleted on sticks the way we'd seen the Indians do it, but we did it on our own, all of it.

I suppose it's somewhat prideful to be always touting doing things without the help of others, but when one has been under the thumb of a leader strong as an oak but just as unbending, it's difficult to resist the celebration of what we accomplished without him. I couldn't remind Mary and the others enough that here we surrendered to no one.

Sometimes, when I heard the *we* and *us* of the Giesy brothers and his father talking about Keil's colony, I did wonder if they saw the colony as "separated" in the way I did. I kept my tongue quiet. I wished to avoid arguments while I lived under their roof. The Giesys, too, tended to ignore me unless I asked a direct question, even when we were gathered together for family meals. They weren't unkind, really. They treated women and children as grass beside a main trail; sometimes it got stepped on, but it didn't really matter to the journey.

Except where our oystering was concerned. My in-laws had strong opinions about that and expressed them. "Christian would do well to come back here and prepare his house and farm," my father-in-law intoned over gravy and beans, "instead of playing with the oysters. He receives a payment now, for his marshalling. He'll need to know what's happening here to best represent us in the territorial legislature. How can he meet those obligations while he is busy playing at sea farming?"

"Karl Ruge thought it a good idea," I defended. I stitched in the candlelight, kept my eyes to my work. "And this way he'll represent not just us Germans but others, too, when the legislature is in session." My husband was seen as a leader by those outside of the colony. Another reason for *Herr* Keil to want us to come back under his wing, no doubt.

"We Giesys belong to the soil."

"When was Christian named the marshal?" I asked.

"I'm surprised he didn't tell you," my mother-in-law said. "It was during the Indian scare, before we got here."

"Maybe he didn't tell me because he felt embarrassed that he was a marshal with a gun but not allowed to use it, not even for hunting," I said. "*Herr* Keil acted like the marshal."

"Christian has nothing to be ashamed of," my father-in-law said. His tone left no room for my reply that I hadn't said Christian should be ashamed at all, just embarrassed. Maybe to this family these were one and the same.

I looked over at Andy and wondered if as young as he was, he could sense the disapproval in his grandfather's voice.

"Oystering gives my husband a new pearl to seek," I said.

"A pearl he would not be looking for without the influence of his wife, *ja?*" I knew he meant it as an insult but that isn't how I took it.

———

Even though my children and I stayed in the Giesy Place—what had once been the meager home Christian and I shared—and daily took tea with my in-laws and sewed while Andreas read the Bible each evening, we talked very little toward any topic that satisfied. I'd propose a question, about service for example, and how in the book of Luke, the apostle pointed out that John and Peter, two of the Lord's disciples, performed "women's work" by being sent to prepare the Passover meal and looking for a man carrying water.

"Ach," Andreas scoffed. "He did not call it women's work."

"Well, no, but it must have been. Women usually prepared meals, and they always gathered at the wells getting water. That's where our Lord found them. Or they washed men's feet to be hospitable to guests, so they gathered water for that. Here, Sarah tells me that Indian men serve meals when guests come. And they handle canoes and help gather the food too, even though the women prepare it. I think that's very enlightened."

"Women's work is defined biblically," my father-in-law replied. He took a draw on his pipe. "Women are less able to perform heavier tasks or ones that require a weighty mind."

"Those water jugs must have been heavy. I certainly feel it in my shoulders when I carry the bucket from the river. And didn't women work together with the apostle Paul? I'm sure I read where he sends greetings to women who work with him, which couldn't mean just serving food *to* him. They studied with him. And isn't that what Mary and Martha argued about?"

"They serve the men," my mother-in-law cautioned. "That is what women do, and Martha was right to bring our Lord's attention to Mary's wishing to be like the men. Women need to know their place."

"But our Lord didn't chasten Mary. He told Martha not to complain. And then later we read about men helping with the water so—"

"Enough, Emma Giesy," Andreas said. The Swiss men always seemed to shout. He looked over his spectacles. "You don't want to set an argumentative example for your children." He nodded toward Andy, who watched me the way a blue heron studies fish.

Andreas was right about one thing: if Christian wasn't oystering, we'd be living in our own home now, and I'd be out from under the wary eyes of Andreas. Maybe Christian would take me with him to Olympia when the legislature was in session. Maybe that was why he hadn't told me about his election, because he knew I'd want to accompany him if we had no home of our own. Mary and Boshie's home had been finished first, then the mill, followed by harvest and then building a barn on the Giesy Place with stalls. We would milk cows there when someone went to Oregon to retrieve the cows that had been here before Keil himself sent them south. We needed hay storage as well and root cellars for our garden supply. And smokehouses for the meat. None of us wanted to repeat the winter we had just survived. We'd be better prepared and would use our ammunition for game when we needed, too. We weren't a colony but a community able to live separate lives.

———

In August, we women gathered up the mat grasses from the cattail flags. Mary and I loaded the bundles onto the mules and led the animals to Sarah Woodard's house at Woodard's Landing. Sarah knew how to make the mats, though first we'd strip the flags to dry them in the sun. "In the winter, when it's raining, we'll weave these," I told Mary as we walked along. "The Indians wrap belongings in them to keep things smelling fresh and dry, and they line their walls with them to help keep out the wind and rain, and they lay them over soft moss to sleep on. Sarah says they aren't as attractive to bugs as our feather mattresses."

Andy carried his own little bundle, and Kate rode like a veteran in the board I carried on my back. Mary's little one also rode on her back and we both giggled once when I said I wondered if we'd be mistaken for Indians walking single file along the path with babies on our backs. "Not likely," Mary said. "My straw-colored hair will give me away, and you're slender as a cattail. Most of the native women I've seen since we've arrived in this country are built of sturdier stock."

"I'm sturdy," I protested.

"In your mind, maybe." She crossed her eyes and I laughed.

"No, seriously, even if we look fragile, like Sarah does, we're still strong as oxen. You ask Sarah. She'll agree. It's something I've learned about myself since coming here. What we can do on the inside isn't always reflected by what's on the outside."

"Sounds like an oyster shell," Mary said, as we reached Sarah's and laid the bundles near their warehouse.

I laughed. "Women of Scripture were capable, and we can't look much different from them. They were small-bodied too. They must have had good minds to have even decided to follow our Lord in the first place, to take that risk of being ridiculed or even killed. What was on the inside wasn't reflected by what was on the outside." I settled that thought with a nod of my chin.

"You're not saying women were like the men who followed him, are you?"

"Don't you ever wonder that if we were made in God's image, man and woman, how then God must be like us, too, and not just like our men?"

Her eyes were as big as horse apples but I continued.

"I mean there's all that talk of blood in Scripture, and we women know about that, don't we? And we understand water and baptism, feeling like we'll die before we give birth."

Mary stopped in her tracks. "That's...repulsive," she said. "I could never imagine God as being...soft and...sideways, tricking people into things, without saying something outright, the way we women do. Or silly thinking. God's nothing like a woman."

"But that's just it, Mary. We aren't soft all the time or we'd never have survived last winter. You wouldn't have come across the plains pregnant with Elizabeth. And as for being sideways, well, think of scriptural Jacob who tricked his brother and his father. That's sideways thinking not left to women. And we wouldn't do it nearly as much if we could just be ourselves, nice and direct, without having to worry about offending the men. And silly? *Ach,* look at how we have to plan ahead and organize so our children are fed each day, or learn how to dye wool and spin it into clothing, or use the land to gather these very stalks so we can have mats to sleep on. We know how to live in…Eden. We've learned to read, even to speak another language. We're born with those abilities to learn. Don't you want Elizabeth to grow up feeling that she's as capable as any brothers she might have? I want that for Kate. I don't want her thinking she isn't as important as Andy."

"You better not let Andreas hear you spout such things," Mary said. Her voice shook. "Even if Christian lets you."

"Christian's never heard it before," I said. I took a deep breath and quieted my voice. "Sometimes I come to wisdom by saying thoughts out loud and I hear it myself for the first time, just when you're hearing it too."

"Oh, Emma," Mary laughed then. I know she thought I teased but to be certain, she added, "I think I'd keep that kind of talk buried inside your oyster shell." She tapped my head.

"You couldn't have said anything more uplifting to my soul, except for the part about having to keep it all quiet," I told her.

———

Christian and Joe both came from Bruceport, and along with his brothers, we all worked together to build my house at last. Our house, I knew, but it was difficult for me to think of "ours" knowing I'd be alone there with the children more often than not.

Even with the help, the construction still took two solid weeks.

Ours was a crude building, ten by fourteen feet with a loft and two cutouts for windows and, of course, a door facing east to catch the morning sun. The men pegged the cedar beams so the loft would be sturdy and a safe place for storage, and as our family grew, it could accommodate more feather ticks, mats, and children too. The scent of the beams would fill the house. We built a fireplace and cat-and-clay chimney so the loft would be warm in the winter. This was perhaps a luxury, but one we could build with the availability of more tools like the big auger that Rudy brought, which pegged the beams, and the frow with its slender blade set at a right angle to the handle. Shingles! How I coveted them, especially after the memories of living under a canvas roof.

If the scouts had carried such tools we'd have made better time in building up our colony, but we traveled light and fast and despite *Herr* Keil's belief, we were frugal with the money and didn't pay to buy many tools.

We all worked to make the fireplace, stacking logs over, each other, then mixing mud and riverbank clay with dried grass and boughs. I tried to think of some herb or spice to mix in with the clay so when we heated our supper there'd be an added aroma, but spices were scarce. For now. Andy loved playing with the mud and forming it into little loaves that Christian called cats. My husband helped his son pat the mud dry and both of them nodded approval at each other with smudges of dirt on their faces.

Christian and Martin worked late to build a little cover for Opal, the goat, so I'd have some place out of the wind and rain to milk her. Goats are hardy but can't stand the rain. That first night, I laid on the floor the elk hide we'd been given by a helpful Indian, and there Christian and I whispered. I would have liked to go outside but the mosquitoes raged after sunset. "When they finish the other houses, the men will come back and build a half barn for the mule and cows," Christian said, keeping his voice low so he wouldn't wake the children.

"We're to have a cow?"

ve worked it out," he said, his eyes sparkling in a tease. Bugs buzzed at the lantern sporting new tin slats Christian had made.

I said, "Maybe from your marshal pay or legislative allotment?"

"Maybe," he said. He dropped his eyes.

"Why didn't you tell me?"

He shrugged. "I wasn't named for doing anything grand," he said. "Indeed. Just recognition of the stockade being built, that we did a good thing to help people. Sam suggested me since we have more Germans here now than other Americans. If someone away from here has a problem, then I can bring about a solution. I don't expect much of that in our colony."

Our colony? "You mean here in Willapa?" He nodded. "Won't you have to make arrests?"

"Indeed. But there's little crime, and the sheriff will handle most things."

"But winning an election as territorial representative. I didn't even know you campaigned."

"I didn't. It was a vote at a meeting same time as John was elected school superintendent and Sam elected sheriff and John Vail as fence viewer."

"I wish you'd told me yourself," I said. "So I could honor you too."

"Ah, Emma," he said. He reached his arms around me. I felt the strength of him. He smelled like a man of the sea, not the earth. I kissed him, tasted salt on my lips. "You honor me by being my wife and staying here through all that has happened. But we're as different as flowers and bees. You bloom vibrant while I, I just want to slip by, have a taste, but never stay long enough to be noticed."

"It's no sin to stand out," I protested. "You do no one a favor by pretending you aren't a worthy man. You're a good leader with a fine mind. A loving husband and father. Responsible to others. Inventive. To deny that means to question your Creator, doesn't it?"

He was thoughtful. "Maybe."

"And besides," I said snuggling beneath his shoulder. "We may be as different as flowers and bees but I believe both are needed to make things grow. And the flower definitely needs to stand out so the bee can find her!"

The fresh scent of peeled logs filled our heads. It was the first night in four years of marriage that we were together, just our family. I wouldn't hear the snoring of a brother or sister, or the sounds of the scouts turning in their tents right beside ours, or the entire community gathering together in the stockade to survive the winter. We were alone at last.

———

I'd preserved wild strawberries in the spring, dried them, and now added them to goat's cheese to make a kind of fruit pudding that each of us could eat. It tasted sweet and the lumps mixed in our mouths. "This is good, Emma," Christian said. I beamed. "It is good to be with you and the children. Good to be home." He kept spooning the soft food into his mouth, feeding Kate just a taste as she'd wakened, then fell back asleep. His blue green eyes looked darker in the shadows. But they had life, pools fed by the rivers of wrinkles beginning to flow into them.

He finished, wiped his reddish beard with his hand, then set the bowl down on the mats covering the earth floor. "But you should have made enough for all of us," Christian said. "All those who helped with the house. It would have been a godly thing to do."

"I didn't have enough berries," I said. "Besides, I wanted to celebrate with just us, for our family. We don't have to do everything together here, do we?"

"Everyone here is our kin," Christian said. "Even the scouts. Joe. Karl Ruge."

"Well, I know, but I meant—"

"I know what you meant. I just wish you didn't have to enjoy so much being separated from them, Emma. They love you and want to make your life easier. They're generous people. They open their hearts to strangers and friends alike."

"They love Andy. And Kate," I said. "I know." I defended against his eyes raised to disagree.

"You don't know," he said. "You are afraid you'll disappear in this large family, but you will always stand out."

He knew me so well. "They love me like a child of God. But my earthly ways and my ideas, well, those the Giesys could probably do without."

"Not this Giesy," he said and reached for me.

That night we lay on mats and he held me while owls hooted. Treetops split the moonlight that spilled through the open window. Tomorrow I'd tan hides to cover the opening. There were shelves to make, pegs to auger into the walls to hang drying herbs and our few clothes. So much to do.

"Emma," Christian said. "Be here with me now."

"*Ja,*" I said. Staying in one place with another is as difficult sometimes as praying. But I became as whole that night with him as I'd ever been alone. With his caresses I lost the questioning in my mind. My thoughts of things to do were silenced by arms holding me, soft words whispered at the nape of my neck. The busyness of my hands found calm as I pressed my fingers against his bare back and tasted of the sweetness of his mouth. His temple where my lips brushed that soft depression was as sweet as a baby's breath. And when he kissed my face, holding it in the cocoon of his hands, I lost myself in him, my husband. I surrendered, unafraid, as unfurled as an apron string in the wind. I marveled later that I had.

In the morning, I thought I'd tell Christian about the images that washed up before me as he held me close, but I decided I couldn't find the words to speak out loud so I'd hear what I knew. But I wondered if what I'd felt that night with my husband was what a holy relationship should be: safe, attached to someone loving, sinking into mystery, surrendering, receiving, finding meaning in the unexplained, being refreshed from the encounter.

I was in love with Christian Giesy as I'd never been before. Such love was marked by trust, surrendering one's all as though to a watery world without the fear of drowning. He knew me well and loved me still, my husband. I imagined that these were the marks of a spiritual relationship as well.

Just for a short time I imagined that, forgetting that even great tenderness can be a harbinger of change.

4

Louisa

My husband, Dr. Keil, set the rules for constructing *das grosse Haus*. Each team of men—four to a team—must cut one entire tree down before they can eat their breakfast. If meat is scarce, they must shoot a deer, and I imagine Rebecca had quite a time dressing out four deer between breakfast and noon. But then, it was easier to cut the trees on Deer Creek near the Pudding River, where we're building up our colony, because they are not so big as those in Willapa. Not that I excuse what happened there, the poor progress the scouts made. Well, maybe I do excuse it some. They had fewer men and they had Emma. Rebecca was chosen for her skill at doing what she's told without retort.

A dam is already on the creek, so there's a mill race too, Dr. Keil tells the others and I overhear. Twice each month, at first, he took the riverboat from Portland to Oregon City and then, by prearrangement, one of the carpenter teams would come to pick him up in a wagon and drive him from there to Aurora Mills. He often took our little Aurora with him. I would have liked to go along but with so many children to tend to and the laundry I took in, it was best I stayed here in Portland.

We all visited for the Fourth of July. It was a joyous time. How I love the music! I think I could endure most anything in this life as long as there is music to return to. Dr. Keil composed a march the band played and it was a happy tune, not the dirge that we'd listened to all across the continent following Willie's casket.

There I am again, always thinking about Willie. But the rains have begun in Portland, so I think of him more often. It was in this month of November last year that we buried him. I still can find no cause within myself for his death; I know it must be my fault, my error, for my husband is perfection. That he has never accused me openly is a mark of that.

I did not cry, not then, not when he died. Some might have thought me cold. I'm not. I am practical. Death can be hastened by man's action, but death visits everyone. Still I will someday ask why Willie went before me or his father. Somehow this does not seem divine, but then I have no wish to question God. I'm sure there is a reason.

I plan for Christmas here in this Oregon Territory, for the delivery of *Belsnickel's* kind gifts. We'll find fruit perhaps or maybe some small wooden toy for each of the little ones. The band will play. Perhaps we will all go out and stand in the *gross Haus* and sing even if it is not yet completed. It will feel like church. We need to work to finish up the *Haus* so we can move forward and build the church. My husband says we must prepare the farmsteads, plant the orchards in the places where the men have cut the timber. Much to do before we build a church, and even then it will not be so grand as the one we have in Bethel.

I do wonder how they fare in Bethel.

Dr. Keil named Andrew Giesy, Christian's younger brother, to be in charge of Bethel when we left. This surprised me as I expected Andrew to travel west as so many of his brothers did. Maybe my husband had spoken his reasoning and I missed it. I did seem to miss things during those days.

Jack Giesy has been here of late. He makes me laugh and sometimes I forget that he is already thirty years old or more and should have put aside childish pranks like changing sugar in the bowl for salt when I was not looking, or staying up all night "drawing pictures" he tells us. When he doesn't tip his flask too much he is a kind companion for the little ones. He likes to keep them awake late, though, and often misses breaking fast in the morning while he snoozes. Once I heard he tossed a cat against a wall when it ventured near his face as he recovered from his partying. Disturbing. But he has a cheery smile. Willie would have had a smile like that, if he had lived.

Why can't I let him go?

I can't speak to Dr. Keil of such things. They are trivial in the world of import and detail he attends to. A flash of feeling so intense swells up into my face sometimes, making it hot and my breath short all at the same time. I want him to stop being Dr. Keil and *Herr* Keil and our leader and to just be the father of our children, my husband who would hold me through this pain.

But this too is envy, selfishness. "Why do you worry, woman?" he told me one night when I felt the tears coming and asked if he might pray with me for something soothing to fill the gaping hole within my heart. "Why do you worry?" he repeated, adding, "I am doing our Father's work."

These were scriptural words spoken by our Lord to his parents when they had thought him lost but he was instead teaching in the temple.

I am a weak woman. Soft. Thinking only of myself. I am commanded not to worry so long as my husband does the Lord's work.

Despite the routines of my day, there are surprises, small treasures I take as signs that God is with us: enough grass to feed our stock; a child pulled back from a fast wagon racing through the streets of Portland; a leggy yellow flower brought by Jack Giesy and tucked into my apron at the waist.

While we brought no sheep with us—a decision I thought an error as we would need the wool for weaving clothes—I had brought lanolin along, and mutton tallow laced with lemon. Neither ever went rancid and at night I rub the cakes on the feet of the children and our own, soothing the blisters on our feet. Even a good cobbler can't make room for every corn or callus. I give out my healing salve as needed. One night as I fell onto the quilt beside Dr. Keil and spoke my tired prayers, I told him, "I am pleased I brought the mutton salve for our blisters." It was such a little thing to bring me pleasure, this packing something that could serve. "So many say it helps even with wind-chapped hands."

"No need for it," my husband said. "Have them step in their own urine and let the air dry their feet and chapped hands. Each will be clear by morning." He rolled over and I heard him snore within minutes.

I lay awake wondering if there was something sinful in offering up a simple joy. There must be. Otherwise, why would my wise husband find need to offer an alternative to what I'd said? Yes, urine would soften hands, but was it so wrong to be pleased that lanolin could do the same? Hadn't God provided that as well?

I must put these pages away. I'm tired and that's when doubt abounds.

5

Emma

Kindling Your Own Fire

I didn't mind not having anyone around but my children. I liked tending to their everyday needs and preparing for my husband to come home. I could make my own decisions about what to eat or what task to do next without having to please a man's stomach or his clock. In the evening, I lit my candles and burned them for as long as I liked without anyone complaining that I interrupted their sleep with my drawing or reading. All in all, it was the best of both worlds: I had a husband and children to love and care for, and I had time for myself within my own home. I wondered if women married to soldiers carried such thoughts, wanting their men with them but not minding that they could rule their own roost and collect eggs when they wished while their men were gone.

The first week after Christian returned to the Bay, I reveled in that aloneness. It slipped into the late evening after the children slept in their beds. The days were filled with weaving mats or pulling heavy needles through tanned hides to make winter breeches. I ground cornmeal for mush, milked the goat, filled the hollowed log with the grass of last summer. It would have been a pleasure to have a cow through the winter, but Christian said that tending the animal would have been too much for me with the little ones underfoot and the goat to milk as well. On the cold, rainy mornings when I could bring the goat inside to milk her, I agreed with Christian, though good butter would have been a salve against milking in the morning chill.

In this house I felt no fear from the outside world. It was built with love and the door was sturdy with a latch from the inside. During the day I left the latch string out so anyone coming past would know this was a friendly place. Sarah said that was the custom here. If the string was pulled in, it meant no one should knock or stop by. Not that I expected anyone to visit, but I heard that the Shoalwater people sometimes stopped to trade milk for fish or fresh bread for berries.

From my in-laws' house, we'd moved the trunk my parents had sent out with them. Its rounded top stood at the end of the rope-mattress bed that fit in the back corner of the house. The men had made a bed along with a rough table and chairs cut out of smaller tree stumps to add to the table chairs the Giesys brought for us. One finely made rocking chair sat at the hearth. Mary has its mate in her home. It was another bonding of us two women. She and Boshie lived but two miles from us, close enough to call for in time of help; far enough distant we never feared eavesdropping on each other's lives. It was the perfect arrangement, and we had chosen it all ourselves.

At my leisure I could read my sister Catherine's letters and write back, though I did the latter more infrequently than I might have. I wasn't sure why.

Karl Ruge made his way to visit once in a while after the misty rains began in earnest in November. He'd split wood for me. If he saw me dragging out a pail of ashes to my soap pit, he would lift it from me saying, "By golly, I'm not so old I can't lift a bucket. Even if I am so old I'm ready to kick it."

"You're not that old, Karl," I told him. He was but a few years older than Christian. I wished he wouldn't bring up his age. He'd grin and sometimes stay to smoke his pipe while I heated hot tea and he spoke with Andy. I knew he stopped by for Andy's lessons, but sometimes he'd bring me the loan of a book. I preferred the titles in German, for I could read and disappear inside the story. The English ones made difficult reads but Karl said I could keep the books for as long as I liked. Once he brought *Uncle Tom's Cabin* and when I finished reading it, he said we could discuss it together, to see if I had captured the meaning in a book written in English. Imagine, a man willing to discuss a book with a woman! A book about people and lives and change and not just about Scripture! What would my mother-in-law say? *Unseemly* came to mind. Well, just the idea of it spurred me on to test myself against the English words. I stoked the fire later than necessary to keep its reflected light upon my page.

Still, a house without a husband reeks of separation. I thought about Christian often through the winter months and spring and seemed to see him everywhere. Andy had his deep-pool eyes and he held his hands on his hips, elbows out, when I scolded him. Christian often stood that way too when I raised my voice. I had to turn away to keep from smiling when Andy reminded me of his father. I had to be stern at times, for Andy's safety. He played too close to a honey tree, ran without looking into the denser trees and could become lost within them. It is a parent's role to be dour at times. For protection of the ones we love.

Kate's hair was blond at birth but now at a year old, it was coming in with a kind of reddish tint and in the sunshine shone like her father's hair. I often talked to the children about their father, what he might be doing, what he was eating for supper, that he was probably already in bed while my Andy persisted in asking questions just to keep himself from falling asleep. "Does he cook?" Andy asked. I wondered. I'd heard that fur trappers took native wives; maybe Christian had found a Shoalwater woman to cook for him and Joe. I'd have to ask. I didn't know how I felt about that.

The children carried Christian's kindness in them too. On more than one occasion when I hadn't returned to the house from milking the goat as fast as I wished, I'd see Andy bent over his sister, patting her little hand while she cried, hungry, sitting on the floor. He was not the least bit mean or jealous, that boy; he had a naturally giving heart.

Christian was missing these moments, and yet I felt closer to my husband with him gone than I ever had when we'd been separated before. I'd been annoyed when he left me behind after we were married, heading into Kentucky to recruit for *Herr* Keil. If he'd been a bug I'd have smashed him with my slippers when he left me to birth Andy alone at Fort Steilacoom. But now while he was at the Bay, I carried a low flame for him, one that flickered with longing when I thought of him, one that I knew would ignite when he came home and blessed my face with the brush of his mustache. Until then, something in our joined spirits kept us linked though physically we lived apart. How strange a marriage is.

When Christian came home every other week or so, he stayed but a few days, so it was as though we had a honeymoon. I giggled when Christian first used that word. It was December and we'd had a rare respite, a patch of clear sky that revealed a full moon shining on the river outside our home. The children were fast asleep. Avoiding the muddy path, we walked through the timber to the river's edge. The air smelled fresh as new cut flowers and was so full of moisture from the dripping trees that I wiped my face with my shawl, thinking it must be misting. Clouds could roll in and drown the moon in an instant but we wouldn't know until the rains began again, as we couldn't see the arrival of storms or clouds. The hills and trees kept us from anticipating much. I pulled my shawl around me to ward off the chill. Even the insects had flown to their bunks. The river gurgled, carrying its cargo of rain and tree branches and needles and lichen to sea. We could hear splashing, likely where a tree-fall cut the water, forcing the stream surge to go around it. Under the canopy of trees, our voices carried.

"Honeymoon," Christian said as we stood together. "The word means sweetness as in *honey* and the *moon* means the sweetness leaves like the moon fades. It's a part of life. The ebb and flow of things. A good descriptive word."

"I'll pray our marriage will be a harvest moon, then, filling us up with good memories. Then when it threatens to fade, we'll have the return of the honey to look forward to."

"Indeed, you would find the hopeful part of the waning moon," he said. "But it won't just threaten to fade, Emma. It does fade."

"Two honeymoons a month would keep us from noticing the darkness in between," I said.

"The Americans call two full moons in one month a 'blue moon' and say something is as 'rare as a blue moon.' Indeed," Christian continued, "a happily married man, for instance, or so my father says. Little does he know." He kissed my nose.

"Look at us," I said. "Our waning did not last. We are renewed here."

"But it is not our doing, Emma. God controls, not us. Remember the scripture: 'Behold, all ye that kindle a fire, that compass yourselves about with sparks: walk in the light of your fire, and in the sparks that ye have kindled. This shall ye have of mine hand; ye shall lie down in sorrow.'"

"Well that's just…dour. The idea that all we get for kindling our own fires is the hand of God giving us sorrow. What kind of hand is that?"

"One to help us when we're grieving," he said. "To remind us that we cannot do anything on our own. We will grieve. We are not asked to move by our compass, Emma."

"But we have to kindle our own fires. We have to read the compass. We can't wait around for others to do it for us. Look what happened with Keil. We waited for him to fan our flames here, and he doused them with buckets of outrage. We looked to him for our compass and see where it took us! He'd take us south to Portland and Aurora, but we went to the sea and found oystering to rescue us." I pulled away from him, disappointed that he couldn't see how pushing ahead, following the course we had, had rescued us. Oh, God had a place in it, but we made it happen, didn't we?

"No matter what we do, there will be sweetness and there will be bitter. To think differently is to find disappointment in God where none is warranted. I worry over you, Emma, that you try too hard to see all good things as coming from your effort. When tragedies happen—and they will as sure as the moon wanes—then you'll blame yourself. This will not be good."

"*Ja*, like you blamed yourself," I said.

It was an unkindness of me, to poke in my husband's freshest sore. Loving someone was in part knowing their deepest wound but choosing not to poke it or to pick at the scab. But did the man think that his deciding to work on the coast had nothing to do with me? Did he think that every good idea came only from God, or that God couldn't speak through another? Didn't God make us all creative creatures?

Still, I should have countered what I said, apologized. Instead I pitched the thought away.

Worse, he reached for me with tenderness. I shrugged my shoulder.

"Stick to the tenth verse, Emma," he said. "We pay a price if we try to do things ourselves. Indeed, we must kindle God's fire to light our path in darkness, trust in Him, not anyone or anything else. 'Who is among you that feareth the LORD, that obeyeth the voice of his servant, that walketh in darkness, and hath no light? let him trust in the name of the LORD, and stay upon his God.' "

He pointed toward a black form wiggling along the riverbank then. "Otters," he said. "They play even at night. They've not a worry in the world. We can be like that if we but trust."

He'd forgotten how sad he'd been. He'd forgotten how defeated he was before I convinced him to try something different. *Ja,* it was easy for him to trust now. He sounded more like a preacher or maybe a marshal or some legislator to me than my husband.

Rains began then, having slipped past the moonlight while we talked. The drops softly pattered my woolen shawl. When he took my hand to help me as we walked the muddy path back to the house, all I wanted was to pull away.

———

Christian still oystered at the Bay when our little community celebrated *Herr* Keil's birthday (and Louisa's) on March 6, just as we'd done back in Bethel. I confess, I resented the celebration for the Keils' birthdays. The Keils didn't live here, hadn't wanted to live here, and weren't a part of this community, even if they had buried their son Willie on the hill. Equally annoying, the celebration occurred on a Friday, not even a day when we'd otherwise have gathered at the stockade for worship, so I had to make the lengthy trip with the children and stay over, then return the following day to milk the goat.

Living seven miles south of the stockade made it no simple journey. Not that I'm complaining, just explaining.

Before I left, I rose in the dark, carrying the lantern to the lean-to where Opal rested. I wished I could milk her later instead of earlier since I wouldn't be back to milk her until tomorrow. Her little bag would be swollen for sure. I had to have time to skim yesterday's cream and leave today's milk in another tin Christian had made for me. When that was finished, I packed a few items, brought ingredients to make a special dried-berry dessert, then woke the children and they dressed. We ate a simple breakfast of oats with molasses and then I saddled the mule—on loan to us from Andreas—hanging the lantern by a rope over the animal's neck.

We rode the mule, the three of us, with a sack of goodies draped over the saddle horn. Andy hung on behind me, his little legs stuck out on either side; Kate rode in front, tied to me with a sash around her middle. A saddle was a luxury Christian had purchased for us. And no, I did not ride sidesaddle, and I didn't care who knew it.

The path was muddy but the mule surefooted. Little squalls sprayed water on us and of course the branches overhanging the trail wetted us down, but the cedar capes I'd woven worked well to keep us dry. The smells were rich with loam and leaf, and the beginning spring colors stood out against moss and tree bark. A red mushroom shaped like a small tulip caught my eye. Little prince's-pine moss that worked well for diapers spurted up from old logs, and there were leaves that looked like reindeer horns and bore the same color. I wished I knew the name of every single one. Perhaps I'd make that a school lesson with Karl Ruge. These small treasures of the landscape made the day a gift.

When we reached the river ford, I had to put the children in the little boat we kept there, stake the mule, then row the boat and the babies across the stream. Once I'd have lost my breakfast at the mere thought of being on the river at all, but now it was part of who I was, this calculating where to put the boat in and imagining where I'd take it out on the other side. Sometimes we got spun around in the current, but I knew where I was headed and kept my eye on that certain tree or log to keep me ever forward.

Once on the other side, I left Andy to look after Kate, grateful for the moment that she was occupied and sitting while I rowed back to the other side. I unstaked the mule, tied his rope to the boat, then once again made my way across the swift-flowing stream. I docked the boat, untied the mule, loaded him back up and off we went, knowing we'd be repeating the event the next day.

We'd spend the night with my in-laws. We rode along the trail, clopped through one or two little streams that appeared in the spring. Blackberry vines threatened the trail; moss-thickened branches hung from the big cedars, forcing us to keep watch and for me to duck, but still there was time for musing. My in-laws loved seeing the children, and I know they missed them, but my mother-in-law never failed to say things to the children that I knew were meant for me. "We hardly ever see you, Andrew. What's your mother doing that she can't come visit more often, hmm?" Or to Kate, as my daughter sat on her knee, "Why, your little hands feel cold. Didn't your mother put gloves on you when you traveled? *Oma* will warm them up." She'd kiss my daughter's hands and I'd feel the layers of guilt flatten me out like the batter of a cake.

I countered those negative anticipations by remembering that today I'd see my friend Sarah Woodard when I traveled north, and she was the reason I headed out early. She was the pearl in the bottom of this oyster. Sustaining friendships has a cost attached. This one meant managing two children and a mule and a rowboat on a swollen stream and enduring the disappointments of my children's grandparents in order to spend a few moments with Sarah and Sam.

On the Keils' birthday, I rode the mile or so beyond the stockade to invite the Woodards to our event. The foliage was thick enough that my in-laws wouldn't see me riding by. Sometimes Sam and Sarah attended our extended-family events, though usually not on a Friday. *Ach,* such a poor time for a celebration!

At Sarah's, I unloaded the children and Andy scampered toward the Woodards' dog, who lapped his face in happy recognition. I received Sarah's surprised hug, watched as she lifted Kate into her arms while I set a tub of goat cheese on her table. The cheese was tart and aged; the way I knew she liked it. In return, she gave me butter and eggs and we spent a few hours catching up, discovering what news she had about the territory.

After Kate fell asleep I asked Sarah if she knew about Christian being named the territorial marshal and being elected to the legislature.

"Oh yes," she said.

"He never told me," I said.

She pondered for a bit, then said, "Men are like that sometimes. They don't let you notice who they are. They think it's prideful."

"*Ja,* prideful," I said, deciding then that Christian didn't want to set a bad example for me by enjoying his honor. Or maybe he thought I'd dote on him, tell it to others as though it were *my* honor. I didn't think of myself as a woman who always made sure that others knew of her husband's goodness, but maybe Christian thought I was. "I wouldn't have gossiped about him," I said.

"No. You don't gossip. Your mind is too busy thinking." She paused. "He maybe didn't want to worry you. The marshals have to enforce the laws and the legislators make them and, well, with Governor Stevens, it can be unpredictable. That man hates all 'evil-disposed persons' as he calls the Indians and anyone who disagrees with him. At least the martial law's been lifted."

Christian had been carrying this responsibility on his shoulders, too, and never said a word to me.

"Maybe he thought he had told you," Sarah said. She smiled. "Sometimes that happens between Sam and me. He thinks because everyone knows that I must know too."

"These men, so complicated," I sighed.

"While we women are as easy to see through as glass."

We both laughed at that, and I was reminded again that journeying to visit Sarah was worth the river crossing and the little irritations I'd find later with my in-laws.

"So, here you are," my father-in-law announced when I arrived just after the midday meal. The table would be filled again as more people joined us so I didn't feel badly that they were just finishing up as we arrived. "We celebrate *Herr* Keil's birthday."

"And Louisa's," I added as I handed Kate to my mother-in-law and stepped down off the mule. Andy had already slipped off the back of the animal and missed the swish of the mule's tail as he jumped aside then ran to his favorite uncle, Boshie.

"You almost missed the festivities, Emma," my mother-in-law said. "Did you have trouble with the mule?"

"*Nein.* I went over to invite the Woodards. I hadn't seen Sarah for so long."

"*Ja,* you don't get up much this way. Not even on New Year's Eve this year. Too bad." She paused as she cleared a pan of cake from the table. "You missed some time with your husband by coming so late."

"What? Christian is here?"

"Was here," Rudy said. "He came very early with the tidewaters but couldn't stay. Still much work to do he said, and so he headed back."

"He said to tell you he'd be home before too many days," Boshie said.

"He missed seeing the children," my mother-in-law noted. She smiled at Andy. "His housekeeper brought fresh clams that we finished right off. So good."

What was wrong with Christian? Why wouldn't he have told me, sent a message at least that he was coming? I suppose he couldn't have. It was an impulsive visit made because he had some moments free and the river agreed with his plan.

"I guess he knew we'd be celebrating Wilhelm's birthday," Martin said.

"And Louisa's," I added, again. *Who was this housekeeper?*

"*Ja,* hers too," Henry acknowledged. "So he assumed you'd be here."

Rudy told me that Christian had almost set out to find us, thinking something might have gone wrong, but the rest of the family assured them I could take care of myself and would be along shortly.

"None of us ever figured you'd pass right by and go visit Sarah first," my mother-in-law said. "That's too bad, isn't it? I know he missed seeing the children."

She's already said that.

I felt sick. I missed my husband and regretted having the chance to see him and hold him if only for a moment. Why hadn't I just stopped by before I went to Sarah's? Well, I hadn't wanted to get caught by the family and maybe not had a chance to see Sarah at all. I should have expected Christian might come since it was a festive day, one we always celebrated back in Bethel. But things were different here. My husband was a law enforcer and I hadn't been told of *that*! I swatted at a spider crawling up my skirt and sent the poor thing skittering past a distant stump.

Some of Christian's brothers got out their instruments and played German marching tunes. They sang later and for a moment I was back in Bethel, swept away with the music. The women sewed awhile, then chattered until it was time to put out bowls of potatoes and deer meat and an array of *Strudels* using the berries of last summer. They invited me into their chatter, talking about their children's antics or their latest success with a recipe or two. Christian's youngest sister, Louisa, played with Kate and I was grateful. The day turned balmy and while clouds scudded across the treetops, it rained in little patches that sent us running for the stockade, our shawls wrapped tight around us. It was a pleasant day.

But I couldn't let go of how I'd missed seeing Christian. The children too, as my mother-in-law reminded me. Why hadn't he stayed just a little longer? I wondered if he often made little side trips that far upriver, but not far enough to reach his own home. The most annoying thing of all: that he had remembered Keil's birthday and took the time to come celebrate it with his family but hadn't waited around long enough to see his wife and children.

"Papa didn't want to see us," Andy said, leaning his head on my lap as I sat.

"*Ja,* he did." I ran my fingers through the silkiness of Andy's hair. "He just had work to do so he had to get back to the sea."

"I wish he lived with us, Mama. I'd like a daddy around."

"He lives with us," I said. "He'll be back before long. Summer is better. He can be home more often. He's taking care of us."

Even my son felt deserted. His father and I had agreed that we could manage the separations. I could kindle the fires alone in the morning; he'd bring home the resources we needed to see us through the winter. But Andy had no say in it. *Ach,* that was the way with children.

We finished the meal and I heard myself sighing more than once as the evening approached and we put the children to sleep. "Don't let it upset you," Mary Giesy told me. She sat down beside me on a stump chair, my oil lamp beside me. A breeze picked up, chilling the hair on my arms. I wouldn't stay out here for long.

"What makes you think I'm upset?" I asked.

"Your hands tell," Mary said. She nodded toward my fingers that had apparently been working on their own, my thumb and forefinger rubbing against each other.

"*Ja,* Andy heard everyone say that Christian was here but didn't stay. He thinks that's his fault."

"I heard him," Mary said. "But you got to see Sarah. That was a nice treat, wasn't it?"

"It cost me seeing my husband. I chose something pleasurable, but had to pay the price. That seems to be my way."

"Maybe not," she said. She looked away.

"What do you mean?"

"Oh, nothing." She picked at a grass stem. The light of the lantern flickered against her face. We heard a swish above us. An owl settled in a tree. She wouldn't look at me. She bit the side of her cheek. The night cast strange shadows. Or no...

"I'm just sorry I missed him."

"I wonder how it was that Christian could have gone downriver without at least seeing your mule tied to the Woodards' post. Surely he'd have stopped by when he saw the mule."

"*Ja,*" I said. "That is a mystery."

She cleared her throat. "You're good at puzzles." She stared at me.

I stared back. "Christian didn't miss me, did he?" I said. "He never even came. You all just told me that to...tease me."

"Don't tell I said." She leaned into me to whisper. "Rudy saw you riding by and he said we should play a trick on you, for wanting to spend more time with your friends than with us."

"But that wasn't it at all," I said. "I had cheese to deliver and eggs to get and—"

"Emma, it's me you're talking to," Mary said. I dropped my eyes. She did know the truth. "I wasn't supposed to tell but you looked so miserable. And then I heard Andy leaning his head on your lap…"

"But why let me think about it all day?" I said. "Couldn't they see too?"

"Not really. You hide your feelings pretty well. I just know you and I knew you'd feel awful about keeping Andy from his dad. So I had to give you a clue. They didn't mean any harm, Emma, really they didn't. And when you tell them you know, they'll laugh and be as happy as anyone that you bested them and figured it out. They might accuse me of telling you, but—"

"But it's cruel, just as they were laughing over Jack's antics with that girl in the outhouse. They let Andy think his father didn't want to see him."

"They think of it as joking. They've been doing it to each other for years. Think of it as a…as a compliment that they involved you in an elaborate plan and each kept the secret. You were the center of it even though you didn't know. Think of it that way and when you tell them, you'll be the center again."

"I won't tell them. Let them feel miserable that they let their grandchild or nephew think his father didn't wait for him. I'll tell Andy but I'll just let them live with their guilt. I'll plan something…I'll stir them up one day and they'll see how it feels."

"Oh, Emma, please. Don't make this a big thing, now. Laugh with us. Don't stand out in this."

"It's not a laughing matter," I said. I stood up, my chin thrust out. "It was hurtful. If a woman can't feel safe with her family, then who can she feel safe with?" I woke the children and we began a night ride home.

6

Louisa

"Food is the servant of the heart, Louisa," Doctor tells me. "Bring them food that their hearts will be warmed."

I hurry to serve. This is how we win new converts to the colony. I know that only men are permitted true recruitment, heading into other territories or states to invite people into our communal society, but we women contribute through our service and especially our food.

People in Portland pay the doctor in food. Wild turkey, venison, chickens, eggs, milk. The latter we don't need so much of since we brought our own neat milk cows across the continent, their little neck bells ringing as they ripped at grass. But several died on the journey west and now we are sending a herd north to Willapa, so perhaps we'll welcome payment in cream.

Chris Giesy made the request. After all, he told my husband in his last letter, the cows had been planned for the Willapa Valley and there is good grazing on the prairies and the Giesys know how to run a dairy. They just need the milk cows that my husband sent to Portland for safekeeping during the winter last. Chris thinks there might be some contracts to be had with the Russians for cheese and butter, sending the produce north by ship. Apparently the British did something like this. They never allowed their people to own cows; they were always working for the British, to be sure they met their contracts. I think Chris added that about the British to make sure we knew this wasn't some wild scheme of his. Or Emma's.

Chris has a cross to bear with his Emma.

So Jack and some of the other young men who like adventure will take the cows north. Jonathan Wagner remains at Aurora Mills. He is helping with the accounting of the new buildings going up there, some using milled boards and not just logs. So responsible, that Jonathan, though I imagine his little nephew Andy would like to meet him. Well, maybe on the Fourth of July they will all come this way to celebrate, though I doubt Emma will ever leave that place, not even for a visit. To do so would be to admit the error of her ways in staying there. She'd have to confess to her part in the separating of our colony. She must come to understand that we women have no real say in the colony life. We are like that Dred Scott, who we learn is not a free man after all. The chief justice has ruled and the Missouri Compromise has been repealed. Slaves, like women, have no voice. It is the way of things.

So I serve meals to people the doctor brings home with him. By their clothing they look important, maybe investors in our colony efforts. The doctor says they are kind men, just ordinary travelers seeking new adventures. But they speak loudly as they tell of Yakima uprisings in bloody detail. They scare the children with their wide-flung hands, and words, like rifle blasts, boom out. I recognize more of their English words each day. Virginians they are and Americans too, who keep telling their stories of the Indians and their trials on the journey across.

As I watch them eat, standing aside to notice when platters need refilling, I think about our crossing. We had no trouble with the Indians, and I think people knew that, so they asked to travel with us. But like these men, I don't think they shared our expression of faith. They used our faith as safety within the confines of our trouble-free journey. I wonder if that is the interest of these American men who see our colony as an easy way to live, not having to work too hard because there will always be food and shelter even if they act lazy. They misunderstand. We Germans are never lazy. And if the war comes, I think our boys will go, if asked, though this is something my husband and I have never spoken of. Might these men I serve have sons they wish to harbor in our colony?

We Germans must always be prepared to be hospitable, not question the motives of others, that's what the doctor says. I pour corn juice into their tins, and they nod, raise the cup as though to toast me as I step back into the shadows.

My husband has a big heart, inviting strangers in. Once, on the journey across, a Sioux brave rode in with his two sons. The doctor invited them to eat at our table too, along with Americans. Because he is so good to communicate even with those of another language, the doctor understood that these Indians were reluctant to eat for fear there would not be enough for all of us. The doctor assured them they were guests and should eat first, that there was plenty for his wife and children. My children did go hungry that night but for a worthy cause.

The Americans traveling under our safe harbor scoffed and left the circle around the fire.

The Indians stayed late into the evening with the rest of us, who watched with empty stomachs as the doctor carried on conversations with his hands. I wondered if they'd ever leave so we could go to our beds. Hunger is easier to manage when asleep. The Americans laid their bedrolls farther from our campfire, and I noticed they slept with their rifles across their chests.

The Indians lingered. With the palm of his hand, one pointed toward me, and later my husband said he spoke of my black hair, as black as his, and that like him, I parted mine in the middle. Something in common. Then Aurora stood up, my sweet little daughter. I would have put her to bed earlier, but the doctor liked her company, and she snuggled beneath his arms as he made signs with the Indians. She gave them her comforter, her little patched quilt I'd made for her with the wool I dyed myself.

"Are you sure you wish to give that away?" I said as she carried it toward them.

She turned to look at me, then back to her father. "Of course she will be generous," the doctor told me. "That is what we do." He beamed at her.

I remembered how the red madder root stained my fingers when I dyed the yarn. I thought of the days I spent stitching the little squares. With each poke of the needle I said a prayer for her. Others in our colony stitched it too. It was a gift of love from all of us, not just from me. I didn't want her to give it away. It was as though I was losing Willie again, a precious thing departing.

I scolded myself as I saw the happiness on the face of the Indian. It was wrong of me to remember an object so fondly and to compare it with the loss of my son.

Then the doctor gave the man an oxbow so he could make for himself a bow of fine Missouri wood. I wondered if the doctor expected each of us to give them something. I had nothing I wanted to part with.

"Bring your friends in the morning," my husband signed. Where he learned such signing I will never know. Neither did I know what we'd feed them except dried peaches.

Just before dawn, twenty-five Indians drove a dozen oxen and neat cows into our camp. They were animals we'd lost, and we were grateful to see them. The natives brought fresh meat, too, and berries. We made ready, my girls and I, to serve the men and their families with them. My girls were eleven years, eight years, and six years old then, but they all knew how food was the servant of the heart. We served them a *Strudel* with dried peaches I baked in our dutch oven, as people called it, rising at four o'clock to do it. The Americans ate heartily though they sat at a distance. The Indians squatted to eat the baked goods and when they had their fill, the women and children ate. We sang for them then, and they grunted agreement with bits of *Strudel* falling on the men's bare chests, catching in the ends of their silky hair.

Then one meandered toward Willie's hearse.

I wanted the hearse left alone, but the doctor stood and as though he showed off a new horse or a new wagon just completed, he spoke in loud words, calling August to help him. They lifted the top of the coffin. My stomach twisted like a snake as I watched them view my Willie.

There was no need of this. I rose to protest, but the Indians all moved toward the hearse now. They lowered their heads as though in prayer and stepped back, seemingly aware of the sanctity of death. The doctor continued to tell them about the whiskey and how it kept Willie pure until we could bury him in the West. The Indians kept their eyes down and then the doctor put the top back on.

The Americans grumbled things I couldn't understand, though they made motions like men who drink too much and pointed to the Indians. But the Indians mounted up then, and waved to us when the trumpet sounded and the *Schellenbaum* tinkled its bells as we headed out once again behind Willie's hearse. Like Lot's wife, I looked back. I did not dissolve into salt. The Indians stayed as silhouettes against the horizon for as long as I could see.

"I have power over the Indians," the doctor told me that afternoon when we rested. "I could get them to do anything I wanted."

"You are worshiped by many, Husband," I told him.

"*Ja, ja,* I know this." He tugged at that tuft of hair beneath his lip. "These Indians, I have a special way with them. Did you see how they looked at Willie?"

I ached. Yes, I saw.

So why he was frightened during our time in Willapa still confounds me. So frightened he would not let the men use guns to hunt for food and our children went hungry at night, again.

I suppose we do things we cannot foresee when trouble drops onto our doorstep. We may try to step over it, go around, but usually we walk through. By God's grace we walk through.

And now, here in Portland nearly a year since we left Willapa, the doctor is happier, at last, as he used to be. His trips out to Aurora Mills excite him, and he returns full of ideas for how the colony will prosper. He carries no ill will toward the Willapa branch that I can see.

I've made a bread pudding with fresh milk. I serve these Portland Americans, and my husband says Jack Giesy will take the cows north. The Americans finish their pudding and leave our Portland home, tipping their hats at me and saying, *"Danke."* My husband gives me no indication of who these Americans are, but he seems happy. So, Jack Giesy is in charge of taking the cows to Willapa. "Big Jack" is what many call him.

"Would it be good to send others with him who have more experience with cows?"

"Jacob needs the challenge, to know that people depend on him. When he has others around who will pick him up, he can act the *Dummkopf.* Sometimes it takes a challenge to help the children think no longer as children but as men."

"Maybe Peter Klein could go," Aurora says. She is now eating the pudding that I held back for the children. "Peter went to Will-pa before anyone else arrived." She is seven and is still troubled by that Willapa word. I smile at her. She can almost read my mind.

The doctor taps her little upturned nose. "Ah, my Aurora, always thinking. But no, you women lack understanding. I will send some of the younger boys along, but Jacob will be in charge and we will see if he can live up to the challenge."

I pack a bag of food for Jack and the boys he takes with him and pray he will not stop by Chris and Emma's or stay for long if he does. Emma has a way of serving ideas into men's heads while their stomachs are filled up with her *Strudels.*

7

Emma

The Waning Moon

On March 26, 1857, I turned age twenty-four. Christian came to spend the day even though I knew it took him from his work, it being a Thursday and during the season when big schooners anchored outside the Bay looking for baskets of oysters to buy for San Francisco.

"Like newlyweds," Martin said, when Christian appeared at noontime still wearing big rubber boots he said were a part of his uniform. Martin said "newlyweds" not with disgust but with a tone of envy, as though he too might like such a marriage arrangement. We met at the stockade, of course. It was our gathering place now. I didn't even mind the journey by mule and boat and mule again, suspecting that Christian might actually come for my birthday.

There were presents for me too. Karl Ruge gave me *Germania Kalender* published by the famous Geo Brumder of Milwaukee. It was filled with stories and cartoon pictures and ads for pharmaceuticals in the back, and Ayer's Sarsaparilla. Martin leaned over my chair as I turned the pages. "New herbals," he noted.

"Very thoughtful," Christian said. "I know Emma likes to write what she's done on the dates, and she hasn't been able to do that with only a calendar from 1855 that Mary brought with her."

The book had a hard cover with a lovely drawing of a lion on the front. It was written in German and I loved it. The stories I could read to Andy and

Kate. It contained advice and information about lots of things, such as when to plant, the tides, days of full moons. How someone figured out all those details and still got them printed in a book in time for use always surprised. This one had recipes in it and a little word trivia. I read that the Italian word for "religion" translated into English as *ambassador.* "An ambassador offers us help in a foreign land," Karl said. "Religion does, too."

"Thank you," I said, holding it to my chest. "I'll treasure it."

"*Ja,* by golly, I thought you might," Karl said. He dropped his eyes. A hint of pink formed on the circle of weathered cheeks framed by his white beard.

Barbara Giesy gave me an embroidered handkerchief, and my mother-in-law said she had something new to eat for the occasion. She called it coconut. It was green and in the middle had a substance that felt smooth but tasted quite fine. "It comes from the Sandwich Islands," she said. "On board a ship. I thought you'd like it. It's...different."

"It is," I said. Andy took a taste and so did Kate, who scrunched her nose at me. "She likes tart things," I said.

Mary's gift was a new needle for my chatelaine and a thimble made of bone.

They were being terribly kind to me, my husband's family. I suspected Mary had told them that I knew of their petty joke and they wanted to win me over so I wouldn't come up with something back in kind. Maybe they felt a little guilt.

I wasn't planning anything, not that I hadn't tried. But every idea that had come into my head seemed silly or cruel, though I believed their joke was too. Still, I wasn't sure I was willing to let their generosity on my birthday buy their way out of guilt.

"And what did you get your wife?" my father-in-law asked Christian.

Christian pulled a tiny misshapen pearl from the knotted bag he wore around his neck. "Just this," he said. "To add to her string of them."

"Pearls," my sisters-in-law cooed.

"Extravagance," my father-in-law scoffed.

"Not when you don't have to purchase it," Christian told him.

"Ah, but you've paid for it. With your time and hard work and being away from home," he was told.

"I have another gift," Christian said. "But of course I don't know for certain when it will arrive."

"That cow," I said, knowing. "Andy, let's look for the cow your papa gave me." I set the presents aside and took my son's hand. We pretended to look for a cow under a leafy fern and inside a rotting cedar trunk.

"Cows don't grow in trees, Mama," Andy said. "Do they, Papa?"

"Indeed they don't. They should have been here by now. Wilhelm said he'd send a dozen from Portland, so we can begin dairying and give the goats a rest."

I hadn't realized he'd contacted Keil. I wondered when he'd done that. I hoped Wilhelm wasn't bringing the cows himself. Well, of course he wouldn't be. He was tied to his precious Aurora Mills.

Before dusk drifted in along with the usual evening March showers, we left the partiers to their music and dancing and began our trek home. Christian planned to stay the night, then take the boat back down to Bruceport in the morning. At the river crossing he said, "Someday we'll have to build a bridge so you don't have to struggle so much to take the trail."

"It's only bad a few weeks out of the year," I said.

"Indeed, but it looks dangerous, so swift as it is."

When we crossed to the other side I helped tie up the little boat, then loaded Andy up on the mule while Christian held Kate. I turned to reach for her and saw instead my husband staring at me. The expression on his face warmed my soul.

"What?" I said.

"You've changed, Emma. Once crossing this river would have made you physically ill. Now, you take the boat without effort and cross even when the river runs high."

"*Ja*. The children need me to know what I'm doing," I said. "I don't want to frighten them."

"So it is true," Christian teased. "Children do raise their parents up."

We slept soundly that evening so I didn't hear the cowbells the next morning until they were nearly upon us. "Yahoy." I heard the shout. A man's voice.

"Christian." I shook my husband's shoulder. "Wake up. Someone's here."

My husband rolled off the rope bed, grabbed his britches, then opened the latch. A drizzle of rain silvered the door opening, but I could still make out yellowish animals moving in the mist. The bells sounded muffled now under the rain.

"Are these Bethel cows?" Christian shouted.

"*Ja*. For the Giesys," a man answered.

"Leave them and come in out of the rain, man. There's plenty enough fodder to keep them content for a time. How many are there of you? Come now," he called to the herders, stepping back to invite them in.

How many men were there? I threw on my shawl around my nightdress and pulled the nightcap down over my ears. The air chilled. I'd have to fix a meal quickly. I'd build a fire, stir up johnnycakes. We had venison sausage I could fry, fruit preserves to spread on the cakes. I gave some of the goat cheese to Kate to keep her happy until I could milk the goat, handed Andy a bite of biscuit, then told him to dress as I set about my work.

While I was busy tending my family, being happy in my home, and while my back was turned, Jack Giesy stepped into my life.

———

Jack looked harmless all wet from the drizzle. He removed his hat when I turned around and swatted the wet of it against his thigh. "*Ach*," he said. "My mother taught me better manners than to baptize a woman's floor first thing in the morning."

"It'll soak in," Christian said, coming in behind him. "No matter. Here, take one of the stools. You too, Gus. What about the others, won't they come in?" Christian asked.

Jack shook his head. "We've got the other along, you know, that 'surprise' you wanted." He grinned at me. "The cows were nothing coming across the Cowlitz Trail," Jack said. "But those…hogs," he said. "Whooee! They'd rather rut in the underbrush than be herded."

Still, they'd had no trouble to speak of, to hear Jack tell the story. They brought the stock from Portland across the Columbia up through the thick brush to our home, the one farthest south of all the Giesy claims.

"It was cold," Jack said. " 'Cept for yesterday when the sun shone on us, when it could penetrate the trees. This is some country you've chosen, Chris. Alluring though, all the ferns and birds and I bet butterflies too, when there's time to let them land on your hand." He put his hat on his knee and motioned to Kate, who sat wide-eyed on her raised mat. She smiled and lowered herself from the mat then waddled, falling but once, to his arms.

"That's Cousin Jack," Christian said to her. "You've just met a distant relative."

I handed Gus, one of the herd boys, a mug of hot black tea and hesitated before Jack, not sure how he'd manage a hot tin and my daughter on his lap. With the ease of a dancer moving his partner from one side to the other, he transferred Kate to his opposite knee, then reached for the cup. *"Danke,"* he said. He obviously knew how to juggle a thing or two. "Two lovely girls you have here, Christian." He sipped, then let a slow grin move across his lips. "This may be a wet boarding house, Christian, but I like the service." He lifted the mug up as though it were a beer stein, nodded to Kate, and drank. I smelled the slightest scent of ale with his movements.

That was all there was to it, that first meeting. Jack joked about the journey, talked of moving through the night as the moonlight held. Gus frowned with Jack's talk of having energy enough to go all night. He told us the whiskey flask had kept them warm and he still had some left. They'd had no difficulty with the cows at all. "I don't know why Wilhelm was so opposed to this valley," he said.

"He was right," Christian said. He kept his eyes from me. "There were too many to prepare for, so taking the others to Portland, that made sense. But with these few hardy souls left, we'll make a go of it."

"Music comes from the river and trees like a symphony playing," Jack said. "I'm anxious to see the Bay, see what this river flows into. Who knows, maybe I'll stay."

Jack set his empty cup down on the earth floor, then responded to Kate's reaching for his mustache. He trimmed it, I could tell, for not a single hair reached down over his full upper lip. Mindlessly I touched my own lips. They were sore from Christian's beard and the kisses he'd left there. The taste of my husband still lingered.

"Don't let her pull your mustache," Christian said. "She has a wicked grip for just a little one."

"I'm used to little women," he said. I don't think the look he gave me was anything more than to enjoy his own joke. Jack took Kate's fingers in his hands, then blew against them, making a funny sound that caused both Andy and Kate to break into laughter. He was a natural with children. It must have been a Giesy trait.

"I'd better get you fed or you'll eat her fingers off," I said.

He popped Kate's fingers into his mouth as I said it, and she squealed, a sound that quickly turned to fear, perhaps as she realized what I'd said. Jack laughed.

"No, no, Kate." I reached for her. "He won't eat your fingers. It's all right. *Ach,* I'm sorry," I said.

"No matter," Jack said, then turned to Christian to begin their talk of cows and hogs. I put Kate back on our bed, then served the men their breakfast.

It was lighter outside now, the sun not showing itself but reflecting against the drizzle. Christian put on his canvas-waxed slicker and boots and stepped outside with Gus to send in the other two young men who'd traveled north with them. These were boys I didn't know, but when I asked as I served them, they did tell me about Jonathan and described Aurora Mills with steadied glumness.

They joked with Jack, though, who sat back from the table to take another cup of tea. He crossed his long legs at the ankles and each time I brought something to that end of the table to serve the boys, I had to step over them, my skirts catching on his brogans.

"Guess I could make your life easier," he said after the third time.

"*Ja*. You could, but then I don't know many men for whom that's a priority," I said.

He laughed.

Christian called to him and he stood, put on his hat and tipped his fingers to it. "My thanks to you, the infamous Emma Giesy," he said, then ducked his head to go out of the door.

Infamous Emma Giesy. Where had that come from?

I stood in the open doorway, shouting directions and pointing at which cows I thought would be good for us to keep. They all looked pretty similar, with wide bony back hips and neat short horns at their heads. Ayershires they were, a sturdy animal known for both meat and milk, though sometimes prone to opinion. They'd fit in well.

Their selection made, Christian, with Andy close behind, led the two cows toward the lean-to, where the goat resided. At least the cows were docile. I'd heard of some of the wild cows with long horns that roamed the Territory, orphans from Spanish herds brought north some years before. At least these with Christian could be led. We'd have to work on the barn soon though a stanchion would have to do for now. The winters were wet but mild and the mules had fared well just standing out under big cedar trees. We'd raise the barn in the summer when oystering wasn't so demanding.

The hogs would be a little different to manage. "I'll ask Boshie and Karl if they can build a moveable corral," Christian said. "I don't want the hogs wandering too far. Bears could get them, or they'll meander away and we'll never get them back."

"I can return later and help," Jack offered. "But wouldn't it be better to just keep all the hogs in one place? You're raising them in common. Separating the cows because it's just easier for a family to handle them two at a time, that I can see, but the hogs, well, why not keep them all together?"

I looked at Christian.

"Maybe it would be better for you to take the hogs on. Rudy might be willing to manage them all."

"I believe you're mistaken, Jack," I said. "We're not a branch of the colony at Aurora."

"Not the way I heard it," Jack said. He stretched. "But whatever way you want to go, Chris, it's fine with us. We're only what six, seven miles from Rudy and the rest?"

"Indeed. Take the hogs," Christian said. "There's too much going on now to ask Martin or Rudy to come here and build while I'm at Bruceport. Rudy'll do well with the hogs."

My husband avoided looking at me. He handed Jack the pack of food I'd prepared for them, then set about arranging a standing place for the cows. I heard him and Andy talking softly to the animals. When I walked out to get Opal, the goat, to milk her, I made sure I didn't look at them. One wrong look back and I knew I'd say something I could only later regret.

———

Christian returned that day to the Bay, and I kept my words to myself, not wanting to start talking to hear what I thought, not wishing to stumble into an argument that couldn't be resolved before he left. I kissed him good-bye and told him to have a safe trip and wondered when I'd see him again. "Next month, for certain," he said. "It's too much time away from you and the children."

I also didn't ask him to explain the present tense of his last words, a sentence that sounded like he was having serious second thoughts about being away, oystering. I decided to keep my own counsel or talk with Mary later to see if I could sort out how I felt about the "common fund colony" that had returned like a counterfeit coin promising riches but taking a toll instead.

Did Mary and Boshie see their work at the mill as contributing to the common fund? Maybe until the redwood was paid for or the time devoted to splitting the spruce wood. Maybe all was just an exchange until people got on their feet, not the return of the common fund. I refused to believe we were somehow just a stepchild of Keil's colony.

In the kitchen later I spoke out loud, though I knew Andy didn't understand. "How will we have something to leave you if your father keeps with the old ways of the common fund?"

I stomped the stick in the washtub, thumping so hard that the pepper mill fell off its shelf. I picked it up and slammed it back onto the shelf, causing the lid on the saltbox to jar open. I took a deep breath. I needed to calm down. *Ach,* even the seedlings I'd nurtured through the winter shivered with my outrage in their potato skins filled with dirt.

This was his family's influence. They saw this community as a branch, just as Nineveh had been a branch to Bethel. We were all to be one happy family here with Keil as the trunk of the big, happy tree. Maybe that was why his family didn't chastise Christian too much for taking risks with the oysters. They assumed he'd bring resources to help them with their needs. Maybe that was why they teased me, knowing that I was the *Dummkopf,* the one kept in the dark, the only one who didn't know anything about it.

But we'd put our own money into oystering. Well, Christian's physical labor was our part. Karl had put money in and so had Joe Knight, money he'd earned laboring in San Francisco.

Maybe I was the only one who assumed that we chose to remain as independent people, not replicas of Keil's vision. That might explain why there was no rush to build a church; any church would be constructed in the main community, now Aurora. Maybe that was why there was so little push toward a school even with a superintendent. The main community would offer that.

Well it was not to be, not here, not under my kneading hands. *Nein.* If I was in the dark, then I would be like a mushroom and grow there, learn what I needed. I'd get Karl to think about offering a regular school schedule as soon as the weather changed. April to September were good months for schooling; Andy was still too young, really, to take the mule on his own to the stockade and back, but John Giesy's children were old enough and the Stauffers and Schaefers had school-age children. John could order the schedule, free children for harvest, then offer school for a few more months until the rains came in earnest. I'd talk to him. And I'd ask Andreas and John to consider regular preaching on Sundays, like a real community. Sarah and the others might come if we acted like people who knew where our bounty came from and took time each week to express our gratitude.

When Christian returned in April, I already had the garden dug up and the small seedlings I'd nurtured through the winter set into the prodigal soil. I'd planted tiny flower seeds, too, totally impractical. He and the mule worked a larger field and we planted potatoes. It was already decided, he told me, that though it was expensive to have wheat brought in from Toledo on the Cowlitz, wheat raised by the Hudson's Bay Company, that's what we'd do. Growing wheat on the Willapa was toil in disaster. The grist mill already handled seventy-five bushels a day. "Sam says oats can make it, but you saw for yourself the small heads of the wheat you grew last year," Christian told me.

But I wanted a harvest to call my own.

"Ah, woman, you are stubborn. You cannot change the seasons to your wishes." But he let me plant wheat. I'm sure his brothers called it "Emma's indulgence."

That spring I had little time for complaining even to myself. The cows needed milking twice a day and the cream skimmed and kept cool in the river. I churned butter, hands on the plunger and my foot rocking Kate as she sat in the rocking chair fighting sleep. I was secretly glad I didn't have the pigs to tend to as well.

When Christian was gone, Henry or Rudy sometimes brought over meat that I smoked, keeping the fire going at just the right flame. I asked after everyone's health and was told all were fine, even Jack, they said, who had gone south to the Columbia to pick up the next load of wheat. "He didn't stop on his way through," I said.

"It would be unseemly," Henry said. "A young man visiting with his cousin's wife while her husband's away."

"I only meant I could have offered him something to eat," I said. "Shown the Diamond Rule." My words must have bristled if the raised eyebrow of Rudy and the way he looked at Henry were any indication. But then they were both safe in my presence, doing nothing unseemly. It just took two of them to deliver a ham.

Weeding took hours, and keeping my eye on the ever-moving Kate and Andy meant I had little time not already devoted to simply surviving. When Christian came home, I sighed with relief, though it meant cooking bigger meals and washing clothes whether I felt like it or not. But by the next morning, his presence was enough to buoy. Just knowing he was there, within the call of my voice, gave me rest. I did raise the common fund issue with him, finally, one day in June.

He sighed. "It is the best way here, Emma. We should have good return on the oysters this year, a good return. Some of what we make must go to *Herr* Keil, as they too struggle to build up the colony and have so many more to worry over. We agreed to pay back what the colony loaned us. You remember."

"*Ja,* but not beyond that. I didn't believe we would simply go back to where we were before," I said. "We set out on a different path by staying here."

"Was it so bad to know the weight was shared by others?" he asked. "To know we can care for widows and children, those in need beyond ourselves, is that so hard? It's the way to live the Diamond Rule, making life better for others."

"We were to care for our own first," I said.

"Emma. That isn't what you told me long months ago. You said we should reach out more to others. How else would the world read the story of our faith, if we just kept it to ourselves, our own little community?"

"Is that why you've taken in a housekeeper?" I asked.

"What? Who said that?"

I shrugged my shoulders.

"They tease you, Emma. I've no housekeeper. If you saw our hut you'd believe."

"Well, good. But this common fund made up of only former Bethelites does keep us as our own little colony. It doesn't reach out to others. People don't even come to the church services because they feel it's all us Germans. Andreas won't use English. How unwelcoming is that for our neighbors? I don't think any of the other settlers are sending their children to the school, either."

"John tells me you had words with him about that."

"*Ja.* I did."

"But because we take care of each other, we *can* give to others. Not just the tithe, but beyond the tithe. John will come around. My father will speak in English if there is someone there to hear him. Don't you see that, Emma? We are a generous people, passing good things on."

"So Joe's investment, his own money, he returns that now to the colony?"

"If he wishes. Karl too. But our share of the earnings, a portion each year, will go to pay Wilhelm. The rest, into a common fund. It is the best way I know how to take care of my family. I could not be away so much, Emma, if it wasn't for the others carrying my weight here."

"I haven't asked them for anything!" I said.

"They tend the hogs. We'll have good bacon and hams through the winter. They grind the grain and bring it. They helped build this very house. They bring you game."

"I could shoot my own game if you'd teach me how. But then how would I get the ammunition if not from your brothers? Or would you provide it for me? If I begged? If I used the proper words, nothing unseemly?"

"Whatever you need you may receive by just asking."

"You will not allow a discussion of this?" I asked.

"Indeed. Discuss all you wish. But the decision is made."

I gathered up willow branches for the mats and took them out to dry in the sun. Nothing had changed. Nearly four years of working side by side with my husband, holding his hand when he thought to drown in disappointment, praying for him, doing all I could think to do and still, he made the decisions. I was still just a woman, a wife, a mother, allowed to have an opinion but, like an unwatered seed, never see it grow into harvest.

The late-afternoon sun soothed my face as I sat with my back to the wall. With a stick, Kate patted at a spider as she sat. The goat followed Andy through the grasses while Christian lifted the bucket and went out to milk the cows. I closed my eyes. There had to be a way. I wanted more for my children than having to beg every time I had a desire. Andy was a smart child. He'd be a good student who might one day want to go far away to school, the way my uncle had, the worldly ambassador. How could I fuel my children's dreams if all we worked for poured into a pool others could take from? And if they could give when we asked, they could also withhold, those Giesy brothers. Just as Keil could. The man still ruled us even though he was miles away!

I started weaving a basket from the fronds left over from last year's mat-making. The baskets I attempted through the winter months were poor results fit only to hold the roots I dug. They made good storage at least but wouldn't be anything I could possibly sell. I lacked talent. I lacked gifts. The weather worked against my wheat. How could I be independent?

I got up and went into the cabin, put the fronds back up in the loft. They'd continue to dry there. When I came down the ladder, a letter lay on the table. Christian must have brought it from Bruceport, though I hadn't seen it that past evening. It was from Catherine. Dear, lovesick Catherine. At least that's how I saw her. Jack was much too charming for Catherine, too old for her as well. He was a bit of a buzzard with a songbird's voice.

But I read the parts about Papa now having property in his name. So not all that he earned had gone into the common fund in Bethel. I tried to remember what he might have sold or where he might have worked to earn his own money. Somehow he had found a way to earn resources that didn't go into the colony. So it was in my Wagner blood to do something innovative. Christian hadn't said that anything *I* might earn had to go into the common fund. And didn't he give me that twinkle in his eye when I teased him about his territorial marshal pay? Maybe he would withhold something for his own. Maybe he wouldn't object if I did as well.

Ach, there is always a way. Begin to weave; God provides the thread. How could I have forgotten?

———

The Fourth of July celebration was the greatest joy of my days in Willapa. Christian came to get us and we all went back with him to Bruceport. I liked the sense of a bustling town, with street vendors serving pork on sticks and hard-boiled eggs for sale right on the street. A band played, though not our German one. We'd heard the Giesys playing when we stopped at the stockade just to say hello as we made our way back to the Bay. His brothers didn't seem to mind that we weren't staying for the Giesy celebration; at least no one said anything to me that suggested that. At Bruceport people made speeches standing on the steps of Coon and Woodard's Store and Public House (Sam Woodard had a branch he owned here). I saw a few women and Andy made eyes with tykes his age. Christian pointed out where the justice held court. I listened to talk of events back East and the obstinacy of Governor Stevens. Posters about the martial law still hung on a board outside the wooden hut that passed as the sheriff's office. One hung upside down.

When Christian bent down to remove a stone from inside Andy's boot, I noticed his thinning hair and a tiny mole I'd never seen before at the back of his head. He needed to wear his hat. I wondered where he'd left it.

It was a slow-paced day with few worries. Karl Ruge would milk the cows and tend the goat and mule. That night, we placed our blankets and mats on the beach, far enough from the incoming tide but not too far to see blasts of fireworks sent out over the water and the long island that separated the Bay from the sea. We set the lantern behind us. Andy pressed his hands to his ears with each loud sound, but he grinned. We heard what we thought were "probably a few happy Americans celebrating," Christian said. "Or gun shots."

"Will you have to keep the peace?" I said. "Take someone to jail or something?"

"Not likely," my husband said, pulling me toward him. "They'll wind down and sleep it off come morning."

The mosquitoes buzzed about our heads, but I'd put a mud paste on the children's faces and hands and at their ankles, making sure they kept their shirts and pants on. We'd pitched netting over us like a tent and kept the fire going. When the children fell asleep and the mosquitoes were carried off by an ocean breeze, I asked Christian if we could walk just a little way along the beach. "To see if we can find a glass jar or some other shipwrecked treasure," I said.

"We'll stumble around like drunkards more likely."

I laughed at him and he indulged me once again, allowing me to hold the lantern as I scanned the driftwood exposed by the light as macabre shapes. What was so clear in the daylight was so easily obscured in the night. Christian sniffed the salty air, then pinched his nose to wipe away the drainage. It was an act of his I detested, but I let it pass without comment. I must do things to annoy him too, I thought. There was no sense in making this pleasant time a misery.

We found no treasures, nothing delivered from a distant sea. We walked past piles of discarded oyster shells. "A settler built a kiln one year and tried to burn the shells into lime," Christian told me. "But he decided the hard-shell clams yielded a better lime. Might be something to consider down the road. Lime makes a fine fertilizer, which we'll need in time as we use up the land."

My husband the innovator, always thinking of the future.

Back at the netting, I recognized that I had found a treasure: my treasure was the companionship of my husband and sleeping family. It seemed the time to give Christian my Fourth of July gift. I pulled the rolled parchment I'd brought with me out of my bag. "What's this?" he asked when I handed it to him. He sat up, hunched over it in the lamplight.

"It's a drawing I made of you," I said. "A likeness."

He didn't say anything as he stared. I thought he might have been disappointed.

"I'll get paint one day and it'll look better," I said. "And the light isn't good here. But Andy recognized it when I showed him. And I made a little tiny sketch of it in my letter home, and Catherine knew exactly who it was though she couldn't read the medal. There." I pointed.

"Who told you about the medal?" he said.

"Your father. It's an artillery service medal, for your marksmanship, he said. You didn't actually ever shoot at any…person, did you?"

"*Nein.* They give medals out just for being ready in a time of war," he said.

"We weren't really at war," I countered.

"Not how Governor Stevens saw it. Anyway, it is a good picture, Emma. You have a talent I didn't know you had. But you ought not waste your time on making a likeness of me. Draw the children instead."

I shrugged but beamed with his praise. I didn't let his alteration of an idea serve as criticism.

That night my husband showed me how he loved me in the quiet while our children slept. He kissed me with a tenderness that brought shivers. I thought I might tell him in the morning of my plan to earn money of my own, but at that moment I didn't want to speak of common funds or independence. I only wanted to be with him, to know him and let him know me. That night we spoke all the words of love we could imagine, tasted of the honey of our full moon.

8

Emma

A Compass Lost

"But why? Can't you just send it to him? Why do you have to go to Aurora?"

"And why must you always question what I do and the way I have to do it, Emma?" Christian said. "Besides, I want to see how the colony there progresses."

We stood at the water's edge. Joe Knight held Andy's hand and the two stood a distance away, being polite. I suppose we did sound as though we'd had this argument before. Soon Christian would be lifting me and then the children, carrying us out to the tender to get into the boat that would sail us up the Willapa.

This argument annoyed more than others, though, because I'd misunderstood, thinking he planned to return to the Willapa with us after this captivating weekend of the Fourth. Instead, his plan sent us home while he headed across the Bay then down the Wallacut River. He'd take a steamer up the Columbia to Portland. To see *Herr* Keil. To make our payment. "It would be too dangerous to put something so precious into the mail," he insisted. "What if it were stolen?"

"You're the marshal. You could catch the culprit," I said. I was being difficult, my back lifting like a frightened cat's.

"I won't stay there, Emma. I'll be back. Maybe I can talk your brother into coming for a visit. Would you like that?"

"Don't wheedle your way through my annoyance by offering up my brother," I snapped. "If he wanted to come he would have. He must be holding some grudge I don't even know about to have stayed away so long."

"Not every act that you don't like has something to do with you, *Liebchen*." I frowned at him. "Indeed. I can bring back things we need. Treasures for the children. Some pigment and resins for that painting you want to make. Maybe I'll look for a ewe."

"Something more to place in the common hold I suppose," I said. Into his silence I blew like old sheets in the wind, knowing soon they'd wear thin. I sighed. "A bred ewe would be nice. To make our own yarn would be good and we could start our own little flock. *Ja, ja,* I know," I said, holding up my hand before he could comment on things held in common. "Maybe you can make me a spinning wheel so I won't have to use Mary's." I wiped Kate's face with my handkerchief. "I do wish your family had thought to bring out more of our household things when they came. Though I realize we had few household things in Bethel, having never had a home of our own before, you always being gone."

"I can see this is the day when everything I say upsets you and reminds you of past indignities. You have an amazing memory, *Frau* Giesy," he said, "and I can tell you are about to share that gift with me if I stay here any longer."

I sighed again, this time motioning for Joe to bring Andy. We'd had such a good weekend together at Bruceport. I wished we could just stay; maybe build ourselves a house on stilts over tide flats. I'd have to mention that to Christian.

But not now. Now it was Monday and a new week and Christian was going to Aurora. I hoisted Kate into my arms, then Christian lifted us both and sloshed across the shoals and shallow water to our waiting boat. Joe Knight followed with Andy.

"I wish they had a dock," I complained, just for something to say. My husband settled us onto the craft. "When will you leave then?" I asked.

"Tomorrow, barring anything going wrong here that needs my attention."

"Is Joe going with you? Maybe we should come along."

"One of the herd boys is heading back with me. He's just arrived. I'll be back in a week or so. Think of me as being here working instead of there at Aurora. Then maybe it won't seem like such a terrible separation."

"*Ja.* Tell a story to my mind."

"Draw another picture," he said. "I'll look at it when I get back." He kissed my nose then, a rare public expression of affection. His hand lingered in mine and he squeezed it, then turned and sloshed his way back toward the shore.

I watched him and remembered a dream I'd had where we'd gone underwater together. I asked him if he knew how to get where we were going and he said no, that he'd lost his compass.

"Do you have your compass?" I shouted. He held his hand to his ear as though he couldn't hear. The wind whipped the sail insistently. At the water's edge, he turned and I waved a last good-bye. The boatman pulled his anchor and we moved out into the stream.

I'd have to think of this separation as just like the others, with him oystering while I tended the children. It's no different. Nothing to worry over. *Tell ourselves stories,* ja. *That is what we must do when we pull up our anchor and have only our compass to trust as we sail away.*

———

Maybe it was the dream. Maybe it was the idea that he was leaving me for Keil, doing Keil's bidding once again. Perhaps it was nothing more than women's intuition. I wasn't sure what compelled me, but about a half hour up the Willapa, with the seagulls crying above us, I shouted to the oarsman, "Turn back, *ja*?"

He frowned and I spoke my English more slowly. "I want to go back."

"The Mister won't be liking it," he said.

"The Mister will understand that you listened to his wife," I said. "Besides, you'll earn twice the fee."

"We'll stay with Papa?" Andy asked.

"*Ja.* We'll stay and if nothing else, see if we can convince him not to go away at all." I imagined Christian's frown when he saw us but I pitched that thought away. I could turn his frowns to laughter.

Kate patted my cheek as the oarsman began rowing the craft back toward the Bay. Now that we headed west, I was in an even greater hurry to arrive. It was silly. I'd just said good-bye but I felt a joy in heading back toward him, in surprising him. I'd change his mind, I would.

A dark bank of clouds formed in the western sky and I told myself it was wise we'd turned back. Why, there might be a squall or something. This storm would blow over tonight and then we could both leave together in the morning—if Christian still insisted on going to Aurora after I tried one more time to convince him otherwise.

I held Kate against my chest and she slept. Andy shouted up at the seagulls. This was what a woman did, try to convince her husband of reasonable acts to take. Christian would forgive me the extra cost of the oarsman having to bring us back.

As we approached Bruceport again, I watched as an old man loaded chairs and a bedstead and barrels onto a raft tethered to a piling at the river's edge. His long white beard caught in the swirl of breeze. Shoalwater women culled oysters. Tiny drifts of smoke from cooking fires reached up to a sky now dotted with a mix of dark clouds. The sun still warmed our faces. I licked my lips. The oarsman clanged a bell and I watched as Sam Woodard stepped out of his warehouse. He put a telescope on us and I waved. Then Christian soon stood beside him and I waved again, my whole arm sweeping across the sky. They walked toward us, both wearing their oystering waders, followed by shadows on the wet sand. The herd boy joined them from off to the side and before the oarsman could say anything I said, "I forgot something."

"What did you forget that was so important?" Christian said. He crossed his arms over his chest. He didn't look angry but wore a small frown of concern. Sam smiled and shook his head.

"We forgot that we had one more day to spend with you," I said. "One more day before you leave for Aurora Mills. A chance to spend it with your family and here we'd sailed away. We can all leave together in the morning. You go your way; we'll go ours. If you still insist on leaving us."

"*Ach,* Emma." Christian said. "You waste this oarsman's time and other people's money in this foolish return."

"Maybe," I said. "But you can't deny you'll like having someone tonight to share your bed."

"She has you there," Sam said and the herd boy laughed with him.

It's the details one remembers. The way the sun slanted through the clouds. The perspiration on my face. The lack of premonition. I stood with the children at my side on the riverbank, where Christian had sent me while he helped the old man at his raft. I don't think Christian would have seen the old man if he hadn't come out to greet us again. I don't think the herd boy or Christian would have been at that place where the river poured into the Bay. But he was. They were. I stood with my children cluck-henned against my hem. Christian said he had to help that man who was going to lose everything on that raft if he didn't get things tied down. The next thing I knew, he was on the rickety craft with the man, tying the pieces of furniture down, the herd boy helping with ropes and a canvas tarp. "I'll just be a minute," Christian had said. "Just wait up there on the bank with the children."

Sam had gone back inside. We stood waiting, watching them work.

Then came the squall.

It was a freakish burst of wind and rain that tore at the tether, then spun the raft and its cargo out toward the Bay. I'm not even sure of how it transpired. I'd turned my face from the blast of rain and wind, then looked back. A cedar dresser shifted against a barrel on the raft and then as though in slow motion, the old man reached to resettle it but instead fell backward into the sea. I heard his shout, an "Oh!" of surprise. I watched as Christian moved swiftly to that side of the raft, his tall body leaning down, then he dropped to one knee to reach his hand out, the black heel of his waders etched against the skyline. The herd boy grasped a bedstead as it shifted with Christian's weight on that side and the wind acting as a swirling agent, pushing then lifting. They were no longer attached to the piling, had become like a leaf in the sea.

"What's Papa doing?" Andy asked.

"He's helping someone who was foolish enough to move furniture out in a squall," I said.

Christian reached for the man. I couldn't see him. He must have slipped under the raft. Christian jumped in then. *He didn't remove his waders.* He held on to the raft, but by then it had swirled out farther and waves washed over it. I lost sight of the herd boy, hoping he stood on the far side reaching for Christian or pulling the old man up.

"His waders. They'll fill," I whispered.

The wind took their shouts from us, if there were any. And then with relief I saw the old man swimming toward the shore, leaving the raft of his furniture. The herd boy wasn't on the raft; I couldn't see Christian gripping it. They must be on the far side. Surely I'd see him and Christian any moment following the old man, swimming to safety.

But I didn't.

The raft drifted away.

The old man stood dripping on shore looking back at it.

"Christian? Christian!" *This can't be happening!* I ran, sweeping Kate up into my arms, screaming. "Christian! For heaven's sake, where are you? Where?" I sloshed toward the water, moved back and forth along the shoreline. "Christian! Please. Where are you?"

The old man stood panting, his hands on his thighs as he breathed heavily. "Where is he? What have you done to my husband?" I wanted to pummel him, but Kate clung to my neck.

"Papa? Where's Papa?" Andy asked.

The old man coughed up seawater. He shouted for Sam, who had already run from the warehouse at my cries, I suppose. "He's out there!" I screamed. "Christian is out there. And the boy. They were with the raft. They went under. Please, please, please. Sam! You have to save him! I don't even know if he can swim!"

Sam signaled the oarsman who had already pushed his craft out to the sea. Together they rowed toward the raft that bounced and jerked toward the long island that separated the Bay from the sea. Wind still whipped at us. Maybe Christian was hanging on and I just couldn't see him.

It was Sunday, July 6, about four in the afternoon. I dropped to my knees in prayer.

"I'm so sorry, Missis." The old man coughed. "So sorry. The furniture was just old stuff."

———

They recovered Christian's body in the dusk, cut him free from the ropes, brought him to me.

I could not believe my eyes. I could not. A swell of outrage surged through me. A waste, that's what it was. A complete and total waste of two lives. Christian, always doing for others, always acting the Diamond Rule, making one's life better than his own. But at what cost? The old man saved himself! He didn't need fixing or helping. He did it on his own! Oh, the irony, the irony. God must be laughing at me, I thought, to take my husband over such a trivial thing as old furniture and to save the man who'd caused it.

But there he lay, on the wet sand, his face the color of gray stone. I threw myself across his chest. Tears did not come. "Oh, Christian, how could you? How could you leave me here?"

Christian lay still as I brushed the sea life from his face and straightened the collar at his neck. "How could you?" I whispered. "We had so much time before us."

The herd boy's body washed ashore the next morning.

———

I don't remember much of what happened next. I know I wanted to take Christian home. I told Sam that and he nodded, said he'd have a casket made up quick as he could and he'd row us up the Willapa himself. I guess we must have stayed in the cabin, but I didn't see Joe Knight until the next morning when he put his arms out to me, his eyes as red as sunset from the tears he'd shed. The children said almost nothing. I think they must have seen my eyes, my constant shaking of my head, my muttering words: "Such a waste. Such a waste."

In the morning, I carried my children and walked by myself to the river. We piled into a wide craft with the caskets at the center and headed home. *Home.* Things would be better if I could just get Christian home. I knew I should grieve the herd boy and his parents but I had only so much room for grief and I gripped it tight in my fist, held it just for my husband. The outrage I held for the nameless old man, for Keil and for God.

How would I tell Christian's parents? How would I tell his friends? Karl Ruge, Martin? His parents would say Christian shouldn't have been at the ocean anyway, "messing with oysters." Karl might say it as well, perhaps blame himself for being our partner. Would they acknowledge that if he hadn't been planning to return money to Keil, he would have been working the oysters that day? Keil had some part in this just as he did in every bad thing that happened to us. If Christian had been working oysters, he might not have seen the old man—that wretched, surviving, old man—and then he'd still be with us, brushing the hair from Andy's eyes, kissing Kate on her nose, telling me I cost him extra money by coming back. *Maybe I'd cost him more than that.*

At Willapa, Sarah came out with a smile on her face. Then she saw the look Sam wore. She stared at me, the children, and the boxes in the center of the tendering craft.

"Oh, Emma," she whispered. "How..."

"Stupid," I said. "It was all such a waste." She held me in her arms then, and at last I could weep.

"You will leave the casket here," Barbara said after we arrived at the stockade and Sam told her what had happened. She rubbed her hand along the wood. "We will prepare the body properly."

"I want to take him home," I said. "We can bury him on his own place."

"*Nein,*" Andreas countered. "He will be buried beside Willie, on the hill. Leave him here. Leave your son here as well. Take the girl and go home if you must. Martin will come get you when we are ready."

I bristled. "My children will go home with me," I said. "And my husband."

"You no longer have a husband," Barbara said. "I no longer have a son. You go." She patted my back. We shared a grief. "You will find comfort at your cabin; I find comfort in preparing my son's body, *ja*?" I could let her have this time with Christian, I decided. I nodded. "I will take the children," I said.

"I'll go with you," Martin told me. "Karl too. We'll see you safely there."

The air felt balmy as we rode in silence. How could the weather be perfect on a day dripping such grief? I held myself together until we reached the house. Opal bleated her greeting and I felt tears burn against my eyes. I blinked. "I'll milk the goat," Martin said. "Go on inside."

I carried Kate on my hip. Andy removed the lantern from the mule, the lantern Christian had made for me, the light that had last illuminated our lives as we walked the beach seeking treasures. Had that really just been a few days before? Karl opened the door. Andy ran in with the lantern and just the sight of it there on that table, knowing Christian would never again light that lamp, took my breath away.

Karl reached for Kate before I fell.

———

Darkness already shrouded when I awoke. A pinprick of light glowed from the candle on the table. Strange shadows danced against the walls. The candle shouldn't be lit over there, away from me. My tongue felt thick and my eyes were gooey. I scanned the room stopping at Mary, who sat beside the light. I could hear the scrape of her needle through cloth as she found the hole in the cross-stitch she worked on. Her face held no features. Where were the children? What was she doing here? I tried to sit up.

Then I remembered. My breath came from an empty hollow welled out in my heart. I suppressed a sob, I thought.

"You're awake," Mary said. She set her needlework down on our rough table and came closer.

"Where are the children?"

"Andy went back with Martin for now. Just for a little while, to give you time to come to the understanding of this. Kate's asleep, bless her. She patted your head for the longest time and then finally just dozed off. I carried her to the cradle. I'm so sorry, so very sorry."

"What time is it?"

"Midnight or so."

"You should go home, be with Elizabeth and Boshie. It isn't necessary for you to be here. I'll be all right. I'll get Andrew in the morning. I want him with me."

She patted my shoulder. "You can get him at the service. You need your own rest."

"Is that possible? Do you know what's happened? Of course you do. I just mean—"

"I know what you mean. But please. Let me just stay with you. I want to be here."

I lay back on the pillow but in doing so I smelled my husband, the salt of him, the brush of his mustache on my mouth, the weight of his head on my breast. I jerked up.

"What's wrong?"

"It's him. Here." I shook my head. "I need to get up, work, do something. There's the funeral. His clothes. I need to give them clothes for the burial."

"Yes. John and Henry are taking care of those things, Emma. They all want—we all want to help. We're all just so sorry. They're making the arrangements, digging the…next to Willie's grave. Martin can dress the body. He knows about those things with herbs and whatnot."

"I should wash his body. It's what a wife does."

"His mother will help with that. It will help her grieve."

"Yes. Help her grieve a senseless death."

My mind swirled to capture the image of Christian's last moments alive on this earth. The flailing, the rush of water, going under the raft, getting tangled in the ropes. Maybe he tried to save the boy, but the young man's panic pulled him under. Did the old man try to save Christian or just himself? *Does Christian know how to swim? Did he?* He'd joked about it once. Perhaps it was no joke. What courage it must have taken for him to work the oysters, to be brother to the water if he didn't know how to swim. *Why did I have no foreboding? Were we not as close as I imagined? Surely if we had been as one, I would have heard him crying out to me or been warmed by the presence of a comforting God preparing me for loss. I felt nothing. I, who feared the water, hadn't been worried when he decided to help the old man; just annoyed that he would take the time from us.* "I had every reason to fear water," I told Mary.

"It was an accident from what Sam says. Just an—"

"It's Keil," I said, interrupting. "Christian insisted on taking the certificates to Keil so he could pay our debt. Always it's been Keil, driving our lives and now Christian's death." I stood, paced. "The goat," I said. "Someone needs to milk the goat."

"Boshie did that. And fed the mule. There's nothing you need to do but rest. Build up your strength. It hasn't even hit you yet, Emma. That much I know. When we lost the baby, well…"

Her voice trailed off. I couldn't listen. My mind rolled around thinking that when Christian came home I'd tell him all about this, how strange I felt, how empty, how my husband had squandered his life in a meaningless way.

He's not coming home.

I resented Mary then. I resented her having already grieved and lived through what I had yet to bear. I resented that she still had a husband she'd go home to. I resented her knowing what to do when I didn't.

I gazed at the door, expectant though I knew that he wouldn't walk through it. Could the human mind hold two opposing thoughts at once? Mary had grief's ritual down. Everyone knew what to do except me.

I wanted Andy with me. I wanted to decide about the casket. I wanted my husband buried here, on our property. Why did it have to be in the place Keil picked for his son? Why was it Keil, always Keil? Didn't I have say in any of this?

I picked up Kate and held her to me, her sweet little face like a full moon, so round, so glowing in the lamplight. I brushed at her nose and the crackled sound she made as she breathed ceased. I watched her chest move in and out. I wanted to hold her tight to me but I didn't want to wake her. My fingers made round motions on her skin. She and Andy were all I had now. All that mattered.

"Emma? Are you all right?"

Who knows how long I'd stood there. My heart felt snowed on, wet, thick, suffocating snow. Mary lifted Kate from my arms, my daughter's little legs hanging over Mary's forearm, relaxed, her head lolling in safe sleep. Mary pressed her onto the bed, pulled a light cover over her legs.

"My mind feels foggy." I inhaled, couldn't get a deep breath. "I'll fix tea. I need tea."

"Let me do it for you," Mary said.

"He's my husband, the father of my children. Five years, Mary. That's all I'm to get? Five years? What kind of God would be so unloving that—"

"Oh, Emma, don't. Don't blame, not now."

I looked at her. I wasn't sure what I was supposed to do, but here was something forbidden, something I *wasn't* supposed to do. My contrary ways, what Emma Wagner Giesy was known for.

My husband understood me. Maybe he was the only one who had ever understood me. And now he was gone.

That thought finally brought the tears I hoped would cleanse my angry soul.

———

They stayed with me three days, the Giesy women. They helped me select clothes for Christian to be buried in and carried them off. I compelled them to bring Andy back despite my mother-in-law's suggestion that Andy stay longer with them, "where he would have male influences to guide him during this trying time."

"He has the memory of his father to guide him," I said. "And me."

Having Andy home gave me strength. I needed that success. Power, after all, is setting a goal and gathering resources to make it happen.

When my mother-in-law brought him back to me, she spent the day. It was her first visit to our home since the house was built. We looked at my garden with a good stand of peas and onions and potatoes. The wheat field looked paltry. "Planting that was a waste when you can get wheat ground at the mill," she said, pointing with her chin toward the field. She looked to the flowers. "And posies." She clucked her tongue. *Waste. A life given for nothing, that was a waste.*

I didn't defend. I had no energy. Christian understood my efforts.

"He loved fishing," she said then. "He'd plop his line into the water, even little puddles of water in the spring. Then he'd come running to tell me he'd seen a fish there. He was always so hopeful." She sighed. "He loved the mountains. I always thought we'd go back one day to Switzerland, just to see them and what we left behind. Did you know that he broke his arm once, running and falling? He didn't even cry but it was so crooked I knew it was broken. His father set it. I nursed him and now…" My arm brushed hers and she reached to grab my hand. She squeezed it firm, and the warmth of it and its strength brought tears. She was perhaps the closest anyone could come to knowing of the emptiness I felt. "A parent isn't supposed to outlive a child," she said, wiping at her eyes. "Especially not a child who has lived to forty-five." She released my hand, fumbled at her sleeve, then blew her nose in the handkerchief she'd kept there.

Andy ran past us, chasing the goat, grabbing for the animal's twitching tail. It bleated in unison with my son's laughter. I could not imagine my life without that child. How would I survive the loss of his laughter or of Kate's? What must it be like for my mother-in-law to have given birth and witnessed a son grow to manhood, and then to watch him be buried? Death was difficult enough, but to lose a part of my own flesh? Such courage it takes to be a mother.

My mother-in-law said, "Such strange events we see in living. I must cherish the years I had with him. You too, Emma. Others, Mary, had only minutes with the child she lost. And you, just five years as a wife." She took my hand again. "But you're young," she added.

I braced myself for the words, "You'll marry again," but they didn't come. I would never do that, not ever marry again, and so I'd never have another child that I would worry would one day be lost to me. These two were enough to worry over.

Christian wasn't supposed to leave a wife and two small children, but I didn't say this to her.

"The service," I said. "I—"

"It is being handled, Emma." She patted my hand. "You have too much to think about now. His brothers and father will take care of those details."

These were details I wanted to take care of, but my tongue fell silent under the weight of her grief.

———

I fought sleep, fearing I'd have to face the loss again each time I woke. The children both slept with me, something my mother-in-law suggested. "It will ease the pain of not sharing a bed," she said. She forgot that my bed stayed empty for weeks at a time when Christian traveled, when he farmed the oysters. In the night, a child's elbow now pressed against my back; a tiny arm draped across my face. I dozed and woke from dreams where Christian fell over a cliff all tangled up with a mule; or where he sank into deep mud and I couldn't pull him out; or, the worst, that dream where we together dived underwater in a craft and I'd asked if he knew how to get where we intended to go and he said, "No, I've forgotten my compass."

I planned to grieve after the service. I'd simmer until then, temper the slow boil I felt brewing that without watching would spill over and sear a hole clear through my heart. When everyone left us alone, my children and I would decide what we would do, not Christian's family, not everyone else who thought they knew best. When we were our own island, then we'd decide when to cross the water to the mainland or whether to stay all alone.

Karl and Boshie came to escort us to the stockade for the service. It was one of those glorious summer days with every sweet scent of wildflower imaginable floating in the air and yet one could not hold on to any particular scent. Birdsong became so loud at times I didn't even hear the clop-clop of the mule crossing the river. A bridge might be there one day, but my husband wouldn't build it. Tiny flashes of memory of trips taken with Christian formed, then darted like dragonflies, away. I'd never hear him call me *Liebchen* again. Never feel his mustache prick my lips. No physical sensations; no recognizing his gait from a distance. Just memories and perhaps not even them if they sifted through my mind forever as they had this week, like seeds scattered in wind.

I didn't want to arrive. I didn't want to see his family's faces, be "Emma" for them, behave as they expected. I wanted this over so I could be alone with my children. Alone with my grief.

Outside, people spoke in low voices and stopped talking when we walked past them. Even my black dress hushed against my legs. I'd put lumps of sugar in the hem pockets, something to soothe the children with later, and the tiny weights tapped my ankles. I stepped inside the stockade where I expected to see the casket and my husband, one last time.

Sarah and Sam stood there, a few others from the area. All the Giesys. The Stauffers. George Link, John Genger, the other scouts. And then as they parted for me, I saw him.

He opened wide his arms to me and I rushed into them trying desperately not to sob, not to bring attention to my wails, but I could not contain the mix of joy and agony his presence represented.

"Ah, Emma," my brother Jonathan said. "It's with great sadness I come now to see you. Great sadness."

"*Ja*, I know, I know. But you are here. I so need you to be here. Thank you. *Danke*." Shared blood comforted as none other.

"Thank Wilhelm, too, Emma. He brought several of us." He said these words as whispers in my ear. Frozen water replaced my blood.

I stepped away from Jonathan, scanned the crowd until I saw him standing with that beard, those eyes that never seemed to blink, eyes that took people in and kept them, that drew people across water they couldn't swim in, just to please him. I felt a buzzing in my head, but my breath came short and I didn't trust myself to speak. I just prayed, yes prayed, that Keil would not approach me, would not attempt to offer sympathy.

"We come today to help our sister, the Widow Giesy, put her husband to rest," Keil said then to the group. "She is among family and friends who know how to serve widows and orphans as our colony has done for years. She is like a daughter to me. We come to say good-bye on this earth to our friend, Chris Giesy, her husband, the father of this fine boy." Andy stood against my hip looking down. Keil touched the top of his head. "We come to light these candles and climb the hill where we will place this man who was like a son to me into the ground next to"—his voice croaked—"my son, my Willie." He cried now and tears rolled down his face. Others comforted him, patted his back.

Singing began, men's voices rising in a German dirge. I saw the *Schellenbaum*. I heard the tiny tinkle of the bells. Keil had brought the staff of honor to be carried before my husband's casket.

When the dirge ended, Keil regained his composure and he continued. "We prepare to lay Chris Giesy's body in the ground, but we know his spirit has already gone before us. It waits for us in heaven where we will all be united one day. All of us, sinners all and yet forgiven by an act of grace."

At least he does not blame me for Christian's death. At least not yet.

He motioned then for the men inside to lift the casket they'd been shielding from my view. It was made of redwood, leftover from the mill, I imagined. A second, smaller casket sat off to the side; the herd boy's casket. "We go now to the burial site," Keil commanded.

This was the service? No talk of what Christian had meant to so many people here? No scriptures I could cling to for their comfort? What about the way he led us here and protected us, couldn't we talk about that? Jonathan had my arm but I pulled back. "I…I want to see him. My husband's body. I need to see him."

"The casket has already been sealed shut, Widow Giesy," Keil said.

Already I've become the Widow Giesy. No longer Frau *Giesy. No longer* Emma.

"But you…you saw your son every day coming across the prairie. You said good-bye to him over time." I heard a gasp from some of the women, but it didn't stop me. "Now you deprive me of one last time to touch his face, to hold him just once more?"

"Emma," Jonathan said. "The lid's already pegged tight."

I wiggled free of his arm. "They wouldn't let me wash his body and dress him. They deliberately didn't want to wait before they pegged it shut."

Keil asked, "What does the Widow Giesy say?"

Jonathan said, "She is distraught. That's all. To be expected."

"I'm not! I only want to see my husband one last time before I never see him ever again." The group, silent, parted when I pushed through them and stopped at the head of the casket.

"Open it," I ordered.

A part of me prayed they'd refuse, begged in my heart they'd deny me so I could place my anger onto all of them instead of where it was.

Joe Knight held one end of the casket and he motioned for the men to put it back down onto the saw horses. His eyes looked swollen from crying.

I stared, as desperate as a prisoner waiting for a pardon. I wanted to see an empty casket. Maybe it was all an elaborate joke. Maybe Christian was alive. Maybe I was mistaken in having witnessed his drowning. Maybe I'd turn and see my husband standing there, strong, tall, healthy, waiting to take me home, the joke elaborate and cruel but one I'd forgive. *Oh, God,* I prayed. *I will forgive them, forgive You; I'll not carry a grudge, I'll not.*

Jonathan said, "She won't believe until she sees."

"*Ja,*" *Herr* Keil said. "It is like Elijah and his servant, Elisha. The servant had to see his master's death in order to believe he must put on the mantle of his master and carry on."

But it was my brother whose grief became the face of truth, my brother's orders that lifted the casket lid so at last I could believe.

The women had lined the wooden box with quilt pieces and given him a pillow filled with herbs. My nose filled up with scents of lavender mixed with the unmistakable smell of death. I touched his face then, felt the rubbery wrinkle of his skin, ran my fingers across his cold lips. Was that a bruise on his cheek? I patted the artillery medal he wore on his chest and removed it. No one stopped me.

Andy pulled at my skirt and asked to be lifted up. I held Kate now, not sure when I'd lifted her. "Andy, I can't...," I said. Then Big Jack Giesy stepped in and with ease hoisted my son.

"Daddy's sleeping?" I nodded. "He slept from the water too." How else to explain to one so young? Andy asked to be set down, and then he leaned his head against me, pushing the ruffles of my crinoline and the hard hem sweets against my legs.

I had two children to remember him by, that's all I had. These two children would keep his memory alive while his friends placed his body in the ground.

I turned, my breath a weight stuck in my chest. They pegged the cover shut. Jonathan directed me outside, up the steep hill. Those gathered carried candles and began following us, the bells of the *Schellenbaum* tinkling in the wind.

"Papa's lantern," Andy said pulling back. "We carry his lantern, Mama?"

"It's with the mule," I told him. "We don't have time to—"

"But Papa's lantern has Papa's light. It—"

"Never mind," Jack Giesy told Andy. "There's enough light with the candles."

"But—"

"Go get it," I told him.

"You maybe could indulge your son a little less," Jack said.

I saw Jack raise an eyebrow of warning. His intervention annoyed. "Go," I said.

Andy raced to the mule. He returned with the lantern, and we trudged up the hill behind the casket, my son's small hands gripping the lantern handle as though he gripped his father's hand.

I really don't remember what *Herr* Keil said at the grave. The wind whipped the dirt, reminding me of ash. All the candles blew out. We didn't need them for light; it was still afternoon. The lantern light continued to glow. My mind took in only small tidbits of his words. A raccoon scampered through the graveyard behind Keil.

I wanted this to be over. I wanted to plant the cedar sapling Jonathan carried for me, then saddle the mule and return home, curl up with my children and my memories, uninterrupted by what others thought I should or should not do. I wanted to lie there, maybe until we all died.

Jonathan helped me tap the seedling into the ground at Christian's grave, then we left the cemetery to eat. *How can I die if I eat?* All had brought food. People did tell stories then of Christian, food being appetite for memory. They spoke of his adventuresome spirit even as a child. His teasing on Ash Wednesday, how as a boy he called the last child out of bed the *Aschenpuddel,* the ash puddle; how his brothers and he wrestled; how his older sister Helena taught him; how his younger sisters adored him.

Then *Herr* Keil suggested they replay the funeral dirge he'd composed for Willie. The men agreed and their horns intoned a heaviness. It was too much.

"Here are Christian's papers," Sam told me as I rose, gathered up my children, and walked out to our mount. I retied the lantern, making sure we wouldn't lose it. Sarah and Sam stood on either side of me. He handed me the folded leather satchel. "It was on his person, tucked in a belt."

"We took everything out," Sarah said. "Sam dried them. They're all in German so you mustn't think we pried."

Her words made me smile. "You would never pry," I said. "Thank goodness you were one of the first to be there, Sam." I clutched the papers to my breast. "Thank you for this."

Sam said, remembering, "His last words the day you left were of you, Emma."

"Were they?" I wiped at my eyes with the sleeve of my dress.

"He said if you needed anything, to remind you that the family would always take care of you. Oh, and just before he left, he pocketed his compass and said to let you know he'd found it, hidden under his books. Did he get a chance to tell you himself?" I shook my head, no. "He was quite adamant that I tell you. I suspect you know what it means."

He'd found his direction; I had now to find mine.

9

Emma

Water-Stained Wisdom

Those first weeks after the service were like the water-stained pages I unfolded from Christian's leather wallet. I remember moments of clarity but mostly I couldn't make sense of much at all. Even before I left the service, that arbitrary time I'd given to myself to begin to face the future, even then my thinking had begun to warp.

I felt obsessed about seeing what Christian carried in that wallet. I could have found the certificates to pay off *Herr* Keil and get that out of the way, finish what Christian had started. But I didn't want to open it with everyone around. It was something tangible of my husband that I could hold on to, and I didn't want to share it. Keil could wait. This was his fault anyway. Christian wouldn't have been on the Bay if Keil hadn't insisted that the real colony form south of the Columbia. If he had accepted what the scouts claimed, none of this would have happened. If he'd realized how much Christian contributed to the larger community here by his marshalling, being the justice of the peace, a legislator, he'd see why we could not follow him to Aurora. Christian and I had come to this place so certain of God's guidance, and now this.

I lacked shelter in this storm.

My brother would be returning with Keil in a few days, though he offered to take me back to my home. *Our home. My home. Did it matter what I called it?*

Once again I would have another adult in the house, but this one was my brother, whom I dearly loved, and I trusted it would be a soothing time.

"We're going to go back to Aurora Mills, up the Willapa," Jonathan told me while still at the stockade. "And Wilhelm will come in a day or so with the others, bringing the herd boy's casket. I can join them then. He's brought you apple cider too. For the children's teeth."

I wanted nothing from Keil but the children did need cider. I had no dried apples to give them. "We can take the cider with us now," I said. "That way Keil won't have to stop by. It'll be easier for him to take the casket across the Bay and up the Columbia rather than carrying it overland. That's the way he brought Willie's casket." *It was the route Christian took to his death.*

"He had a hearse then. Now it is just us and the mules. The boy is light. Keil has decided. I'm coming back with you now, Emma," Jonathan said. It wasn't an offer but a directive. He stepped back into the stockade to let Keil know, I supposed. He came out with Jack Giesy.

Jack tipped his hat at me. "I'm sorry for your loss, *Frau* Giesy."

I looked for the tease in his face, but his condolences sounded sincere. Right then hollow platitudes would have angered me.

Jack had been the one to lift my son up for a last look at his father. Jack touched Andy's hat. My son didn't jerk away. The two had twisted a thread together. "Thank you," I said. I nodded my head to him and finished saddling the mule.

Boshie and Mary stood near my brother and Jack when I finished and led the mule to a stump, where I stepped up into the stirrup. Sarah lifted Kate up to me, the child all wide eyes and smiles. Mary wiped at her eyes.

I caught a look in Jack's eyes, a blend of surprise and disapproval, I thought, and so I said, "Sidesaddles aren't much used in these parts. Certainly not when one is holding a child."

Before stepping back Mary whispered, "We could see your crinoline ruffles when you lifted your leg over."

"*Ja*, well, fortunately for me, I don't care," I said.

Jonathan mounted up and we headed south toward my house.

Christian wouldn't see the garden harvest. He wouldn't be there to tell me that my wheat had been a waste. He wouldn't find another perfect small cedar tree to decorate with blown egg shells like the one we had last Christmas. Last Christmas. Christian had seen his last Christday, my last birthday, our last anniversary. How many "lasts" could there be? A last senseless death. I wondered then if I'd ever have another thought that didn't carry with it a reference to my Christian.

———

Jonathan stayed busy those days he shared with me. He milked the cows while I handled the goat. He chopped wood in the late summer dusk when the air cooled. He often knelt to weed with me and surprised me with his love of words, something we shared that I hadn't known of. "The word *therapy* comes from working with decay and decomposition," he said. "As in a garden. Yet in that decay, the soil builds up if we add to it, tend it. It's the way of life."

"I like the gardening but it's just that, work. Not much tenderness in ripping out weeds."

"More though, Emma. Your grief, it must be worked and reworked through your own thinking until you come to a place of resolution. So you can go forward. From dust to dust. We are all built up eventually, again. If we allow it."

He failed to engage me with such talk that Christian's death was somehow related to an act of nurture, soil decaying and being restored. I wasn't ready to be restored. I planned to have a few words with God, once my brother left me alone, about what had happened here, words about the life of a worthy servant being taken in exchange for an old man's insistence and inferior furniture. "Doing for others. Helping our neighbors." Keil and this whole act of servitude had taken us from Bethel to here.

For now, I'd change the subject.

"Christian planned to bring back a bred ewe for me, for wool," I said.

"We will bring several up. *Ja.* Andreas and John talk of sheep too." He looked around. "Lots of twigs and such will get in the wool here unless they're fenced and fed," he said. "Be difficult to clean but the fodder would be good. Christian must have talked with his father about it."

"He was going to bring one just for us," I said.

My brother let that pass without comment.

That evening when I served him bean soup with fresh lettuce from my garden, and biscuits with molasses followed by a cake with berries and freshly whipped cream, he pushed his chair back and stuck his hands in his waistband and said, "That was good, Sister. Good flavors, filling but not heavy. I like that."

"A compliment's a rare thing," I said. "Especially from a brother."

Andy and Kate both licked spoons full of the cream. Jonathan cleared his throat. "I should do it more, then." He picked at his nails as I cleared the table of the tin plates that Christian had made. Andy, wearing a mustache of white, came to sit on his uncle's knee. Jonathan bounced him as though he rode a horse but then said Andy was getting too big for him. "See how I huff and puff?" Jonathan told him.

"Like the wolf and the three pigs," Andy said.

"Like that."

I washed Andy's and Kate's faces, then picked up my stitching and wasn't looking at Jonathan when he said, "Emma, now that you are widowed, it will be foolish for you to hold on to this idea that you can have your own sheep and whatnot, without the others to help you." I looked at him. "Christian understood that communal care is the best care. Each has a gift that can be shared, and together no one has to bear the great weight of doing all, alone. It is the Christian way, Emma."

"Obligations come with gifts," I said. "Accept the cows and then one must meet the obligation of the contract for butter someone else signed. Take on the sheep and then one must shear when others shear, not when I might want to."

"Ah, Emma. When we give something away, our hands are empty then, right in front of the person receiving our gift. We stand exposed, admitting that we're needy too. Then they give back. It puts us all in the same place. We are part of the colony. The community."

"I'm not alone. I have the children. We'll do *gut* here. *Gut.*"

He ran his fingers through his hair, a habit he had. "It's for the sake of the children…that you should think about coming back with me. There is room in the *gross Haus*. Louisa would welcome you, I know."

I laughed. "Louisa would take me in, but welcome me? That I doubt." I took a needle out of my chatelaine, changed thread, and continued mending. "Louisa didn't come to Christian's burial."

"Their children, she has them to care for."

"But in a communal place, wouldn't someone else care for them while a woman took time to grieve with her sister?"

He sighed. "You always could find fault."

"Not faulting. I don't complain, just explain. I see things how they are."

"You see things how you want to, unique but not always right," my brother said.

As if being right mattered to me. Only where my children were concerned or my husband, well, then it mattered that the right choice was made, the right decision carried out. "I'm not a welcome member at Aurora. It is foolish not to admit that. Even your offer to bring me there would not remove the stain."

"You're not thinking clearly, Emma. There is no stain. All is forgiven: your rush to join the scouts, your push to keep Christian here, the oystering, all of that is overlooked in the wake of this great loss. We only want to help."

My face felt hot. I had no need of forgiveness. Keil, now he ought to be seeking forgiveness for what he'd caused here, for the suffering and hardships and even Christian's death. But it would do no good to attempt to convince my brother. I stepped over his words and merely told him once again that we'd remain here, in the house Christian had built for us. "We'll be *gut* here," I said. "Just *gut.*"

"We've planted hops at Aurora. Our brew masters will have good work to do," he continued as though I hadn't made my stand. "Oregon has scheduled a constitutional meeting and will become a state before long, long before this Washington Territory with all its arguments over Indians and martial law. Your children would have more chance to find meaningful work one day if you came with me to Aurora."

"There is progress here," I said. "That man Swan who first invited Christian to this region, he supports the building of a canal from Puget Sound to the Columbia River coming right through Willapa Bay. It would mean great economic growth. We have a future. Right here."

My stomach burned at any words of the future. I couldn't imagine my life without Christian. Each morning since his death had been trial enough, to wake up, face the empty pillow beside me, rise and tend to the children as though nothing had changed. At times, I pretended that their father would be coming home any day now in the summer lull of the oyster harvest. I supposed that was a gift of sorts, that the children were accustomed to being without their father for long periods of time. Now, even though Andy had seen him "sleeping" on the beach and in the coffin, Andy might simply be waiting for him to come back. And Kate? Kate would not remember his face at all. She would know him only as a memory. She'd know her mother only as a woman, bitter, widowed.

One evening while Jonathan chopped at logs so I'd have firewood for winter, I finally opened Christian's wallet. I'd been longing to do it, yet dreading it, as once it was done I'd have no more tangible thing of his to anticipate discovering. It would all be memory from then on, nothing unveiled as something new. It was the last of my connection with him as an undiscovered man.

I unfolded the wallet. Inside was the certificate that would pay off our debt. It was smudged, water-soaked but decipherable, its intent clear. Maybe I could invest the money back into oystering with Joe so he could hire the labor that Christian would otherwise have provided. Or I could use the money to purchase the ewe or pay outright for the cows or buy a hog myself. Maybe I'd use it to make my way in this world by traveling to Olympia or Oregon City to paint miniature portraits of prominent people there, people who would pay to have a good likeness made of them. Of course doing so with two young children posed a problem, but I pitched that thought away. The certificates offered a future, though the one I envisioned opposed Christian's hopes.

To pay Keil…I could barely stand the idea of it.

A smaller piece of paper was folded into the leather. I could be grateful that they'd quickly recovered Christian's body, or the sea and salt would have ruined everything inside. I held a piece of paper that looked like a letter. I unfolded the layers.

It was one of my own, sent to him when he traveled in the South that first year we were married. He'd saved it. I read it again, filling in the words smudged by the creases and the water. I'd told him I'd support his work, do what must be done to make him grateful he had come to marriage late in life. One day we would have a family. He wanted that. I'd forced myself along on this journey west because of that. Well, that and other reasons. If I hadn't, he wouldn't have known his son and daughter who were his legacy, nor this place, this valley he'd felt called to and trusted. I'd helped him find a way to be here. Staying here would honor all he'd sacrificed; leaving would mean the work he'd done here had been for nothing. I folded the letter back into the wallet. Those were the only two things he'd carried with him.

At some point, Keil and the herd boy's casket and those who'd come to the funeral would head back by way of our land. I could simply hand Keil the certificates that would pay off our land debt. We had no donation land claim; Christian had purchased our three hundred and twenty acres from a former settler. If I kept this certificate and converted it into cash, I'd have enough to purchase all we'd need to get us through the winter—the grain, cloth, whatever else. I'd be independent of the Giesy clan and Keil too.

Or I could give the certificate to Keil and end the debt, knowing to do so meant I'd be in debt to Christian's family. There was no way out of the obligation, not the way Keil set up the colony, not the way he controlled and mastered everyone to do his bidding, not the way Christian had followed Keil through the years. *Such a senseless death.*

I would ask Keil to forgive the debt. That would be the Christian thing to do for a widow and her children. Indeed, to not do that, I decided, was an unforgivable act.

I prepared meals and offered additional food for their sacks. The latter they rejected, saying they'd been given enough by the Giesys and Schaefers and others to make it back to Oregon well fed.

"You'd reject the Diamond Rule?" I asked. "How can I make your life better than my own if you won't take my offerings?"

"*Ach,* Emma," Keil said. His dark eyes bored into me. "While it is true that it is more blessed to give than to receive, it is also true that all of us must receive. When you accept a gift, you practice accepting forgiveness."

I'd done nothing requiring forgiveness, and I felt the hair at my scalp tighten. Maybe I needed forgiveness for my un-Christian thoughts about Keil. Perhaps for coming back and bringing Christian out to the water where he saw the old man in need. Perhaps I needed forgiveness for that. No. I was doing what a wife did, making time to be with her husband. My thoughts were pure and simple theological explanations of his actions. Considering holding on to the certificates, to not carry out my husband's wishes, that was an act of caring for my children. If I handed over the certificates, we'd be at the mercy of this colony. I'd be dependent. I and my children would be required to accept help from others. Our life would not be better than Keil's; we would never be on the better end of the Diamond Rule, a rule that had taken my husband's life.

But to withhold the payment denied the vow I'd made to further Christian's work, his ministry, his wish to serve the colony and Christ.

Ach, jammer! These men put me in such a whirlwind of confusion.

In the end, I behaved without courage. I gave Keil the certificates. I suppose it was my own letter Christian had carried with him all those years that was the deciding factor. I'd made a vow to support his work. Even being in this valley was a sign of my willingness to support his work. He'd made a vow to Keil and the nurture of the colony. And while I resented that he'd done it, that he'd kept his lifeline to communal living, I wasn't sure I was strong enough to keep the certificates and turn them into independence. I wasn't sure I could live with the consequences of reaching for something that Christian might not have supported had he lived. And if I failed, then I'd have lost Christian's last hope along with my own.

With the payment, the land was free and clearly mine as Christian's widow, the debt to the colony paid off. I had not even a half dime of my own to do anything without the help of others. I read the letter again in the quiet of the night, the light from Christian's lantern reflecting on the smudges.

"Here it is, *Herr* Keil," I'd said. "Christian meant to give this to you."

"Not '*Herr* Keil' but 'Brother Keil' to you, Widow Giesy." He patted my hand like a child's. "Your husband was one of my best friends. You must know that. He was like a brother to me." I said nothing. "As it should be," he said then. "This payment will help all of us at Aurora Mills. We'll remember your husband. He was a true saint in the work of our Lord."

"It's too bad you couldn't have told him that while he lived," I said.

"It was a hard time when we were here. My son…then the Indian wars. No houses ready for us. All the rain. Here today, this, this climate in August is lovely. But the rains will come again and there will still be much work to keep the cows from disappearing into the woods. The rivers will rise and you will struggle to get your crops to market. We have a better site in Aurora Mills." I straightened my shoulders, prepared to defend. "But I honor the effort of the Giesys and the building of the mill and the work of the scouts who stay here. We're friends, all of us. You must see that too, Widow Giesy. You are still a part of the colony. For the sake of your son if for no other reason."

"For the sake of both my children, then," I said, "I give you the payment as Christian wanted." I paused. "Though I am prepared to receive it back, to have you make my life better than yours. The Diamond Rule—"

"Emma," Jonathan said.

"Which way is it then, Brother? If I receive, then I'm a good and noble widow; but if I ask, then I am somehow a sinner?"

"You ask for something that would take away from many, Widow Giesy," Keil said. "I cannot grant such a thing that would rob those in Aurora of their needs."

"My children have needs too. They are robbed of their father's love and care because of his generous willingness to save an old man from drowning."

"You and Christian chose this place. Remember that."

Oh, I'd remember that. But this bitter exchange would mark a new time. I knew this as I watched Keil and Jonathan and others leave to carry the herd boy back to Aurora. I vowed that I would do whatever it took to keep my family together and free of influences I rejected, influences that had taken Christian's life from me.

I vowed it again on the day after Keil left, when I faced the first days of morning sickness.

10

Emma

Holdfast

That day, weeks ago when Christian and I walked along the beach, the day following our nighttime excursion, he pointed to a stringy plant, seaweed that clasped its greenish tendrils tight around a rock. "Holdfast," he told me.

"It does appear to be holding fast, *ja,*" I agreed. "Clinging tight."

He corrected me and said that was the very name of that attachment. It was a holdfast, a noun. The seaweed was made in such a way it could not loose its hold on the rock's surface. They were bound together by their very nature.

"As we are," I told him that day.

"It's how we are in God's sight," Christian corrected. "Man and God, a holdfast." He clasped his wide palms together. "Woman and God too," he added and smiled, a deference to his independent-thinking wife.

"But are we not a holdfast, too?" I asked. "You and I?"

"Human beings can separate," he said. "But not each of us from our Creator. We are bound in storms, in trials, even unto death."

He was right, of course, at least about the two of us not being so attached the bond could never be broken. On this first day when I was alone with my children, I dismissed Christian's observation that a holdfast existed between the Creator and all created ones. I didn't feel anything holding on to me, didn't want to even talk to that Being I had once believed would keep us safe.

There were details to tend to. Christian's clothes, for one. His brothers could wear the pants or the shirts. Those nearly worn out could be cut into pieces and crafted into quilts. The boots might be kept for Andy. They were a good pair, heavy. Those waders, they brought on his death, filling as they did. I would burn them one day when I burned out a stump. But I didn't want to give any of it away or cut any of it up. To do so meant saying he would no longer need them and that meant, well, it meant that he wasn't coming back.

As I went about my day heating water for laundry, fixing a meal for the children, wondering if the lettuce looked ripe, I heard myself saying, "I'll ask Christian about that." Other days I knew for certain he was gone, but then I'd set an extra place at the table and not even notice it until Andy started counting.

I feared I'd forget what he looked like and often took out the sketch I'd drawn, just to stare.

Then one day when my bonnet hung drying in the sun, I wore Christian's flat-top hat out into the garden to shade my face. It offered more protection than my bonnet, and I could see if something moved at my side better too. The next day I pulled one of his shirts over my head. I fell to my knees, overtaken by the scent of him. When I stood again, I found comfort, my thin arms lost within the blousy sleeves, the barrel of the shirt covering the new life I carried. I wrapped a cord around me to keep the cloth from billowing out and decided I would wear it daily. Later I pulled on a pair of his pants and rolled the legs up and tacked them with thread. It was easier to milk the cows in the pants, and if people stayed away as I hoped, no one would know that I'd taken to wearing my husband's clothes. I could keep Christian with me, and when they became too worn by wearing, I'd sew a tiny dress for the infant he'd never know, or make a quilt from the scraps.

My initial reaction to the baby I carried was one of disbelief, then anger at the injustice of it all, then resolution. I'd been left to raise not two small children but three. This infant would be a constant reminder of what he could never hold fast to. A father.

I carried that fatherless child through the September harvests and into the mild October breezes. I began to talk to the baby, a sure sign that I accepted it was there. Maybe I could talk to Christian that way too, accept that he was gone but still with me.

Some days, though, talking to my husband felt like praying, and I didn't want to give God that satisfaction.

I wrote letters to my family. I made candles and soap. I dried herbs from my garden. I dug potatoes. I used the handsaw to cut some of the twigs to size for cooking and while I did, found myself annoyed again at Keil. Why hadn't Keil sent handsaws with us when we'd come here? So many things I did each day made me remember my outrage at Keil.

Despite the morning sickness, I dragged myself out of bed to milk the goat. Andy learned to stoke the fire, carefully, but it proved a huge help. I tried peppermint-leaf tea to settle the sickness. I hadn't remembered having morning bouts with either of the other two children, but this one, this one protested its place within me. I thought often of Keil's words spoken long years before about the fate of a woman, how she would suffer for her Eden brashness of seeking knowledge, daring to want more. In return, her punishment was pain in childbirth.

Yet he'd been encouraging young men and women to wait to marry and even seemed to bring to sainthood women like Helena Giesy who chose to never marry at all. How would Helena come to know her place if painful childbirth was the chosen path for women? He never had answered that question for me, saw it as one more challenge to his authority.

I moved through the days as though in a fog, still. Andy could take me from it with his questions, and Kate could sometimes make me smile as I watched her get her legs beneath her now and run without as much falling. She'd plow toward my lap and throw herself at me, sure that I would catch her. I'd swoop her up into my arms and blow air bubbles on her belly. She'd arch her back in laughter and almost flip herself from my arms. Standing, she'd toss me a kiss from her tiny palm just before she lowered her head to run toward me and start the whole routine again. She always began again, even when she stumbled. She was strong, my daughter. And yet fine grained. Like flint.

I saw in Andy more of his father as the days went by. He seemed to know what time I needed to go out to milk the cows. Young as he was, he tended Kate carefully while I milked them, then skimmed the cream. His eyes were Christian's, especially when he couldn't untie a knotted rope or when the goat bunted him when he least expected. Once he said, *"Ach, jammer!"* and I smiled rather than chastised him for his close-to-cursing words.

In the house one day Andy asked me when his father was coming back from the Bay. I finished scrubbing the potatoes, gaining time. I sat him down and pulled up a stool beside him. "Remember when your uncle Jonathan was here? He stayed for a time after the funeral. That was when we said good-bye to your papa because he can't come home anymore. Jonathan can come to visit us again, but not your papa. He's not a living being anymore. He doesn't hurt, but he doesn't breathe or eat. He's gone to heaven." Did I believe this? Was I telling my son a lie? Yes, I believed there was such a place, and surely Christian would be there. It was here, the hellishness of this earth, where I thought God had forsaken us. "To heaven, Andy, where good men go."

"Why didn't he take me with him?"

I pulled him to me. "He didn't mean to leave you behind, or me or Kate or his friends. It just happened, and when it happens like that, he doesn't even get to say the words good-bye or reassure us, though I know he would have wanted to." I made it sound like it was perfectly understandable that death followed life. But I still woke every morning hoping I'd hear his footsteps at the door or smell the salt of him when he turned toward me and kissed my nose. How could I expect a four-year-old boy to understand? "That's hard, isn't it?" He nodded. "We must be like flint," I said. "Hard but firm, and when we think of Papa, it will be as though we struck a spark like we do when we light the cooking fire. We'll remember lovely things about him then. We'll keep him with us that way," I said and patted his chest with my hand. "We'll hold him fast in our hearts."

"Like when we slept at the beach," he said.

"*Ja*, that's a good memory. We had to fight off the mosquitoes, didn't we?"

"Papa put up netting. They went away then. We could only hear buzz-buzz."

"He took good care of us, didn't he?"

Andy stayed quiet a long time and then he said, "He didn't want to go, did he, Mama? He just wanted to help that man, didn't he?"

"I'm sure he didn't wish to leave you, not ever. But one day we will all go, and—"

"Not you!" He startled. He pushed away, then hugged me tight, burying his face in my lap. "Not you!" I could feel his shoulders shake and then the sob.

I patted his back. "Not me, not anytime soon." No one can ever know such things, but it was a lie I thought I'd be forgiven for, as it seemed to comfort my son. He reached up around my neck as though to have me lift him. "I can't right now," I told him. "I'll hold you here, beside me. You'll have another brother or sister before too long, and you're so big that lifting you isn't good for the baby."

He patted my stomach then. I told him to put his ear to my belly, to listen to the heartbeat. I knew he'd hear my heart beating, but in time, if this pregnancy progressed well, he'd be hearing the sounds of his sibling. Kate waddled over then, and she too put her head to my stomach. "We three," I said, caressing their heads. "We three will be all right. We must just hold fast."

———

The work I had to do now lost a certain luster. I no longer milked the cows so we'd one day be independent. I milked them for the milk I would make into butter. It wouldn't be long and I'd have no more milk; the cows would be bred back and they'd need what they made to prepare for their own calves when they came in the spring. I suppose I was grateful in one way that no one had brought a bred ewe up from Aurora and that Rudy had taken the pigs to raise. A ewe would have been one more thing to manage. When the cows dried up, we'd rely on the goat then for our daily milk. I wondered if this next infant would have trouble eating, if I'd have trouble feeding it as I had my others. Time would tell.

For the first time in my whole life, I felt like I had too much time and nothing I cared to do with it.

I had hurts and no one to salve them, and few reasons to treat the wounds myself. I had ideas but nowhere to go with them, no one to listen to them, not even to tell me that what I thought about wasn't worth the trouble. Malaise. That was the emotion that haunted me those first months after Christian died.

"You're a wealthy widow," Mary said one day. She'd brought Elizabeth over to play with Andy and Kate while we churned butter. She'd take the round molds with her when she left, and they'd be transported to the Woodard's, where they'd be shipped north or south. Contracts had to be met, and those of us in Willapa were meeting the needs for butter in faraway places. Soon we'd add pork to our obligations. John and Andreas had found markets for our products just as Christian said they would. But what was earned went to the common fund. Or so I supposed. I didn't see any payment for my labors.

I also hadn't seen much of Mary since Christian's death, and now that she was here there was a strain between us.

"Wealthy?" I asked.

"You own your property. Isn't it what you always wanted, to have your own place?"

"It isn't how I imagined it," I said.

"I know, but still, you have property and value in your own name. Christian left you taken care of."

"All I can do with this land is sell it," I said. "If I stay here, then I have no choice but to depend on all of you to take care of me. To be…communal, again."

"Is it really so bad to share?" she asked.

"I'm adjusting," I said. "I can't contribute much myself except the butter, and before long that'll stop too. So that adds to my…beholding, something I've never liked."

She churned for a time then said, "Maybe you could hire Jack. To do your work."

I laughed. "I don't have any way to pay anyone, let alone a wanderer like Jack."

"You could pay him in shares to the property, for each year worked or something like that. You could keep accounts. You can't chop wood or do the hard labor, not with your baby on the way. And the others can't always get here after their day of work. I mean to be helpful, as we should be to widows and orphans."

I raised an eyebrow, more interested in how she knew I carried a child than in the thought that others might resent having to help me after completing their own day's work.

"How did you know?"

"You're starting to show," she said. "Only a little, but your face, it's rounder already. I noticed at the last gathering at the stockade."

"Do Christian's parents know?"

She shrugged. The children's laughter rose, and Mary motioned for Elizabeth to come to her so she could say a few settling words. She sent her back with a finger of warning. "He's…good, Emma," she said, turning to me.

"Who?"

"Jack. He doesn't complain about my cooking and—"

"Jack's living with you now? You and Sebastian and Karl?"

She shrugged her shoulders. "I don't mind and Boshie likes the conversations with the others. Oh, Jack keeps odd hours sometimes, but usually he helps with chores so Boshie has less to do when he gets home. I think he wants to help, if you let him."

"You mean work without being paid?"

"You have such a difficult time letting anyone help you."

Her avoidance confirmed my hesitance. "There's something about him, Mary. When he first came here, with the cows, there was something…I don't know, he's…cocky."

"Confident," Mary defended. She was a good judge of character, at least I'd always thought that about her. She shared my dislike for Keil. Or had.

"Arrogantly pert," I said. "He…swaggers."

"He's young."

"He's older than me, if I remember correctly."

"Is he? He likes his brew, but it seems to make him happy rather than demanding as with some men. And Boshie doesn't like him to drink and Karl doesn't either, and Jack honors that. He even goes outside to smoke. He's… funny. He does unexpected things, sort of like you do. That's why I thought he might be someone you'd enjoy talking with. It was just a thought, a way to make your days easier," she said.

"My days aren't hard, Mary. They're…lonely."

"Well then, maybe Jack could bring you laughter. Laughter wipes out loneliness like ash to a stain."

———

While my husband was alive but working at the Bay, a man could not visit me alone without some consternation. Karl was sometimes deemed safe enough; he was twenty years my senior and he offered lessons to Andy. But otherwise, the men honored civility and didn't come alone.

But now that I was a widow, men could come by without hesitation, in the name of service, in the name of helping me out. They could sit at my table and be served noodles and *Strudels* and never once feel out of place. I was set apart, as different as I could be from every other woman along the Willapa as I wore the widow's robe. *I am set apart.* That thought brought a wry smile. *Oh, one must be careful what one wishes for. There is a chance it will arrive in peculiar ways.*

Jack Giesy showed himself one day, tipped his hat and said, "Mary Giesy says you maybe could use some help."

"I'm not in a position to hire anyone. I have no cash and—"

"Well, let's just see what we can work out," he said. He didn't push past me as he stood, hat in hand. He stomped his feet in the wet. It was November and the rains were with us. I'd have to invite him in. It would be the neighborly thing to do. "I'm flexible," he said. He blew on his hands to warm them. *Why won't I invite the man in out of the rain?* "About pay, I mean. We maybe could get…creative with the books." He added a grin, one that slid its way from my eyes down over my body to my toes. It made me want to slap his face.

I didn't, but it did confirm my instinct to send him packing, which I did.

"I've no need of wood chopping," I said. "I know how to do it and in my own time. I thank you for the offer. Let me give you some cheese to take back to Mary."

Fortunately, he didn't step inside or follow me while I got the cheese. I held the bag out to him and he put his hat back on and took it from me. *"Danke,"* he said, still wearing that grin.

I watched him saunter down the path with an axe over his shoulder. Something about his swagger told me he'd be back. I just hoped I'd be ready, and able to hold fast to what really mattered.

11

Catherine

My Dearest Emma,

Papa tells us that you have seen Jonathan but for sad reasons, as we learn of Christian's death. Jonathan tells us you saw your husband last on the Fourth of July. While the Aurora Band played in a town called Butteville, you were at the Bay having your last days with Christian. I'm so sad for you, Emma. We celebrate Christmas here and wish that you and your children were with us so we could put our arms around you and warm you in the cold of your suffering. To lose a love, oh, how tragic that is. How do you ever stand it? But we are grateful he was acting the hero in saving another's life. That must bring you comfort.

Herr Keil writes to our teacher, Herr Wolfer, so we learn of his traveling to your remote country for the funeral. How that must have comforted you to have him there to stand beside you, to speak last words over Christian's grave. We miss him here. Papa says the spirit of the colony is missing something without Wilhelm, so the men are talking now of when they'll take the second wave out from Bethel to Aurora Mills. Sometime in 1862 or 1863. That's still five years away! I'll be an old maid by then.

Do you ever see Jack Giesy? I just wonder.

Mama says I should write of everyday things, that talk of thread and harvests bring comfort more than other words. So I will tell you that the hops harvest was good this year. "Never let September winds blow across your hops," Papa says, and so the men spent August bringing in the harvest. Mama says the hops poultice is what saved her bad tooth, so it is good for something besides making beer. I always think it grand when something can be useful for more than one thing.

Women in Shelbina are wearing puffs and pads under their skirts called bustles! I've seen them. You could hide a child inside one they're so big. Mama says we girls can't wear them. It would make our sister Lou look less like a chicken leg, all straight up and down, though. I don't need one. I carry the bustle God gave me, or so Mama says.

We heard word of a terrible massacre not far from where Tante Mary lives in the Deseret country. Mama is worried, as Indians killed an entire wagon train of people heading to California out of Arkansas. She worries about her sister and wishes Tante had never married a Mormon saint who took her far away, especially if it means they might be in the middle of an Indian war. Tante Mary says it was a terrible thing, the people being killed in a beautiful meadow in the mountains, and that more terrible things may come from the story. She doesn't say what, but the army is sent to investigate because it was Indians against Americans. A few children survived and the Deseret saints who came upon the train and chased the Indians off found them and took them in. Mary and Uncle John Willard took one in. A girl. I don't know her name.

Does Uncle Jonathan write to you from France and Germany and England? Our cousins write too. How different their lives are from mine here in Bethel! But they learn of wars too. There is a war with other Indians in a country called India. Uncle Jonathan says they are warring against the British even though both have lived side by side there many years. Uncle Jonathan has returned to France and Papa's pleased he is not being sent to that India to negotiate a peace.

There are uprisings everywhere in this wide world. I wonder why. There are rumblings about slave and free states here, and Papa says a war will come and Missouri will be the black powder that starts it. Is anyone fighting in your Washington Territory? I just wonder.

There is not much more to tell you. So I will write you these words even though Mama says everyday mentionings bring more comfort than Scripture when a wound is wide open and needs more time to heal. I try to imagine what it must be like to have had love taken away like a boat drifting out to sea. Oh, I should not use that image. I'm sorry. (I can't erase on this thin paper.) Maybe it is more like having a leaf blown from a tree. A red maple leaf wider than Papa's palm, one that would cling for a long time to the branch, resist the winds and make one think it would stay through the winter and hang on forever. Then in an instant, it waves like a limp hand and is gone. I think if I'd been watching the leaf and loved it and came to expect to see it there every day, well, when it was gone, I'd be very sad. I think I might even be angry at God for having allowed it to happen. God is all-powerful, so why not stop the wind? Why not let a young girl enjoy the beauty of that leaf? It means nothing to hear someone say it is just the way of things, that leaves form, cling for a time, then die and go back to the earth. But why? That's what I ask.

I think I'm not supposed to ask such questions, but I would if it was my husband. I would ask and would grieve for the answers.

Mama says it is a sign of maturity when one can form the questions but not be frustrated by the lack of answers. She says wisdom is when we have gratitude in the midst of all uncertainties.

Since there are so many unanswered questions, every question must not have an answer. I just thought of that. Maybe that's what confuses people, that belief that there must be an explanation for all things. It makes me feel defenseless to not know things, though. I don't like living as though I'm standing in my crinolines with all the world to see. I don't want to fear something happening as it did to those Arkansas travelers who ended up dead. I don't want to have to decide what to do next if I survived that. How would those children understand that all they'd loved had been taken from them? Maybe living with Tante Mary and Uncle John Willard will be their answer on this earth.

Papa says you never should have talked Christian into staying at Willapa and instead should have gone to Aurora with Father Keil. I wouldn't say that to you because if I were you, I'd feel badly for having encouraged Christian to stay. And the others stayed too, so poor Keil doesn't have all the help that he needs now, and he urges us to come from Bethel soon.

Lou and Johanna and David Jr. are helping William with egg scratching for the Tannenbaum. He has a nice eye for detail and holds the blown egg as though it was a young rabbit about to hop out of his hand. We will hang the ones you made as a young girl. William looks at them as though to copy what you've done and Mama says that's good, for you always did make scratching pictures well. We boiled the eggs in onion skins longer than usual and they have a chestnut hue, nearly the color of a tintype picture, Papa says. We will put Christian's name and date of death on one, Emma, as a remembrance that he will be forever in our lives. We'll hang it on the tree.

I found this verse to give you from Isaiah, who says there is light to follow, that your face may be like flint, hard and firm and ready to make a spark when touched by the loving hand of God. Be like flint, Emma, and not like one who makes her own flames. It is best to rely on God for the fires of your life. Father Keil will help you. Please don't be angry if the words are not what you want to hear. I just felt I had to tell you.

Your sister, Catherine

12

Louisa

My husband the doctor preaches today. Every other Sunday as is his way. Whether it will be on simplicity, humility, self-sacrifice, or neighborly love none of us knows. Even I don't know, though some might think I do. The doctor doesn't share his views with me before he expresses them. Like the others whom he serves, I pull out the threads of his weaving that speak to me. I don't mean to suggest that he has anything to say just for me, only that today he preaches and it will be well with us all when he is finished and I will take a tidbit away that will help me learn to live better.

It is February, a month here balanced like a good quilt with warm days of sunshine backed with rain showers and occasionally snow. The snow never lasts. It merely covers things up for a time until light and heat melt it or the clogs and boots of workmen walk the snow into mud.

The men work hard at building yet more houses. They will not be set close to each other as they were in Bethel but instead will have a block of area around each one, giving room to build a barn and a summer kitchen later. Each will have a small garden, a smokehouse, and pens for hogs and our sheep. This is a new concept that my husband adopts. I think he might have seen the merit to the Willapa sites being somewhat separated. Or maybe here in this Oregon Country he could see that we didn't want to make our "community" appear too tight-knit, so that people from surrounding areas fail to come here to buy our goods. All things change in new places. It troubles me at times to know what few things one can expect to remain the same.

This land is an Eden. We'll have fine crops to sell to the hundreds of settlers who arrived last fall, many in poorer shape than when our colony reached Willapa. We may have walked across the country, but we had enough food, thanks to my husband's good planning and the Lord's provision.

Yet as hungry as those settlers looked, they recovered with the help of friends. They plan a dance. Our men practice, for the band will play for the Old Settlers' Ball at Oregon City, which should be a grand affair. We won't attend, of course. But our musical men will get to watch the candles shimmer against the finery of the dresses requiring yards and yards of cloth. One can only hope they've sewn such gowns with easy seams so all that material can be put to good use later making clothes for their men and their children. Imagine leaving such a hoard of cloth sewn up in a dress worn but once a year, and then just to dance!

Still, I do love to dance.

Neighborly love. That is what the doctor spoke of today. It always makes me think of Emma Giesy and her struggle with being a good neighbor. She was such a giving girl back in Bethel. Oh, self-centered as young women are, but kind too. It's been some months now since the doctor traveled north to attend the funeral of Chris Giesy, yet we have heard not a word from Emma, his widow. Oh, I know, one does not always behave as expected when in the swirl of grief, but I did think she might have sent word by way of her brother, perhaps thanking the doctor for his sacrifice, traveling there in the heat of summer. It was a fine service, the doctor told me. The men played a Beethoven piece. Beethoven followed by one of our German family tunes familiar to all of us, lighthearted, the doctor said, for a service commending a body to the grave should be a joyous time. A man's soul has already left and gone on to a better place. We bury but the body.

I know this is a terrible thing to admit, and I would never tell the doctor this, but I am grateful that my Willie will not have to lie alone now on that hilly site so far from us. Chris Giesy lies beside him and that's a comfort to me. His mother will visit the grave and as she does, she'll be there for Willie too. No one wants to be alone, not even in death, though of course we are. For the living, there is a comfort with two graves there. I hope Emma sees it as such. We placed a stone for Willie with a willow tree on it, weeping for him always.

We prosper here in Aurora. We women work side by side to feed the men, who work long hours to build more homes. We're readying our fields to plant, though spring will not find us until all the Easter eggs have been eaten. That was the rule in Missouri. The Pudding River runs full but within its banks, and there is the smell of spring in the air, that scent of a Missouri root cellar sprinkled with birdsong that marks the ending of a long winter of despair.

The almanac says today it will bluster and blow so I should work inside, on my *Fraktur*, perhaps. I'm to make the letters perfect for writing special papers and documents so they look as they did from the old country, when our German printer of renown, Gutenberg, printed the earliest books. It is one of the things the doctor does not object to. The lettering is beautiful when completed by one who works hard to make the *w* just so or the *m* look like a lightning-split hickory tree. It might be that I could earn money by making baptismal certificates with the lovely letters so they might be hung on the walls of our neighbors, who are mostly Methodists and Catholics. Our colonists could hang them as well. Not baptismal certificates, no, we do not celebrate that sacrament. But perhaps a marriage certificate could be written out with the *Fraktur*. I'll ask the doctor if this might not be an act of neighborly love, to commemorate a marriage day. The doctor will likely tell me there's no time for such foolishness. He still does not think marriage is what young people should put their hopes in. "We have too much to do to be ready for our neighbors from Bethel," he'll say.

I have clothes to mend, more to wash, food to prepare, and the young ones who fall in love, well, they are of no good for getting things done.

At least I can sing while I work. There may be foolishness in singing or playing in the band, but at least it can be done while one is being useful. Perhaps that is what the doctor objects to in my suggestions: they do not appear useful, only pleasurable, like enjoying the look of the lettering on a page. Being useful is what the doctor says God calls each of us to be, though I'm not sure how the band is useful. Oh, it raises money.

Rudy Giesy arrived this past week. He has bought a farm in our country from a man named Anderson. It's close to us in Aurora, and Rudy will raise any sheep that the colony wishes to keep. He's also going to take a sheep or two back with him to Willapa, where Henry will now keep the pigs. Rudy says he'll give a ewe to Emma Giesy as she harps on it so.

Forgive me. He did not use the word *harp*. He said she asks for one. I imagine that means repeatedly. She knows what she wants. I must be kinder especially now that we learn she is with child again. This must be a trial for her, long and odious, to grieve her husband's death while tending his children and then to learn another comes. Or perhaps she sees the child as the gift it is, sent by Chris from beyond the grave in a way. Some of us count, but we have not seen her so we don't know when this baby might be due.

Karl Ruge too visits with Rudy. It's been months since I've seen the old teacher. Karl and Rudy brought fence posts of yew wood all the way from Washington Territory. They'll surround the farm that Rudy bought.

I am hopeful Rudy is the first of many who will leave Willapa and come here to stay. It is what my husband prays for.

They brought news of Big Jack Giesy too, that rascal. He's been working at the Bay, helping where Chris Giesy died. Chris made good money there, the doctor tells me, and paid off the Colony loan. Chris left his widow a landholder in her own name now. She should be happy, though I do wonder what makes Emma happy.

When he's not oystering, Jack stays with Mary and Sebastian, along with Karl. It must be the season as he didn't come to help with the yew posts. I don't know why this matters. He's just a young man but he so reminds me of what my Willie might have been if he had lived, though without Jack's lust for liquor. Still, he is a joyful, unpredictable soul, and any sin can be forgiven if one can be made to laugh.

Gloriunda and Aurora are a big help to me and the other women. Rudy brought a big spinning wheel for us to use, almost as big as those we had back in the textile mills in Bethel, where we had to walk the thread to and fro. With this one, we can sit and use one foot to move things forward. It was a gift from the Giesys. Well, what is a gift when one shares everything essential with one's neighbors? Was it theirs to give, or did it belong to all of us?

We've been finding what we need for dyes. That is a gift! God provides even the smallest things. Red from the madder root that flourishes in the garden. We've found black walnut trees, and since it stains the fingers, it stains wool brown too, and when left long enough, black. Peach leaves brought with us from Bethel give us green. And thus we weave the cloth for quilts or clothes.

Some of us are excited that there's to be a harvest fair this fall at a place called Gladstone. We plan to take our woven goods with the colors of the earth and trees to be judged. We can take baked goods as well. They welcome essays and music entries too. Perhaps the men will earn certificates for their baskets. Perhaps we women will.

Maybe I could make up such notifications of award with my improved *Fraktur* letters. *Ja,* this would be a good thing for the Aurora colony women to be working toward. It is good to have a goal to look to. The men have theirs: to build the colony, to plant and prune, to make a way to tend each other through the common fund. Why not the women? Why not let us have a special goal, something to mark our days in some interesting way? So long as our goal includes the tending of others, this should not be troublesome to the doctor.

I can almost see my *Fraktur* lettered certificate hanging there against the logs.

I suggested this to the doctor later in the week. He said nothing for a time, then told me that his next sermon must need be on humility.

———

We hear of difficulties in the Washington Territory. Two Indians have been hanged, though some say they were innocent wretches. Any of us could make mistakes; any of us could falter and fall and once hanged for it, there is no way to earn redemption. Not that redemption is earned, exactly. It is freely given. But any of us can be wretches in need of that gift of forgiveness.

I used the word *wretch* to mean someone exiled, in distress because they are alone and are, as in German, full of *Elend,* of misery. Some days this is how I feel here, as though I travel in a foreign land, exiled from what once gave pleasure. This is not to blame anyone, not my husband or God or anyone else. But I feel wretched just the same.

I worry about our friends on the Willapa with such wretched happenings. We learn too this month that the Indian uprising of last September, which took the lives of one hundred and twenty sojourners in that Deseret country, may not be blamed entirely on the natives. It is now believed that saints also took part in the killings. I find this nearly impossible to believe, but some children remembered. They saw the white flag of truce flown by their parents and uncles and older brothers. When the Deseret saints came in to say they'd negotiate the peace, they instead attacked, killing everyone save those few children they thought would not be old enough to remember. But they were. They do. Poor wretches.

So I fear for those in that country too. We hear they have rebelled against the governor appointed to the territory, and the military has moved in to make the peace there. Emma Wagner's aunt lives there. I pray that she is well.

I pray for us here too. Whenever some bad news comes about a group set apart as the Deseret saints are, the Americans around us get nervous, or so my husband tells me. They wonder if we will attack our neighbors or pretend to be neighborly when we really aren't. They weave us into the same pattern as those they do not understand. Soon, instead of coming to our storehouse to purchase pear butter or to buy up a new bed that one of our men made, they'll stay away. Maybe start rumors about us because they cannot understand our tongue, and then like others who stand out, we'll be asked to move. All of us here in Aurora would be wretches. Yet not alone at least. In the colony we always have that hope, that we will never be truly alone.

I hoped that Rudy's purchasing land near us meant he'd be coming here for good. He's a laughing soul, and my husband needs that to lighten his efforts to keep this colony prospering. I thought Karl, too, would stay but he returned. He purchased school items from the common fund for those Willapa children. But what of ours here? Our children need learning all year long. They should speak English so they won't stand out as different in this land.

My husband says we can teach our children as we go, as we did along the trail. We'll build a school after the church. But first we need more homes, and also more buildings so we can manufacture barrels and chairs and weave our cloth, all things these people of Oregon need. We will win them over by having what they want. "Who needs a church when we have the *gross Haus* in which to meet?" he asks me.

No one needs the church building to worship God, it's true. But back in Bethel, what my husband did not know is that many of us found solace in that building, even when he wasn't there to lead us. We women slipped in, sometimes together, sometimes alone. We sat in a quiet place, the scent of cooled candle wax and brick mortar falling gently on our shoulders. We prayed. We felt less wretched. And when we left, we could resume the work, serve the people, tend our families. It is harder for me to find that place of peace when there are people always around us, living here, needing cooking, mending clothes. A child needs a nose wiped, another a napkin changed. I wonder if I sin by wishing for time alone, by longing to make my letters pretty, to dream of recognition at the harvest fair, or to find a joke to laugh at. Maybe to enjoy a little teasing.

At least I have the choir to sing in. I wonder if Willapa has a choir. Does Emma sing in it? Probably not. She is honoring her husband's death, preparing for a new arrival, tending her children. She must feel wretched indeed. There must be something I can do for her even from this distance. I don't know what that is or why she comes to mind so often. I will listen harder to my husband's next sermon on service. There is always something in what he says for me.

13

Emma

Chipping Flint

That winter wore like a threadbare cloth, covering just enough to keep me breathing but offering little warmth. I struck my flint to start the February fire. I must be like flint. Strong. My young sister's letters urged me to let God lead the way for me so I could avoid more of His harsh lessons. What more could He do to me than make me a widow? My sister wrote of a spiritual world both confining and remote.

I sparked the riven wood with my chipped flint and hung the pot filled with water on the crane, then pushed it back over the flames. I tried to imagine the convenience of starting a fire without having to make the spark from the stone. Maybe if one waited long enough, all things changed for the better.

Karl's visits offered sparks of interest. My threadbare cloak of grief warmed a little more when he stopped by, filling me in on various news items of the day. He took a German newspaper, and while it was rarely current, having to come from Bethel or Milwaukee or beyond, he did still seem to know more about the outside world than any of the rest of us. It was easier to think of events back in Missouri than to face the struggles just down my road.

Mary came less often, and when I attended church, something felt different with the other Giesy women. I blanketed their festivities, I feared. They must not tease a widow, just offer help to her.

Karl was easier to be with. He gave his time without reminding me that I had so little to give in return, save a good meal for him, a little conversation about words. We talked of tending Christian's grave and how even that word *tend* has many meanings: looking after, caring for. Yet it brought images of fragility too. I felt tender, not strong like flint. Karl sat and talked while I rolled out egg noodles. Sometimes he gave Andy guidance on a lesson. I welcomed the sound of his voice, his thoughts about life, and the smell of his tobacco reminded me of my father. We spoke of him.

"Have you written and asked your father to come here?" Karl asked. "To help you now that you are widowed?"

I shook my head. I stuck my arm inside the fireplace, testing the temperature. The hair on my arm singed slightly as I pulled it away. "I doubt they'll ever come west, even when more of the Bethelites do, sometime in 1862 or 1863 my sister tells me. That'll give the colony leaders there more time to sell things, but also time for Aurora to be ready for them, I suppose. Keil doesn't want a repeat of what he found here." I heard the disgust in my voice.

"*Ja*, some of us take to change, and some of us find it troubling because we don't know how things will turn out." He drew on his pipe. This one had a foot-long stem. "We want to live in certainty and there is none save faith."

"It could have been better if Keil had waited before bringing the first group out. We scouts wanted a better welcome instead of what Keil turned it into, a huge mistake and disappointment."

Karl took a long time to respond, the draw of his pipe filling the silence. "It might still have been too much to hope for, Emma Giesy, that this would be a timber place where we could cut and sell the harvest. Sam Woodard tells us that he and his partners logged and hand-hewed timbers square so they would not roll when shipped on the boats. A lot of work that took. Their first shipment went through fine to California and they got paid."

"See," I said. "We just needed time to hand hew." I picked up a pan for the noodles.

He raised a hand to silence me. "The second load was lost at sea. The third load became frozen at the water's edge and was carried away in the spring. The fourth load rotted because they could never find anyone to buy it. Imagine such frustration! The first turned out well so they kept going. But eventually, they had to face what was. That's when Sam built his warehouses and moved inland to farm."

"So you're saying that even if we'd had more time to prepare, the people would still have been better off in Aurora?"

"By golly, I think so."

"Why don't you go there then?" I asked. I slammed the spider down, the three-legged frying pan clanging at the hearth. My children stopped their activities and stared.

Karl looked away. "Willapa helps Aurora now, as does Bethel," Karl said. "It all works out."

"My husband is dead. I don't see how that's 'working out.' "

"*Ja,* I misspoke. I meant that Willapa contributes to Aurora now just as Bethel does. All things do work out as Romans says, 'to them that love God and who are called according to his purpose.' " He set his pipe down to cool the bits of tobacco left. "Though what Bethel contributes could be impaired if war comes. I'm glad to be here, apart from all that. You can be glad too, Emma Giesy. Your children will grow up away from the battles. Maybe your father will want to avoid war too. Then he'll welcome an invitation from his daughter to come west to meet his grandchildren. You could give him a reason to bring his sons west."

"I can't ask him to come just to help me. And he has daughters too."

Karl nodded. "Ask, Emma. A parent does what is necessary for his children."

"Not for grown children," I said. "They should manage on their own once they leave the nest."

"*Ach,* one never stops being a parent. Or so I'm told."

"Unless one loses a child," I said. "Maybe by coming here I am lost to them."

"You think of Christian, *ja?* It was a hard loss for Andreas and Barbara. Even so, Christian's parents, they are still his parents, still with memories of him and with his children alive waddling around before them. If you asked your parents, I think they'd come to help, by golly."

I imagined them all here in this house with me. My mother would mid-wife my infant, my father and brothers would joke and laugh, and I would hear the sound of a man's voice and perhaps not ache with longing so for Christian's. My young sisters, Lou and Johanna, they could play with their niece, and William would take Andy by the hand and give my son a chance to be a little boy instead of a little man who looks after his mother and sister. And Catherine, well, she'd talk of love, tell me to put my husband's clothes away and read me hopeful scriptures that promised goodness if I just obeyed. Such words made me feel empty, sometimes angry.

It would be good, though, to hold my mother in my arms again. Maybe in giving her comfort I could receive a bit of my own.

———

My mother-in-law and Christian's aunts, the other scouts' wives, brought me food that spring and helped me dye the yarn I'd spun. They brought me eggs to boil at Easter. Their husbands came by to chop more wood, see to the fields, make sure this widow had what she needed. How I wished I could have received their gifts of time and labor without feeling embittered by my need. I remembered a sermon Keil had once given about true Christian community requiring honesty among its members, especially about our weaknesses. Once shared, each could support the other, he said. He quoted something from James about our confessing to each other, then praying for one another so that we might be healed. What courage that would take, I decided, to confess how I felt about God, my life, everything here that kept me in an anxious, often angry state. And praying? I hadn't done that for some time. It would take courage to confess or pray. I didn't feel safe here without Christian, and safety is surely the first requirement for a healing heart.

I'm not sure when I admitted to the growing resentment of the women that their husbands had to tend to me and my children in addition to their own. They said how good it was they got to act on the Diamond Rule by helping me. But I could tell. Mary mentioned more often than needed Jack's willingness to stop by. I'd already told her Jack made me uncomfortable. Christian's sister-in-law, John's wife, noted how busy her husband was with the school and the mill and so many other things, and wouldn't it be nice if someday I found someone else who would take me as his wife. She said it all in the same breath and then asked my forgiveness if she spoke too soon after Christian's death.

"Yes," I said. "It is too soon and will always be."

"You're young," John's wife said. She patted my hand. "A whole life awaits you."

It wasn't a life I looked forward to.

———

My mother-in-law sent shivers through me when she noted that in some parts of the world when a son dies, his oldest son is given as a ward to the father's family, a grandparent or an uncle. "This has happened even among fine Americans," my mother-in-law told me as she calmly stitched her husband's pants. We worked side by side at her table. "Meriwether Lewis, who came across the land with the American Clark over fifty years ago, he was raised by an uncle after his father died, even though his mother was perfectly capable. Of course if she'd remarried right away that might not have been so."

"Are you suggesting I can't bring up my own son?" I asked.

"It was just an observation," she said. "How Americans do things."

I tried to remember if such a custom had occurred in the old country, or even as part of the colony. But of course in Bethel, all lived close to each other, so it wouldn't be difficult to have a fatherless boy influenced by his uncle while still living in his mother's house. Maybe that's all she meant.

Still, I found myself feeling ill after that conversation with my mother-in-law and vowed to do much more of the work here in the cabin myself. The men could stop by to do their duty to the Widow Giesy, but they'd see that I already had chopped wood aplenty, that the goat was already fed, that I'd put bacon grease on her udder to be a healing balm, that I'd kindled my own fires just fine. They'd leave and could tell their wives that their help wasn't needed, that they didn't have to stop by the widow's place this week at all. With the cows dried up, Boshie would put them in with their two animals. John already had the mule.

It was a fantasy, of course. Maybe if I hadn't been carrying this infant, maybe then I could do it all. But I could barely swing the axe. Keil had been right about one thing: my small frame worked against me in this landscape. He expected it to mean I'd have trouble delivering an infant, my punishment for being Eve's daughter, still seeking more. But so far, that punishment hadn't happened. My two babies had arrived with relative ease.

I avoided the men when they came to help, set by the door the packed bags of *Strudels* or dried fruits I'd prepared for them in return for their effort so I would be less indebted. On Sundays, when otherwise we might have made our way to the stockade for Andy and Kate to see their cousins and relatives, I rested at home with my children cluck-henned under my arms, and I read to them from the almanac, or we made cookies and decorated them with dried fruit. If anyone asked, I claimed the weather kept us away.

I did have difficulty putting Karl's suggestion from my mind. Perhaps my parents might come out to help if I asked. My longing for them surprised me. But truth be told, I suspected that within a very few weeks of their arrival

I'd be wishing them gone, as uncertain for the cause of my agitation as I had ever been. *A contrary woman* was my Americanized name.

———

My second son and third child arrived as I expected on April 4, nine months to the day after his conception. I awoke with a familiar ache in my back and milked a bleating Opal that morning, suspecting this might be the day. The day before, I'd brought wood in so we could heat water, and I made a huge pot of beans for the children to eat. I talked to Christian, said things out loud, and reminded him that once all those male doctors had insisted I was wrong about the date of Andy's birth. But I was sure this time, I really was, just as I'd been before.

When my water broke late in the April afternoon, I sent Andy for Mary. But by the time she arrived, I held my baby in my arms. It seemed right that I delivered this child alone. Doing so affirmed my strength. Kate sat off to the side, quiet as a mouse. "You have a new brother," I told her after I'd cut the cord, then washed the child and wrapped him in the gown I'd made from one of Christian's shirts. The scent of my husband was still in it, nearly a year after his death. Kate ran her finger over the baby's forehead, looked up at me and smiled. "Mine," she said.

"All of ours," I told her.

I named the baby Christian. He had a fuzz of reddish hair, not unlike the wisps of red that sometimes showed in his father's beard. "Your father would have loved you dearly," I told my youngest son. That night, with the baby satisfied by Opal's milk, I felt my eyes fill to overflowing. "You're missing all this, Christian," I said. "It isn't fair. You should have lived and not me. You were the better person, the finer parent. But you were so…good, too good, and look at how we're left now?" I kissed the tears from my son's forehead. Andy came to me and pressed his head against my arm. Kate slept.

This was my family now. Christian's life did go on, but not with him in it. With this Christian's presence in my life, I'd have no time for wondering about the meanings of words. I'd have no time for anything but keeping three children alive and showing without doubt that I didn't need an uncle or a grandparent to fill a father's void. I didn't need anyone at all.

———

Renewed purpose filled my days. I dried lovage to sweeten the cabin and ground the root into powder to pepper my venison stews. The cabin smelled fresh; food nourished. Spring meant renewal to me, and with it a change in how Christian's memory filled my days. Christian and I had married in the spring. Baby Christian smoothed the rough edges of the loss. I thought of my husband a little less, not every waking moment as my baby was my first morning thought now. I heard myself laugh out loud once when the baby blew bubbles, again when he greedily consumed the goat's milk fed through the finger of a glove. I didn't blame myself for not being able to produce milk on my own. It was the way of things for me, something I needed to accept. I adapted. That too was a sign of strength.

When the goat took Andy's handkerchief stuffed at his waist and shook it as though it were a flag, running away when Andy tried to grab it, we all laughed.

It was spring, when the unexpected can be more innocent than romantic, when creativity proves delightful rather than calculated.

I could see why people fell in love in spring.

I decided to fall in love too, but with sketching and drawing. I planned to talk with Sarah Woodard about my idea and see if she and Sam could help. They knew everyone in the region, and Olympia would be the logical place to try to find customers. How I'd get there and what I'd do with the children, I pitched those thoughts away, but the germ of the idea was there, that tiny irritant inside the oyster shell that might one day grow into a pearl. I'd begun to think of the future with more than just dread. I didn't know when that actually happened, just that it did.

Big Jack arrived carrying an egg etched with this new infant's birthday on it. It had fancy lettering, almost like the *Fraktur* that marked our German documents. It was beautiful, with the flowing letters scratched onto a kind of chestnut-colored egg, and an intricate border on the top and bottom. I had no idea who'd made it. Jack had knocked on our door, placed the egg in my hand when I opened the latch. His palm was as wide as a butter paddle, dwarfing the delicate egg. He said nothing, just turned on his heel and left.

A present, most likely from Christian's grandparents. I felt a twinge of guilt keeping my children from visiting time with them.

In early May, Sarah brought me a laying hen. It had been a long time since I'd seen her. We put the chicken in the smokehouse and together we made a little roosting nest for her, though Sarah assured me the chickens would roost in the trees at night if left out. "They're like seagulls that way," she said.

Back in the cabin, Sarah held the baby to her and sang softly. I knew she longed for a child of her own, but though she was nearly twenty and had been married to Sam for nearly five years, this had not happened. I wondered if it felt strange for her to see me with three children all without a father while she and Sam, all ready and willing, still had none. She bowed her blond hair to my son whose eyes had closed.

"He takes to your singing," I said. "I can't carry a tune in a candlestick."

Sarah smiled and when she looked up, I saw tears in her eyes. She sat in the rocking chair while I heated tea. It was May but still chilly. I lifted Christian from her arms and placed him in the baby board I'd used for Kate. Sarah lifted her cup, and that's when she noticed the scraped egg on a shelf I'd tacked to the logs. I'd placed the egg on a little stand I'd made of twigs. "That's beautiful," she said. "Did you do that work?"

I shook my head. "I don't know who did it, but Jacob Giesy brought it by."

She laughed then. "I should have recognized it, though this is a little fancier than what I've seen. He makes charcoal drawings on rocks and signs his name." She looked at the egg more closely. "See. Right here is a little *JG*."

I'd thought the lettering was just a part of the decoration, but she was right. I hadn't remembered seeing any such rocks with charcoal drawings on them, but then I hadn't gone very far from my hearth. "He draws well?"

"Oh yes. He made a likeness of our old dog on the side of the warehouse. It would wash off in the rains, so I asked if he'd do one on paper and he obliged. I think at first he thought I'd be upset with him, or Sam would. He hadn't asked if we wanted that picture on the warehouse." She set her cup down and turned the egg around in her hand. "Was it a baptismal gift?"

"No. We don't celebrate baptisms," I said. "Dr. Keil doesn't think it a necessary sacrament for either children or adults." Karl Ruge, who remained a Lutheran, did consider infant baptism important, though. I would ask him about that. "Maybe I should have Christian baptized. If for no other reason than that Keil wouldn't want it," I said.

"Oh, Emma." Sarah laughed. "When we have a child, I'll want him baptized." She stood over my son as he slept. "It means he'll be forever in God's hands." She fluffed Christian's reddish hair, pulled it between her fingers so it stood up like a cock's crown.

I wasn't of the opinion that being in God's hands was always that comforting. I studied the egg. "I didn't know this about Christian's cousin," I said. "I assumed someone else had done the etching."

"Jack's very talented. He speaks good English, or at least I can understand him." I was still trying to imagine the artistic side of Jack when she added, "Sometimes he's a bit…unpredictable, but very generous too, it seems, to have given you this special gift."

I'd thought he'd been merely the delivery person who at last understood that I didn't want him around. Why on earth would Jack give my son such a precious gift?

My fingers fidgeted.

"I wonder if maybe you and Sam might have some ideas about how I could earn money on my own, sketching people or painting portraits or making drawings of their homes that they could send to their families back East. I know there are no printers here, none needing lithographers, but maybe in Olympia?"

"I'll ask Sam. But I think it would mean you'd have to…travel. I'm not sure how you could do that, with the children so young. And you a woman alone."

"You're not going to tell me that it might be 'unseemly,' are you?"

"Never," she said. She lifted an eyebrow. "But I'm certain there are those who would."

"*Ja,*" I said. "But maybe, since so many have been telling me they don't mind helping, maybe they'd keep the children for me when I made such trips. They can act the Diamond Rule by doing so and send their husbands over to milk and feed without worry about what the Widow Giesy might do to them." Sarah frowned. "They wouldn't have to be long journeys, a week or so at a time."

"How could you be separated from him for even a day?" Sarah said, nodding toward Christian.

"If it meant I could provide for them on my own it would be worth it in the end."

"You say that now, but I don't know. Don't you remember how it was when Andy stayed with his grandparents after Christian died?"

"That was different. I was confused and frightened. I'm more certain now of what I need to do."

Kate came over then and I made a cat's cradle for her out of string. Andy asked to use the corn mill that Karl Ruge had brought us at Easter. It made grinding corn so much easier, and we could use just enough for the corn drink or the mush we wanted for breakfast. He swung his little arm round and round, dropping corn kernels into the hopper. They clinked like tiny pearls dropped into a tin cup.

It would be difficult to leave my children. Sarah was right about that. But Andy would be old enough to come with me.

"Maybe you could make some drawings that Sam could show to people," Sarah said. "That way you wouldn't have to leave here. You could draw our place or maybe the children's portraits. Or the trees. That might be a place to begin. You wouldn't have to worry then about tongues wagging over your leaving your children behind."

She was right, of course. This next year must be devoted to my children. But I could make some portraits in between. I'd have to borrow money for the charcoal and paper, but I could pay it back when I sold something. "Would Sam make a loan to me for the supplies?" I asked.

"I'm sure he would. But you might also think of asking Jack. He seems to have a good supply of paper."

I didn't ask Jack Giesy, but I did find another way to take the next step. I wrote to my parents. I told them of Christian's birth and drew a small picture of his face, his eyes like Christian's, his mouth with a wide space between his nose and the top of his slender upper lip. "Room for a fine, bushy mustache one day," I told them. "As his father always had."

Asking for the money was the easy part. I told my father what I planned to do and that I thought I could make a living this way, so I wouldn't be so dependent on the colonists here in Willapa. My father had somehow accumulated independent resources or he couldn't have purchased property in his name. He'd understand that kind of inventive thinking...at least if I'd been a son he would. *I'd have you send the money to me when the other colonists come out,* I wrote. *But that might not be for a long time from what Catherine tells me, so perhaps you could send it to me by ship.*

Then came the hard part, the expressing of my real need. *The children should know all their grandparents, not just Christian's. The future may hold changes for me, travel if I'm to do this work successfully. I could do it more easily if you came to visit and perhaps even stayed. I'd know then that the children were in good hands.*

Would I move across the country to an unknown wilderness in order to help my child? Would I move my family if my father or mother needed me? Would I make such a sacrifice for my children one day? Yet here I was, asking this very thing.

If they agreed to come, I'd be sinking deeper into debt.

14

Emma

Keeping All Together

I marked the first anniversary of my husband's death by going to his grave. I took the children, of course. I decided we'd also spend the day with Christian's parents, as they'd seen little of us through the spring and now into the summer. Maybe with a little time together I could shake the agitation of my mother-in-law's comment of some months ago, about the eldest child being given to the grandparents to raise. Enough time had passed, surely. I could be generous with my children's time.

We made the trek walking, then climbed the bare hill to the cemetery. Someone had built a small fence around the two graves, probably John, since he seemed to be in charge of so many things now that Christian wasn't. A warm breeze brushed against my face and Baby Christian's reddish hair. Andy acted solemn but Kate was a typical *Kinder*, running about and doing somersaults near the cedar sapling I'd planted.

From a distance I could see the stone that marked Willie Keil's grave. I wondered when they'd set the stone and felt an immediate sense of guilt that I had no such marker for Christian. That I'd not known of the occasion when Willie's stone had been set also discomfited. Perhaps the family was protecting me, not wanting to invite me on the occasion of a grave marker while I still carried a child. More likely, they thought I'd be uninterested in anything having to do with Keil.

But then we approached Christian's grave, and it had a marker too. Not a stone one, but wood, laid flat. Someone had cut his name and birth and day of death into it. No one had bothered to tell me of its setting, either.

The whole community probably clucked their tongues even now that it had taken so long for me to comment on this gesture, which could only mean that I hadn't spent much time grieving at my husband's grave. True, I hadn't spent much time at this grave. In fact, this was the first time I'd come since the day he'd been buried, and that only because it was the anniversary date, a time designed to be the end of mourning. I could only hope. Sarah said a husband's family set the time of mourning for an Indian widow, established ways she must behave during those years. It had sounded constricting when she'd told me, but at least the rules were clear and there was an ending time.

I imagined Christian's family thinking ill of me that I'd stayed away. They wouldn't understand the difficulty I'd had in traveling seven miles with the children. I didn't always have the use of their mule. Walking and carrying three young children wasn't an easy task at all. They might think of that.

Still, if I made my way to Olympia to paint or draw, the family would say that I could travel when I wanted to.

After we put dried flowers on Christian's grave, I took the children down the hill and over to where Andreas and Barbara lived. I waited for the inevitable comment about how long it had been since I'd visited them, but instead they opened their arms wide to the children.

Henry continued to work in the fields, but Martin waved when he saw us and moved toward the house. He wiped his hands on his jeans. He had a pleasant face, this brother of Christian's. He was tall, almost too thin, and leaned into his walk as though to resist a wind that might otherwise blow him away. He shook Andy's little hand and smiled into the open face of Baby Christian. He nodded his head to Kate, too, who was sitting on her grandfather's knee.

"Emma's brought the boys to stay for a bit," my mother-in-law said.

"That would be *gut*," Martin said. "For her to stay too."

"Just for the afternoon," I told them. "We need to go back before dark."
I gave Barbara some salal-berry cakes I'd carried with us. I'd dried them and
stored them through the winter. These were the last that I had, but soon the
bushes would be filled with the small berries as purple as a bad bruise, and I'd
make more cakes again.

"Oh, *ja,* but it stays light till after ten now," Barbara said, unwrapping
the berry cakes from the leaves they were wrapped in.

"So we have time to catch up on news," Martin said.

"I don't have much of that," I said.

"Time or news?" he asked. He smiled.

"You don't come to the Fourth of July celebration," Andreas said. He
looked tired and moved a cane I hadn't remembered his using. It must have
been a difficult winter for him too, having lost his oldest son to death.
Andreas wouldn't have stayed at Willapa without Christian's being here, and
I wondered why they remained now. Probably because his brother John was
here and his other sons.

Barbara said, "We'll give you news, then. John says the children should
go to school from June to harvest and then stop, starting again in October
until the rains come too much. Andy should stay here for that. You want
him educated, *ja*? The travel would be hard for him and Martin enjoys his
company."

"He's never been separated from me," I said, wishing now I hadn't taken
the time to come here, wishing I hadn't even considered being generous and
sharing my son with this family. It always seemed to end with suggestions for
how I could do things better.

"That's not so," Barbara corrected, "when his father—"

"They're planting teasel," Andreas said. "To card the wool. Down at
Aurora Mills. That's news."

"It grows wild along the river here," I said. "We just need wool to card. No one ever brought up sheep."

"We have sheep here," Henry said. "Rudy brought them."

"There's talk of building a teasel factory in Aurora," Martin said. "It'll be a good sheep production place. And they're beginning to build furniture to sell to nearby settlers. It's a busy place there."

"I suspect one day some of our young men will head that way if things pick up," Andreas said. "Rudy bought a sheep farm there."

"They have a cemetery," Barbara said. "Can't have a village without a cemetery."

"Speaking of cemeteries, who made the wooden marker for Christian's grave?" I asked. "I'd like to thank them and apologize for taking so long to do it."

"Imagine growing teasel. Stuff is like a weed back home," Andreas said.

"The Shoalwaters use it to brush their hair," I said. "I've seen them once or twice doing that by the river." They sometimes came to trade with me, offering up fish for my bread. I didn't tell my in-laws that. "About that marker," I tried again, but then the conversation took a troubling swing.

"Those Indians will be in trouble for not staying on their reservation," Andreas said, "if they're coming so far south as your place. Could be dangerous. You should live back with us."

"Ja. Why don't you leave Andy with us for a few days at least," Barbara said. "We miss seeing him, and you have the baby to look after."

"Andy's a big help to me," I said.

"Ja, that's as it should be," Andreas said. He tapped his cane on the floor. "But he must miss having a man around to show him things."

"Karl Ruge comes by," I said. My thumb and forefinger made circles against each other and I bit the inside of my cheek.

"What kind of wood did they use for Christian's marker?" Martin asked. "That might tell us who did it."

"Wood? I don't know. It looked like cedar. It was nicely done."

"It's too bad you're so busy," Barbara said. "Maybe whoever did it would have asked you to be there when they set it. But they know how much work it must be to come this way. We so seldom see you."

"I'll ask around if you'd like," Martin said. I nodded.

"What's the point of living near your family if you don't take advantage of them?" Barbara continued. She handed Andy a cookie and a big glass of milk. He sat on the chair, his legs swinging beneath him. He looked happy and I realized I hadn't seen that smile much since his father had died. Maybe I was selfish in not letting him come here more often.

"I was under the impression that I took too much advantage," I said, "having to have so much help since…Christian's death."

"Well, that's what we do for each other," she said. "We take care of each other. And having a little time for Andy to spend with his *Oma* would just be a nice way to repay."

"I should have made a marker for my brother," Martin said.

"You might think about how you could be generous to others since you want to not be beholden to people." Her words were sharp.

"We really need to be getting back," I said.

"What's your hurry?" Barbara said, softer now.

"Generosity, that's a good thing in our colony," Andreas said. "But why they want to plant teasel, *ach,* that's beyond me."

———

Surely I was strong enough to resist any real effort by them to lure Andy from me. I'd never heard of anyone in the colony having their child raised by another against their will. But it reinforced my view that showing few signs of needing them was the better course of action for our future.

My fields were plowed and planted into oats, not wheat, as the men suggested. They'd harvest the crop on my land just as they did on their own. Whatever they sold would be brought to the common fund of the family; whatever was milled would be shared with the families both here and probably at Aurora. I had no say in it. I stayed out of their way. When the cows had their calves and they were weaned, Boshie brought them back. He kept the calves, the increase, so the bulls could be sold and the heifers kept to expand the herd. The increase was payment for his tending them through the winter. I could once again have the milk for butter and to supplement the goat's milk for the children, and of course to meet whatever butter contracts we Willapa people had.

Sometime late that fall, people began calling the stockade Fort Willapa, and a post office was even established there with John Giesy as the postmaster. He wore so many hats, that John. Christian wore many hats too. He'd been a legislator for less than year. My brother Jonathan wrote that Oregon had indeed held its first election of state officials. Next year for sure, Oregon would be a state, or so Jonathan said. He didn't invite me to come there in his letter, but it was clear he felt Oregon the better of the two places.

A few of the Willapa women sent some of their weavings down to Oregon for a harvest festival at Gladstone, not far from Aurora. Mary suggested I bake a special *Strudel* for the event. I scoffed. "By the time it arrived it would be either hard as a rock or worse, covered with a hairy mold they'd have a hard time passing off as a frosting."

"Maybe we should hold our own fair," she said.

But there weren't enough people for such an event in Willapa. There probably never would be. That very thought made me feel disloyal to Christian, and I apologized to him out loud.

Mary and Elizabeth and Boshie made plans to go to Aurora, though. It was to be Mary's first visit. "Karl Ruge is going with us, but Jack's staying so he can look after things." Her face was flushed with excitement about the trip. "He'll come by here too. I've asked him to do that, so don't be rude to him."

"I've never been rude," I said.

"You can be...hard," she said.

I wanted to ask why it was that when women said what they wished that they were considered "hard," but when men said what they thought they were just wise and authoritative, a quality to be admired.

"I'd really rather Jack didn't come by," I said.

"What's wrong with him?"

"I just...he looks at me strange. Like I was some sort of exhibit at a fair," I said.

"Maybe you're just not accustomed to having a man show interest. Maybe you're suffering a bit of lovesickness. You pursued Christian. He never really had a chance to woo you."

I turned to her. "Lovesickness? I'm so far from such a thought. And Christian chose me, he did. That you'd—"

"People do marry for things other than love, you know," she said. She looked away, acted as though my table needed dusting, and she did that now.

"Mary, I...I don't know what to say to such strange thinking."

She shrugged. "It's what is, Emma. Most women who are widowed do remarry, and not all of them are so fortunate as to fall in love before they do it. Think of your children."

"They're all I do think of."

When Mary returned from her visit to Aurora she was full of stories about plum orchards that had been planted and how a new railroad was running a short distance along the Columbia River in the Washington Territory, and that in Oregon City there was a school that women attended and that she'd seen an advertisement for people making daguerreotype portraits, for a fee.

"Daguerreotype portraits. They must have been lovely," I said.

"Much too expensive for the likes of us. And probably too worldly," she added in a whisper, "though I'd love one made of Elizabeth."

I hadn't shared with her my plans to draw portraits. She might think that was too worldly also. Neither did I tell her about my limited interactions with Jack Giesy while they'd been gone. Jack had come by, tipped his hat, and acted the cocky gentleman.

Andy warmed to him, running right up to Jack as he swaggered into the yard. I kept my face emotionless but I could hardly deprive my son of time with the man who'd helped him say good-bye to his father.

I let them stay outside. It was October and the air smelled fresh as mint. Jack showed him how to make a whistle from a bird carcass Andy handed to him. Then Kate begged to go outside too, as she squatted beneath my legs, pushing my skirts aside. She ran to where Jack and Andy sat beneath a cedar tree, her little face so close to what Jack worked on that her eyes must have crossed.

Jack laughed and patted the cedar boughs on the ground beside him, and she sat. Andy raced toward me when the whistle was finished and the sound he made was that of a hawk flying high overhead. I stopped my butter churning and picked up Baby Christian, the forlornness of the whistle haunting. Kate shouted, "Me too, me too!" and Andy ran back and gave her the whistle, though she couldn't make the song.

Christian watched with careful eyes all this activity while I held him, standing in the doorway of my cabin. I wondered what he could see from that distance. Could he feel the dry air? The vine maple had turned red already, announcing the coming of autumn. I would welcome the rain.

"Come over, Mama," Andy shouted. He motioned with his arm.

There'd be no harm in that, I supposed. The grass was crisp as I walked across it to where Jack sat, to where Kate had returned the whistle to him telling him it was "lame."

"*Lame,*" Jack said. "There's a new term for something broken."

"She sees the goat sometimes limping," I explained. "We have to take a stick or stone from his hoof."

"Let's see if we can heal it," Jack said and blew on the whistle to Kate's delight. She studied it and then she grabbed for it. Andy grabbed back and Kate started to cry, a high-pitched wail. "You best stop, little lady, or you'll get yourself in trouble," Jack said in a stern voice. *A little too stern,* I thought. It just made Kate cry louder.

"I'll handle my children," I said, bending to take the whistle. "Andy, go get your sister a drink of water." He hesitated, then accepted that what I recommended must be the correct course of action.

"You spoil the girl," Jack said.

"She's considerably younger than her brother and can't solve problems without bringing attention to herself," I said. "You have no children. It's hardly your place to comment."

"*Ja.* Not my place," Jack said. "But your boy will lack proper respect for himself and your daughter will neglect her role of silence if their mother's words aren't balanced by a good man's words to guide them. Their mother too."

"If you came here to tell me how to behave, I'd say it was time for you to leave."

"Maybe I could chop that stack of wood for you," Jack said. "That's the reason I came. To help a widow out."

Furious, I ignored him. "It's all right, Kate," I said. She'd calmed a bit. "When you're older you'll make the whistle work."

"Andy go."

"I know. For now, you go drink the water your brother's getting for you." She gave in reluctantly and I saw myself in her eagerness to do all things that her older brother could.

"About the wood?" Jack asked. "I maybe could chop you up a winter's supply."

He made offers with a ready escape when he said "maybe could." If I turned him down he could say, "I only maybe offered," and if I accepted, well, then he had the upper hand. If I took something from him, he'd want something in return. He had obligation written all over his high forehead, wrapped into that lazy, almost leering grin. In another time I might have flirted back, just for fun, but not now, not with Jack.

"The work is good for me," I said. "A good change from churning butter."

He cocked his head in that way he had. "They always said you were a stubborn woman," Jack said.

"They?"

He stood up and when he did, he stood too close. I could smell the soap that had scrubbed his skin and see the pores in his chin. I shifted Christian into the crook of my other arm and stepped back.

"You know who 'they' are," he said. He stepped away, leaned against the cedar tree, picked at his cuticles. "The relatives. They say it with some admiration, though," he added.

"I doubt that." Baby Christian squirmed against me. I put him onto my shoulder and patted his back. He burped and the smell of sour milk filled the space between us. "There's little room for the admiration of women in this colony."

"Not true, not true. Look at Helena Giesy. Never married, just gives her life to Bethel. She's coming out to help Keil, did you know that? And we all think Louisa Keil is a saint. She never makes demands or questions. Mary Giesy is a generous woman too, taking me and Karl Ruge in, treating us like family though we're two old bachelors. So you see, women are noticed."

"For what they *do*," I said. "Not for who they are." He squinted at me. "And you are hardly an old bachelor." I wished I hadn't added that last, but his characterizing himself as someone like Karl annoyed.

"I'm not? Well, that's good news. Must mean I'm young enough to chop that wood for you before I go." I shook my head. "You don't want me to go?"

"No. I mean *ja,* I think it's time you left."

"Is there anything else I *can* do while I'm here?" Now he lifted an eyebrow and with it came that half leer, eyes twinkling. His legs crossed at the ankles, arms folded across his chest. So self-assured.

"You've treated my children to a pleasant hour. I'd say that was more than enough. The rest I can take care of myself."

He jerked himself forward off the tree trunk, an act that startled me and caused Christian to begin to cry. The children had returned, Kate carrying a tin cup and Andy now chasing at the goat. Jack moved in a little closer and patted Christian's back. Anyone passing by might think it the perfect family scene.

"It's not easy raising three children on your own, Widow Giesy. It is a man's duty to tend to the widows in his family. You and I've grown up with the colony's wishes about widows. Christian would want that tradition carried on. You know that. A woman is meant to be with a family, with a man to shape her life." He squatted and picked up dirt and rubbed it between his hands. "Pitch," he said by way of explanation. He looked at me then. "I'll return to the oyster beds before long and won't be so available to…help you out. So you might think of tasks you'd like done before the rains come hard. I can oblige. I'm as decent a man as you'll find in these parts with all sorts of hidden talents, lots of time to give. I rarely sleep. Mary will tell you. And I'm a patient man despite what you may think of me."

"I never thought you weren't patient or anything else," I said. "You flatter yourself, Jack Giesy, that I think of you at all."

He laughed. For a moment he looked less like the wolf of the three little pigs' fame and more like Mary's little lamb. *Can he turn on that boyish grin at will?* Apparently so, for he added, "Oh, you think about me, Emma Giesy. I bet you put that little egg I made for you in a nice prominent place in your house. Will you let me see where it sits? Or are you too frightened that once I'm inside your home you might not get me out?"

"It was a gift for Christian. And I should thank you for it. I do now. I hadn't known you made it, just that you delivered it. And nothing about you frightens me," I lied. "I'm just cautious about what sorts of critters come into the house."

I went inside, brought the children in with me, then seethed in silence as I heard him chopping wood that he must have known I'd one day burn.

———

After he left I chided myself for not asking him about his drawings. But to do so invited an intimacy I wasn't prepared for. An artist's work exposes, and one wishes to do it on one's own terms. I might have asked him what he thought about selling portraits, but I didn't want to know his opinion enough to risk his rejection of mine. Maybe with daguerreotypes being sold now even in the streets of a small town like Oregon City, there'd be no need for my making drawings. Maybe photographic likenesses would be preferred.

Once the children were in bed at night, though, I did light Christian's lamp and take out my charcoal and the last of the papers I had to draw on. I ironed the damp paper flat, then filled in the sketches, made the ferns detailed, darkened the bark so it looked almost real enough to pick up. I hadn't heard anything from my parents about sending me money or supplies, or coming to this land. They probably didn't realize what courage it took to make the request.

My days were filled with diaper changing, though Kate had trained herself. The first time she successfully found the privy of her own accord we were at Fort Willapa at the last service I thought we would attend before Christmas and the truly heavy rains came. Kate told Christian's youngest sister what she needed, and Louisa took her out. Kate came roaring back in and announced to everyone that she'd "wee'd all alone." She carried the word "all" out as though it was a long song. John was giving the sermon that day. He stopped short, turned his head toward the women's side of the building. He

A T E N D E R I N G   I N   T H E   S T O R M

smiled at her and then the rest all laughed. I loved him for that, for noting that a young girl's early success should be shouted to the world.

Christmas came and then the New Year which brought treasures from my family. The joy I felt with the gifts surprised. They sent wooden toys for the two older children and a silver rattle for Christian. I realized they must have begun gathering up gifts and sending them as soon as they learned of the baby's birth in order to get them here at this special time.

For me, my parents included charcoal and paper as gifts. The latter was crinkled from the damp weather and the days it took for it to reach me. Still, it would be my beginning, and I hadn't had to ask a Giesy or a colony member for this start.

My father wrote nothing about coming either to visit or to stay, though. So, that was the way it would be then. Whatever I could do with the drawing would be my next step toward independence. I would have to do this on my own. I'd keep my children with me, and perhaps we'd travel together to make my sketches. Never mind that my parents weren't going to be able to make the journey or did not wish to meet their grandchildren. There were good reasons for them not coming, I was certain.

I'd always wanted to live on my own, and so I would. I might even sell this property. It was in my name. I could sell it and use the money to begin my newest life. Why not do that? Why not leave this place behind?

The thought of leaving what Christian and I had built together left me breathless.

Here, I was as close to independence as a widow with three children living in a communal colony could come. The money received from any sale would eventually be used up. I couldn't take the risk. I felt like a harlot accepting the work of others on our behalf, but I refused to be like other widows who married someone they didn't care for because they couldn't make it on their own. I would find ways to pay back Christian's family, I would.

And if Andy hadn't gotten ill, I might well have made it work.

15

Emma

The River of Transport and Hurdle

Andy's fever spiked and waned for days. He coughed so hard he seemed to bring his insides out. I kept him cool in baths of agrimony, the water turning yellow from the plant we dyed wool with back in Bethel. Here I used it to make him teas to help the vomiting, but it did little good. I put a mustard plaster on his chest, went through my shelves to see if there was anything I could give him that might help. Catnip tea did nothing but make him sleep. His round face poured into tiny hollows at the cheeks. His lips quivered and cracked. Little ones had no reserve against a storm like this, I decided. His face sank pale with pain.

He must have picked it up at the Christmas gathering with all the others. I remembered now hearing Joe Bullard and the fence viewer, Mr. Vail, coughing. Children played in spite of runny noses, their little hands lifting doughnuts from the table, then putting some back for those more heavily sugared. I tried to keep Andy and Kate from the ailments of others. But it was Kate's birthday celebration, too, and I hadn't wanted to deprive her of what I thought would be worthy attention.

For all the good that did. Her grandparents were kind to her, giving her a cookie and patting her on the head. The aunts commented on her pretty curls, but it was Andy and Christian they doted on that day, commenting on Christian's reddish hair and Andy's stance with his hands on his hips, just the way his father used to stand. My daughter didn't garner much interest.

My present to her of a special covered basket made of tulle pleased her. "For treasure?" I nodded. I could have as easily given it to her at home. A good reason to stay the winter closed up in our cabin, alone.

But my insight came too late. Now the January rains poured themselves out like wretched tears on our cedar-shake roof, leaks forming in places where the shakes were saturated by the constant downpour. Mornings when it didn't rain we could barely see the cows in the half barn for the fog. I hated leaving Andy even for a moment, but the cows had to be milked. I'd come back in, wash his soiled clothes, and hang them at the rafters, but they took days to dry in the dampness, even with the fire burning hot. At least I had plenty of chopped wood, thanks to Jack Giesy. I gave him that grudging thanks.

I brought the goat into the house to stop her mournful bleating and so I could milk her. I cleaned after her, but nothing seemed to stop the stench of the mix of her *Dreck* and Andy's illness.

I knew I should go for help but I couldn't take Kate or Christian into the weather and I couldn't leave Andy alone. With this discouraging rain, they probably took to heart my constant insistence that I needed no help.

Midweek I stopped milking the cows because I didn't want to be away from Andy. Taking all three of the children to Mary's seemed overwhelming and unsafe, but I had to do something. I had to get additional herbs or get him to the doctor. There was only one thing to do.

"Mama!" Kate cried as I pulled on my scarf and Christian's heavy oiled slicker.

"It's fine, *Liebchen*," I said. "I'll be right back. Don't worry." I swung open the door and stepped into the downpour. It chilled but it wasn't icy, wasn't about to become snow. Water ran like spring freshets along the muddy path, so instead I walked beside it. I slipped my way to where the cows mooed in the half barn. They stood, heads up when they saw me. They hadn't been milked since the morning before. They wouldn't like what I was about to do. I untied them, then I picked up a stick and shouted, startling them both. One mooed and switched her tail at me.

"Get out! Go! Go on now!" I swatted again but they merely moved a little and stood looking at me, the rain making their short horns as shiny as the Bay. "Please, you've got to go. Go to Mary's, please." I switched them again. They moved but a foot, the cold evident in the moisture at their nostrils.

If I'd wanted them to stand still and not move despite my shouts, they would have run in all directions.

I put the rope around the neck of one of them, the one with the bell, and began to drag her forward from the comfort of the half barn. They could be so contrary, these animals. We'd tamed them into dogs who didn't want to be in the wet and the cold. Who could blame them? But it was all I could think of to do, to let loose the cows and swat at them and head them in the direction of Mary and Boshie's and hope that when the Giesys saw the animals loose and needing milked they'd know that something was wrong.

Finally I dragged the recalcitrant cow out onto the path. The other followed at a desperately slow pace. *How long have I been gone from Andy?* "Shoo!" I shouted, getting behind them now. "Shoo!" They both turned back toward me. Then, as though they shared a signal, each began running toward me, back into the half barn. "No, please!" I felt the tears come. *"Ach, jammer! What is the matter with you?"* They split around me as though I were an island and they the moving river, their hooves splashing mud onto my dress, my slicker, my face. They stood inside then, chewing their cuds, their bags swollen out between their legs.

I stomped to the house to get Christian's percussion gun. One shot, that's all I needed. Thank goodness Christian hadn't left me a flintlock. In this rain, the powder would have been nothing but mud and I'd not have gotten off a single shot.

Before I left with the gun, I tended to Andy, his face so hot. "Katie, you put this cloth on your brother's forehead. Do it now. I'll be right back. Never mind the gun. It'll be fine, *ja.*" Christian cried now too. He was sitting up by himself and had just started to crawl. I scanned the room to see if he could reach anything that could hurt him. "You watch Baby, too, Kate. Make sure he doesn't get too near the fire."

"You're crying, Mama," Kate said.

I wiped at my eyes. "It's just rain. Go; do as you're told now."

Outside I hit at the cows with the butt of the gun and this time, as though to humor me, they moved out single file down the path. "Go! Go!" I shouted. Instead they stopped. But before they could turn around and race past me again, I aimed the rifle and shot. The recoil forced me flat against the ground. I knew I'd have a bruise the size of the Territory in the morning, but I looked with joy to see them both running down the path toward Mary and Boshie's, their full bags swaying out between their legs as they ran.

"Oh, thank God," I said. "Thank God."

It was the first time I had prayed since Christian died. At least it was a prayer of gratitude and not one of complaint.

Heading back toward the house I thought that I should have tied something in writing to the bell! How could I have not done something so obvious, to tell them what I needed? *Ach.* There was no calling those cows back now. I'd have to hope that the cows arrived and that Boshie would bring them back and not decide to "help me out" by keeping them.

"Please," I said out loud. "Please bring someone back who can help us." I wiped my son's forehead with a cooling cloth. At least the cool rain was good for something.

So when hours later I heard the cows bellow and I opened the door to hold up the lantern and look out, I believed even Jack Giesy could be an answer to prayer.

Jack led with that sly grin, and said something about my not letting him come in "until the cows come home."

"Of course I want you in here. Those cows did their duty bringing me help."

"You? In need of something?" His smile broadened if it was possible, one hand still holding the lead rope of a cow.

"I need you to take care of Kate and Christian while I get Andy to Woodard's Landing and Dr. Cooper."

The smile vanished. "The boy is ill?" His concern seemed genuine.

"You think I'd send my cows out for some silly reason? A fever. He's had it for a week, sometimes a little less, sometimes a little more. He hardly eats. I've done what I could but he needs a doctor. I need to take him to the doctor."

"Don't be troublesome, Emma Giesy," Jack said. He moved with the cows toward the barn and tied them, then walked as quickly as I'd ever seen him back to the cabin. "The boy is ill and must be taken, as you say." He stomped water from his brogans. "But I can do that faster and safer. Your place is here with your other children."

"But Andy needs—"

"To be taken care of quickly. Let's bundle him now. No more about it. I'll look after him."

I stared. It was the best choice. I'd have to trust this man. I found the blanket, wrapped Christian's oil slicker around Andy, then lifted this bundle so light into Jack's arms. "I want to come along, Andy, but I can't. Cousin Jack is taking care of you." He lay still against Jack's chest. "Thank you," I said. "Please. Let me know what's happening. Please."

"As soon as I can," he said.

So I let Jack take Andy to his grandparents, where Martin was and where the doctor could be called from Woodard's Landing. I let him take my son.

———

True to his word, Jack did come back two days later, with news that filled me with relief. Dr. Cooper said Andy rested quietly at Andreas and Barbara's. "It's a kind of bronchitis," Jack said. "Doc Cooper gave him baked onion juice, a little sugar and glycerin. Calmed the cough some. He doesn't look so tired. And he slept they said."

"Is he well enough to travel?"

"Oh, not for a bit yet," Jack said. "Your mother-in-law said not to worry, to just take good care of Kate and Christian. She said she hoped you'd accept their help for once with this."

"I wouldn't have let you take him if I wasn't willing to do what was best for him," I said.

"Something I know," Jack said.

"Did he give you any idea of how much time before I can come to get him?"

"Martin said he'd bring him back when he got better."

"Martin did? Oh, good."

Knowing Martin tended him brought comfort. He'd understand my need to have my son back and could remind my in-laws about whom Andy really belonged to. I sent Jack off with thanks, grateful that he left without resistance or suggesting any future obligation.

———

By February 1859, the rains let up. Sun breaks came occasionally, chasing off the fog, and one morning I bundled up the children and we set off. I stopped at Mary's and asked if she would mind watching Kate and Christian while I went to fetch Andy.

"Is he that much better then?" she asked.

"Jack says he makes steady improvement and he's been there two weeks. It's time for me to bring him home."

"Or at least visit him," Mary said. Her cheeks were rosy as though she'd been out in the sun but it wasn't that warm. "I'd be lost without Elizabeth for that long."

"I have been," I said. She rubbed her belly as I talked. "Are you…will you have a child?"

"*Ja!* We are so happy. I wanted to tell you but it's hard to share a joy when someone is in sorrow in her own life. I thought Jack might have told you."

"I don't like to have him around much," I said. "Except now, to share news about Andy."

"You should talk more to him. He's funny, sometimes, Emma. He could make you laugh. You used to like to laugh."

"That was before my husband died and I had three children to raise. I don't have much time for frolic," I said.

"A little light conversation with Jack wouldn't take much effort," she said.

"When is your baby due?" I asked.

"Summer. It will be a good time for a little one with fresh vegetables from our gardens. Elizabeth will have a new brother or sister." She smiled at her daughter working diligently on a stitching sampler. Kate already had her face in the sampler, looking closely. "I can watch the children for you but you'll come back today, won't you? I don't have goat's milk here."

I'd brought goat's milk along just in case, but I assured her I'd be back, hopefully with Andy, before it got dark.

"It gets dark early," she warned me. "And the river's running high, you know."

"Then I'd better be off."

When I arrived at the crossing, my boat wasn't moored where it was usually left. Other people used the craft; it was a custom, just as it had been back in Bethel. I thought of it as "my boat," since Christian had bought it. I moved up and down the shoreline trying to find where whoever used the boat last might have tied it, muttering beneath my breath about the inconsiderateness of them. I looked across the water to see if someone had already used it to cross and sure enough, I saw it there, tied to a willow, the water pushing against it so it was nearly flush with the opposite bank.

The river was way too high to attempt to wade it.

Letting Jack take Andy had been the right thing to do. I'd have risked all three of my children in that boat with the Willapa so high. I'd have lacked the physical strength to cross it, much as I would have wanted to. Will was sometimes simply not enough. Timing was as much a factor in success as effort.

There was nothing I could do on this shoreline. If I waited for whoever had taken the boat to return, it would likely be too late to make it to Fort Willapa to get Andy and come back. The river ran swift, and managing the boat with Andy on the return trip could be a challenge too. But if I attempted to wade it I could at least see him, at least know that he was doing well.

I couldn't.

The rush of water darkened before me. I'd ridden on boats. I'd taken a mule across a stream. I'd stood in the water and clubbed fish to survive a winter. But I could not imagine myself with water to my chest pushing against the strength of the current and being strong enough when I reached the other side to then bring Andy back.

I told myself this obstacle was nothing out of the ordinary in a place like this where the rivers acted as both transport and barrier. There was nothing strange in having family look after a child, especially a sick child.

Watching the river rush, undercutting the banks while it carried swirls of trees and branches, I came to one conclusion that day: I couldn't leave my children behind while I traveled off to follow a scheme to paint or draw and make money of my own. If I went, they'd have to go with me.

I hoped my in-laws explained what would keep me away. Andy would see Jack or others coming and going and might not understand that a younger brother and sister and a raging river kept his mother from being with him.

I can't even cross a river to visit my son.

My routine continued through that month. I milked the cows. Karl came by once or twice, but without Andy there to teach, he seemed uncomfortable. He didn't even take time to smoke his pipe. Jack picked up the butter, spent a little time talking. He wasn't going back to the oyster beds, he said. Too much work for a laboring man with no potential for ownership, not that Jack wanted that. "I think communal living is the perfect answer for a young man's life. No worries, labor that helps others, never without a roof over one's head."

"Don't you ever want to just have something to call your own?" I asked.

He shrugged. "Owning property doesn't give a man much over one who doesn't. Why, we had neighbors back in Harmony who worked twice as hard just to keep everyone fed because they had land, property, and slaves. If war comes, they'll die for that property, and why? I don't see the point. Not when you can live taking care of your neighbor while your neighbor…takes care of you." That last he added with that grin again telling me he had more than one intent to convey.

"I'm sure Joe Knight's been pleased to be working for himself."

"Maybe could be. But I think he'll tire of the effort before long and head back to San Francisco. Maybe even Bethel. Oystering is a constant job, and the beds are property, so he has to watch them diligently so no one steals the shellfish. He stays awake nights worrying. None of us colony members do. Not worth it if you ask me."

"I thought you said you rarely slept."

He grinned. "True enough. But I'm not awake worrying."

"Christian never felt the need to own things either," I said.

"But you, you're one to believe that if you own a sheep you'll soon have wool and yarn and weavings to sell."

"*Ja,* and if the sheep belongs to the community, then no one cares especially for it. No one calls it by name or worries over it. Instead of it being an animal with wool becoming a weaving, it'll be but a sheep growing old."

"Don't let those who tend sheep in Bethel hear you say that. They looked after the animals as though they were children."

"But they aren't. And if the Bethelites would want to do something different, they don't have the authority to sell those sheep now, do they? They own nothing after all that work. Everything is in Keil's name. *He* has property. What'll happen when he dies? His sons will get all the work you've put in."

He shrugged. "I've had a good life."

"Don't you ever…want something else?"

He smiled then. His dark eyes told me I didn't want any answer he maybe could propose.

———

He was an interesting man, Jack Giesy, I had to say that for him. I could see a few of his virtues. But he presented a caution as well. I wanted to keep on his good side, as I might need his help bringing Andy back so I wouldn't have to wait until the river lowered. Meanwhile, I would treat him like a brother, listening to his news.

One day, when he'd kept his distance, made Kate laugh with the faces he made and so seemed safe and predictable, I asked him if we could plan a time when he could go with me to pick up Andy. "You're asking me for help, again? If I was a betting man, I'd have lost such a wager, that Emma Giesy would ask a man for help more than once in a lifetime."

"Am I really as difficult as that?"

"Maybe could be you are."

"So I am, then. Your answer?"

"*Ja*, sure. I'll go with you. Let's make it for Sunday next."

———

He brought a mule. "We'll need it here to work the fields anyway soon enough, so Boshie said to bring it. I'll leave it here when we get back." We loaded Kate and Christian up on the animal and the two of us walked the mile or so to Mary and Boshie's.

"You'll be back by dark?" Mary asked, as we unloaded the children.

I assured her we would. Karl was there. He drew on his pipe, asked after my health. I told him I missed our visits and he said, "*Ja,* by golly, I'll have a new almanac to bring to you soon. We'll check the best times to plant." Then he nodded to Jack and headed back into the house, taking Kate by the hand while Mary held Christian on her hip.

Jack led the mule to a stump step so I could get astride the animal. He frowned again and I remembered his discomfort with my swinging my leg over the animal. "You don't have a sidesaddle," I said.

"You had one. We should have taken it."

"And made it impossible for the children to ride? No. There's nothing wrong with a woman riding in a way to make her secure."

He grunted but swung up behind me.

"Feeling secure?" he whispered in my ear as he pressed into my back, reached for the reins and clicked his tongue at the mule that started off throwing me into Jack's chest as it fast-trotted toward the river.

Jack didn't want an answer, which was just as well. I felt secure enough that I wouldn't fall off the mule but I resented this man breathing so close to my neck. I resisted the scent of him against me. I bristled at the warmth of his body seeping so close to mine. How could he be upset by the impropriety of my leg swinging over a mule's rump but not have the slightest discomfort with an unmarried man's body heat warming a widow's robe?

Recent rains left the ferns and trees sparkling with raindrops. As the sun hit them, it reminded me of candles on the *Tannenbaum* at Christmastime. Birds twittered and I heard one lone seagull flying upriver and wondered for just a moment if it might be our Charlie. Andy would have been delighted to see a gull. It somehow marked the coming of spring.

Jack's arms held me on either side of my shoulders, like a cow's stanchion, as the mule plunged and pushed against the water, but we crossed the river without incident. On the other side, I suggested that I'd like to walk a ways. Jack complied and the conversation went easily back and forth between us talking of wheat and sheep. Safety. Walking was safer.

At a rock outcropping I noticed what looked like the remains of a drawing of a flower maybe or a dragonfly. "Look," I pointed. "Could that be a natural design of lichen or is it a…drawing? Yes, I believe it is."

"Maybe could be," he said, grinning.

"You did that."

"*Ja,* sure. I have hidden gifts you know nothing about."

"I know the egg you scratched for Christian showed a fine talent," I said.

"As if you'd know how to evaluate such talents, Emma Giesy."

His retort had been said in jest, but it stung just the same. I wasn't going to say anything to him about my own artistic bent. "Don't you worry that it'll soon be washed away?"

"Maybe could be it's all the more precious that way, knowing it's fleeting, not long for this world. If we lived that way, knowing we're on the way to dying, we'd take more time to do the things that bring us a little pleasure, don't you think, Widow Giesy? I bet your Christian wishes he'd spent more time in his marriage bed than with his oyster beds."

He was so brassy. Did Christian have regrets? Could those who died still harbor longing the way those they left behind did? I couldn't imagine that. It was a theological question, one I'd have to explore with Karl, not with this man who sent signals of friendship wrapped up in tempered heat.

As we approached Fort Willapa I could feel my heart start pounding. It would be so good to see Andy! I'd clipped pictures from my almanac and glued the tiny pieces with flour paste to form entirely new designs, ever grateful for my sharp scissors that let me practice the craft of *Scherenschnitte.* I'd made him a tiger and a parrot and wrapped the cuttings in cloth for Jack to deliver to him. I imagined Andy opening them and finding pleasure in the little pieces of paper that were transformed into something new. Little pictures I'd sent so he'd know that he was constantly on my mind. Kate even took some stones from her treasure basket and sent them with me. "So's he'll know I got them for Andy," she told me. "I wants them back."

"He'll be bringing them back," I'd told her as I kissed her forehead good-bye.

Now at last I'd be seeing him and taking him home. I'd ask Martin for as many herbs as he could spare so if the cough came back I'd have a way to stop it before it got so bad he fevered and I had to be separated from him again.

Martin came out of the house as we tied the mule to the post. "Such a long way you've come," he said. He leaned forward, always leaning into things. He looked over at Jack.

"She wanted a visit," Jack said.

"*Ja,* that's good, but there's only me here, don't you know?"

"Where's Andy?" I asked. I looked toward the field. He must be well enough to run and play outside. How wonderful! But then they could have brought him back. I felt a rush of heat to my face but held my tongue.

"They've gone to Aurora Mills," Martin said. "Jack didn't tell you? Just for a visit, don't you know. They'll be back in a week or so."

I turned to Jack. "You knew he wasn't here and yet we came all this way, for nothing?"

"You needed an outing," he said. "Tell me it wasn't a pleasant journey?"

"When will people stop deciding what I need or don't need?" I said. "What I need is my son back. What I need is to be able to take care of things without other people cutting up my life like it was some little piece of paper they could recompose into something else entirely. How dare they just take my son! How dare they!"

"He wanted to go," Martin said softly.

"*Ja,* and if a five-year-old wished to ride a mule across a swollen river you would let him? This is what a grownup does, make good decisions for a child."

"Mama and Papa had never gotten to share their grandchild with their friends at Aurora. It's been nearly two years since they've seen the Bethel folks. They're going to bring back sheep when they return. It'll be fine, Emma." Martin reached out to offer me his hand. "Come inside and have tea."

"No tea. I just want to go home." I swung around swiftly and began walking out ahead of the mule and Jack. My mind burned with the outrageousness of it all. They'd had to come right by our place if they went to Aurora crossing the Cowlitz. Maybe they took a ship, crossing the very bay that had taken Andy's father's life. Without talking to me, his mother, about any of it!

I heard Jack shout something about not being in such a hurry.

"I must get home before dark, remember?" I said. "I have children to attend to." I stopped short. "Don't I?"

"Of course Kate and Christian are there, waiting for you," Jack said as he caught up with me. He moved the mule to stand before me. "Why don't you get up here and ride with me."

"I'll walk," I told him, pushing past the mule. "At least it's some small portion of my life I still control."

16

Louisa

If it weren't for the music I should think we colonists would have taken much longer to find our place of belonging in this West. It soothes us when the day's work shifts from outside to inside and the candlelight becomes our comforter. Through the open windows (where there are blessedly few insects despite our closeness to the river) the men's chorus lifts its melody above the treetops, and even while we women sit and spin we can hear them, sometimes their rhythm a perfect fit for the thump of our wheels. Beethoven's Ninth with its lovely chorus makes me feel as though I am at home in Germany; the words bypass my heart and go directly to my soul. I love the rousing songs they sing too. They practice for the festivals. The settlers here enjoy festivals. There seems to be one scheduled nearly every month somewhere within carriage distance. I suppose it is something to look forward to. It breaks up the monotony of difficult fieldwork, all the adjustments needed to find the way in a new land. We Germans know how to celebrate with our brass horns and dances and wonderful food. It is good we brought those customs with us along with the drums and brass horns.

My husband has actually composed some pieces, though more for the band than for voices. I like "Webfoot Quickstepp" because it makes me tap my feet and I have to stop my spinning! I don't believe he composed that one but it is one of my favorites. Sometimes he lets others think he has composed them all. I notice he says "I made up some strongly medicinal wine from Oregon grape" when in fact someone else did the work but he oversaw it. I think "we" might be a good word to use there instead of "I," but of course I'm not likely to suggest it.

We Bethelites are becoming "webfoot" people. After last winter we started calling ourselves that because of the incessant rains. Andreas and Barbara Giesy, when they visited this spring, said the same was true of the Willapa though they claimed those ocean breezes bring in sunbreaks more often than we saw here through the winter past. I wonder if people back in Missouri would understand a sunbreak.

Then in the summer the ground becomes dry as old coffeecake and we smell smoke sometimes in the morning where a fire to burn brush or stumps has gotten out of hand. It can take over an entire field and lick at trees the farmer hadn't planned to burn at all. Fire is a terrible thing but oh so necessary in these parts, where the stumps must be burned to clear the ground and then dug at with a crowbar so the workers are covered with soot.

Our mill turns out lumber for houses and we are building steadily. The doctor rises early and he has tasks for everyone. It is as though this journey west has given him new vigor. I worry he might decide that we need to expand our family. I pray not, though I know Eve was admonished to submit to her husband's wishes. I wish only to keep my eight living children healthy and well, and to do so I must keep myself healthy and well. Women die in childbirth. I see it. It is almost as dangerous as cooking in the summer kitchen with the fire sparking as we stir; a woman's dress is suddenly aflame. Such morbid thoughts I think! Eve did as she was bid by her husband after she ate of the Tree of Knowledge. The doctor forgets that the man ate of that fruit too. Maybe, just maybe, Eve wasn't tempting him as the serpent had but instead was hoping to feed him, the very thing a woman is called to do and a man will complain about if she doesn't.

I would never say such a thing to the doctor. Never. But I think it. In this diary of sorts, I write it.

So far, the doctor's diligent work, the young people's problems he has to solve, his music pleasure, and the laughter with his children before they go to bed keep him willing to be held in our marriage bed without requesting the fruit that would bring another child into the world.

I still think of Willie every day.

The children are good. They don't speak his name but the grief sneaks up on me like a black cat racing across my path, unexpected and promising to make the day go badly. I wonder if Emma Giesy has that experience too. I don't know why I think of her as often as I do. Perhaps because we share a grief now, having lost someone so dear to us, someone who was the chalice of our lives. It surprised me to see that she'd let her Andy from her sight to come here with his grandparents. It is a side of her I must assess through different eyes.

The boy and his *Oma* and *Opa* remained here several weeks. Andy enjoyed the other children living in this colony, even though it is a hike to the distant farms nestled among the firs. In the town proper there is still just this big house and several smaller dwellings and the colony store, but we keep working. As in the old country, we go out to the fields and orchards, returning back home at night. The doctor says the new arrivals, those not of our colony of course, look for land separated from each other where they can't see the smoke of a neighbor's house. We've adopted this western way somewhat. Hiking is good for children the doctor says. Even little ones like Andy.

He has sad eyes, though, that child of nearly six. He has seen trial in his young life, with his father's death. I asked about his sister and brother and he answered clear and firm, "They're well, *Frau* Keil." Like a little man he is, so like his father, ready to take on responsibility at a young age. Watching the boy makes me think of when his father first came to the doctor and said he wished to be in service to the colony. My husband beamed. He groomed Chris for such a role and my husband is a grand teacher. This is not to malign George Wolfer back in Bethel or Karl Ruge in Willapa. These are both great teachers with university degrees. But my husband, who lacks such schooling, is a true teacher, a true guide, and he helped Chris see what must be seen in order for the colony to be successful.

His death was tragic indeed, as the doctor led Chris to the understanding that taking the Bethelites to Aurora Mills and not staying there in Willapa was the only sane course of action. It was so good that Chris came to accept this before he died. Imagine if he had carried thoughts that my husband betrayed him; imagine if he had died with such beliefs? I wonder now if his wife encouraged him to persist at oystering as a way of helping Chris save face. It would be a grand gesture on her part if she had. But I suspect she liked more the idea of having her own cabin to stay in far from others the way these eastern settlers seem to like their land in the West. That oystering scheme suggests that Emma had no intention of letting her husband come here one day to take his chosen place as the heir to the doctor's work. At least it earned him good money and Chris met his duty and sent the money to repay what the colony had put out for him.

In time, they'll all come here, the doctor says. Every one, and then they'll know this was truly God's plan. He says we can "rest assured we are following God's plan when things go well and in time, all things go well."

I have questioned this in my mind. Not that I would share such thoughts with the doctor. *Nein.* But Willie died. And Chris died, a man meant to lead this colony, perhaps share in the doctor's work so he could rest a bit. I get confused then between what is suffering meant to compensate for our sins and what is suffering that will one day bring God's plans to fruit? Who to ask? There is no one. I know the question alone would be seen as challenging the doctor, and so I won't ask it. I'd not do anything to add to the weight he carries here.

It was good to see Andy Giesy closer to the true activities of the colony. He could learn from the doctor. But I can't imagine Emma letting him go. It amazes me still that the boy has spent such time apart from her at all.

I suppose she is busy just doing woman's work with that new baby. I've set aside my *Fraktur* work. There is too much washing, mending, cooking, planting, harvesting to do. But this fall, the doctor let us take two days to attend the fairs at Linn and Benton counties. We prepared the wagons with food we'd need for the travel and the stay away from our home. The children jabbered in excitement as we took four wagons of people to the events.

Some of our harvest was entered to be judged, including our apple cider vinegar, some hogs, a sheep, our oats, a quilt, a *Strudel* or two. Food. We women put so much of who we are into our food. The doctor said the fair is a way of announcing our wares and thus while we cooked and played and offered venison sausage and spoke about its special flavorings, we invited others to taste. Thus we worked to let others know that we value quality and are easy people to be among. We also bring business to the colony. Sometimes it seems no matter what Dr. Keil chooses to do, he can find a way to turn it into good for the colony.

The children scampered around, and while there were many people we didn't know in attendance, the atmosphere was one of neighborliness, of goodwill. People smiled and the women nodded their bonnets at each other as they walked on the arms of their men, serenaded by distant fiddles and the smells of cooked beef wafting through the air.

There were booths with lovely things a woman might have decorated. Tin pots painted with bright colors. I was reminded of the pottery my mother had in our home in Germany and for the moment felt all wistful. I saw whittled figures made of soft woods that must have been brought from the old countries by settlers in the region. Miniatures. Even a scene meant to be Adam and Eve in the garden. Several people painted landscapes of trees and that mountain they call Hood that has snow on it all year round. We can see it from Aurora Mills. What pleased me most, though I did not tell my husband, was that I peered at the lettering on the bottom of the paintings and read first names like "Nancy" and "Mary." Women's names! Imagine. Here in this wilderness, women painting pictures for display. A woman even sat in one booth and handed out papers in English I could not read. The doctor had turned aside to talk to someone about horses, so I took the leaflet. I will save it and ask Karl Ruge when I see him next. I thought I heard the woman say the English word meaning "school," but I can't imagine there'd be a school here for women to learn to paint.

I saw show towels embroidered with scripture, so there are other Germans here, not just of our colony. My favorite item was a butter mold. A flower was carved with intricate leaves that one would press against the butter. Such butter would sell more quickly at a market than a simple mold or none at all. And it was beautiful, nearly as lovely as my *Fraktur*, which I saw no examples of at the fair. I brought the doctor by and hinted here and there until he said we should make such a mold. "Something unique to the colony," I said, "yet grand enough to be the centerpiece at a fine table."

"I've had a good idea," he said and nodded. I know he meant it was his idea but for just a moment it felt as though he'd paid me a compliment.

We walked the uneven grounds, surrounded by the scents of venison and even a beef being turned at a spit. Chickens and hogs, fruits and flowers; the displays were like music to my eyes. Our band would be playing in the evening.

Then came my husband's finest words to me in weeks: "See all these people, Louisa?" the doctor said to just me. "See them all coming from near and far, leaving their homes in the East, arriving here? They'll need all we have to give them." Soon, the doctor said, we'd begin weaving and tailoring and making shoes and we'd have these items to sell and display at the fairs. "We'll have furniture and blacksmith's work. Helena Giesy will come out, and she'll help weave cloth and piece quilts to replace the ones people had to leave behind or that are so worn out from being room dividers and sick robes and warmth to wrap around a woman's shoulders when she steps out to milk her cows. We'll make new quilts made with the wool we raise and dye and spin right here." His eyes were shiny with the possibilities. "Whatever they have need of, we will sell to them. Helena will come and she'll be followed by others. All will go well here now. It is God's will."

That "will" question again. I wished he hadn't said it, for it took me back to my lost Willie. Instead of feeling as warm as if I'd been wrapped in a quilt, I was chilled, even in the hot October afternoon; even with the band playing the "Webfoot Quickstepp." So quickly grief could transport me. I guess my mind knew before I could remember that as in life, the band would follow the joyous piece with the heaviness of a funeral dirge.

17

𝕮mma

A Prayer Against the Sail

My Kate put a piece of cloth as a sail on a cedar bark boat she'd made, then set it afloat in the barrel of collected rainwater. She'd made a twig mast and somehow drilled a hole through the tough cedar bark, then stuck the stick there so it bravely held the sail. She set it afloat. It twirled around once, twice, then tipped over. She lifted it out, reset the sail and set it afloat again. Her breath pressed against it; it toppled again. She kept picking it back up, setting it on the water. The cloth sail was saturated, the bark too uneven to keep the mast upright. Before long it would be waterlogged and probably the whole thing would sink. But still, time after time, Kate continued, doing the same thing, expecting her sail to stand upright and her craft to move where her breath sent it, to get a different result even while she hadn't yet come to realize that she must change what she was doing. I couldn't stand it.

"It won't work," I told her, swiping the bark, pulling the cloth from its stick mast and squeezing the water from it with my fist. "Why do you keep doing it over and over? Can't you see it's finished? Done. You're defeated."

She stared, those wide blue eyes looking into mine, and then I saw her lower lip quiver.

"You broke it," she accused.

"It was already broken. It won't float. It isn't balanced right for one thing. The sail is saturated; it's too wet. It isn't ever going to do what you want it to."

She blinked. I'd never yelled at the children, not ever. My parents had never shouted at me. They might not talk to me for a time when I upset them; they might raise an eyebrow as an indicator that I'd gone too far, but they never shouted, never grabbed at me the way I'd just grabbed at Kate.

"Andy could make it go," she said. She crossed her little arms over her chest, her lip still shaking.

"*Ach,* he's not here."

"When's he come home, Mama?"

I didn't know. My shoulders sagged. I pulled her toward me and she let me comfort her. "I'm sorry, *Liebchen.* I'm so sorry. I miss him too."

"Did he go away like Papa did?"

"No. Not like Papa. He's with *Oma* and *Opa.*"

I was like that little sailboat tipping in the wind and no amount of setting it back up would take me to where I wanted to be. It wouldn't do any good to try to get Andy returned, I knew that. My son was healthy—at least if I believed Martin—and maybe Andy wouldn't even be alive if I hadn't handed him off to Jack.

Yet I felt betrayed and had since that day.

I walked hard all the way back that day, resisting Jack's cajoling that I should ride. At the river crossing I did let myself be pulled up—behind Jack this time—onto the mule, but as soon as he splashed across the water I slid off over the animal's rump and continued my purposeful stride.

"Did you know that Andy was gone, Mary?" I asked when we reached their homestead.

"Gone where? Didn't he come back with you?"

She was either a marvelous actress or didn't know, for her grief, when she looked behind me and realized Andy wasn't with me, was a gasp that any mother would recognize.

"Andreas and Barbara took Andy to Aurora. They didn't say a word to me, not one. They just rode off with my son, probably putting him on board a ship and sailing across the very sea his father died in. With not a word to me, as though I were nothing more than a heavy anchor hung around their necks."

"Maybe they went to have *Herr* Keil look at him, give him special herbs?"

"No one said anything about his still being ill. They were just 'traveling,' enjoying themselves and stealing *my* son." With the last of the words my fury caught in my throat and I felt the lump there clog and strangle.

"How awful, Emma." Mary patted my arm. "I can't imagine that they did this to harm you. Andreas and Barbara are loving people. It's only for a family visit."

"Why not tell me then?" I swallowed, my breath short. "Because they don't have to. Because I'm just this widow and they can justify anything they want by pointing out to all how much they're helping me. 'She has three little ones at home, you know. A widow, too, and not all that skilled in her needle-work, don't you know. Helping her son is the least we could do.'"

"Emma. They're not like that, they aren't."

"I feel so...useless."

She put her arms around me and that touch of comfort, warmth against my shoulders after so very long, brought the heartache to my eyes. "Just wait," she said. "It will get better."

Jack had put the mule up, and I heard him come up toward the house. He stayed silent, for which I was grateful. No teasing comment about the strong Emma Giesy withering like the last leaves of fall, nothing funny to try to set aside my powerlessness pouring out as tears.

"What you're going to do now is have some tea," Mary said. "Karl and Boshie are at the mill and won't be home for a time. We can just sit and be. Your Kate missed you, and Christian, well he's quite the chunk. You're feeding him well, Emma. Come along, now." She urged me toward the door.

"Opal and the cows feed him well, not me," I corrected. One more in-adequacy pointed my way.

Jack opened the door and I let them lead me into the house like a lamb.

"Where's Andy?" Kate asked when she saw me.

"With his *Oma* and *Opa*." I wiped at my eyes. "He'll be home shortly," I said, hoping it wasn't a lie.

"I miss him," she sighed, looked at my tear-stained face. She patted my hand as I sat at the table, then returned to her play with Elizabeth.

Later, after the tea had soothed me and the children's laughter had pierced the afternoon malaise, I lifted Christian from his nap and told Kate we needed to go home.

Jack did not protest when I declined his offer to help me take the children to our cabin. "This is something I can do myself," I said. I had to keep finding those things I could make happen, or like an untethered boat, I'd simply drift away.

———

I did drift during the following weeks. I felt as though I walked while asleep doing just what I must, answering the children without inflection. Later in the week, Jack came by again and startled me out of my lassitude.

He made an offer. He proposed it like that, that he "maybe could have an offer to make," and I thought it probably had something to do with the work around my cabin in return for my sewing up his clothes. Or to maybe go to Aurora and bring Andy back. That thought perked me up. Or at the very least to go there and find out when they planned to return. For a moment I wondered if he'd offer to take us there and I wondered if I'd go. All those thoughts in the span of a few seconds.

Instead Jack asked for my hand in marriage.

I laughed. "Why would I ever consider marriage, especially to you, Jack Giesy, a confirmed bachelor?"

"I wouldn't be such a bad catch," he said. I thought I smelled alcohol on his breath and he had a bit of a glassy look in his eye. Maybe that was why he was being so bold as to "maybe could" make his offer.

I sighed. I had little time for such nonsense. "Are Mary and Boshie moving you out with their family expanding?" I said.

"Maybe could be. But that's not the reason I'm—"

"It's out of the question. Simply not possible," I said. I brushed my hands at him as though shooing flies. "I thought maybe you'd offer to find out when Barbara and Andreas were coming back. That's an offer I'd consider."

"Has it occurred to you that if you were married and Andy had a father that maybe Andreas wouldn't feel the need to have Andy with them? They'd know he had a man to look after him, raise him up correctly."

I stared at him. "That would never be a reason to remarry," I said.

"Haven't heard about wagon-train weddings, I guess. Women do what they gotta do to survive." He walked to the saltbox I kept near the fireplace, lifted the lid. He wet his finger then stuck it into the salt, returned it to his mouth, his eyes holding mine while he sucked on his finger. "There are worse reasons to marry," he said at last. "For money. Now that's not necessary in our little communal lives, is it?" He licked his lips of the salt. "Or for convenience. Maybe could marry because it's easier than courting. Or because your bed's been cold long enough." He reached for the salt lid again but I grabbed his wrist.

"There's no sense in spoiling the salt," I said. "I'll get a spoon and salt dish and you can have your own."

"Will you now?" His look darkened. I still held his wrist. He was close enough I could smell the rye on his breath. I felt my heart pound; my face grew hot. I hadn't touched a man with any kind of emotion for over a year. I was aware of the strong bones of his wrist, how my small hand didn't begin to surround it. Confusion rattled my thoughts.

Christian crawled between us then, and Kate followed him as though Christian was a mule leading a wagon. Kate shouted, "Gee! Haw!" I released Jack's wrist and he stepped back to let the children pass. Then before I could catch my breath he reached for my arm and held it tight, pulling me toward him.

"Why not marry so you can show your saltiness in the way God intended? And have your sons with you?" Jack said. "Seems like a mother would do anything to accomplish that."

"You're hurting me," I said. He wasn't but I couldn't explain what was happening, how uncomfortable I felt yet how…invigorated. *This is insane.* "Let loose. Please."

"Aren't you the salty *Frau* Giesy?" he said. "Can't you break the hold?"

"If you don't release me I'll—"

"There's nothing you can do or say to make me do a thing, Emma Giesy. Time you learned that." He reached his free hand past my ear, flicked the saltbox lid open, then licked his finger. He stuck it into the saltbox, pressed it toward my lips. "We're to be salt and light in the world, *ja*?" I tasted the salt, had all I could do not to bite his finger. "A good wife knows how to be such salt." He released me then, like an animal trap sprung open.

I stumbled back. My hearted pounded like the butter churn. "There has to be another way for a mother to raise her children without having to…to marry for it." I was certain that I could do this without the Jacks of this world. I just hadn't thought how. And now I couldn't think clearly at all because Jack stood before me and he was smiling, head cocked, dark swath of hair angled across his eyes, his face flushed.

"Ah, Emma." He crossed his arms over his chest. "In time you'll cease to resist."

"Never," I said. Oddly, I felt as though a light breeze pushed wind at my sails.

———

I made the trip back to Fort Willapa each week, hoping to see Andy returned. I talked briefly to Martin, hearing his "don't you knows," resisting a retort that no, I didn't. I held no ill will toward him, not really. He spoke quietly and carried on the work that needed doing to manage the farm. I knew it wasn't easy work they tended to. A twinge of guilt came with our having chosen this landscape that made so many demands on everyone. Maybe the thing for me to do was to go back to Bethel, to be with my parents. Go to Aurora, get Andy, and then head back East, though I wasn't sure how I'd finance that. Sell the land, perhaps, but I doubted any of the colonists would purchase it and I might be many years finding someone wanting to move into the region and live in our little cabin. My life had taken on twists as tangled as a tobacco string.

During the school term, Karl stayed at Fort Willapa, so I seldom saw him. He was busy with the students. Andy should have been among them. I did see Sarah. I didn't tell her about Jack's offer. I put that evening in an oyster shell, clasped tight the hinge. I didn't want to find the meaning of my confused emotions by blurting it out without having considered every aspect of it first.

Instead, I heard Sarah's news. She was pregnant. "December," she told me. Her blond hair looked silky and the luster on her skin shone like a fresh peach. "Maybe he'll have the same birthday as your Kate," she said. "We can celebrate birthdays together."

"*Ja,* that would be *gut.*"

She knew about my frustration with my in-laws and how they'd taken Andy visiting. I still considered them just "visiting." I had no need to see *Herr* Keil or any of those colonists again, but I'd given Andreas until fall, feeling certain they'd return home to help with the harvest. If they didn't bring Andy back then, I'd go to Aurora Mills and get him. Somehow. Meanwhile, I clung to the thread that said what everyone else did: my in-laws were simply trying to be helpful, and they'd bring Andy home in due time.

I also told Sarah about the day I'd been abrupt with Kate, had taken her toy boat and chastised her for trying to do the same thing over and over with no hope of it ever getting better. "Sometimes I think I do that myself," I said.

"We do what we know to do and hope it will work. It takes great courage to change. Anytime we do something new, it's risky. I'm nervous about this baby," she said. "Sam says I'm so soft that I cry when the chickens squawk. I don't know how I'll be with an infant to watch over."

"You'll be *gut*," I said. "The very best. And you won't have in-laws living close by to make you question yourself."

"I talked with Sam about your drawings," Sarah told me then. She rocked Christian on her lap, his head against her breast, eyes closed in comfort. "He says he could take one or two to Olympia to see if there's interest."

"I'd pay him for his time," I said. "Out of whatever was paid me."

"It would be a gift to you, Emma." She patted my hand. "Sam wonders if you might have someone take your pictures south into Oregon City. There's a teacher there, a woman, who has taught painting now for over ten years. She shows her work at fairs and sells them. There must be enough interest if she's taught a class that long."

I hadn't imagined people could be taught to paint, that it was something more than a natural bent. But even a gift could be made better with practice, wisdom, and time.

"Maybe my work isn't good enough yet," I said, suddenly cautious. "Maybe I should take some classes, if I could afford them, if there was an instructor close by."

"Don't be afraid now, Emma," Sarah said. "You make lovely drawings. Let Sam take them. I'm not sure I can be a mother but I'm going to do it; you have to have confidence that you have natural talent and can do this, even without lessons." She hesitated. "If you feel strongly that you need lessons, maybe Jack would—"

"No. Jack has nothing to teach me."

I wrote again to my parents. I told them about Andy being with the Giesys and how much I missed him and how if they were here, if David lived here or Papa, then there'd be no question about where Andy belonged. I even asked my father if there was some legal means by which I could make sure Andy wasn't kept from me. We seldom used lawyers for anything in the colony. I wasn't sure there were even agreements signed about the land people worked in Bethel. It seemed all was in Keil's name and there hadn't been a lawyer involved in any of it except between Keil and whomever he bought the land from. The sellers never knew that the money they received came from the efforts of many.

But I heard nothing more from my parents. Just school-girl letters from my sister Catherine that reminded me that once I'd been young, with problems no larger than whether to put ruffles on my crinolines and wondering if I'd ever grow up enough to marry.

Finally, in time for the harvest, Andreas and Barbara returned home and this time, when the leaves were turning their vibrant red and the air begged for the rains to begin, this time when I made the trek with Kate, Christian carried in a sack on my back, this time when we arrived, Andy was there to meet us.

I was never more soundly greeted in my life than by my son that day. "Mama," he said, running to me. "Mama."

My heart pounded and I could hear his too. I felt relief in his arms clinging to my neck as I squatted to him. He enclosed Christian too, then Kate threw herself into the bundle of us. "I'm so glad you're here, so glad," I said and kissed his hair, his forehead, his cheeks. Such a reunion! "Look at me. You've grown taller. What do you have to say to that?" I said, not expecting an answer.

"Why didn't you come get me?" he challenged. "Why didn't you ever come back?"

I hadn't planned what I'd say to my son, an amazing lapse on my part, for here he was, asking why I'd abandoned him. How to answer without creating a greater rift between his grandparents and me? Or maybe that was just what I should do; put a distance between us that wouldn't be easily bridged.

I had dreamed of what I'd say when I finally saw Barbara and Andreas eye to eye. No, I did not pray about it despite my sister's insistence that prayers were like kisses sent to the wind. I'd had little time for prayers of late, and when I had in desperation sent one out, Jack had been the answer. One could never be certain with Jack, and that's how I felt about prayer.

The speeches for my in-laws I'd composed in my head would have made the president of the States nod his head in approval for their eloquence and passion. But once these two people stood before me, once Andreas's cane tapped unsteadily and Barbara's eyes filled with tears, once Andy shivered beside me, I said very little at all.

Instead I inhaled and breathed out slowly. "I knew you were safe, Andy," I said. "I knew you were all right, but when I came back—"

"We trust you had a good summer," Barbara said. "People in Aurora send greetings."

"That's good of them." I kept Andy in the crook of my arm, my fingers firmly planted at his elbow. I didn't look at him. I knew there'd be more to say to him but better if I could do that when we were alone, in our home, safe. I could protect him under my wing. I didn't want to let him go. He did look healthy. I was certain they'd been good to him. It was just the separation that confounded and their unwillingness to acknowledge my authority over my son.

"He's had no recurrence of the bronchitis," Barbara said. "And we've returned with extra supplies in case it happens again this winter. We'll be prepared."

"I'll be pleased to take the supplies with me along with Andy's things," I said. I held my breath, waiting for resistance.

"*Ja.* I'll get them for you," she said and turned back into the house. Her compliance surprised. I'd thought I might have to demand that they let me have Andy back. Once again, I appeared to have little intuition.

Andreas tapped with his cane. "We enjoyed the boy very much," he said. "Good boy. Smart. Needs good tutoring. Needs to be in school."

"He missed most of his schooling this summer," I snapped. "John had any number of children enrolled. Karl taught them, but Andy was with you."

"*Ja.* We gave him an education in traveling from here to Aurora. He saw the orchards planted there. He heard the band play. He could play a brass instrument himself before long. They have no school yet in Aurora. Still, you should let him stay here to go to school now, until the rains come, *ja*? Then he comes home to be with you for Christmas."

Here it was: the demand had just been delayed to throw me off my guard. "I've missed my son. His brother and sister have missed him as well, and you heard him ask why I didn't come to get him."

"Young children must not make these decisions. It is up to us, those who know better," Andreas said. He coughed.

"I'll get him into school in a day or so. I'll do whatever it takes. I'll do it," I said. "Me." I tapped my chest. "His mother."

"Maybe we erred," Barbara said, handing me the cloth bag tied with a braided rope that held his things. She didn't let go, so we held it in tension between us. "We meant no harm. We wanted only to help you, Emma. This is all any of us wants to do for you. Yet you seem so unwilling to allow it."

"Asking might be a good way to begin," I said pulling the bag from her grip. "Imagine if I just took your Louisa for months at a time, just whisked her away while you weren't looking?"

"And would you have let us take Andy?" Andreas said. "If we had asked?"

"He belongs with me, his family."

"He needs us in his life too," Barbara said.

"*Ja,* and it is the grandfather who must lead the child now. We let you have your mourning time. Now you must come to your senses. There must be a man in this child's life. It is the right way."

"Karl Ruge, his teacher, is in his life. You lead him. Martin does, don't you know. He has many good men to influence him. Isn't that the very benefit of the colony? He needs one good mother to tend him. He's only five," I pleaded.

"The age of *Kindergarten* in the old country. Some in the States, too, begin school at such an age and the *Kinder* stay where they can be easily schooled."

"*Ja, ja,* I know." I'd stepped back and Andy leaned heavily into me.

"Then we will see him in school," Andreas said. I nodded. "And you will bring the children to visit."

"I always did."

"More often."

"Yes," I agreed. "*Ja.* And in return, you will never take him away from this valley and from me without my agreeing."

"We will never take him away again without you agreeing," Andreas said. "But you must think about the possibility of the benefits for the boy living somewhere besides with you."

"It will never be better for him to live anywhere but with me until he's old enough to be on his own," I said. "Never."

"You speak boldly, Emma Giesy," Barbara said. "Yet one never knows what life holds for us."

"My children come first, that much I can know."

"We'll see," Barbara said. "We'll see."

Andy took the knapsack from me. "Let's go, Mama," he said.

We turned, me carrying Christian at first, then as we moved down the road, I let him walk. Kate skipped beside her Andy, swinging his hand. Andy hadn't spoken after I'd interrupted him except to ask that we leave. As we walked, though I cajoled him, he didn't say a word.

But the farther we got from Fort Willapa, the more he relaxed. He smiled at Kate, who kept hopping beside him, or jumping in front of him. He laughed once at Christian, who attempted a somersault and landed with cedar boughs blanketing his hair. At the river we waded across, it was so shallow in this season before the rains. Since Kate and Andy were barefoot, they splashed on ahead. I took off my leather-soled shoes, tied the laces and swung them over my shoulder, then lifted Christian as we walked across. The mud felt cool and oozed between our toes. On the other side, I decided to stay barefoot, to feel the dry grass beneath my feet.

The water splashing freed Andy and he laughed now with Kate and then came beside me and took my hand in his. It felt cool.

"When you were sick, when I saw you last," I said, "your hands and face and legs were hot to the touch, you had such a high fever. It's good to feel how cool you are, even on this warm day."

"You didn't come to get me."

"I did try, Andy. I couldn't bring the babies that far with the weather so bad and sometimes Auntie Mary couldn't watch them. But I did try. Did you get the little paper pictures I cut for you? Jack said he'd bring them to you."

"They weren't you."

"I know. Then one day I came to take you home, but they'd already taken you to Aurora. When I learned you'd gone my heart felt broken, as broken as when Papa went away."

"I thought you'd gone like Papa!" He wiped at his eyes. "They told me you were home. Then we left and I didn't know why you didn't come with us."

I should have tried harder.

"Did you like Aurora?" I asked.

He shrugged his shoulders. "I liked the orchards. We went to a fair before we came back."

He'd found good things to like despite his disappointment. This was the sign of a wise child in the making. Secretly, I was relieved that he hadn't said he loved Aurora or that he wanted to go back or that he wished he could stay with Barbara and Andreas forever and ever. He'd forgive me in time, I felt sure of it.

"I'll make it up to you, Andy. I'll take you to school each day and wait for you if you want, so you'll know that I'll be there. Would you like that?" He nodded. It would take a great effort and the younger children would have to come too, but it would be worth it. "We'll get up early and I'll milk the goat and we'll pack something to eat and we'll get you to school. We'll make it a festive time."

"What will you do all day?"

"Why, we'll visit Sarah and sometimes we'll stop at Fort Willapa and see your *Oma* and *Opa,* so they'll know that you're where you're meant to be, in school. It'll only be for a month or so before the rains start and then we'll be at home, just you and us. Our family."

We walked a ways farther, passed where Karl and Jack and Mary and Boshie lived. No one came out to greet us and I was grateful. I just wanted for us to be home.

When we rounded the path where our cabin stood in the distance, Andy sped up. He pointed at "his" special cedar tree that shot up beside the barn. He called for Opal, who offered happy recognition bleats and a swinging tail. The cows mooed, more for their need of milking than Andy's call to them. He danced around and then he stopped. We caught up to him. "Is everything all right?" I said.

"It'll be hard for you to take me and Kate and Christian to school every day, Mama."

"We'll do just fine."

"I wouldn't leave you if I didn't have to go to school," he said. "It's all right. I know how to get there and back. I wasn't sure I'd remember."

I squatted to his level and pushed the hair back from his face. Barbara had kept it trimmed well. They'd done all the right things—except let him be with his mother and brother and sister. "You'd remember," I said. "You have a good mind. But we'll take you. That's what we should do."

"Because sometimes we do what's hard, even when we don't want to?"

"Yes," I said.

"Because it's what's good for everyone."

"*Ja.* Exactly that, my little wise one. How did you get to be so wise?"

"It's what *Opa* always says."

18

Emma

Gruel or Guide

I rose in the dark, milked the cows and goat, gathered the eggs and fed the chickens, then woke Andy up to grind the corn for mush. I packed us cheese and venison cakes with berries and a hard-boiled egg for each—good, hearty food for our journey. I even told myself that this was the true calling of a woman, to prepare food for her children and keep the hearth warm and ready, and perhaps that's all Eve had intended in that garden long ago, nothing tempting at all. The thought—and how *Herr* Keil would cringe at it—made me smile.

Next I roused the children, dressed them, checked their road-hardened feet for slivers, then put Christian on my back. We could probably get leather shoes if I asked a Giesy, but it was one more "generosity" I wanted to avoid. Instead we'd save for Sundays the thin-soled shoes, or for when the weather changed. Our clogs we saved for muddy days. Kate walked sleepily beside me, carrying a doll I'd made for her out of one of Christian's socks. I'd wound yarn for curls and painted on the face and given her an ever-present smile. I wished sometimes I could do the same for me.

Dawn lit our river crossing. Sunlight shining through the trees revealed an opaque sky sliced by sharp cedar boughs. At first it looked like giant balls of spider webs hanging as though ornaments in a Christmas tree, but it was bouquets of sky peeking through the branches instead. A small gray bird sang to accompany us and the smell of earthy loam near the river richly marked our way. Christian awoke at the water and then walked partway. But he tired easily and I soon put him on my back. We arrived at Fort Willapa, the schoolhouse, just as other children arrived. Andy walked inside and before we could head to Barbara and Andreas's, Karl Ruge came to stand at the door.

"By golly, you made it," he said. "*Gut* for you."

"*Ja*, it took some effort," I said, "but we are all here for Andy."

"It makes a long day for the *Kinder*," he said. He nodded at Kate, who leaned against my leg. Christian hadn't stirred so I knew he still slept.

"I keep my commitments," I said.

"*Ja*, by golly, I know that about you. Even when they're tough ones." He smiled and waved me off as he turned to respond to loud voices I heard coming from inside. Andy nodded at me like a little man and turned toward the sounds of children.

I pasted on a smile as we headed for my in-laws. My exchange with Barbara and Andreas was strained, but we passed an hour or two. I helped Barbara spin while she cuddled with Christian, showed Kate how to thread a needle. "Begin to weave," she said. "God provides the thread." It was an old German saying my mother had given me. It once encouraged my days, but I hadn't thought of it much since Christian's death. I wasn't sure God cared much about the weaving of my life.

We had a light dinner and in the early afternoon, I said I needed to talk to Sarah and we spent the rest of that day visiting with her. We picked up Andy midafternoon and began the trek home. I knew once there I'd need to skim the cream from the morning milk and churn. I wanted to grind the corn so Andy wouldn't have to do it at dawn. I'd split some kindling so each day we could have a hot meal at the beginning of our day. Dinner and supper would be cold. It was just the way it was.

I reminded myself that we only needed to keep up this pace for a few weeks. I could do this until the rains began. A person can do most any dreadful thing for a time, as long as one knows there's an end.

The first day was the hardest, as we had not yet made it a routine. It was dusk when we arrived back at the bend that marked our property. Christian bobbed on my back. Kate begged to be carried too, but we were so close to being home I told her I couldn't. She scowled and sat down in the path, arms crossed over her chest. She reminded me of my sister Johanna when she was little, marked by a stubborn pout. "I won't go 'less you carry me," she said.

I sighed. "Don't be difficult."

"Carry me."

"I'm carrying your brother. It isn't much farther until we're home."

"I'm hungry. I want to eat now."

We were all hungry. Tired and hungry and discouraged by effort we knew needed to be repeated. Trying to convince Kate that she wasn't hungry or could keep going would be a useless effort too. Sometimes one just had to face a troubling thing straight on and see if it could be converted into merit.

"*Ja, ja,* I'd like to eat now too," I said. "I'm hungry enough to eat an entire…tree. Maybe that one there." I pointed to a giant fir rising up so high Kate fell over trying to see the top. She looked up at it, lying on her back, then back at me, and little lines formed across her brow. "I'd chew the bark and have toothpicks already in my mouth to clean my teeth." I bared my teeth at her the way a horse does when it's smiling. "After that, I could eat a whole…horse if there was one here."

"I could eat a cow," Andy said. "That's how hungry I am." He'd stopped for us.

"Eat cow?" Christian said, waking.

"Not our cow," I told him. "I could eat…the river," I said.

"You drink a river, Mama," Kate told me as she pushed herself up to sit.

"*Ja,* you're right. Such a smart girl." I reached for her hand and pulled her up. "Come along then, what would you eat?" She offered up the house. Andy laughed at that and I smiled too. "Now that's a hungry *Kind,*" I said.

She went on to describe things inside the house, and Andy added the barn, and before we had eaten the fence rails, we were home, hearing the cows moo, and the goat bleat its discomfort with this new routine.

I fell onto my rope bed that night as tired as I had ever been. My shoulders ached from carrying Christian, from churning late into the night. And yet I could not sleep. The soothing breathing of all my children underneath this roof should have been all the lullaby I needed, but instead I lay awake, the low embers of the fireplace casting the merest hint of pink against the logs. My throat had a scratch to it that I hoped wouldn't go into my chest or worse, be something contagious. That thought forced me to sit up in the bed. What if I got sick? I coughed. Seven miles was simply too far to go twice a day. I lay back down. That could not happen, not now, not after all we'd been through. I turned on my side, the ache of my shoulder causing me to gasp out loud. I listened. The children slumbered on.

Out of my aching came the words of a psalm, the sixty-ninth: "Save me, O God; for the waters are come in unto my soul. I sink in deep mire, where there is no standing: I am come into deep waters, where the floods overflow me. I am weary of my crying: my throat is dried: mine eyes fail while I wait for my God." A psalmist somewhere once felt as disheartened as I felt. Yet if I remembered well, there were psalms of rescue too. What happened in between seemed far removed from me.

I'd never prayed for the rainy season, but I did that night, my words hopelessly self-centered, asking that the rains might come early so I could keep my commitments. I did everything necessary to be the holdfast for my family, but when I imagined expending this much effort for the rest of my life, the floods overflowed.

That night I dreamed of the river. Our small boat was moored for when the water became too deep to walk across. A ship of safety waited. But it was on the other bank, so far from where I needed it to be to help me make a safe crossing.

In the second week of October Andy made his request.

"No," I told him.

"Just until school is out, Mama," he insisted.

"No." I coughed. There was something on the trail that made me sneeze and sniffle. It would pass. "There are only a few more weeks until the rains come, and then Uncle John will declare the school year over until spring. We can do this until then."

"Kate's grumpy," he said. "You stay up late. It would be better if I—"

"*Nein!* It is a mother's job to decide such things. You will not stay with your grandparents. You will not!"

"Karl's there. I could study at night. Now I'm too tired, Mama."

"I'll ask Karl not to give you so much work to do."

"Just let me stay at *Opa*'s. I don't want to see Christian all tired and you carrying him so much. You'll get sick. It'll be my fault. Because I have to go to school or I can't live with you anymore."

"Who told you that?"

"That's why you make us go every day and take us all. So you'll know I'm there and no one takes me away again. I know."

He'd come to his own conclusions and however distorted they were, he may have been right about a portion of it.

"I want you not to worry about my leaving you again."

"But sometimes I fall asleep in school and Karl Ruge hits my fingers with a ruler to wake me up."

"He does?" I didn't like hearing that. "Well, it doesn't hurt you very much, does it?" He shook his head.

"I don't like the ruler. I don't like sleeping when I want to stay awake. To do good for you, Mama. To do good for you, that's why I go."

An obedient child, pushing every day, just to take care of me.

"We'll finish this week out and then see if the weekend comes and brings us rain. Then we won't have to make any decision about it at all. All right? We'll let things be and just wait and see."

"If it rains on Sunday can we stay home?"

"Your grandparents will expect us. When the time comes, Andy, I'll make the choice. It's what mamas do. It won't be on your shoulders, I promise."

The weekend was a balmy one, the perfect weather for picnics and harvest festivals, so we made our way to the Sunday meeting. At least we'd had one day without having to leave the cabin. And we didn't have to pack food for each of us for Sunday. Instead I'd gotten up early to make a *Strudel* and we carried it in a pan wrapped in a show towel. I knew there'd be plenty of other food for after the Sunday sermon, meat and harvest vegetables brought by those who lived closer.

After the sermon I tied the strings beneath my bonnet and watched Andy stay away from the other children as they played. He looked tired and listless.

Sarah and I talked, as she and Sam had joined the gathering this day. A few more of the settlers not affiliated with us Germans had begun to share our Sabbath time. If Christian had lived, he would have thought that a good sign. Sarah beamed in her pregnancy, her face flushed and smooth, her eyes sparkled as though they were diamonds. I so hoped that things went well. Mary was due anytime now too. In fact, she hadn't made the trek this Sunday. Neither had Jack, and I found myself surprised that I noticed he was missing. Well before the afternoon waned, my little family headed back. We stopped at Mary's and she was abed but said she was only tired. The baby was still a month away by her calculations. I told Boshie to be sure to come get me when needed. He nodded but had that confused look on his face. "You could stay with my children while I come back and midwife," I clarified. "Or send Karl if he's here, or Jack. They could do the same."

"*Ja, ja.* That would work," he said. "Plenty of time, *ja*," he said, and I could tell by the tone of his voice that he remembered their first child, who had died at birth.

"Elizabeth was born strong and healthy. This one will be too," I assured him, though of course, who could know?

Upon arriving home I knew instantly that something was different. The cows weren't mooing. The goat barely looked our way. A small stream of smoke rose up through the chimney, though I'd been certain I put the fire out before we left.

"We have visitors," I told Andy.

I guessed that it was Jack, making himself at home. He'd probably told Mary and Boshie he was laboring at the coast when in fact he was hanging around, trying to make himself useful. I felt a mix of irritation and anticipation. I didn't want to have to deal with any of his "maybe could" offers, but fire in the fireplace meant we could have a warm supper for us all. I was certain that was where the anticipation came from.

We approached the house. Of course it might have been a traveler just assuming a welcome, as so many did where settlements were few and far between. I'd left the latch string out, suggesting invitation. I pressed against the door. The inside was dark but for the little window light and the fire. I smelled venison and beans.

"*Gut* evening," the visitor said, and when my eyes adjusted to the inner darkness, I recognized him and his voice. There stood my brother Jonathan, an apron tied around his waist.

———

"Papa wrote you could use some help," he said. "So here I am."

"You're better than early rains," I said as I crushed myself against his chest.

"I've been called many things, Sister, but never better than rain."

I removed my bonnet and Kate's too while Jonathan served us a hot supper that tasted better for the gift of it. Over the meal my brother met Christian for the first time. It was good to hear him and Andy exchange words, and just the sound of his voice, a gentle man's voice in the house, felt like music to my ears.

Jonathan took Andy to school in the morning. Work still called my name, but I could stop in between chores and sit for a moment with my children. I even napped, something I hadn't done since Christian was born. I prepared a big meal, hot food with fresh biscuits fixed in the dutch oven, for the "men" when they arrived home at dusk.

They made better time than our little troop had and arrived in higher style: Jonathan and Andy rode home on one of the colony's mules. "They made a loan to you," I said. "That makes for an easier day, doesn't it Andy?"

"Would have done it for you too, if you had asked," Jonathan said, stepping off the mule.

"The mules are always in use for the fieldwork," I said. "I didn't want to be a bother and make someone have to come and get it."

Andy led the mule to the half barn as Jonathan put his arm around my shoulder and pulled me into his side and kissed my forehead. My brother had one blue eye and one brown eye. That mix always fascinated me, and when I looked up at him both those eyes had a twinkle in them. "You make everything so difficult. All I had to do was ask for the mule. People want to be helpful."

"You're his uncle. They would do things for you."

"Emma…"

"You know they took Andy to Aurora without my knowing it." I shook myself free of his one-arm hug.

"Maybe they should have said something, but what they did caused no harm, not really. Except that now you push yourself until your clothes nearly fall off your bony frame, for what? To make sure they know you are up to doing the impossible? That's not the way we Wagners do it," he said. "We persevere, *ja,* but we cut our losses before they cut us."

I crossed my arms over my chest. "Meaning?"

"You have choices, Emma. They are not all bad."

"Ach," I said, dismissing him as I walked toward the house.

"For one, your life and that of the children's would be easier if you lived with Barbara and Andreas. They would extend such an invitation, I know this. The community would add a room perhaps, that you and the children could call your own. I know this is important to you to have your own place. But then Andy would not have to travel so far to school; you would not have to drag the children out each day. You would be close to others so your spirit could be filled with friendships. You could stay and work with your mother-in-law, together raise your children."

"And who would keep up my cabin?"

"Maybe Karl would move into it. Or Jack Giesy. They could manage the land. The cabin isn't what matters, Sister. It's the people; they're who matter."

I scowled at him and Kate looked up at that precise moment, her eyes drawn from the wooden blocks that Jonathan had brought her. She scowled then too, mimicking me.

I made my face look calm. "And my other choices?" I said.

"You could come back with me to Aurora Mills." He silenced me with his open palm to the air. "Think of this. You would have all the help you needed with the children. You could have people close to give to you but more, you could help others. This is what your life misses now, Emma. Christian was devoted to making other lives better, and that kept him a good and faithful servant. You've turned…inside yourself, leaving no room to look after others."

"Ach, no," I said. "I only look after my children. Should I sacrifice them in order to help someone *Herr* Keil thinks needs tending? Is this why you came here, to talk me into coming to Aurora? Because I'm not welcome there

and never will be. *Herr* Keil made that clear to me when he said we'd failed him by choosing this place. To leave it would but confirm his view of our error, and I'll not do that to Christian, I won't."

"Christian is dead, Emma. And Aurora would be better for your children."

"They don't even have a school there."

"Ah, Emma. Then we go back to allowing your son to stay with Andreas, to make his life easier. And yours."

I asked him why he didn't take Andy with him if that was what everyone thought my soon-to-be six-year-old son needed, to be living with the guidance of a man rather than his mother.

"I travel too much. I shouldn't even have traveled here as they have need of me at Aurora. But *Herr* Keil suggested I come."

"You said Papa told you to come."

"He did."

It occurred to me then that Jonathan was here not to offer me support, but to do business with the colonists, talk about farming and harvests and contracts for butter or cheese, look into fields that would serve sheep or goats or hogs, all for the good of the colony. The Aurora colony, of course. Helping his sister and his niece and nephews, well that was secondary.

"I'm sorry you had to take time away from your colony duties," I said. "I can take Andy to school tomorrow and I'll ask if the mule can be made available to us until the end of the term. We'll take care of things here."

"Emma. I'm here. I'll stay until the term is over. You'd still have to take the children with you. Andy's not quite old enough to go it on his own."

"Maybe he is. Maybe he just needs to learn young that you have to take care of things yourself. *Ja,* he can ride the mule. Then you won't be inconvenienced and you won't have to feel guilty that your niece and nephew are spending their days walking back and forth and going nowhere, as you suggest."

He shook his head. "You'd slap a hand rather than grasp its strength."

I pitched his thought away. He didn't know what it was like to live on the outside, to be a woman alone and dependent on the generosity of others. He didn't know how weak and empty it made a person feel to take hold of a strong hand and not know when it might gruel rather than guide.

———

It was my cough that made me relent and let Jonathan continue to take Andy to school. By the end of the week, the rains came and with it congestion that filled my lungs until I sounded like the wild geese that flew overhead, barking with their plaintive cries.

Jonathan described my symptoms to Martin who said the catarrh could be helped with powdered ginger made into a tea. I was to lie beneath as many quilts as we could spare and "sweat the inflammation out," Jonathan told me. I was grateful my brother stayed through this ordeal. I recovered, but the best news was that the term then ended and we had no need to travel anywhere for a time.

We might have enjoyed the remaining days with Jonathan before he headed back to Aurora Mills except that Jack Giesy made himself known again. He arrived to fetch me for Mary's delivery. I felt well enough to go. I still coughed some, but nothing as I had.

As I readied my few things to take, my brother and Jack talked about crops and weather and people they each knew back in Phillipsburg, Bethel, and Harmony. They had an immediate camaraderie even though they'd shared little time together for years. A part of me envied that. We women were always eavesdropping, rarely a part of the sharing. Jack talked of boat building at the coast; Jonathan spoke of the wine-making at Aurora. Then Jack chided Jonathan, telling him he should find himself a good woman and my ears perked up, wondering if my brother had been courting. When Jonathan teased him back, I wished I'd kept my eavesdropping to myself.

"I've got myself a chosen one," Jack said. "She just doesn't want to accept it." He looked over at me. "But she will."

I wished Jack hadn't offered to walk me back to Mary's, but obviously the man lived there. Jonathan assured me he had the children in hand and then he smiled, those two-colored eyes shining. "Don't you two get lost along the way."

"Ach, jammer!" I said.

"Methinks the *Fräulein* complains in jest," Jack told him.

"I'm a married woman," I reminded him. "That's *Frau* to you." I stepped out into the rain.

Fortunately, the rains were steady enough to dissuade conversation. The patter against my oil-slicked hood—Christian's old one—served well to keep my head dry and my mouth shut.

Mary's baby, a girl, born without incident, they named Salome. Elizabeth looked on in wonder at this doll whose arms moved with jerks and starts that matched her legs. "She's dancing, Mama," Elizabeth said.

"Like a good German girl should," Boshie told his daughter. He ruffled Elizabeth's hair and gazed with tender eyes upon his newest daughter and his wife.

The love I saw pass between them, the raising of their spirits by this newness in their lives, made my heart ache with its emptiness. I'd had no one to share Baby Christian's new life with, save the children. No one who looked upon me the way Boshie looked at Mary. I supposed I never would again.

19

Emma

Waiting to Be Found

There is something to be said for customs that keep men and women separated unless chaperoned by those who care about their souls. I remember when Christian courted me back in Bethel, my parents walked before us, where they could quickly turn around if I called out. When he came into our home, my parents sat at the far end of the room, working, but with one eye always on the two of us, making sure nothing untoward might happen. They felt responsible. It annoyed me as a young girl but now, at twenty-five years of age, the widowed mother of three, feeling lost and alone in an uncertain world, I longed to know that someone I loved and trusted looked after my interests, that someone else might know what was best for me and cherish my soul in their hands.

Fatigue now framed my future. I was tired of a life promising only the drudgery of every day, of keeping my children alive rather than contented. I failed to even have the energy to paint, to get my drawings to Sam Woodard to see if they might sell. Even the path toward something better took too much from me and I chastened myself for my sloth. If I hadn't had the children to feed, I would have failed to eat, for it didn't seem worth the effort to feed the emptiness. My life was a walk in the deepest beach where if the blowing sand didn't cover me, the pounding surf soon would. It had been only two years without Christian. It seemed like dozens, and the almanac of living loomed before me without a hopeful story in between the calendar of days.

I suppose in part the sight of Mary and Boshie and the comfort of their family proved the crowning blow for my state. The whole time Jack and I walked back the night of Salome's birth, I thought of Mary and Boshie and of Christian, and then about the man walking beside me with no chaperone to even care what we did. I waited for Jack to do something, say something that would strike the flint of his interest, give me a reason to snap at him, at anyone, to relieve this irritated frame of mind.

But he chatted little through the rainfall, and when he did it was to point out a drier place to step along the trail. He whistled a marching tune. Once, when I slipped, he reached his hand out and caught me, but instead of holding it as I thought he might, as I hoped he might so that I could challenge his forwardness, he let me loose, faced forward, and kept whistling.

Maybe because Jack had been the only man to offer interest to me, maybe that was why I half expected him to do so now, while we were alone, no children, no one else to monitor what was said or done. We were two grown adults. What did it matter to anyone else what two grown adults said or did to each other? No chaperones necessary when the woman was a widow, her virtue already molded into wisdom she could carry on alone. I didn't feel wise so I said nothing.

Then just before we reached the bend where the cabin would be in sight, Jack stepped in front of me. He put his hands on my shoulders. "Consider, Emma Giesy. Consider how long you want to work as hard as you have chosen to do these past years. Consider how two are stronger than one, as Ecclesiastes notes, and three strands are best of all. You and I would be those two strong strands, and the third would be our children."

I thought he'd translated that verse with a theological error, that the third strand was meant to be God. It was why marriage was a sacrament for Karl Ruge, a Lutheran, and many other communities of faith. Marriage wasn't such a sacrament for the colonists. Karl had officiated at marriages back in Bethel as though it was just a matter between people and the state. But I suspect that Karl prayed for them and saw his role not just to say the words but to weave people together, forever, in God's sight.

Still, Jack offered his children as a third strand woven together within *our* marriage. He appeared to say that he'd accept Christian's children as his own, as though they were his responsibility too. Maybe he understood their importance to me. It was a side to him I hadn't considered.

He lifted my chin. His fingers were warm despite their being wet from the rain. He had a solid jaw, gentle lips he opened now, just wide enough to slip a pumpkin seed through them, if he'd had one to chew. "Emma," he said, "the time for playing has passed. You're a grown woman. Time to step up to it."

He kissed me then.

His lips were thinner than Christian's but the pressure he placed against my own felt firm. When I moved my head back, uncertain as to what churned within me, the pounding heart one of hope or shuddering with fear, his lips came with me. I pushed him back gently. His face stayed close to mine, so close, but he released my lips. "I know you compare me," he whispered. "This is a natural thing. But in time, I'll make you forget Christian Giesy. I'll replace whatever you cling to about him with something real. Alive. You won't be carrying around the memory of a tired love of an old man. If you admit it, you long for a young man, one meant to meet your challenges. That's me."

He didn't say he wanted to take care of me for the rest of my days. He didn't say he cherished me. He didn't say he loved me. It was as though he'd confessed to wishing to win a competition, a race he ran with a dead man.

I gave no answer, just said we needed to get back. I walked past him, half expected him to grab at me and twirl me around, but he didn't. He was quite the gentleman after that. At the cabin, he came inside, talked with Jonathan, and then nodded his head at me. He slapped his hat against his jeans leaving water like a dog shaking itself of the rain. He smiled.

He seemed harmless there in the presence of my brother and my children. I took in a deep breath. I wasn't ready yet to risk that this Jack who stood before me, gentle as a lamb, was the real Jack who would stay that way forever. I wasn't yet that tired.

———

Jonathan left the following morning to return to Aurora Mills. He made one more encouragement that I consider letting Andreas and Barbara keep Andy, or that all of us move in with them, or perhaps all of us come live with him. But I discouraged him from thinking that any of those options would ever come to pass. I didn't tell him about Jack's vision for my future.

I missed my brother, put the longing into work. I pulled the last of the cabbages and buried them beneath the grass hay in the lean-to beside the half barn. Then, because the flour was a little low, I decided to tend to that myself, not wait for "the men" to take care of it.

On my own, I made my way to the mill. I still had the mule we'd borrowed and decided to use it to bring home a sack of flour that would tide us over for the winter, then return the animal. It had rained in the morning, so I waited until the November mist lifted in the afternoon. Often we had sun-breaks in the late afternoon, and this day proved no exception. Andy said he'd watch the little ones, and though he seemed young to do so, he had an old man's soul and I knew somehow the children would be safe, perhaps behave even better for him than they did for me.

There were many things that caught my eye as I rode. I vowed to come back and draw, then chastened for making commitments I failed to keep, even to myself.

The mill had weathered into gray over the years, and mosses already dotted the shingles of the lower portion of the roof. The oyster schooners carried redwood for ballast as they sailed north from San Francisco, sold it for a profit, and then refilled their cargo holds with baskets of oysters they marketed when they reached that city. Maybe if Christian had lived they'd have branched out and owned their own ships. But likely Christian would have just used the money to pay off Keil and contribute to the colony. Always for Christian, it was the colony that mattered.

Still, seeing the structure in the distance brought a comfort to me. "Oh, Christian," I said out loud as the mule twitched its ears. "How I miss you." Christian would have loved taking his sons to the mill, would have cherished seeing how the lumber weathered to this settled, sturdy gray. He would have scowled at my doing this work, riding the mule, gathering supplies for the winter. He'd have claimed it as his duty, his obligation as a husband and father, and he would have expected his family to have tended me in such a way there was no need of my doing it for myself. Of course for one to give there must be a recipient. "They would have done it," I told the bird that flitted through the air, "if I wasn't so stubborn, if the cost wasn't so great to let them place me into obligation." Repayment was always required of any charity received, of that I was certain.

I arrived to human stillness though I could hear water rushing through the mill race. The mill door stood open. It was late in the day. I should have come earlier. But Boshie would have ground extra bags of flour, and I could load two on the mule to balance the load and leave a note saying that I'd taken them and to make a mark against what I owed.

I tied the mule to the hitching post and when no one answered my calls, I pushed the door and went inside. Dust mites rose in the air toward the shafts of setting sun that came in through the upper windows. It smelled of grain and earth and the powder of flour crunched against my feet. The huge millstones stood quiet. I looked up toward the tower where the windows looked out on each side and wondered what the view from there might be, standing at the ledge, looking out. A ladder reached to it from the main opening. A loft with windows that was the office looked out over the grist stones and there was probably a stairway to the top of the tower from there. The ladder would be a long climb up, a difficult one, but the view would be spectacular.

I was about to decide if I was up to that ladder climb when I felt a breeze behind me and turned.

"I maybe could think this was destiny, my finding you here," Jack said as he pulled the door shut behind him. More dust mites rose up.

"I was just getting some grain loaded."

"You were thinking of climbing that ladder to the window ledge," he said. He smiled and the tension I'd felt with his presence lessened.

"I wasn't sure I had the stamina for the climb."

"Risky thing to do, but then you always did like a little risk." He moved closer to me. I swallowed. "This is your lucky day," he said, reaching past me toward one of the interior posts, his breath just inches from my ear. "I have a key to the office and we can take the stairway from there. It's a much easier route to the view of paradise." He held a key that had hung hidden behind lengths of rope.

Doing it the hard way was my way. But the day ran late. Why not do it the easy way? He had a key.

So we took the steps up to the office loft. Jack opened the door and at the back a stairwell twisted its way up to the window that looked up the creek. I climbed the steep steps. Actual glass was used in this window, and my fingers felt cool against it when I brushed a circle into the grain dust. The perspective was spectacular, with the sunset pouring over the rain-coated trees. The willows sported red and the ferns had just the hint of rust color at some of their edges. I could actually see beyond the treetops to the sky. The world of Olympia lay that way. Fort Steilacoom, where Andy had been born, bustled miles beyond. Another world. A better world. There was something more, something worthy of all this effort to just live.

I lost all sense of where I was for the moment. It seemed that the view promised something greater than what my life had shown so far. Hope rose up in the forest mists, a hope of life filled with moments of joy yet to come.

"You can see the northern lights from there sometimes," Jack said. I turned to look down at him. He stood below me as there was only room for one person at the window ledge. "Dancing colors, late at night. Early morning. Quite a sight."

"You're a poet," I said.

"Makes me want to paint it, but I doubt one could capture the vibrancy of the colors. At least nothing I've ever attempted satisfied."

I almost told him that I shared his love for drawing, for capturing on paper something in the world that could nurture later. Instead I said, "You're here at such hours?"

He shrugged. "It isn't easy for Boshie and Mary always having someone about."

I looked down through the staircase and saw the bed then on the red-wood floor. My fingers began making circles on their own. I noticed drawings on the walls I hadn't seen before either, drawings of faces with strange features, heavy lines around eyes, swirls of hair that moved off one sheet of paper and onto another. They were tacked up nearly covering the wall by the bed. Jack's work. Jack's dark and heavy work.

I took one last look at the view, the promising view, then stepped back from the window ledge. He reached up for me and took my hand to help me. He didn't release it but instead pulled me to him. Not in a possessive way as he had in front of the saltbox, but with a gentle firmness, offering security.

The drawings stared at me. The bed reminded me of an animal trap covered with deceitful familiarity and harboring something troubling beneath it. "This isn't a good place for me to be," I said.

"*Good* is a relative word," he said. "I can help you load the mule of the flour. That way it won't be a wasted trip." His breath was sweet as though he chewed mint leaves.

"I wasn't thinking it was wasted," I said. "I loved seeing the view from the window. Thank you for that, for showing me that. I hadn't realized there was a stairwell. Did John design the mill? I can't remember who—"

He put his fingers to my lips. "Quiet, Emma Giesy," he said. I let him pull me to his chest. "Just let yourself be cherished for this moment."

He moved his hands across my back and held me firm. And in that space of safety, I succumbed to comfort.

Not that we did anything untoward. He did not even try to kiss me. He just held me and I felt myself sink into his arms, the first time since Christian's death that I'd felt comforted without an expectation.

I really don't know how long we stood there, my head on his chest, my fingers fanned up toward his collarbone, then pushed together as though in prayer; between us yet, my hands. He stroked my hair, the back of my head, and I blinked back tears. It was all I wanted, just this salve; the reassurance of a man's hand against my head.

I closed my eyes to the pictures on the walls.

"Andy's watching Kate and Christian," I said finally. "I really need to go home."

He nodded, his chin tapping gently on my head. I was aware of his height, his bigness. I felt so small beside him. He inhaled, a deep, long breath, and something in the sound of it or maybe in the way he held me made me acknowledge that the world is full of wounded souls. I pulled away. He preceded me down the winding stairway from the office, locked the office door behind us, and we took the stairwell past the redwood flour bins to the main floor. Outside and in silence, he hefted the sacks of flour into the panniers on either side of the mule's rump, then put his foot out so I could step into the clasp of his palms as a stirrup. I grabbed the reins then swung my foot over the back of the mule, lifting it high to keep my skirt from catching at the packs. I remembered his grimace when I'd done that at Christian's funeral. He did it again now.

"A woman does what she has to," I said. The animal's ears twitched as I settled onto his back.

"Maybe could be," he said.

"Thanks, Jack," I lifted the reins. "For the help with the flour. And the view."

"I thought maybe I startled you when I first came in," he said.

"*Ja,* well, you did. Truth is I'm never quite sure…about you, Jack Giesy."

"I'm an uncomplicated man," he said. He cocked his head to the side. "Maybe could be you're not accustomed to such as that." He stepped back, swatted the mule on his rump, then let me and the mule pass.

The twilight was enough to see by, and the mule made his way along the trail, surefooted. I patted his neck, ducked beneath low-hanging branches. I realized I didn't even know the mule's name. It struck me as odd that I would think of that now. Other questions came too: Had Jack walked to the mill? I'd seen no other mule around. Or maybe he slept there often, to have so many drawings up, and such strange ones. His life carried a bit of emptiness in it too: a man alone, moving from site to site to work, but without a place to call his own. Did men need such things? Many of the Bethel bachelors lived together in Keil's house, and no one seemed to think they'd even want a home of their own. Maybe it was a woman's dream, that desire to make one's nest, fix the quilt on the cot the way she wanted and not have to negotiate with someone else about it.

For just a moment an image flashed of me, sitting on that quilt on Jack's bed in the mill office, sitting beside Jack Giesy, not frightened but desired. Was that the promise the mill view offered? Or something more? I didn't know. I kicked the mule into a faster trot.

———

The winter months wore on with their usual sheets of rain. Andy rigged up a stick marked by inches and kept it standing in a tin set on a stump out near the half barn. "Three, Mama," he shouted. It couldn't be. I'd just emptied it the morning before. But it had rained so hard the whole day that at times I thought the barn was gone because we couldn't see it. Each time I left the house to milk the cows, the path became more mired in mud, so I made new paths. The old ones just didn't work anymore.

In December, Henry and Martin came to take the cows away until spring so I wouldn't have to milk them nor worry about churning the butter. We'd do well with goat's milk, and Martin assured us we could have butter whenever we wished. With fewer chores to do, I'd have time for drawing. But I found time to create new excuses for not doing so too.

There were Christmas presents to make and eggs to scrape, letters to write. I wrote cheery things to Jonathan about how well we were doing, and to my family in Bethel I made it sound like my begging them to rescue me the year before had been a momentary lapse. On Christmas Day we made our way to my in-laws' without incident. The men brought out their instruments and we tapped our feet with pleasure to the music. While there I learned of the arrival of Edwin Woodard, Sarah and Sam's first child. For a few hours, I left all three children with Andreas and Barbara and rode the mule, whose name I learned was Fritz, to Sarah's. She was radiant and her son wailed a healthy cry until she fed him from her breast.

"He's a fine boy," I said. "Look how big his hands and feet are. He'll grow up to be a strong man."

She nodded. "Like your Andy. I wish you'd brought him. All the children."

"Letting them have time with their grandparents is a good thing," I said. "It keeps the lid on the teapot that is our life with them. I never know when the fire will get kindled again and things will boil over."

Sarah understood and despite the changes in her life, like a true friend, she still made room for me. "Did you bring them, your drawings?" she asked as she stroked Edwin's fine hair. I shook my head. "You won't go forward if you don't put your foot out," she said.

"I'm not ready to get that foot stepped on just yet. Maybe this winter, when the rains keep us inside, I'll make more. The mill makes a good subject."

"You already have some you could send with Sam," she said. "What are you afraid of?"

I didn't know.

"I'll bring you one in honor of Edwin," I said.

"We won't sell that one, Emma. You know that."

"I've come to accept that there's no future in the drawings." It was the first I'd admitted that even to myself. "It won't make me independent. I'll still have the obligations of my husband's family. Even if I had the money to hire help so I could make my own way, I wouldn't want to travel without the children, so what would be the point? I just can't see a future with any kind of creativity in it, Sarah. I'm just to raise my children. That's my life now. I'm not complaining, just explaining."

I made it sound beleaguered. Not every life was meant to have peaks of joy scattered throughout it. Or maybe my peaks had all come within the first years, when I was a desired woman, a wife and member of a scouting party that had carried out a worthy task. My peaks had been the births of my children, though even Christian's had been laced with melancholy.

"Your life could be more," Sarah said as I left. "If you'd let it."

"I can't let go of Christian's wasted death," I said.

"You have to forgive yourself," she said.

"Me? I didn't do anything. It was that old man. And Keil."

"It's hard to receive good things when your hand is a fist against the world, Emma."

"*Ach,*" I said. "You just don't understand." But then, neither did I.

———

With the rain and the rise of the river I begged off of the New Year's Eve celebration, even though it promised to be festive with this new decade inviting us out of the old: 1860. We read of rumors of war back in the States. A new president would take office soon. Those changes felt far from our daily lives.

I half expected Jack to knock on our door on New Year's Eve but he didn't. I hadn't talked with him since our encounter at the mill. He'd been at the Christmas gathering but we kept our distance. Perhaps our last encounter proved too intimate for him, too exposed as he simply stood beside me rather than attempted to lead me here or there the way men tend to do. It was pleasant to remember just the safety of that moment when he held me with no demands, nothing to indicate that he needed, wanted, or would take more.

We waited out the rains, watched for the dusting of occasional snows. Andy and Kate played games and we read stories from the almanac. I even read a few stories from the Bible my sister Catherine had pressed into my hands before Christian and I left Bethel. I'd put Christian's away, to be given to Andy one day. Andy liked knowing that Luke was a doctor, "like I want to be one day, Mama," he told me. It was a new admission for him, a wish he'd never expressed before. Maybe his time with Martin had influenced him well. I told him he'd make a good one and I meant it, though I wondered how we'd ever make that happen.

Kate liked the book of Luke too, especially the story of the woman who'd lost her coin and couldn't find it. Kate misplaced everything, it seemed. We were always on a search around the house, the loft, the half barn, or wherever she might have been, seeking her stocking doll. Andy proved the tidy one. And Christian appeared to be in between. I liked the lost coin story too, for it showed a woman at the hearth, looking for something that mattered to her even though she already had other coins. She kept seeking. I wondered how she'd lost that coin. She must have been a good manager to know just how many coins she had. Maybe it had fallen from her purse. It had rolled away, perhaps, was missing through no fault of her own. The woman understood that. Things happened that separate us from what we loved through no fault of our own. But the woman kept searching until she found it, and then she had a festive party with her friends.

"Mama finds me, *ja*?" Christian patted my hand, taking me back from my own losses to this room filled with warm scents of food I'd prepared, of my children freshly bathed in heated rainwater and ready for bed. "Find me, Mama." Christian moved to hide under the bed, sure that the story was something about hide-and-seek.

"*Ja*, I'll find you," I said. "If you ever get lost."

During the days, deer munched outside our window, then startled if we opened the door. Near the river, we found otter slides and sometimes the air was so quiet, the trees so still, that in the distance we could hear the crunch of a large animal, maybe an elk blazing its own trail through the wilderness. Karl Ruge visited once or twice, the pleasant smoke from his pipe staying in the cabin for hours after he left. A few times I bundled up the children and we walked to Mary's to see how Elizabeth and Salome grew. We found Karl there, reading and smoking that pipe, and Boshie when he wasn't at the mill. But no Jack.

I split my own kindling that winter. My arms gained muscle and I began to feel healthy again. The little outrages that flushed my face happened less often. A sheen returned to my skin that had been missing in the months since Christian's death, and I thought it might be the result of my body finally adjusting after my last baby's birth. Or maybe as I made sauerkraut, or added vinegar to the warm potato salad I prepared nearly every day, and watched the children take pleasure in the rolled cakes I made, I'd come to some level of peace in this widowing life. I even wondered if I'd one day not think of myself first as a widow, then a mother, but once again as a woman. Perhaps I too was a missing coin, cherished, waiting to be found.

20

Louisa

Many days pass by without my writing in this notebook.

We learn of illness at the Willapa. Not the fever and ague that people suffer from here but of some lung discomfort. Emma has let her sons stay with Andreas and Barbara again, though I understand it is she who is ill and not the children. Little Kate apparently remains with her, and Mary and others stop by to look after them, though I cannot imagine that this suits Emma well. I know I hate being ill almost more than anything for it means others must tend my needs, so while I feel sick I also feel a burden. Well, worse is when the children fall ill. I struggle even more when my husband ails as he has this past winter. I suspect it is his worries that bring him down. He sees what must be done but hasn't been accomplished yet. He wants Aurora ready for those coming from Bethel, and yet he needs them here to build. His need to be ready weighs on him while his need to have more help, to build up the businesses here, presses on him too. His leadership is a balancing, just as the way one pieces a quilt requires measuring this and that in order for things to come out as they should.

I would offer to assist him with his worries, but he would not see of it. And truth is, I am not much able to help with financial things. Jonathan Wagner carried that skill from what I overheard as my husband talked with our son, August, before he and Jonathan headed back to Bethel. My husband hopes these two boys, well, men now, can spur along the sale of homes in Bethel so people will give up the comforts there to serve each other here. Jonathan can perhaps help the Wagners too, as their daughter, Louisa, injured herself at Elim while at a dance. She fell from the second story of our old home and now has trouble standing at times. My husband says bad things happen there because of the delays, but I believe bad things just do happen. They are part of the ebb and flow of life. I do not attach all suffering to sin as does my husband, though these words to him I'd never say. No need to add to his burdens.

Now there are more worries here for my husband, as neither Jonathan nor August are here to help him. But Helena Giesy has come. She traveled by ship up the Columbia and did not even visit with her parents first in Willapa. She didn't even stop to visit her brother's grave before coming here to aid my husband. Well, the colony.

My husband says she is a saint, turning down a marriage proposal so she could devote her life to the work of the colony. He spends long hours with her. She is so helpful and never tires of tending to him.

I can barely manage all the household work with my leg giving me such an ache. I don't tell my husband of it. He healed it after all, and it must be my lack of faith that keeps me limping. I miss August, but my husband ordered him to Bethel so it must be for the best. My Aurora, already eleven, is a help almost more than her sister Gloriunda, two years her senior. Gloriunda has a tendency to laziness while Aurora knows no rest. She's like me in that. While I am honored by the pattern I am also worried for her, as her devotion to family requires the buildup of much steam and the promise of terrible despair when such runs out. One is always seeking fuel. Fuel does run out when one loves others so much. How to fill up again, that is a mother's constant quest.

We will celebrate this March the beginning of my husband's forty-eighth year. All believe that we share a birthday, but his is actually later this month.

It's mine we celebrate on the sixth of March. I'm older than Wilhelm by twelve days, but he honors me by telling all we share a birthday. He does not like a woman being older, I suspect, for he assumes wisdom comes with age. His voice is still strong as he preaches. He stands upright and his eyes burn with an intensity I remember from his youth. But afterward, he pales. I prepare him tea and hover over him as he leans back in his rocking chair, his wide chest taking in deep breaths. Others do not see this; it is a wife's duty to recognize such sinking and to puff up pillions of encouragement to surround her husband's head. I remind him of his birthday and the partying we'll do. Those not yet living here, those still in Portland, will come out to celebrate, I remind him. But he replies that it will sadden him because they cannot stay in Aurora Mills as we have insufficient housing. He wants the next group of Bethelites to come out, and yet where would they stay? More here in our house, I suspect. As Helena is. I asked my husband once if this might not have been the dilemma Christian Giesy and the scouts faced. He sat silent for a long time, his eyes closed, and I thought he might have fallen asleep. Instead he said, "I might have been too hard on those good people. Perhaps I should tell them so. Maybe they might even now come here to help us out if I expressed more sorrow."

An apology? From my husband? I would not have thought of it, but he is so wise! It has good merit. The Giesy family supported him in Bethel. Andrew Giesy Jr. runs the colony in Bethel with David Wagner's help until August arrives. I think my husband longs for such an alliance here and might have had it with Christian if not for Emma's forcing those families to stay in Willapa. I wonder if she carries guilt in that, her husband dying on a bay they had the chance to leave but didn't.

Perhaps that is too harsh. I carry no less a weight wondering if I might have done something different that would have saved our Willie. But no. I have come to believe that death is unrelated to the choices others make. I wouldn't say that to my husband.

Now Emma forces no one to do anything as far as I can tell. So they ought to come here, those Giesys. And Karl Ruge. Why hasn't he joined us, my husband's oldest friend? Karl wrote the letters back to Bethel, dictated by my husband, and I think his good mind added well to my husband's thinking. He should be here. His presence would so help my husband with his trials. And if Martin Giesy came, he could treat the people that my husband has to heal now, in the midst of everything else he's asked to do. He is becoming known for his healing, and even newcomers from Portland make their way here for his herbs and concoctions. So in the midst of business dealings, to serve us all, he stops to heal a small child or offer a salve to a man whose wound weeps. Martin could help immensely in Aurora.

Jack Giesy, too, that man of impractical cheer, he would lighten our days if he lived here. What keeps him in that Willapa country anyway? All the dairy cows, all the farmland, all of that work could be put in place here, near Aurora Mills, and we would join together again as we lived in Bethel. All of us except Willie. And Chris.

Well, I believe I have just uncovered the solution to my husband's strains. If the Bethel people cannot come west sooner as planned, then why not join together those who are already here, who had once planned to be a part of this colony under my husband's leadership? John has leadership abilities. He's the school superintendent there in Willapa. We don't even have a school here as yet. So much would be better if they lived with us. Even with Emma. I must write to John's wife, to Sebastian's wife, to Barbara, to remind them of what they once planned to do and let them know how much we need them, how much Wilhelm needs them. It would be the Diamond Rule if they came to make his life better than theirs. And they could see their daughter too.

Ja, that's what I'll do, write to the women. Paul himself wrote to women who worked beside him in the church. *Ach.* Not that I compare myself to Saint Paul, but women had work then as we do now. Those in Willapa have proven they can endure in difficult times. Now they must prove that they are one of us still. It is time for all God's children to come home. A mother understands that call. "And again, I will put my trust in him. And again, Behold, I, and the children which God hath given me." So says Paul as he writes to the Hebrews. It is a wife's duty to address her husband's needs and to hope those around her will understand how much more they can carry together than alone.

My husband might object.

If he knew.

But I would write as one communal wife to another, a coworker in the service. The women will see the value in our joining up. I will even write to Emma, for all the good it will do. But no one should be left out. All should be called to come home. My husband might even consider me a saint like Helena should I succeed. *Ach,* no. My husband would say that a mother cannot be a saint. She has no time.

21

Emma

Cheers, and Smart You Are!

I shook my head at Andy, wanting him not to approach too close. My throat felt coated by slivers of glass that ground against each other each time I swallowed. My skin ached to the touch. The winter season might have drifted further into hope but it didn't. When I found myself too weak to milk the goat, I sent Andy to Mary's. The child protested, saying he could milk the goat; he could fix our meals and tend me. But he went, returning with Jack and Boshie.

"We'll take the boys to their grandparents and I'll bring Martin back to doctor you," Boshie said. My face flamed from fever. I hadn't considered that suggestion, but fearful as it was, it held merit. I pointed to Kate, but Boshie shook his head. "Kate's of an age she can help bring you water to sip."

"Please," I croaked. "I don't want any of them ill."

"I'll stay to look after Emma," Jack told him. "Take them all. Kate's small. She'll not take up anymore room than the boys."

"She's little. But you here—"

"The widow is ill and in need of care," Jack said. "I'll stay only until the women come to help."

Jack helped the boys find whatever they'd need to take with them. He hurried Kate along as she looked for her stocking doll and nearly had to leave without it, but Andy located it up in the loft. Andy scowled the whole time.

I watched the movements around me as though in a dream, my throat a cave of broken glass, swollen, my eyes throbbing with pain. What might it take for me to get the children to return when I was well? I couldn't begin to imagine. I pitched the thought away.

They left and Jack proved the perfect helpmate, heating tea, helping me sit up and holding the cup to my lips. I knew the women were all busy, had children and families of their own to take care of, but I would have liked to hear the sound of a woman's voice. I would have liked to have a woman help me to the slop jar and settle me on it rather than Jack Giesy just before he turned his back. Oh, he did step behind the curtain. But the sounds one's body makes embarrasses in the presence of others, especially men. A woman would understand.

"Could your sister Louisa come?" I asked Martin when he arrived.

He shook his head. "She looks after the children and is a big help to Mother, don't you know."

He looked at me with sympathetic eyes though, and the next day, when Sarah Woodard arrived, I knew without asking who had suggested she come.

"You should have sent word to me right away," Sarah said.

"Didn't want...to bother," I said.

"*Ach,*" she said and pushed the air with her hand. She grinned. "Now I'm sounding like you!"

Jack came in with an armload of fire logs, and he startled when he saw Sarah. "What are you doing here?" he asked.

"Martin thought I might be able to help," she said. She placed the board Edwin was in onto the rocking chair, then put a stick beneath the rockers to keep it from moving and possibly pitching the baby out. "I'm to let you go, Jack Giesy, though Martin says you've been quite the good doctor for Emma."

"Does he?" He hadn't put the logs down next to the fireplace. "We really don't need any extra help."

"I'm enjoying...Sarah's visit, Jack," I said. My throat pain had lessened, but now I barked like a sea lion. No one could speak while I hacked. "She's my friend."

"She maybe could infect her baby," Jack said.

"As I feed him from myself, he stays healthy. I won't let Emma hold him." Jack scowled. *What is going on with Jack?* "I brought mail for you too," she said digging into her pack. "It came to Woodard's Landing just this morning. I bet it's the fastest mail service you've ever had out here."

I nodded and lifted my hand for the mail, but Jack reached past me, his long arm taking the letters from Sarah's fingers. "She can read them later," he said. "No sense wasting reading time while you have a guest." He pushed the letters into his shirt blouse before I even got to see who they were from.

"Jack—"

"At least one is from someone in Bethel," Sarah said. "And I think the other was from Aurora Mills. Oh, and one from far away in France."

"A cousin," I said.

Jack's proprietary manner bothered me. Maybe he felt I owed him that liberty for the care he'd been providing. Once again I could see how receiving a gift came riding on that horse as obligation. I had no energy to push it off.

Jack fed the fire, and when I motioned to Sarah to help me move to the slop jar, he rose from his squat to assist. "No," I croaked. "Let Sarah, please."

"She's as small as you are," he said.

"I'm small but I'm strong," Sarah chirped. "It's a woman's prerogative to have a sister assist her with her hygiene needs. A gentleman like you should know that."

"*Ja.* Well, I do know that," Jack said, backing off. "But don't come crying to me if she pulls you over." He turned his back to us and poked at the fire.

Sarah winked at me, then put her arm around my shoulder to help lift me up. My head spun with light spots, but I steadied myself on her arm as we took the few steps to the end of the bed, then pulled the curtain that separated the bed and slop jar from the main part of the cabin. The porcelain felt cool against my buttocks. I panted a bit to catch my breath, lowered my head. "Are you all right?" she whispered. I nodded. She rubbed my back in small circles, and when a wracking cough came on me, she squatted and held me with both arms. "I hope Martin's bringing you good teas," she said. I nodded. "He's a little worried that you haven't made the gains he thought you might by now," she added. "Especially when you've been getting such good care."

"A stubborn cough," I said.

"Are you finished?" I nodded but as she went to help me up I put my hand to hers to stop her.

"Let's just sit here for a moment," I said. "A moment…alone." She nodded understanding. "Have you seen the children? Jack tells me so little."

"They are all well. Rosy and happy."

I coughed. "Whatever this is, they might have missed it then."

"You did the right thing."

"How long can you stay?"

"A couple of days. But then one of the Schwader girls will come. And I've arranged for Louisa to help while I look after your children. Barbara, John's wife, will come. Each will spend a night so you won't be alone and before long, you'll be well."

"So Jack can leave."

She nodded. "If you weren't so sick, people would already be talking. But we do what we must, *ja*? See, I speak some German now." She smiled.

"*Ja*." She helped me stand. "Will you tell him?"

"I will," Sarah said.

I took a deep breath. It exhaled as a sigh of relief.

Jack left begrudgingly. I suppose he enjoyed knowing where he'd be each night, and he'd been helpful. But with him gone I did feel as though my strength returned. The women took their turns with me. Each was gracious and gentle, careful not to let me think they didn't want to be there. They had their own families to care for, and who knew how contagious I might be? I was grateful that they stoked the fires, kneaded the dough, gathered eggs. At the lamplight they stitched and we talked as my throat improved and the coughing faded, and time passed as gently as a feather drifting in the breeze. I felt like one of them, as though perhaps Christian's family really was my own. The families were the most gracious when someone was in need, real need, they would have said, not need resulting from one's willful choices. They each showed a charitable spirit that was always there, but I'd never acknowledged it before. I made a point of saying thank you.

When Mary took her turn, Boshie brought Salome to her for nursing, then took the baby back home. I appreciated this extra effort and told them both so.

She shrugged. "We take care of each other, *ja?*"

I nodded. "Have you talked to Jack of late?"

"Ah, a little interest?"

"Not the way you think. When Sarah was here, he received my mail from her and I can't find the letters anywhere. He must have forgotten to leave them. Could you ask him for them? I think one was from my parents and one came from Aurora Mills."

"Perhaps your brother tells you that Dr. Keil struggles with many responsibilities and needs the Bethelites to come out to help, but they're not ready. They're being tardy." She smiled as she stitched. "Like recalcitrant children."

"Things aren't all perfection under *Herr* Keil's direction?"

"No need for sarcasm," she said. "He's sent August back to help your father and Andrew Jr. move things along so everyone can join them soon. Even some of the Portland people haven't gone out to Aurora Mills yet. They like earning wages and having a little spending money for themselves, I guess." She stopped her work to spread butter on a piece of bread that Louisa had made the day before. "I heard that even Joe Knight quit the oyster business and headed back to Bethel."

Hearing that made me sad. One more connection with Christian was broken and Joe hadn't even stopped to say good-bye. "What about Karl's investment?"

She shrugged. "I think Karl lost interest once Christian wasn't involved. He was never drawn to the rough and tumble of keeping the oyster claims guarded or tonging for oysters in the moonlight. Jack liked that pace, at least sometimes. He can stay up all night, that Jack. Karl has the school and that's his first love. He'll get some of his money back if he sells his interest. Who knows, maybe Jack will buy him out."

"Jack has money to invest?" I said.

"He doesn't have much to spend his money on except rum now and then."

"I guess I thought everyone put their earnings into a common fund, so there'd be little room for private investment."

"Not all of it," she said. "Here, we own our land, just like you do, Emma. But we're sharing the increase of the cows, and putting a portion of the butter money into the common fund and keeping some to use as we see fit. This new territory demands that we invest but still work together."

She sounded like Boshie when she said that last.

"I don't recall receiving any money from my work with the butter contracts," I said.

She stood up and busied herself at the pantry, wiping the breadcrumbs into the palm of her hand. "I'll just throw these out to the birds," she said. She stepped to the door. It took her a long time. I guess she watched the seagulls swoop down to get them. Finally, she came back in.

"Mary. Are some people receiving private pay for their labor and able to keep some to invest for themselves and others not?"

"Maybe people thought that because the men tend to your stock and your firewood and look after things as you're a widow, well maybe they thought your share of any increase would be better spread around to those who've been helping you."

I felt my face burn.

"Or maybe they're setting your share aside for your children's needs. For when they might want to go to school. That would meet with your approval, wouldn't it?"

"What difference does my approval make?" I said. "My decisions appear to need filtering by what others think, so I rarely get the chance to make them."

"Oh, Emma. You make it sound so dramatic. We welcome your opinions. Decisions just have to be made whether you're around to hear about them or not. It's not a woman's place to worry over such things anyway. You should be grateful you have so few worries. Think of poor Brother Keil."

———

Decisions. Which ones did I have left to make? I could decide when my children came back home to me and set the date as Christian's April birthday. I'd force myself to be well and able to do for my own family. Though I was still weak, I had the Schwader girl, who was staying with me last, saddle her mule and then asked her to take me to the Willapa stockade and to the Giesys and my children.

Andy ran in from the river when he saw us approach. Kate jumped off a stump she'd been standing on, and even Christian waddled to me. I could not describe the joy I felt at seeing them and having them run toward me, wiping away the fear that separation might make them wish I'd never come.

I slipped from the mule, caught my balance with a lightheadedness. Then I took steps toward them as they threw their arms around me. My children, back in my arms.

"You don't look too well yet," Barbara said when I stood, my knees like *Spätzel*. I used Andy's shoulder for steadying. "Martin, look at her eyes. They're sticky, *ja*?" I sneezed, and instead of the German phrase that meant "God bless you," she said in Swiss-German, "Health to you. Cheers, and smart you are!"

"I don't feel so smart as all that," I said. "It's just the spring foliage making my nose itch."

"Still, you shouldn't push too hard."

"It's Christian's birthday, and I'm here to celebrate and take them home."

"Oh, I don't think that will be a good idea," Andreas said. "School starts just this next week and you don't want to go through what you did last fall, pushing yourself to get Andy here. That might even be why you're so ill now. You're a pretty fragile soul, Emma Giesy."

"I gave birth to that boy in the wilderness, so I'm anything but fragile."

I'd expected resistance, but I hadn't thought about school starting or how I'd counter that. He was right: I couldn't maintain the pace of last fall. At least not for a while yet.

"I think Andy's old enough to ride the mule," I said. "If you'll make the loan of Fritz to me."

Andreas tapped his fingers on his cane. Martin stood beside him in silence. Barbara said, "We'll be in need of the mules for the spring seeding. Andy would have to walk all that way by himself. You wouldn't want that."

"I saw bear tracks this past week, big as washtubs," Andreas said. "Just through the school term. You take Christian and Kate. They'll be handful enough for you while you're healing. Have you even spent a night without help since you took ill?"

They redefined every human foible into weakness. I didn't have a mule to call my own, but that was to help me out so I wouldn't have to winter him. I had no cows, but that was so I wouldn't have to be troubled to milk them nor someone else be forced to come by to do the same. If I became ill, well, it must be because I overworked—but how could that be when I did so little? Everyone else did it all for me. Other people got sick. Andreas needed a cane. Mary caught a cold, though I suppose even that was my fault. Even my effort to meet the butter contracts were considered insufficient compared to what everyone else already provided for me. I wasn't holding my own, and now my son would have to struggle to get back and forth to school because of my self-ishness, my need to be in charge of my own family. That's what they were saying.

A fire roiled inside of me. My fingers moved in their circles, so I hid them in fists.

"Andy," I said. "Your grandfather's right. You'll be better off staying here through the school term."

"But—"

"I'll come back for you. You're not to worry."

"Can I come home when we don't have school?" His eyes pooled with tears. One slid down the side of his face and he brushed at it. "Can I come home on the day before Sabbath? And come back when you come to worship?"

"I don't see why not," I said.

"Such a long way to go for just one day," Barbara said.

"*Ja*, it is. But sometimes being home for even a little while, where he can play with his brother and sister, sometimes that struggle is worth it."

"I'll bring him to you," Martin said. "So you won't have to worry about the bears or whatnot, and you without a mule."

"That's generous of you, Martin," Andreas said. "With my mule and fieldwork time."

"Consider it part of my contribution to tending widows and children," Martin said. He sounded a little testy, something I'd never heard before. "That's what we're doing all this work for, isn't it? To be of help to each other?"

"*Ja*, you're right. I shouldn't have talked so," Andreas said. He patted Martin's arm, seeking forgiveness.

I finished the afternoon holding my children while from time to time they ran to play with the others. They always came back to check on me as though I were part of a game and served as home base. I longed to leave, to take Kate and Christian, but that also meant less time with Andy. I barely heard the conversations going on around me. I was not a part of this community, not a part of the Giesy family, not in the way Christian once imagined we'd be. If he had lived, it would have been different, but he hadn't. It was time that I accepted that.

I sneezed again and Barbara said, "Cheers, and smart you are!" It wasn't a blessing. It was a challenge and a charge.

If I was ever to have control over my children and my life, I needed to get smart.

It was July before Andy came back home to stay. Martin had brought him once or twice on the weekends as he'd offered. His father's quick retort to him on Christian's birthday made me think that Martin might be longing for something more in his life too. He was a fine healer and I'd never imagined him as one who would toil the earth to make his living, or should I say his contribution. I hadn't realized until that day that he probably took care of his father, as the elder Giesy had deteriorated with both age and the grinding of his bones. Andreas needed help to stand and sit. Barbara seemed healthy and strong, but who knew what aches and pains she might seek remedy for when others weren't about. Louisa, their youngest, was nineteen now and like my sister Catherine, I assumed she hoped to find a mate. Instead, she too looked after her parents, cooked and cleaned for them and her brothers, and Karl Ruge during the school term, and now my son too. Helena might have assisted had she not chosen Keil over her father.

Louisa was a good girl, though I didn't think she took much interest in the almanacs or books, and that saddened me. I wanted Andy to be enthused by stories and not just focused on the work of learning. If he wanted to one day be a doctor, he'd be filled with science and medicine and studies far beyond anything I could ever help him with. But he'd be a complete man, one able to come up with solutions to problems no one else could if he matched his scientific mind with art and music and stories. The arts were the keys to imagination's door. Louisa didn't have much imagination. She'd been a silent caregiver the nights she spent with me and went to bed before the sun had even set. Perhaps she longed for rest the most: rest was her key to survival.

I knew the fall school term would begin after harvest and Andy'd go back to school, back to Andreas and Barbara's. Andy knew it too. One evening while we sat beneath the cedar tree taking in a cooling breeze before the mosquitoes came to call, he asked, "Isn't there any way I could stay here with you, Mama, and still go to school?"

"You are with me." I hugged him. "Look what a fine artist you're becoming. I believe that's a woodpecker you've drawn."

He tapped the pencil lead against his lip and I saw myself in that behavior. "Couldn't you come live with *Opa* and *Oma* while I'm in school? I miss you so very much."

"There are just too many people there already, Andy. And we have Opal to care for here. I know it's hard, I do. The shape of the bird you've drawn is perfect. Have you been practicing?"

"*Opa* says drawing is a useless thing," he said. He tapped the lead against his lip. "He says Jack wastes his time with pencils. He doesn't want me to draw things when I'm there."

"But music is fine. The men's band, that's fine, but not art?"

Andy looked confused at my outburst. "He says I need to have a man to influence me."

"Oh, does he?" Yet Jack Giesy's influence would be with the arts, and Andreas disapproved of that.

"With Papa gone I don't have that," he said. "That's the real reason *Opa* wants me to stay with them. Because I don't have a papa anymore."

"Smart you are," I said under my breath. They could claim they kept Andy due to my health or the distance or Andy's young age or the lack of a ready mule. They could say whatever they wanted, but my son was right about the cause of their attention. I sneezed and Andy said in Swiss, "Cheers, and smart you are, Mama."

I knew in that instant just what I needed to do.

———

It was three years and one month from the date of my husband's death when I sought out Jack Giesy with a purpose. It took me several days to find out where he was, and I did that searching on my own so as not to start rumors before they were facts. I couldn't ask many questions. I used the pretense that I looked for my letters and wondered if Jack still had them.

A part of me dreaded what I had to do, as Jack would see it as a win. He'd made an offer that sounded like a business proposition and I'd declined, because I didn't want my life to be a business arrangement but more because marriage had not been in my envisioned future. But neither had becoming a widow. Things changed. One had to decide what one cherished and what was subject to transformation.

I'd decided not to kindle my own fire but begin to depend on someone else. And I'd be able to tell my sister Catherine all about Jack Giesy now, so she could stop wondering. I felt a tiny twinge of guilt when I thought of my sister and her interest in Jack Giesy, but hers was a girlish longing and it would pass.

Jack must be staying at the mill. I had the children with me as we pushed a wheeled cart there. I pulled the bar and the children pushed and we stumbled over the tree roots out onto the trail, then picked our way through the forest road. We made a terrible racket, which was good. It would keep the bears and mountain lions away.

When the mill came into view Christian looked up in awe. "So big," he said. He rode inside the cart and tried to stand up. I motioned him to remain seated.

"You haven't been here before, have you? Your papa helped build this mill." It offered a kind of peace as I remembered the vista I'd seen from the upper windows. A new perspective, that's what the mill represented. I noticed unused redwood lumber stacked beside the mill and a thought came to me in seeing them. I'd ask Boshie if I could have a few of the boards to add something new to my home.

"Mama?" Andy asked, touching my hand. I blinked and gave attention back to my children. We went inside and I signaled that the children stay close to me as the big stones ground nosily away. I found Boshie and asked if he could help load our cart with two sacks. He scolded me, saying he would have brought flour by, that it wasn't necessary for me to come all that way and to bring the children too.

"I was looking for Jack," I said. He raised one eyebrow. "He has some letters of mine that he forgot to deliver."

"Ah. Well, he isn't here now. There was talk that he might go back to Bethel. They're having trouble getting things ready to come west, and people are worried about a war there."

This had not occurred to me, that he might go back to Bethel. His offer might not even be an option any longer. I blinked several times in my thinking.

Maybe I should talk with Martin. He was kind and generous, and perhaps he'd like moving into a cabin some distance from the demands of his parents and brother. Or maybe Karl Ruge. Why didn't I consider Karl as a mate? He could meet the criteria that my in-laws might require, perhaps even better than Jack Giesy "maybe could."

So calculating I was. So…pragmatic. *Herr* Keil would be proud of my practical process; it was so much like his own.

"If you see Jack, tell him I'm looking for those letters, will you?"

Only Jack had made an offer. Only Jack demonstrated a willingness to take another step with me. Was it a step into a calm or into a storm? That I didn't know.

———

I looked at him anew and saw the bigness of him. He must have been working in the forests felling trees, or maybe he'd been building boats again. His neck and arms were well-muscled. He was tan and he walked purposeful as a mule heading back to his barn. I was outside using a drawknife against one of the redwood boards Boshie had given me.

"I hear you're looking for your letters." He removed his hat, then slapped at his thighs with it, leaving dust motes in the air. "When Boshie said you'd asked about them, I checked my pack and there they were. Imagine."

I put the drawknife down and brushed my skirt of the wood curls, then put my hand out. He held the letters just above my reach. "I didn't even open them," he teased. He sniffed them. "Don't smell of perfumes, so they're from men."

"Aside from my family, there are no men who would be writing to me," I said.

"Pity." He continued to keep the letters above my head. I could see that the seals had been opened and then pressed back but not tight. He'd read them all right.

"Jack. Please," I said.

"Oh, look at that lower lip pooch out like your Kate's."

"I like you better when you talk to me without the teasing or jockeying," I said. He kept his hand raised. I sighed. "Fine," I said. "I guess you can carry

them around for another five months. I'm sure it's old news by now anyway."
I turned to go back into the cabin.

"Can't you take a little teasing, always so serious?"

"If you didn't come over here to give me the letters, why did you come?"

"For entertainment," he said. "I haven't had much of that in the woods."

"I hate to disappoint you then," I said. I held his stare. "You're like some schoolyard bully having his way." I crossed my arms over my chest, feeling like my mother. She used to do that, cross her arms and tap her fingers when her children behaved badly. "It occurs to me," I said as I tapped my own fingers at the elbows, "that some men like to be treated as though they were children. Are you one of them, Jack Giesy?"

He took one quick step toward me and slapped the letters against my shoulder. "Here," he said, holding them like they were a glove and he'd just challenged me to a duel. "Take 'em, fine lady." He used a deep Missouri drawl, exaggerating the *a* in *lady,* but he let me take the letters.

"Thank you. That's better. Now, would you like some tea?"

He raised an eyebrow in surprise. "You're not setting me in the corner with a dunce hat on?"

"Oh, Jack."

"I'll take some tea. Maybe there'll be something entertaining happening here after all."

———

Oh, I can see now the complications I ought to have seen then, but I held fast to just one point of view, one perspective, and it wasn't of the divine. I had one direction I thought that I could take, as I did when I felt compelled to go west with Christian, when I didn't tell him that I carried his child, didn't advise him that I'd already met with Keil and pushed my agenda. This time I'd considered other options, though not a one of them would work.

This was the only real out, this alignment with Jack Giesy, whose marriage to me would grant me a level of independence from the Giesy family of my husband. More, it promised the presence of my sons.

I told Jack that. Looking back, the explanation might have been an error in judgment, but I wanted to be as honest with him as I could be about our arrangement.

"And what would be in this for me?" he asked.

"You'd get the land," I said. "Once married, it would be yours, of course."

"You'd give it up just to have your boys living with you?"

"I'd have no choice. The law would say it was yours, my husband's. And yes. I think that's what Christian would want."

He held a small oyster shell the size of Kate's little palm and just as pale. He plopped it back and forth between the palms of his hands. "Look at this." He motioned Andy to come to him. "See that little tiny hole? That's from a drill, a little snail that attaches itself to the oyster and drills right down through the shell to suck out the meat."

"I know. My papa showed me," Andy said.

"*Ja?* Did he tell you to watch out for them?" Andy shook his head. "They look harmless and they're so small you wouldn't think they could cause any problems to a shell as hard as an oyster's is, but they do. Worse than starfish." He handed the shell to Andy, who took it to Kate and Christian for further study. Jack turned back to me.

"And I'm to assume you want this relationship to be what, like brother and sister then?"

"That would be my preference."

"It isn't mine," he said.

"Unless there's comfort that moves in or lights a spark."

"Such already exists for me," he said. "And it's a woman's duty if she weds."

"I know. But you can understand, can't you? I mean, you did make the offer some time back and were willing then to make a go of it without apparent care if I returned affection for you or not. You've spent a little time in my presence, and though I was ill you were willing to stay with me, to take care of me. It wasn't so bad then, was it, just being in the same place together, making things work?"

"The way this maybe could work is if we try to make it a true marriage."

Oh, I should have prayed then. I should have prayed that if this was my own doing and not God's, that He please get my attention, make me know and tell me whether I was smart here or not, taking some action that I'd later say was wasted. I should have prayed that my sons would be well tended no matter where they lived, that perhaps my being in their lives was not the most important thing for them. I should have begged for God to show me the path so that I might act according to God's plan. That's what I should have prayed.

But I'd stopped praying. And as with the spring rains that forced me to make new paths, that's what I was about. I was a woman of new walkways. A verse from Job drifted into my thoughts: "But He knoweth the way that I take: *when* He hath tried me, I shall come forth as gold." I'd never cared much for the emphasis placed on the word *when*. I'd had enough trials.

"A man has needs," Jack said. "It's a condition of this arrangement."

"If that's the only way this will happen," I told him, "I'll meet them."

22

Emma

On Reflection

I silenced all the cautionary voices that woke me in the nights before I did it. I listed what I'd tried that had not worked and got as smart as I could about what truly mattered in my life.

Drawing could not be my exodus. It was silly to believe a little picture could turn into something grand enough to support me and my children. My parents were not coming to rescue me. I couldn't go to Aurora Mills and be forced to live side-by-side with the man whom I held accountable for all my miseries, even though Jonathan had once invited me there. My efforts to remain on the Willapa and work toward the common fund would never earn me a place among Christian's family; worse, it wouldn't be enough to keep my children with me. Each spring I'd be fighting family just to have time with my son—my *sons,* as soon they'd worry over their youngest grandson's upbringing. As long as I was a widow with male children to raise, my in-laws would seek to "protect" them from unseemly influences. They didn't mind that Kate was under my thumb.

What mattered most to me was *my* influence in my children's lives, *my* presence to nurture them and hand down to them the values of their father and me. Being able to do that required desperate action.

Jack left after we struck our bargain, and I then read the letters that made me ache all the more. A cousin spoke of the good life in France. The one from my sister advised me to confess sins I didn't know about and reminded me of the dreariness that life would hold for me back in Bethel if I returned, once again a daughter living with her parents. Bethelites wouldn't build me a home there, not ever. I learned of my sister Lou's accident and the new worries she brought to my parents' lives. They'd never come west now, that was certain. They had new demands to care for their own family. I could understand that.

From Aurora Mills came a letter from my brother with news that he would head back to Bethel in the spring. He was likely already there. His absence just affirmed my need to do what I did.

———

All three children were to stay with my in-laws for the week of our marriage. "You're going visiting?" Barbara asked.

I took a deep breath. "No, Jack Giesy and I are getting married."

"Well, well," Andreas said. "What does Wilhelm have to say to that?"

"We didn't ask his permission," I said. "There was no need."

"You should marry here then," Barbara said. "Let us have the family around you as you make this change." She smiled. "We can have the band play. A party."

Martin came in while I talked to his parents, and I felt discomfort, as though I was doing something childish and resisted being caught.

"We'll need to transfer the land titles and things in Olympia anyway," I said. "We'll go to Steilacoom too. I have good memories there, of where Andy was born."

"A waste of time lamenting over old memories," Andreas said. "But we always like the boys to visit so they can stay."

He rarely mentions Kate.

"Don't let Big Jack get you into any trouble now," he added. "Get him too close to rum and he becomes another man." He tapped his cane.

"He hasn't done much like that of late now, has he?" Barbara said. "He's a good boy." She clucked her tongue at her husband.

"Kate's looking a little bit peaked," Barbara said the day Jack and I left for Olympia. "I wonder if you shouldn't take her with you. Andreas is fragile these days. He just got over a bad cold."

Andreas did look frail with his watery eyes. Dark reddish spots covered his face and the backs of his hands. "Whatever will work best for you. We'll take Kate along."

"Not possible," Jack said. "We can't be hauling a child around all that way. Wouldn't be good for her."

"I'll ask Sarah then," I said, and she was pleased to watch my daughter when I said I was going to Olympia. "Are you going to take the paintings to show around at last?"

"Shh. No," I silenced her. Jack stood talking with Sam outside. "No more talk about paintings or drawings except for fun, for pleasure. I've other issues to tend to there."

"I didn't mean to pry," she said.

"*Ach*, I know. I'm just nervous." She looked quizzically at me. "I'm going to Steilacoom to get married to Jack Giesy."

"When did this all happen?"

"It didn't happen in the way you think. It's an…arrangement. So that I can have my sons with me and the family will see that I have a man to help me. I'll stop being the Widow Giesy, stop being a burden. Most of all, we'll stop these months of separation when Andy isn't living with me. And I'll have a plan for Kate and Christian, too, when he's of school age."

"Oh, Emma, do you think that's the best way? Wouldn't it be better to go back to Bethel with your parents? Maybe go to that Aurora place where people live a little more closely together so the boys could stay with you and still go to school?"

I shook my head. "There'll always be this tension with the Giesys, this idea that without a father I'm not properly raising my sons. And I can't go to Aurora Mills, I just can't. It would be betraying Christian, and worse, I'd have to live with the gloating of Keil if I threw myself on the colony's mercy."

"Marriage is such a drastic step to take without even love in it to help see you through."

"This is my help. I'm taking care of things myself. I'm getting married."

"I'd always seen Jack as a bachelor," she said. "He has his own ways, seems to like to come and go, work at odd jobs here and there. The artistic person who can be flighty, maybe."

"We both love to draw," I said. "We'll be a perfect match then."

"I guess that is a tie… Does he like your work?"

"He doesn't know of my *work*. I've never told him or shown him. But I like you calling it a tie. It reminds me of that verse my mother always said. 'Begin to weave; God provides the thread.'"

"I hope this is God's thread, Emma, and not just a badly tied knot. I really do."

———

I knew there was a church in Steilacoom and somehow I thought that being married inside it would cover my less-than-sacramental motives for being there. I could have asked Karl Ruge to officiate and wed us in Willapa. Karl was a dear soul, but I guess I knew even then that he held me in a special place in his heart. I hoped that marrying Jack wouldn't tarnish that. I couldn't bear to hear him read the vows to us when this was a loveless marriage I was vowing to uphold forever.

Jack behaved as the perfect companion on the mule-riding journey. The trail across required chopping of overgrowth and he tended to that with ease. He smiled, made light little jokes, and looked like a happy groom-to-be. We met no one on the trail and had to sleep out for three nights in our tent. We talked easily together. He said kind things about the food I'd prepared and brought along. He made no demands. I wondered for just a moment if perhaps this might work out. Two adults looking after children, making decisions to affect the little ones' futures without harming their own.

We reached Olympia and in conversation, mostly Jack's, as his English was still much better than mine, we learned that the church in Steilacoom was Catholic and the priest traveled greatly. Even if he had been there, he wouldn't have married us outside his faith.

"We'll marry here, then," Jack said. "Find a JP."

My heart twinged with the memory of Christian's role as a justice of the peace.

"Can we still go to Steilacoom?" I said.

"What for?"

"Maybe a judge there could marry us. It's where Andy was born. I just want to walk there, to look at Puget Sound again."

"You can see the water right here."

"Please."

He hesitated. "Let's marry now then. Get a judge here. Tomorrow or the next day maybe we'll go to Steilacoom."

"That's a good compromise. See, we can work things out." I said it as much to convince myself as him.

The judge spoke the words to make our marriage legal though certainly not blessed. We moved next door to the land office, wrote the changes to transfer property. My hand shook when I signed the new documents. Christian's home, my home, was no longer mine.

We spent our wedding night in the same hotel Christian and I had stayed in when we'd first come west. Could that have only been seven years previous? A Chinese cook still shouted from the kitchen. In our room, the sheets smelled clean, and fresh water filled the pitcher. Thank goodness it was not the same room. Still, time had skipped across my life like a small stone across the Willapa. It had left its tracks: three children. I was doing this for them.

That night, to meet my wifely obligations, I sent my mind to the salty ocean sands that looked barren but gave birth to green grasses. I imagined the tides flowing in and out, washing away the choices that disappoint, leaving behind reminders of what I would cherish always: my sons, my daughter. All else didn't matter. One did what was necessary for what one cherished. That night in my mind, I was in the oyster beds at Bruceport, looking across to the shiny cobbled flats where the tide unveiled abundant oyster shells. I remembered a lantern light held high that showed me only as much as I needed to see: the oysters, hard shells harboring life inside. Oystermen watched over them to make sure the tiny snails didn't attach themselves and drill inside, sucking out the life from within. I was quite sure there was no one looking out for me. I'd have to do that myself.

———

Reluctantly, two days later, after we'd walked around Olympia, visited a boat-building site, looked at a furniture store but purchased nothing, Jack took me to Steilacoom. He described it as a puny town, but it had a territorial jail built the year after Christian died. There were blacksmith shops and stores and many more houses than when I'd been there before. I was sure I'd seen evidence of a sawmill or two, and a tailor shop opened its doors to the breeze beside a small hotel. A brewery sent smells into the air. It looked like a vigorous town to me. I loved being out in it after all these years. I wished we'd stayed here when we first arrived in the territory. Maybe Christian would still be alive. I pitched the thought aside.

I still marveled at the window boxes of the little houses and the wide-openness of a sea-lapping town. We walked. I carried a parasol and, near Gore Street, I stopped before the orchard that Nathaniel Orr and Phillip Keach had planted beside Orr's furniture store. "I remember this place," I said. Then farther up the hill I saw both the Catholic church and a Methodist Episcopal church. "We could have gotten married here," I said. "In the Methodist church."

"A judge was fine," Jack said. "Maybe could make no difference."

It was in Steilacoom though, in front of that old church, where I asked Jack to halt. The light was perfect, the air balmy. We'd weathered our first few days together with more hope than hassle.

"What now?" Jack removed his hat and brushed at the dust in irritation as I settled onto a stump.

"Just be patient," I said. I drew out some papers carried in my reticule, found the charcoal and began to sketch the town: the way the little houses marched up the sloping hillside away from the water; that wide, square building with its steeple spired into the blue sky. I was going to put us into the picture. I thought Jack would like that.

Jack frowned. "I didn't know you could draw," he said. "Did I know this about you?"

"It's just little sketches. I sometimes draw things in letters, do little portraits. I could draw you sometime if you'd like. I'll sketch you in right here." I smiled up at him. He grunted. "Oh. Well, as I said, they're not very good."

"All this time you never mentioned it."

"Wasn't important." I held the paper on my knees as I sat.

"Maybe could be you don't always know what's important," he said. His voice held a warning that I ignored. "Look at those pelicans," he said then, pointing. As I looked up he lifted the charcoal from my fingers, leaned over me, and began scribbling the birds in flight, making them fly right on top of what I'd sketched. They were morbidlike, his pelicans, as though from a bad dream, all dark with storm clouds around them with lines so heavy I could barely make out what I'd drawn beneath.

"Jack. Don't. Here, I'll give you another paper to draw them on."

"I'll draw where I like." He marked so hard the page tore.

"Jack." I grabbed at the charcoal. It broke. "*Ach.* Look at this now."

"Your pelicans have flown right off the page," he said. He laughed.

"So childish." I threw up my hands.

"Am I? Is that how you treat a husband? You stay here and draw then," he said. "I'll follow those birds toward that brewery we passed a while back."

"Jack, please. What's this about?"

"Jack, please," he mimicked. "I won't stay here to be whipped by a woman." He strode off. *Do I follow?* My fingers made nervous circles at the pads. I should have chosen another time to talk to him about my drawings. I should have never let him see my efforts at all. But I hadn't expected this kind of response. I wasn't in competition with him. I smoothed the paper. The hole was in the very center. Like the drill of a snail damaging the life of the picture. I folded what was left of it, picked up the broken charcoal pieces that had fallen when he'd ripped the paper. My reticule was full again but my heart was empty.

I raised my chin. I wouldn't be cowed by his childish behavior. Let him do what he wished; I'd do likewise.

Jack's behavior shouldn't have surprised me, but it did. He wasn't a man who tolerated equality. He always had to be above another. Frankly, his drawings were better than mine, so I saw no reason for him to be jealous, and that's what the behavior had looked like to me. A bit of jealousy over my simple sketches. I decided to let time do its healing. I walked the few miles out through the trees toward the fort, where Andy had been born. Later I'd reassure Jack that he was the better artist, and that we could put this spat behind us. Until then, I'd enjoy my day.

Like a town itself, the fort was much larger than before, with several more buildings and what looked like officers' quarters. Men hung laundry and others stood guard. The Yakima War of years back would have required greater troops here, which would account for the additional buildings. Or maybe they were readying for the war between the States that my sister Catherine wrote about. I walked along the split rails to where I'd taken the fall that Christian thought had brought on Andy's delivery. I looked for An-Gie, the Indian woman who had been so helpful to me, but I didn't see any other women, not even any officers' wives. I was a woman alone on my honeymoon.

I should return and see if I could find the brewery and Jack. *Honeymoon.* Where the sweetness waned, that's what Christian had said.

I bypassed the brewery and returned to the hotel. The waiter took me to a table without a second thought, which was gratifying indeed, me never being sure of my English. I wasn't sure of much these days. I ordered biscuits and tea and ate it in the dining room alone. People watch, that's what I did, saw how women dressed in this outside world and noted how my plain black dress stood out, my bonnet years out of fashion. The women all wore hoops to keep their skirts billowed out like tulip bulbs. I saw how men and women treated each other in public. I thought about what my next steps would be if my husband just walked away and left me here in Steilacoom. I'd go back and get my children. That would be the first step. I didn't have a second one.

"You're like a cat," Jack said. He startled me, having come into the dining room from a back way, spied me, then sat down across from me, his eyes glaring even as he sat. I slowly sipped my fourth cup of tea, keeping my hand steady. My heart pounded. *Do I bring up his absence or let him?*

"Like a cat...because I enjoy high places?"

"You always land on your feet."

I made myself smile. "Jack, you have your...interests. I have mine." He didn't smell of barley. Maybe he hadn't gone to the brewery after all. "I didn't tell you about my drawing because the pictures are so amateur. I certainly don't think they equal your own in any way."

He grunted. "When you're finished, I've something to show you."

He acted the proper husband in the presence of others. He ordered a coffee and I took my time with the tea. Finished, he pulled back my chair, then put out his arm so that I could take it as we walked. He took me up the street to a gift shop near the Sound. It was almost closing time. "They get imported things in here," he said. "I'll buy you anything you want. A wedding present."

"That's…not necessary, Jack."

"Maybe could be it is."

He urged me to look around, and the shopkeeper talked with him as though this wasn't the first time they'd met. He smiled at me, called me Missis.

Most of the wares looked European. There were German pewter candlesticks, silver bowls, and what looked like Italian pottery. Furniture from England or possibly back East sat nestled in the back of the cluttered store. Nothing practical to speak of, mostly luxury items for people who had others to do their work for them.

"These must be terribly expensive," I told Jack in German.

"Get a keepsake," he said. "It's what a husband does, *ja*, gives his wife something for their wedding?"

I thought of Christian's presents to me months after our marriage, brought back from his journey to the world outside: a ruffled petticoat that we later tore up to use as bandages in Willapa. He'd made a chatelaine for me to hold my sewing needles, and he'd given me a tiny Willapa Bay oyster pearl the year before he died, the most precious gift of all. None of them extravagances like those in this store.

"Look here, for now," Jack said, tapping on my shoulder as I stared. His words brought me back to the present. "Something to remember this occasion."

What was this occasion? Not a honeymoon, not sweetness hoping to return. Seek something practical, something to remind me that I did this for a reason, a good reason, the love of my children. What attracted me first was a plate, made up of six oyster-shaped wells to hold oysters on the half shell. A depression in the center would serve for a sauce. Someone had painted the outside edge and the center piece so it was like a work of art. The shop owner said it was French imported and the thin lip ledge was painted with gold. "This is lovely," I said. It made me think of my cousin in far away Honfleur, France.

"Shall I wrap it for the missis?" the shopkeeper asked.

"Not yet," Jack said, as he saw me set it down and pick up something else. "She's not one to easily make up her mind."

What won me was nothing practical at all. It was a single oyster shell, four or five inches across. I knew it couldn't be a Willapa oyster, as those I could hold in the palm of my hand. This would fill Jack's big paw. On the smooth inside, someone had painted what looked like an old mill beside a sea, using reds and rusts and purples. Mountains marched down to the water alongside the building.

"This is beautiful," I said. "I wonder who…?"

The owner shook his head. "Not signed. But it's a beauty. Wouldn't want to ever serve anything on it but rather hang it on the wall. Or maybe set it on an easel." He pointed to the little stand.

"Completely impractical," I said.

"Would you like it?" Jack asked.

"It must be very expensive."

"That's not the answer to my question."

"Ja," I said. "I would like it." I could sink into that scene.

Jack paid the storekeeper, and I received it as a gift from my husband, though I did wonder what price he might extract for my reception of it. I also wondered where he got the money. Perhaps the Willapa colony, knowing we were marrying, gave him resources. Maybe he did keep some of his earnings to spend as he saw fit just as everyone else appeared to do. When the census taker had come around in June, he'd mumbled something about my own assets being among the highest for the region, but that was the land, of course. I owned the land. *Had* owned the land. Having discretionary currency was a luxury a colony widow did not have, nor, apparently, did a wife.

I held the shell up to the window light to better see it. It might have been a scene from Spain or Portugal, judging from the terrain and the building's shape. Maybe one day I'd go to such a place of promised serenity. It would remind me that peacefulness existed somewhere along with security and calm. The mountains were treeless and the water looked almost transparent. Onto the water, the artist had painted a reflection of the mill and a small boathouse. Inside would be a boat. I could imagine that, a boat to take its owner back and forth to deliver items from the mill. A *tender,* I'd heard such transferring crafts called. I squinted, then gasped.

"What is it?" the shopkeeper asked. "Is it broken?"

"No, nothing," I said. "It's beautiful." I had seen in the reflection something I'd missed in the painting. I looked at it now with new eyes, my keepsake with a deeper meaning. The building wasn't a mill at all, it was a church. A tiny cross had been placed at the top, a cross I would have missed except that I'd seen it reflected in the water.

23

Emma

Flaming Fires

We married on a Sunday, the sixteenth, and returned to Willapa a week and a day later to collect the children and to tell any who didn't already know that we were now husband and wife. We stopped for Kate at Sarah's, who patted Edwin's bottom as she held him on her shoulder. *Does she wear a worried look?* Sam came in and took him from her easily, curling the child in his arms. He was a natural with the boy, as Christian had been. Jack was…fair with my children. He gave distinct orders laced with teaching instruction. Hadn't he explained the drills to Andy well? Gentle words came from him, except for the outburst over the drawing. He'd even made me laugh a time or two. The oyster painting was packed in my valise, a sign of his generosity and that he sought forgiveness with objects rather than words. We were compatible. I stuck tendrils of hope like wispy strands of hair into the braid of my life.

"Looks like Jack's ready to get on home," Sam said. "Declined my invitation to share a meal."

"He's anxious to have some say in the farming of my place. Our place."

"You've married Jack Giesy," Sam said. "Didn't know any courting had gone on. Guess I don't get as much news from you Germans as I thought."

I cleared my throat. "I told him about my drawings," I told Sarah cheerfully. "He wasn't pleased at first. But he adjusted." I picked up Kate's bag, held my daughter's hand in the other.

Sam smiled. "No wonder he's thinking of home."

"For the boys," I said. "That's who I did it for. So my in-laws will stop wondering about their future. Not much courting involved with that."

"A business arrangement, is it?" Sam said.

"*Ja*, I guess."

Sarah squeezed me when I left, whispering in my ear, "You'll have to give me details later."

"Jack'll be fine. A little volatile but that's an artist's prerogative, *ja?*"

I'm not sure what I expected from my in-laws. Were they still my in-laws? I hoped I'd see relief that in their minds at least, I was at last under someone's control. Perhaps joy if they thought our union had been brought about by a romantic inclination. Maybe Barbara would plan a party for us after all. Maybe John would authorize the stockade for such an event.

Andreas tapped his cane as we approached. "You don't even have to change your name, *Frau* Giesy. Very practical." He smiled.

Jack wore a cocky grin. Henry teased him about leaving bachelorhood behind. Barbara offered us something to eat, and Louisa, Christian's youngest sister, ran between her fingers the new bonnet ribbons Jack had let me buy. I did feel as though I'd been brought into a family circle of sorts.

After the pie, Jack said, "Get Christian. We should head home." My son Christian held a wood carving of a horse that I suspected Martin had made for him. I hadn't seen it before.

"*Ja, ja*," Andreas chided. "You'll want to be home a lot now that you have a bed already warmed up for you. Boshie will get you regular at the mill now too, and he won't need to keep that bed there for you." Andreas's laugh turned into a cough. Louisa patted her father's back and Martin said soft words to his mother. She nodded, looked away.

Andy had come into the room again. He'd welcomed us when we first arrived, then returned to help fill the wood box for his grandparents. He stood before me now, his hands on his hips, elbows out. "Jack says it's time to go," I told him. "We need to listen. Do you have your things?" He nod-ded. "Let's go then." He turned to get his bag.

"I said get Christian." Jack reached out to prevent Andy from getting his bag. "No need to have Andy come with us now."

"*Ja,* he wants time with his wife without big ears around," Andreas joked. Everyone laughed.

I looked up at him. "You're joking, *ja?*"

"School term is on. I'm sure Andy went to school today. I'll pick him up at the end of the week." He kept his voice light but I felt a tension there that none of the others seemed to notice.

"But...that was the point," I said. "Why—"

"Oh, their first argument," Henry joked. "You picked yourself a hot coal when you fired up Emma Giesy."

"I know how to manage fire," Jack said. To me he said, "I told you to get Christian. Come along, now. Wife." He patted my hand. "Kate's waiting and so am I."

"But you said—"

He put his hand behind his ear as though he needed a horn. "I can't hear you." I saw Andy flinch out of the corner of my eye. "You said we married so you'd have your boys and Andreas and Barbara here wouldn't have a hold on your sons."

"Jack!" I felt my face grow hot. "There's no need to—"

"That's why you married?" Barbara said. She set the pie plate back down at the table, clasped her hands in front of her. "Because you don't want us to have time with your children?"

"Of course I want you to have time with them. I want Andy to go to school, of course, but he's old enough to ride the mule each day during the term, and with Jack at home, he won't have to help with so many chores when he gets back each night, and if the weather is bad, Jack can take him to school. Jack and I can do the work there; we won't need to trouble the rest of you."

"I'm the hired hand, am I?" Jack said.

"Jack—"

"The owner of the land but a hired hand."

His voice had gone from snarl to a forced banter. I knew from the fire in his eyes that he fumed.

"I meant Andy'd have you to help influence him. In the evenings of the school term as well as weekends. There'll be less need for everyone else, Boshie and others, to come to help us and they won't have to worry about my son's future influences."

Martin shifted from side to side, glancing at the children. I wished he'd take them outside. Andy frowned and now Kate whined, "I'm hungry, Mama." Into her whining, Christian threw the wooden horse. It landed at my feet.

Quick as a snake, Jack grabbed Christian's hand. "You maybe could hurt someone." Christian's eyes were as big as a bear's paw and his lower lip slipped out. Kate whimpered. "You, young lady," he turned to Kate, hovered over her, "have no need to cry about what to eat. You eat well from the way I see it." Kate backed away from him, sniffed, then buried her head in my skirt. I picked her up.

"Jack, please. She's just a child."

"Jack, please," he mimicked.

Jack had provoked this for the audience, I suspected. He understood our agreement. I'd given him what he wanted. He needed to be reminded. He needed to treat us all with a little more respect, but I couldn't say that to him here. It would only enflame the smoldering rage, and I knew one should never feed a fire one wanted to go out.

"By golly, what do we have here?" Karl said. He must have been out walking or working late at the school. He stepped inside, a blend of welcome then confusion on his face.

"A little family spat," Jack said, his voice light again, joking.

"Let's just go," I said, my heart pounding. "I'll bring Andy back in the morning. We all need to be together now. Come along, boys." I didn't want

Andy wondering if he was to be left behind again. He'd already been through that. I turned Kate to me to wipe the tears from her face.

"Andy stays." Jack's words wore hardness of coal. "I'll collect him at the end of the week. It's been decided." He whisked my youngest son up into his arms, not in a gentle way, not in the way Sam had held his son nor as Christian had once lifted Andy. Christian leaned away from him and fidgeted, pushing against Jack's tight hold. "Stop it," he said. "Listen to me. Just listen to me." He shook him. My son looked like a terrified kitten held in the jaws of a dog. He stopped squirming. "Come, Wife."

"Wife?" Karl said.

"Wife, my old bachelor friend," Jack said. He slapped Karl on the shoulder as he passed.

"By golly." Karl looked at me. I couldn't describe the expression in his eyes.

"Auf Wiedersehen," Jack said, all cheery again. He waved to everyone, then meandered out of the room, shifting Christian onto his shoulders. Through the open door, I watched as he plopped Christian on the mule's back, then swung up behind him. "Are you coming, Wife?" He almost sang it.

"You'd better go, dear," Barbara said. "No sense in having a major feud. Andy'll be fine here. You'll see him at the end of the week." She actually sounded sympathetic but I couldn't be sure. I could never be sure.

My hands felt wet. Taking Andy out with me would enflame Jack more and make Andy the target. But to leave him…

I kissed Andy good-bye, held his slender shoulders against me for a moment, then left without my son.

———

We rode back in silence. I slipped Kate a piece of sausage, which offered her comfort. She remained quiet, taking her cue from me as she sat before me on

the other mule. At least I wasn't riding sidesaddle. At least Jack had succumbed to that little practice he obviously didn't approve of. That was a sign
he could change. This was a temporary outburst, a quirk of his character.
He'd calmed after the Olympia drawing fiasco, even became generous after-
wards. He'd do so again.

I thought about his tactics. He used an audience to his advantage, getting other people to help affirm his belligerent wishes maybe even *because* he
was belligerent. Like a school bully. He hadn't threatened force, really. His
abruptness with Christian concerned me; I didn't like how he'd silenced Kate.
But if I complained about it to Barbara, for example, she'd probably tell me
he was just being an attentive father, getting accustomed to his new role. Still,
he threatened in his quick movements, grabbing, moving close to a child's
face. It was a violation, though I couldn't describe why. My in-laws would
simply say children need to behave and I'd spoiled them. A child wasn't supposed to throw things; that was true, but the fright surely did not fit the
crime.

I wondered how Christian fared sitting in front of Jack. I couldn't see
him. I kicked the mule to ride beside them, to offer an encouraging smile to
my son.

Jack pressed his knees to the mule. They moved ahead. The trail narrowed and I wouldn't have been able to ride beside them for long anyway.
Was it the trail or was he excluding me? We crossed the river without incident, rounded the bend.

I'd always found comfort in the sight of my home and breathed a sigh of
relief that in my absence it had not gone up in flames. I'd never lost anything
to a fire as many had, and yet I always feared it. My home had been my refuge
since Christian's death. A warm hearth welcomed, though I knew that if one
wasn't diligent about putting sparks out, they could cause destruction instead.

Jack was unpredictable. Self-centered. I'd known that. But I hadn't
counted on his perfidiousness, nor had I ever seen it directed at my children

before. Being firm had always worked, even when we'd been alone. We were home now, on safe ground. I'd deal directly with him. Such men might pretend strength when underneath they felt weak. His offense at my little drawings back in Olympia supported that. Jealousy was an emotion rooted in insignificance. I needed to weed that out.

"I'll fix us something to eat, Jack," I said, riding up beside him as we came into the yard. The cows munched contentedly and the goat gave a perfunctory bleat, so I knew Boshie had been by and milked them. The chickens cackled from their tree branches, safe from predators for the night. "After the children are in bed we can talk."

"Nothing to talk about, Emma," he said.

"Well *ja,* there is. If this is going to work, we've got to talk things through. Andy's schooling is one of those things."

"Already decided," he said. "You made the right choice in following my directives."

"I wanted to avoid a scene," I said. "I complied though I didn't agree with you."

He laughed. "As if I care about why you did it. Just so you do what I say."

"Jack," I cajoled. "We really can't keep up a lifetime of your giving me orders without my having any say in them. I'll resist every time, and it'll fatigue you if nothing else. Make you old before your time." I gently poked his arm in play.

He grabbed my chin, surprising me. He held me, fingers firm. "I'm not worried about aging quickly," he said. "Though you might be."

He released me, pushed me away. Christian patted the mule's neck and when Jack told him to stop, the action was instantaneous. "Good boy," he said. Then, "That's the response I want from you, Emma, when I tell you something."

"You can't be serious," I told him. At least he was speaking to me in a civil voice. "I'm not ever going to sing every note in the tune you call."

He slipped off the mule, then lifted Christian to the ground. "You've got yourself a challenge, Emma Giesy, learning to sing the tunes I want you to play."

I felt sick to my stomach, even a bit dizzy as he led the mule away. It was the long trip, highs and lows staining each other, the washing of emotions, hope scrubbed now with anxiety and bleached by the uncertainty I'd placed us all in.

He fed the animals while I took the children into the house and started the cooking fire. The room smelled sour from being closed up for a week or more. Even the cedar shelves I'd made needed fresh air around them to renew their fine scent. Spiders flitted across the floor and a new web had been produced in the corner of the only window sill. I opened that window, wiped the stickiness of the web onto my apron. I left the door open to the outside and felt the breeze pull through. My hands shook.

But the children's delight in being home made me forget my discomforts for the moment. They ran around the cabin, bounced on the rope bed. Kate crawled underneath to find a wooden toy she'd been missing. Christian danced a little dance, his bare feet slapping on the floor.

By the time Jack came in, I had a stew going and added fresh vegetables from the garden. The carrots would take a bit to cook, but added to the onions and cabbage and potatoes, we'd soon have a hearty meal. I mixed up cornbread, aware that Jack pulled up a chair and sat at the table. I waited for him to speak, and when he didn't I told him I thought it would be a few minutes before the carrots were tender and the cornbread browned well.

"Take your time," he said. "I'm in no hurry."

"That's good," I said. "While things are finishing perhaps we could—"

"No mood for talking. You'll get used to my moods, but talking won't be a mood I'm in much."

I ladled the cornmeal onto the dutch oven top, slipped the pot close to the fire, then sat. "I'm confused, Jack. I thought we shared a number of interesting conversations over the past months about this and that. We had lovely dinners together in Olympia. We talked about the Pony Express making its first run from St. Joseph to Sacramento, how that would improve communication between us and those back in Bethel. We visited stores. We carried on as though we were two adults. Did I dream that? Did I just imagine that, Jack Giesy?"

"I'm a complicated man," he said, apparently forgetting that he had claimed otherwise not long ago. He leaned back in his chair, crossed his legs at the ankle, his arms over his chest. "Just the sort of challenge I would have thought the independent Emma Giesy would have liked." He grinned. I was heartened.

"I know we both need time to adjust to this…arrangement. But you seem so inflexible suddenly when before you'd been, well, congenial. Surprising, yes, but even your teasing stopped eventually. See, I've already put the painted shell up on the shelf." I pointed to the gift he'd bought me. "But this side of you, this…dare I use the word…this rigidness. Well, that's something I never saw reflected—"

"Don't know how to reign right now do you, *Frau* Giesy?"

"I'm not trying to reign over you at all. I just want to walk beside you and have some say in my own life."

"Christian spoiled you. Everyone talked about that, you want to have words about something. Indulged you. It made you a problem to yourself once he wasn't here to take care of things."

I felt tears burn behind my nose but I wouldn't let him see that, I wouldn't. "I just want a good life for my sons and my daughter, with me in it."

"Your sons. Always it's about your sons."

"And Kate. The children. I'm a mother, Jack."

"You'd better widen your kingdom a bit then, for you have a husband now, in more than just a document. You remember that."

"I'd like to make my home a safe and welcoming place for all of us."

"My home," he said. "And a nice one it is, too." He looked around. "Did Christian make all those lovely shelves with the curlicues at the edge?"

"I did those. It filled my long evenings. Don't change the subject, Jack. You should know this: I'd be a better companion and wife if I knew what I could count on."

"You might at that," he said. He drew close and breathed against my face, then leaned back. "But it wouldn't be nearly as much fun."

———

Jack refused to let Andy ride the mule back and forth, so he still stayed with his grandparents while in school. Jack's swagger increased after Andreas died in late October.

I knew Andreas had looked frail, but I hadn't imagined him so ill as to die. He'd always recovered. His dying made me grieve Christian anew. I grieved for Barbara, too. Losing a son and a husband. Word was sent to Bethel and to Aurora Mills of Andreas's death, but we couldn't delay the burial. John decided we'd bury him in the cemetery with a small ceremony led by Karl, and when the Giesys from Bethel arrived, then they'd have to come to Willapa with Rudy to mourn their father's death.

If only I had waited to marry Jack, I thought the morning of the burial. My sister would have said I should have let God handle things, not kindled my own fire. She might have been right. Now there was no one voicing the need for Andy to have a father in his life. Martin wouldn't try to take the children from me. Barbara had no more standing than me. Rudy and Henry were too interested in farming to worry over the upbringing of their nephews.

I assessed my present status. Maybe if I hadn't married Jack, I would have faced increasing pressure to keep Andy from me. But with Andreas's death I'd gained nothing by marrying Jack, not one thing. And I'd lost a great deal.

We were all together now, though. Perhaps we'd figure out what made

Jack happy or tense and we could begin to function as a family, though a strange one. I imagined the next school term when my sons would be old enough to ride the mule, Christian behind his brother. They'd return to be with me every evening. I'd be the primary influence in their lives, and that's what this marriage had been all about.

Only Jack's demand for compliance of wifely duties brought me sorrow. I had no love for him and any congeniality we experienced together could be shattered in a moment by his teasing or his brusqueness with the children. Before we married he hadn't shown the intensity of such precarious colors.

So when the children were tucked in the week after Andreas's burial and he said, "Wife. Such is the time," I knew of his intentions. It was my duty. I betrayed Christian by being with Jack, by demeaning a portion of our marriage that had been loving and good, trading all that in for this. My mind soared to those tidal places that had been gentle in my memory. They told me I could do this. I could meet my obligations so long as I did not let Jack intrude on this place that was me. During those intimate moments, I traveled somewhere safe in my history or my dreams, far from Jack's bed.

I'm doing this for my children. Those were the words that moved through my head: *for the children.* That loving choice could surely cause no real long-term harm.

———

In November, I threw up my supper. I tried to reach the slop jar. I'd woken up sick. My head throbbed as I fell back onto the bed, the back of my hand wiping the scum from my mouth.

"Ach, jammer!" Jack said rolling over, sniffing the air like a dog. "What kind of sickness is this that wakes you up? What did you feed us that was bad?"

"You won't get this," I said. "I can assure you of that."

The rains came, though not steady as they'd be by December. Already my sickness was greater with this child than with the other pregnancies. I thought back. It had been August when I'd had my last flow: I was probably three months along. I must have conceived the first night as Jack's wife. My bones ached and my legs swelled. I thought of *Herr* Keil and his charge that difficult childbearing was the result of Eve's sin. I'd had no difficult deliveries as yet; I'd count on my stubbornness to see me through this childbirthing too.

There were the usual chores to attend to, milking the goat and the cows, and I continued to do this while Jack worked at the mill. He was good with fixing problems there, making things work. I cherished the time with my children while he was gone, all of us relieved by Jack's absences. I found myself wishing he would find a job that would take him away as it had before we were married. But Joe Knight had sold out his oyster operation and headed back to Bethel. And they wouldn't work much in the woods with the heavy rains, so Jack seemed content to be a millwright and a farmer, a grouchy stepfather and demanding husband.

My stomach roiled daily. When the time came for Jack to arrive home, I noticed that all of us became a little noisier. We laughed a little louder at the antics of Christian attempting to do a somersault. Kate needed greater comforting in the late afternoons. Andy grew quiet, almost sullen. Our world of ease and closeness seeped away from us with the waning of the day.

Would I have prepared the venison stew in the way Jack preferred, or would he fly into a rage about my trying to kill him? Would he object to my using millet flour to make him a berry *Strudel,* or would he object if I didn't? He might complain that I'd wasted time with my redwood shelves that lined the walls now. Sometimes he brought the children little gifts, but if they didn't give him proper gratitude, he fumed. His irritations increased rather than lessened after I'd met my wifely obligations.

"You need to bake things," he said one day as he brought word that several from Aurora would be arriving to honor Andreas's death. I hoped I wouldn't have to attend this second service just because I felt so ill and travel made me sicker. I'd already gained more weight than I had with the other children in just these first few months.

"*Ja,*" I said. "You can take my *Strudel* with you."

"We'll all go," he said. "Let them all see that we're a family and that I've done my part to carry on the Giesy name."

"Jack, the travel, with the river higher now from the rains, will just be troublesome for us all. Why don't you go alone, Husband? It'll be easier on you. I'll stay here with the children."

He stared at me as though I were an unsolved problem. "You don't want to see Keil, do you? That's it. Don't want to face the consequences of your getting Christian to push him aside."

"Keil is coming? *Ach,* that has no bearing. I'm just tired. Your child is—"

"You bore a baby in this wilderness," he said. "Then two more. Don't tell me you're not sturdy as an ox. This is about you whining your way out of something."

"I'm strong, but sometimes women have difficulties that—"

"What you're owed," he said, "for being a woman. For being one who… drives others away."

"What on earth are you talking about?" I sighed. "No one's left Willapa because of me. They chose on their own to head for Portland and then Aurora Mills. I just wanted us to remain here. Christian wanted to remain." I kneaded dough for cinnamon rolls. Cinnamon was the only spice that quelled my stomach.

"It maybe could be you drove *someone* away long after Keil left, long after Christian died," he said.

"*Ja,* well, it can't be the great Jack Giesy because you're still here, aren't you?"

His hand stopped just short of my face.

"You will go with me to the service," he said. "We'll honor my uncle's death and you'll meet up with Wilhelm Keil. Maybe even apologize to him for your part in the separation of the colony."

He was insane, my husband, all interested in the well-being of the colony. I touched the side of my face where I'd felt the rush of air just before he stopped his hand. "You will not go away from me," he warned.

"I'm standing right in front of you," I said. I used soft words so as not to aggravate him. I was grateful the children were occupied in the half barn, tending the goat.

"You go away when we are as man and wife," he said.

That was a truth, and it was likely to remain. I had to keep something of myself, something he could not control. This new infant had to have a strong mother ready for it. I moved away from him. I was going to be sick.

24

Louisa

We are going north to Willapa this December, such a terrible time with all the rains, but then death does not consult our almanac. It will be a safe time to be away from here with all running smoothly, harvests all in, thanks to the help of those joining us from Portland and beyond, from my prayers being answered. Is it prideful to believe my prayers for assistance were the ones God heard?

So we go to Willapa. We remember Willie's burial. We'll have a ceremony for Andreas, my husband's longtime supporter, and we'll honor my boy's life too. It will be good to comfort Barbara by holding her in my arms and not just sending letters. Even good rag paper is a poor substitute for flesh.

With all disappointments come possibilities. Andreas's death is the perfect occasion to urge the Willapites to come to their true home here in Aurora Mills. Giesys have good heads for business and they could manage a colony store for us. My husband misses John's fine leadership and Boshie's good will, and I miss that Boshie's round red face. He shares a limp with me too, and we encouraged each other in the Bethel days.

My husband misses those he sent back to Bethel, too: Jonathan Wagner and August, but they are needed to urge the Bethelites to proceed with haste to sell the lands there so we can purchase more here. Quit claim deeds have been signed and sent back by Pony Express, a luxury of the outside world that we have not had before this far west. There should be no problem selling the land there. No legal problems, though there is much talk of that war, and perhaps people will not want to invest in farms or businesses when one does not know whether blood will be shed on the soil they've purchased. The old country knew many wars, and people in this place have known few save for the Indian wars. They don't know how long wounds fester even after the last shot's fired.

My husband foretold the future and we are safer here in this Oregon State. I want my sons with me on this soil. Maybe they won't be required to fight if that time comes.

The band plays again at Butteville on the Willamette, and the Old Settlers still plan a ball for January. I saved the invitation from a few years back, printed as though the occasion when our band played was for royalty. We attended another harvest fair this fall. The Oregon Agricultural Society formed, so there is strong interest in farming and markets just as my husband predicted. My husband says we will become a part of this in time, when all of us are here together again at Aurora Mills. I wonder if then it will feel like home and this *Sehnsucht,* this yearning, for home will cease its pull on me. Or with Willie buried elsewhere and with Bethel far away, perhaps it never will.

Jack Giesy took a wife! That it is Emma Giesy made all of us drop our soup spoons at the news. Perhaps that's why she failed to answer my invitation to come here. I asked her to let old disappointments go, to let us all be together to help each other as we once did in Bethel. With three little children she might see now the advantage of friends close by, of sharing worry as well as wealth. I even told her that my husband now acknowledged that he was too harsh on Christian Giesy, that he didn't give sufficient weight to the demands on such a small group asked to build houses for so many. These nearly five years since have told well how many hands it takes to build a colony, and there were too few, just too few for the Willapa colony to adequately prepare for all of us. My husband never spoke those words out loud to me, but I have a sense that it's how he feels now. We have not enough hands to prepare for the next Bethel group, which my husband hopes will come next year, 1861, for sure. The Willapa group needs us too. No community can just give; it must receive as well. But without my husband to rein them in each day, well, they'll stray. I can't imagine why Jack Giesy chose Emma except that somehow, Jack strayed.

Truth? Emma did enliven us. She made us laugh with her unique views that bubbled like good brew. Oh, we looked aghast at things she said but she did make us think a little differently about our work. Sometimes, about ourselves. I didn't tell her all of that, of course. I only told her that forgiveness came with the letter and I even asked her to forgive my husband. I didn't tell him that, of course, but it must go both ways I think. Those two are like two strong rivers coming together where there is bound to be froth.

I thought I'd offended her in my letter but now I understand; it was her marriage that took her time. Jack Giesy. *Ach,* who can know the ways of men? Jack's sense of humor will make her laugh, and this is a good thing for a woman as she grows older. My husband finds little humor in life with me it seems, though he does dance at the Old Settlers' Ball, if not much with me. Well, I have a bad hip. Aurora is his favorite partner; she's young and so light on her feet.

We leave in the morning for Willapa. Karl Ruge was here a week ago buying tobacco and shoes and he reminded us that after harvest, the Hebrews held the Feast of Tabernacles where they celebrated God's bounty in their lives. We have had a good harvest. The hops do well. Grain grows tall. The soil is deep and black and truly could grow anything, I think. We have apples and cider in our Eden.

We will rejoice and, as Scripture says, the Lord God will bless us in our harvest and in all the work of our hands, and our joy will be complete. Joy. Perhaps now in her life again, Emma will have joy. Jack can bring that and maybe she will discover that being a wife among the colonists will not be so constraining as she always seemed to think. Perhaps she will find her *Sehnsucht* satisfied at last too. A woman of faith can hope for such things for her sister.

25

Emma

The Keel of Confusion

The Aurora Mills group came up the Cowlitz Trail. They followed the Willapa so they reached us first. We heard the horses and the dogs they'd brought with them as the afternoon waned. In the rainy months, I told time more by when the children expressed hunger than by any afternoon change in light. Pewter clouds greeted us in the morning and dropped rain on us throughout the day. We kept the fire going inside and listened to the drizzle against the cedar shingles. With the group's arrival I began to prepare a meal for ten or twelve. I heard no children's voices, but then a journey with little ones slowed travelers. This was meant to be a quick trip.

Jack was at home when they arrived, and he greeted *Herr* Keil and several of the others as the men now tended to the horses. Three women came into the cabin led by Helena, her presence a surprise. They took chairs, weary from their journey, their dark dresses and bonnets indicating they'd come to mourn. I hung their capes on the pegs near the fire. I fluttered around them, trying to make them comfortable, knowing that Helena would be judging my efforts and that before long *Herr* Keil would be standing in my home. He'd probably begin with chastising me for my being with child, for my having married without asking his consent.

"Well, Sister Giesy," Louisa said. "I hear you wed again. And to Jack Giesy at that." She sounded happy for me. "Perhaps you've calmed that jokester down some?"

Helena said, "It might have been better to let others help you rather than add to your trials with a marriage."

I dropped my eyes. "Widows do what they must to provide for their children. May I get you something to eat? You must all be hungry." I didn't look at them. I didn't want Louisa or Helena to see the pain in my eyes.

"Did the Willapa colony not provide for you then?" Louisa asked, surprise in her voice. "You married our Jack not for love but to provide for your sons?"

"Of course they did," Helena said. "I heard that my brothers had to come by all the time to milk Emma's cows and tend to other of her chores."

"Not that they were asked to," I said. *They've been corresponding with Barbara.* "Not that I didn't appreciate that they did, though," I hastened to add. "Some sugar cookies and tea? We'll have supper before long, but I wasn't sure what time you might get here or how many there'd be. Or even if you'd come this way rather than coming up the Wallacut River as you did when you brought Willie's hearse." I could have bit my tongue for mentioning that. "I meant, I just wasn't—"

"Well, don't go saying that the colony here didn't take care of things," Helena insisted. She brushed lint from her skirt. She must have bought new traveling clothes. The cloth looked new.

"People don't always do so well after the loss of someone they love," Louisa countered.

"Things needed tending after Christian died," Helena reminded.

Do these women argue?

"And then you had that new baby," the third woman said. She had been introduced to me as Margaret. She kept her bonnet tied so tight around her throat it almost disappeared in the soft flesh of her neck. "So soon too. Was it even nine months?"

My face burned. How could they think any such thing? That the Aurorans talked about me and my affairs shouldn't have surprised me, the gossip and speculating, but I'd learned well that one knew so little, really, of what went on beneath another's roof.

"My son's name is Christian," I said. He looked up at the sound of his name. I smiled, shook my head, and he and Andy and Kate returned to pretending to look at my latest almanac, though I knew they stayed curious about these new arrivals. "He is his father's son."

"Oh, I didn't mean to suggest—"

"I'm sure the Giesys did the best they could for you," Louisa said. "But it is sometimes hard to tend to things when people live spread out as you are here."

"*Ja,* it's much easier to help each other as in Bethel," Helena said.

"And Aurora Mills," Louisa added.

"Well, there too, though we're still spread out more than at Bethel."

"And not so many niceties as back there either," Margaret lamented.

Dissention at Aurora?

I hurried to place a plate of cookies on the table, set before them tin cups Christian had made, and brought out loose tea to strain. The hot water steamed through the fragrant leaves. Then I donned my shawl to fetch eggs.

"The men can handle things, Emma. You don't need to help them," Louisa said. She chuckled.

"Oh, see, she can't be without her Jack," Helena cooed. "You always did like to do what the men did. Heading west alone with all those scouts." She clucked her tongue. Christian's sister had never married yet acted like she knew all about men and women's ways. Louisa hid her giggle behind her fingers.

"I'm getting eggs," I said. "So I can make *Spätzel* later."

"The noodles don't take much time," Louisa said, waving her hand in dismissal. "Wait here with us. Sit. Talk."

"I like to dry the noodles," I said.

"They take a time to dry in this damp weather. I noticed that in Aurora Mills, too," Margaret said.

"We adjust," Louisa said. "That's what we women do. You don't have to go to such lengths for us, Emma. Just boil them like we all do. No reason to be fancy. Anyway, we don't need so much to eat now. You rest."

"You must be tired, too, Emma. I notice you're with child." Helena nodded toward my burgeoning girth. Small-framed women always swelled early.

"Oh?" The soft-fleshed woman adjusted her glasses. "You've a good eye, Helena."

"That's why you didn't respond to any of my letters," Louisa said. She fanned herself with her bonnet as she sat beside the fire. "Just so busy with the children, a marriage, and now a little one. When is the child due?"

I didn't want to talk about my pregnancy nor anything else with these people. I wanted to leave to get the eggs. But I hadn't been aware of any letters sent to me. In fact, no letters had arrived to me since Jack and I had married, which was odd now that I considered it. I didn't want to face *Herr* Keil any sooner than necessary either, so staying to talk might be wise. Keil was the reason my life had become so grim, the reason I'd had to make so many decisions. Maybe those eggs could wait.

"June," I said, turning back to the room. "The baby is due in late June. And I've never received any mail from you, Louisa. Only my brother sent a letter from Aurora Mills telling me he was heading back to Bethel, and that was sent nearly a year ago."

"You were married in September or the summer then?" Helena said, holding her fingers up as she counted. So cheeky!

"He and August left together," Louisa said. "But I sent you more than one letter. I wonder where they might have gone." Louisa rubbed her hip. I'd forgotten she had a limp. The ride must have been difficult for her, and the rain would just make it worse.

I thought of Jack's teasing me with the letters I had gotten before I became ill. No doubt he'd confiscated Louisa's letters, read them, and threw them aside as "women's missives" of little merit. I wondered who else might have written to me, offered me encouragement of sorts. Maybe my parents? Even my sister's letters made me smile. They might not after I told her about Jack.

"What news did you share in them? Do you remember? And yes, Margaret, we married September 16 to be exact, in Olympia."

"I just wrote that we missed you." Louisa sat up straight. "And I told you that my husband realized his error in being so hard on Chris, on all the scouts who stayed to help build homes for us before we came out from Bethel." Her words stopped my hand midair. Louisa brushed her fingers to smooth the hair on either side of the center part.

"The doctor made no error," Helena said.

"He would not call it an error. Those are my words. But he's realized the difficulty involved in building a colony in this vast country. I do believe he shared that with Chris, at least in the way men do that sort of thing, and that Chris forgave him his harsh words. Building up a colony in this landscape takes more hands than just to hold hammers; it takes hands to hold each other up. That's why he so hopes those back in Bethel will come out soon and those of you here will find your way home to Aurora. He's such a good, good man who wants the best for all of us."

She made her husband into some sort of saint. It was unlikely that *Herr* Keil would have had any real change of heart. Christian might have forgiven Keil, but Keil would calculate his apologies, especially if he saw some benefit to himself in it. Apparently there was, as Christian had since repaid the land debt. It was what had killed him. I looked at Louisa. She exaggerated her husband's abilities, she so adored him.

"Your parents might come to Aurora soon too, Emma. You could join them," Helena said. She hadn't noticed my absolute amazement at Louisa's words.

"I don't think they'll ever come west."

"That's not what your father wrote to my husband," Louisa said. "He said they would come to be of assistance to you, their widowed daughter. Of course they didn't know then that you'd remarry so soon."

"It was almost three years," I defended.

"*Ja*, well, a bed gets lonely after a time with only one in it." Helena said.

"And you'd know of that how?" I asked.

Well, I just suppose." The other women laughed and nodded their heads. Helena's face took on a rosy hue.

"They've already left to come here?" I changed the subject and knew my voice raised an octave because Andy looked up, a question in his eyes. "Why didn't they tell me?"

"They were going as far as that Deseret place, where the Mormon saints are," Louisa said. "I worry over that because of the skirmishes there. The soldiers were called back to the States, so there's little protection for outsiders."

"My aunt lives near Deseret. They're just visiting, I'm sure."

"*Ja*, I know. They didn't have mail service for quite some time, so it must have been hard for your mother to know how her sister was. They'll be surprised when they get here to find you safely taken care of by Jack Giesy." She sighed. "My Wilhelm will be so pleased that they've come to help him at Aurora Mills."

I'm not sure why this news stunned. Maybe because of the timing. Perhaps my brother had returned to Bethel to handle things and help my parents come out. But they would have written to me if that had been in their plans. I'd not gotten Louisa's letters. I must have missed getting their letters as well.

Their arrival would bless me and my children. Jack wouldn't impose his threatening ways with my father present.

"I suppose they'll go on to San Francisco and then take a ship north. That's what I did," Helena said.

"They could come up here to see you and then of course come up the Columbia later to settle in Aurora Mills," Louisa persisted. "You'll have to come too, Emma. Jack can bring you and we'll be together again."

"Then they'll be here by spring," I said. I didn't want to disagree with Louisa about their ultimate destination. I had no intention of ever coming to Aurora Mills or letting my parents settle there.

"We don't know when they left, you understand," Helena said.

"Just that they plan to. I think my tea is strong enough, *danke*." Louisa put the strained tea on a plate I'd set beside each cup. I wished I had pretty teacups, porcelain, like the ones I'd seen in that shop in Olympia. My mother had lovely tea things. Maybe she'd bring them with her. I'd write to them, tell them of the marriage myself and welcome them to my home. Our home. If they hadn't left yet. Jack would have to build them a cabin. He had to. Lou could heal here. Their presence would bring safety. Maybe with safety I'd let myself become Jack's wife in truth and not just in demand.

Herr Keil and the other men entered then, removing their capes and coats and brushing water from them. They stomped their feet, but the mud was always with us this time of year. I stepped back away from the door; the scent of wet wool mixed with tobacco filled the room. I said to no one in particular that I'd be back in a moment; I was going to get the eggs. My heart felt light as a feather with the idea of my parents on their way west, and I wanted to be alone to savor the thought.

"*Ach*," Keil said. "Jack. You go do that. We need some tea here for these men."

I didn't look at my husband or Keil. I just stood at the door, sideways to them all, waiting for the explosion.

"Brother Jack, you're already wet." Keil's voice rang out in the small cabin. "You go now. Pick up those eggs and bring them back. *Frau* Giesy and I have much to catch up on." He laughed then. "*Frau* Giesy. I don't even have to remember to call you by a new name."

Why would he call me at all?

I wanted to go outside, but I couldn't let my first encounter with Keil be a defiant act over eggs. "Go," Keil ordered. Jack brushed past me without protest, an act that surprised me almost as much as Keil's interest in having a conversation with me.

"Come." He took the only empty chair, then patted the one next to him that the soft-fleshed woman had vacated as he sat. She heaved onto our bed, using it as a chair, the children scurrying behind her. "Sit down now and tell me how things go with you," Keil said.

I couldn't believe he was speaking to me, asking me to sit while men stood. "I…we're fine," I said. I didn't sit. There was too much to do, too much going on. "Let me get you tea."

"Louisa can do that, *ja*?" Louisa nodded and grabbed the potholder so she could pour water into his cup. "How are your boys?"

"My boys grow strong." I motioned for Andy to come forward. He stood in front of me and he lowered his head in deference to Keil.

"He is well taught. This I can see. And does he do his lessons with diligence? My friend Karl is your teacher, *ja*?" Andy nodded.

"It was good of you to let Andreas and Barbara bring him to Aurora Mills," Louisa said. I bit my lip but decided they didn't need to know that Andy had gone there without my consent.

"And that he had days with his grandfather before he passed," Helena said.

Keil agreed, patted Andy on the head. "And your other son, Christian is it?" I nodded. "Where is he?" He twisted around. "*Ach, ja,* there's the boy with his father's name. That was good to call him for Chris." He patted my clasped hand. His flesh felt clammy. I pulled my hands away.

"And here's my daughter, Kate," I said.

Kate stood, her light curls dropping into her eyes as she skipped between the adults to stand before him.

"*Ja,* your daughter." He reached in his pocket for peppermint sweets, and when she bit into the candy the smell of mint filled my head, taking me back to Christmas and my parents. He handed one each to Andy and Christian too. "I miss my little Aurora even though we will see her again in just a few days when we return home."

Does Louisa fidget?

Louisa sighed. "It was hard to leave them, but the weather…well, the journey is better this way."

"Is it true that my parents are on their way here?" I asked, the words flooding from my mouth. I ignored Helena's frown.

Keil looked surprised, turned to Louisa, then back to me. "They don't come yet, though. I've asked them, but…"

"Oh. I thought—"

"They do consider it, and I think they'll come before too long. They know, as do all the rest there, how we struggle. We would struggle less if people from this Willapa country came to Oregon too. I've asked Jack to consider this and will tell John and Henry and Martin and my good friend Karl the same when I see them tomorrow. They've proven that they can make it here. But the work is hard and there is more commerce available at Aurora Mills and less rain." He laughed. "We should gather all the saints together in one place."

He droned on for a time while my mind wandered to my parents. They hadn't already left then. Louisa was wrong. She hoped for something and created a world that wasn't real, just as she imagined things about Keil's great goodness.

Maybe I did the same thing. There'd been no letters from my parents about coming out to help, and yet I'd grabbed onto that thread as though it were a rope thrown to a drowning woman, and I'd plunged my children into a treacherous pool in the process. The only way out meant giving Jack what he wanted and hoping in time he'd see the children were no threat.

I felt my eyes begin to tear and bit my quivering lip. My parents weren't going to rescue me. No one was. I shook my head without realizing it.

"What? What do you disagree about?"

"Nothing, *Herr* Keil. My mind wanders. I need to prepare supper for us."

"Louisa, you help. You go now." He shooed her with his hands. *He treats her like a child.*

Jack opened the door then and gentled the eggs onto the table.

"Sister Giesy needs to rest, *ja?*" Keil said. "She still grieves the loss of her Chris."

Jack glared at me as though I'd caused him some personal grief. There'd be no rest for me.

———

The evening continued in those hop-skip jumps when I felt lightened by an interest Keil took in our lives and burdened by the uncertainty of how Jack would respond to it. I hadn't remembered Keil being congenial before except on Christmas or his birthday in March, and maybe New Year's Eve. My father had always described him as a compassionate man, a fine leader with the colony interests at heart. My family had followed this man from Pennsylvania to Indiana to Missouri. I'd never understood why they absorbed all he said, acting like a sponge. Christian had too. Did they all see a different person?

I'd missed detecting Jack's darker side, or at least recognizing all the behaviors I thought I could live with or change. Maybe grief and change and babies had impaired my thinking about Jack. Now about Keil too. Was Keil the friend my husband always claimed, or was Jack more of a culprit than I thought?

At least my husband did nothing to challenge me in front of Keil while I prepared the meal. I convinced Louisa to rest, too, while I cooked. Busy chattering with the men, Keil didn't even seem to mind that I contradicted his directive to Louisa. No one would prepare my meals in my house, not even at Keil's command.

Jack made jokes while I worked. He didn't bark at the children. He told tales of life in Willapa that made it sound Edenlike. He said "his place" was one of the finest in the valley. Every time he said "his place," a hot poker seared my side.

"Did you do the woodwork?" Keil asked. "It took a fine hand to make the loops on those plate shelves."

"What? No. That's Emma's plaything," Jack said. "She doesn't have time for such little frivolities now." He reached around me as I bent to check the bread baking at the side of the hearth. He patted my stomach and laughed. Louisa giggled. I felt my face grow hot, but as I leaned over the fire, no one else appeared to notice.

"Ah, another child," Keil said. "It will take you from your work, Jack." He wagged his finger at him. "Now that you know the cause of such things, you should be able to stop at just one."

"Give me more hands to do my work," Jack countered. "That is what children are for, *ja*? To work so as we age we will be taken care of."

"The colony takes care of us in our aging," Keil told him.

I prepared a hearty vegetable stew instead of *Spätzel*. I thickened it with flour, then poured it across freshly baked biscuits. We had slaw kept in a wooden barrel cooled at the river, and without protest when I asked him to, Jack brought that in and I sweetened it with dried berries. The aromas filled the small space and Margaret moaned that the food smelled "divine."

"Let's begin then," I said.

Keil held up his hand. "We will bless the food," he said.

It was a custom I'd ignored after Christian's death. I thought of such blessings then as wasted words, since the food had not blessed us with life or good health or a future without grief. My husband was dead. My son had almost died with illness, me as well. What good did blessing the food bring us? But Keil's prayer included my name and Jack's and my children and everyone else who stood in that room, one by one. He asked that each of us would be remembered and blessed by God and he finished by saying, "especially the hands that have prepared this meal."

My shoulders rose.

We ate our fill, all of us, me sitting next to Margaret on the bed. The men finished off what was left of the stew.

"I didn't remember you as such a cook," Helena said. She picked up the tin plates.

"She lived with her mother always back in Bethel," Louisa reminded her. "And we didn't have much to eat during the winter we were here. How many ways are there to prepare those salmon? Remember, Emma?" Louisa laughed.

She laughs! One of the worst times of my life brought about by her husband's demands that we club fish rather than use ammunition to shoot game, and she laughs.

"She didn't have the chance to show her talents until now," Louisa continued. Little bits of biscuit fell from her mouth as she talked. She put her fingers to her mouth in embarrassment. *"Ja,* this is so *gut.* Our Lord has given you a gift, Emma." Her pleasure in the eating was a compliment I decided to accept by staying silent.

I hadn't thought of my cooking as having any kind of talent behind it. It was what must be done to keep my family living. But Louisa was right: I had developed my own style, mixing cabbage with dried berries; thickening stews into sauces as tasty as *Strudels.* Even more, cooking kept me where the activity was, but I didn't have to talk with people if I didn't want to. I was with them yet still apart, and no one would be critical that I acted haughty because I wasn't gossiping or telling stories. I had good reason to be silent: I was cooking. I was serving. Louisa's words put a festive hat on an otherwise ordinary outfit.

After the meal, as people rolled out their blankets and covered the floor with them, Keil offered up words I'd never heard him say before, about the power of sleep to bring us peace, to help us be better servants in the morning. I wished he'd been so comforting during the harsh winter when I was pregnant with Kate. I wished he'd encouraged the scouts through those months. The old feelings of resentment returned with the memory of how we'd suffered. The men lifted the chairs and turned the seats onto the table to give more room on the floor.

"Ecclesiastes reminds us that 'the sleep of a laboring man is sweet,' " Keil said. The men all murmured in agreement.

"A laboring woman, too," Louisa said, then she gave a little gasp with her fingers to her lips. I looked at her. She'd spoken out loud my very thoughts. I looked at Keil but he said nothing. It was as though he hadn't heard. Helena acted deaf as well. Only Louisa and I shared a glance.

"Children, you sleep in the loft," Jack said then. He didn't need to give such an order. It was where they always slept. "We'll give you our bed," Jack said, as Louisa rolled out *Herr* Keil's blanket and mat. It was the common thing to do when guests came, for the hosts to give their finest, the Diamond Rule, making someone else's life better than our own. It surprised me that Jack would offer it before I could. I nodded agreement even though I would have welcomed the softness of the bed.

"*Nein.* Louisa and I will sleep on the floor. This is not a problem," Keil said.

I caught the look in Louisa's eye. She was tired and that hip of hers must hurt her as she leaned to the side.

"Perhaps the men would consider sleeping on the floor and Louisa and I could share the bed," I said.

Jack scoffed.

"*Ja,*" Keil said. "That is a *gut* idea, a better one."

He's so congenial. He must want something. But what?

"*Nein,*" Louisa said. "It is not good that my husband should sleep on the hard floor while I lie in a soft bed. No. The men need to be well rested. Emma and I will adjust on the floor along with Helena and Margaret, and you two men can sleep well on the bed as men should." The other men had chosen the half barn outside.

Keil didn't protest. It served his purpose.

I wished that if Louisa was going to defy him it wouldn't have resulted in my sleeping on the floor. I thanked Louisa for the blanket roll she handed me that was hers; she would use her husband's. I turned to see Jack staring at me. He had a sly grin on his face. He must have known that wherever I slept, I would welcome a good night's rest lying beside someone other than him. I smiled back at him. My sleep that night was sweet.

———

In the morning, I prepared a large breakfast of eggs with slices of ham and a cinnamon loaf I'd made two days before. The cabin smelled like a good home should, and as they washed their faces in the cold water, nearly everyone commented about the pleasant aromas and later, how good things tasted. I took time to fry the bread and put some of my jams onto tiny tins that dotted the table. All of it was gone when the meal was finished.

"If only it would stop raining," Margaret complained as she tied her bonnet. She sighed. "I'm full as a tick and wish I could just stay right here."

"The mules are surefooted," her husband reminded her. "You'll be fine."

"It surprises me," I said, "that you would all come in this rainiest of months. It was never a time that you liked, if I remember, *Herr* Keil."

"Brother Keil. You must call me Brother Keil," he said. He patted my shoulder. "We are of one family, *ja?*" He put on his hat. "That was a difficult time for us all. Willie, our Willie...well, we grieved." He shrugged. "But it is good to come now to honor him again as we did with Christian's burial, to stand beside his grave as we will stand beside Andreas's and Christian's. We'll do this together, all of us."

"Emma, are the children ready?" It was Jack speaking.

I took a deep breath. "I won't be going with you all today," I said. I didn't look at Jack. I could use an audience too. "There's no reason to take the children into the weather, and my stomach is still upset. I'll have a good meal ready for when you return. It will save Barbara and her daughter from having to prepare something there for afterward."

"We'll spend the evening with Barbara's or John's family," Keil said.

"*Ja,* that's good," Louisa agreed. "Emma was sick twice in the night. All that good stew, *kaputt*. Such a shame. You should stay home." She rubbed her hip absently.

"It would be a greater shame for you to miss this service of your former father-in-law," Helena said.

"My uncle," Jack said. "They will set a carving today to mark his grave. You will come and bring the children too."

"Jack, I—"

"No, Jack." Keil stopped him. "Tomorrow or the next day we'll return and your meal will give us a good start back home, Sister Giesy. Thank you. Helena will represent you at the funeral," Keil said. His voice held all the authority that I remembered. "Your wife has served us all well here and will do so again," he said to Jack. "No need to come out into the rain with the children. Jack, you can show us the way."

"You know the way," he said. Keil frowned and Jack seemed to reconsider. "*Ja*, well, you maybe could have forgotten."

"*Gut*. We go then." Keil clapped his hands together. The party packed up what they needed. I stayed out of Jack's way. I knew I'd have a large meal to prepare eventually, but I'd also have a day or maybe two alone with my children. And I had been sick in the night. None of that was anything but truth. A bold truth perhaps, knowing that Jack wouldn't like my using it to get my way.

I watched them saddle the mules and noticed none of the women rode sidesaddle. Pragmatics won out here in this western landscape. The rain was steady but not as hard as it had been the day before. Still, they all ducked their heads into their necks to keep the water from dripping down their backs. I waved good-bye until they rounded the bend. They'd stop at Mary and Boshie's before heading on. The gathering would grow as they traveled north. It would grow without me.

I drank a cup of tea to help settle my stomach, then changed clothes, putting on Christian's old pants and a shirt that worked well to milk the cows in. I didn't wear those clothes unless I was alone with just the children. "You stay in here and stay dry," I told them. "Andy, keep an eye on your little brother."

"Yes, Mama," he shouted down from the loft.

I wrapped a scarf around my head, found my gloves, donned my wooden shoes. I'd get eggs and make the egg noodles for this evening, let them dry over the little pegs I'd drilled below the redwood shelves. They'd be ready by tomorrow even with the moist atmosphere. Maybe I'd make some special dessert. I felt almost happy and hummed a little tune.

I opened the door. There stood Jack.

26

Emma

Marrow and Fatness

Jack pushed me back into the house. "Don't you ever defy me in front of others," he said. "Not ever." He had his hand at my throat. He squeezed hard. "I will decide what you'll do, not you. Do you understand that, Wife? No more of this whining about being sick." He smelled of whiskey and wool. His face glared into mine, the whites of his eyes like a raging buffalo's. His nose flared. Spittle soured at the corner of his lips. My throat throbbed. "I will decide what goes on under my roof, not you."

"Mama?" It was Kate. "I'm come down the ladder."

I croaked, "No, stay there!"

He released me, throwing me back into the table. The edge gouged my thigh. "You enjoy this day, your last day of getting your way. I'll be back tonight."

"But they aren't returning until—"

"I couldn't leave my poor, pregnant, sick wife home all alone, now could I? It'll be just us again. You. Me. And your children. I'll try not to do anything to upset *your* children." He scanned the room and I thought he searched for them, but instead he stomped to the shelf that held the oyster painting of the church I'd come to love. His wedding gift. He grabbed it. "I told them I'd forgotten something and had to turn back. It'll make a nice little addition to the marker on Andreas's grave."

———

I lay awake and startled at every sound; every creak in the roof or the floor made me twitch. In between I thought of Helena. Would she urge her relatives to go to Aurora? Would they all go and leave Jack and me here? I felt sick again. Got up. Lost my supper. How odd that after all this time Keil's prophetic charge that I'd suffer in childbirth should come to pass. An old psalm wove its way into my sleepless state: "When I remember thee upon my bed, and meditate on thee in the night watches. Because thou has been my help, therefore in the shadow of thy wings will I rejoice." The sentences didn't seem right, so I rose and lit Christian's lantern and read an earlier verse. "My soul shall be satisfied as with marrow and fatness; and my mouth shall praise thee with joyful lips."

That was what was missing of course: I'd stopped praising, stopped praying, and so I was hungry all the time, never satisfied. Now in my night watch I didn't feel like meditating. I only knew the shadow and not the sun.

Jack didn't come back that night.

The next day, Andy stayed close to me, getting me a damp cloth for my face, brewing me savory tea to help my indigestion. It was an herb I added to beans to prevent stomach winds. "Where did you learn that?" I said.

"Martin showed me. He gave it to *Opa* when his stomach failed him."

"At least there's something to relieve the constant complaining of my bowels," I said.

"*Opa* got sick, like you."

"Not like me," I said and smiled. "But we all get ill sometimes."

"*Opa* died."

"My sickness will pass," I assured him. I hugged him with one arm. "I'll be fine. Remember when you were sick? You got better, *ja*? Why don't you go work on your lettering or whittle with your knife. Do something restful. Before Jack comes back. He'll have duties for you, I'm sure."

He stiffened at the mention of Jack, then nodded his head.

"Jack's never…hurt you, has he?" He shook his head but looked away. "That's good. We'll just try to do what he asks and make him happy, all right?" He didn't agree but continued to sit with me.

Jack and Keil's party would be back anytime. I needed to rest just a moment longer and then would finish preparing the supper meal that I decided would be meatballs. I had day-old biscuits I could soak with the dried venison, which needed plumping, and enough bacon to add flavor to the sauce. It would feed all of us and wouldn't lose flavor if they didn't arrive until late. I should have planned a dessert, something sweet, but we had no liquor to finish off a great cake and besides, fresh berries were always better. Maybe a thin pancake with maple-sugar chunks would suffice. I just didn't feel well enough to care.

"You should go play now. Do something else besides take care of your old mother."

"I like making you feel better."

"*Ja, ja.* Every mother should have such a son as you," I said. I might have had a headstrong child or one demanding or perhaps one injured like my sister Lou, one who had some sort of accident that changed her. I felt a wash of gratitude that I'd been given this kind of child who was healthy and caring and alive.

"I'll read from the almanac," he said and climbed the loft. The other two entertained themselves with Kate acting as a teacher and Christian her patient student. I knew it wouldn't last for long, but for the moment their brother was free of their care.

I worried about Andy. He was seven but he acted much older. I'd done that to him, I knew, depending on him so much. He easily assumed responsibility for his younger brother and sister, and I had to watch that I didn't just expect him to perform tasks that were really mine to do or might have been his father's, had he lived. Before Jack, Andy milked the cows. He still did when Jack failed to come home until late. He made sure the wood box never stood empty. He even heated the water for the laundry. He was a kind soul who showed no interest in hunting or being present when the hogs were rendered or when we had to kill the chicken for dinner. He'd reacted with my mentioning Jack and I wondered if Jack teased him about his not wanting to hunt. Perhaps Jack hadn't physically hurt him, but physical wounds weren't the only kind.

Jack. When he came back, it would be with Keil's crowd, a different kind of audience. Perhaps he'd be congenial, polite, compliant.

I rolled myself off of the bed, donned my day-apron, tying it loosely around my thickening waist. It wasn't even four months. How large would I be when it was time for this child to be delivered? I began the meatballs, got bacon from the smokehouse with Jack ever on my mind. Jack certainly danced to Keil's tune when the man spoke and Jack didn't ask him to repeat any notes. "*Ach,* Emma," I said out loud. "You've managed to make your life miserable with two authoritarian men plaguing your days. Such a waste."

Keil's authority managed Jack, at least. Once Keil was gone, would Jack be his old self? I considered that Keil's influence was not so strong over people who had been his followers for years. Karl Ruge was here in Willapa. So were the Giesys. Yet the Bethel group delayed. I wondered why.

I could ask Keil to talk to Jack about being less…unpredictable. Jack might listen to Keil. But asking Keil for anything would invite a lecture about how I could be comfortable living in Aurora Mills. He might tell me I wouldn't now be struggling with my morning sickness (and evening sickness, too, it seemed) if I lived a more faithful life, was faithful to his colony. Worse, Keil wouldn't believe me that Jack could be like an angry cat, pouncing and hissing and scratching the people he claimed to care for, then purring as though nothing had happened.

I'd have to comply with Jack's wishes and maybe find more reason to bring other people around for added safety. But I also had to be careful about not granting him an audience.

The second night, we waited again and still Jack did not come. Neither did the others. Jack and Helena probably commiserated about my refusal to attend the memorial gathering. I imagined him giving that oyster shell to Barbara and her even thinking he'd painted it himself. I shouldn't have cared about that luxury item with no practical claim, but it was something lovely that gave me comfort. Now the memory of it would chafe.

When the party finally arrived the next afternoon, I had the meal prepared. The men took time tending to the animals, then came inside. The rain had let up and the sky looked like milk with cream spreading through it. The dogs they'd brought along growled over bones.

Jack came in last. He flopped a rabbit on the floor by the door. "And what did Andy do while I was gone?" he charged.

I frowned. "His usual chores. Why?"

"He didn't check the traps," he said. "If he had, you could have prepared this for us. It's been a long time since we've had *Hasenpfeffer*."

"I prepared a good meal for you," I said. I kept my voice light. "We can fix the rabbit in the morning. It will give everyone a good start." I began immediately to dress the animal.

Jack grabbed my arm to stop me. "Andy can do that. It was his chore he failed to attend to."

"I don't mind," I said. "Please, the rest of you, sit, eat before it gets cold and loses its flavor over our discussions here." I smiled and urged them to fill their bowls with the meatballs and find a place to sit.

"*Ja*, boys will be boys," Keil said. "You missed plenty of your chores as a *Junge*, Jack. Quite inventive in getting out of them, as I remember." He laughed then and failed to see that Jack did not laugh with him. "We will ask the blessing," Keil said, his accent thick as he prepared to pray.

I bowed my head. Once again with Keil's words, a silent comfort washed over me. I felt my shoulders sag with the weight of life I carried and felt warmed by the hope that a special blessing did come to those who prepared the meal with love. Aside from loving my children, I didn't think I loved anything or anyone anymore. Maybe my parents in a distant way, the *Kinder* of my family. But life, or sunrise and sunset, the smell of cedar in the air, the warmth of well-chinked logs, the taste of salt on my lips, even the presence of friends, none of those had warranted the emotion of love or even gratitude. Keil's prayer reminded me that I had prepared food joyfully and that God saw that as love. Perhaps that was enough love for now.

I stood back to make sure all were served, called the children when the adults had finished, and offered seconds to Jack before anyone else. He glowered the whole time. When I'd served all the thin pancakes with the hot maple sugar and butter treats, people made comforting sounds about being satisfied. There were a few scraps for the dogs outside. People yawned, made ready for bed. "We will make the same arrangements as before," Keil announced.

I nodded while Helena, Louisa, Margaret, and I rolled out mats as the men put chairs up on the table so we'd have more floor space. I'd need to boil the water and wash the dishes yet, but having everyone settled down would make that easier.

"Andy will finish the rabbit now," Jack said.

"Please, Jack. It really is easier for me to do it while I clean up. There's no need to have the boy—"

"He must do what he's told," Jack said, his voice loud. "I'll not have you make him into a sniffling rabbit."

"Jack—"

"Get over here, boy," he ordered. "Pull the guts out and skin this animal."

"I don't think he's ever dressed an animal before," I protested. "Let me just show him—"

"Must you insist on defying me, woman?" Jack said. He grabbed my arm, then thinking better of it, he dropped it. The cabin stilled as before a storm.

I watched my son as he made his way through the adults, some already lying down, others still standing or sitting on the floor. He didn't look cowed or defiant either. "I can do it, Mama," he said.

"Your mama is not the one asking," Jack said. "I am. You listen to me, now, you hear?" He boxed at his ear but missed as Andy ducked. "You have a weak stomach, is that it? Can't stand to handle what will feed you?"

I saw just a tiny flash of anger cross my son's eyes, but he held his temper and began the task of gutting the animal. The group went back to their settling in while Andy kept his head low. Tears formed around his nose and he wiped them with his forearm as he worked. He did the work cleanly, using a knife with skill. The odor of intestines and blood was greater than wet wool and old soot. It wasn't that Andy shied from the blood or body juices of the rabbit, I could see that. He didn't have a weak stomach. He grieved the animal's death. Had he gone to the trap and found it still alive, he would have tried to tend it, not bring it home for dinner.

At last he finished and washed up, stepped outside and hung the hare from the rafter, tossed the entrails to the dogs. I'd fry the hare in the morning. I finished washing the tin plates, wiped out the dutch oven and hoped that Jack would be asleep by the time I lay down beside Louisa on the floor.

No one slept yet. Keil had asked a blessing on our sleep, but people chattered as though they were sitting upright on a divan, telling stories in the darkness. The air cooled in the cabin as the fire died. They talked about the service, about Andreas's long and good life. Helena said perhaps she should have stayed with her mother; Keil assured her she was needed at Aurora. Louisa said the oyster shell Jack placed at the grave looked peaceful next to the wooden marker Keil had made himself. Every now and then a person would fail to respond and I knew that, like a star disappearing in the dawn, the person had drifted to sleep. Maybe that's what death was like when one died in their sleep, just a gentle not responding to an earthly voice; listening instead to one from somewhere else. I hoped that was how it had been for Christian when he died…just a change, not so much a challenge. I closed my eyes, hoping for sleep.

Instead, I lay awake remembering Christian. I heard Jack's steady breathing and knew he lay awake as well. Louisa said the oyster shell painting looked good next to a wooden marker Keil had made for Andreas's grave. Then it came to me: *Keil must have made the one for Christian's grave too, all those years ago. How very odd that he should have.*

———

I prepared the *Hasenpfeffer* to kind reviews. "Andy did a fine job in dressing the animal," I said. "A good dressing is half of the flavor." The women nodded. We knew that field dressing made the venison, reduced the gamey taste if a man handled the carcass well, but I appreciated their praising Andy for his effort. The men had saddled the animals and rolled up their slickers to where they could reach them easily. The air felt heavy with rain, but we could see patches of blue sky flirting with the clouds. Jack had gone into the barn to milk the cows, I assumed. I thought it odd that he'd begin that chore before the colonists left, but perhaps he knew we'd be talking for a while. It seemed we Germans were forever talking. Even as our hands were on the latchkeys ready to leave, we'd stop and find some new topic that needed exploring. It had been a while since I'd enjoyed the little gabbing that went on. When it wasn't about me, gossip was intriguing. As when they'd talked themselves to sleep the night before, it was a comfort. Even now I didn't mind Louisa directing her words at me, trying to get me to change and come to Oregon.

"But if my parents are on their way out, they'll come here," I said. "Imagine how disappointed they'd be if we weren't present to greet them. I'd want them to see all that we've accomplished." I spread my arm to take in the half barn and the fields we'd planted, the smokehouse. Our lives these past seven years were written on the landscape. "Besides, Jack won't leave."

"You should come for a visit at least," Louisa said. "You don't even know all the advances we've made at Aurora because you've never been there to see, not once. Come next year for the harvest festivals. Such precious things to look at. Some of the men are weaving baskets in the winter months, and they are highly valued at the fairs."

"I think they'll all come to Aurora," Helena said with authority. She patted her thick braids wrapped tightly around her head. "They'll listen to my urgings." *I wonder how Helena fits into Louisa's life.* I suspected those in Bethel might have been pleased to see Helena go. *Does Louisa welcome her?*

"You could use a basket for your eggs, Emma," Louisa said. "We're back to weaving again. My husband purchased sheep and we're dying the wool as we used to and showing it at the fairs. Maybe you could display some of your woodwork, and Jack could bring his drawings." She got all excited with that idea and clapped her hands. "The band plays as it did back in Bethel, and we are helping our neighbors, just as we did back there. That's why we came. To serve our neighbors, to make their lives better than our own."

She reminded me of…me, five years previous when I'd tried to convince Christian and all the Giesys to remain here in the Willapa country, to see the goodness in the crude huts, the huge timber that took its toll on all of us, when all I wanted was to find freedom for myself, relief for my husband. That's what Louisa wanted too. I could see that.

"You could cook us up a storm at Aurora," Margaret said.

"What's this talk about Aurora Mills?" Jack said. He'd come out of the half barn carrying a bucket of milk. He set it down. "This is my home now. And my wife and children stay with me."

"Well of course they'd stay with you, wherever you went, Jack," Helena said.

"We could all help each other more if we were closer, don't you think?" Louisa said. "That is the Christian way, to help each other. And if all of you were to come to Oregon—we're a state already, not like this Territory—we could better welcome all the Bethelites and be in service to our neighbors too."

Louisa actually meant what she said. Charity was in her heart: charity for her husband, for the colony, even for those of us who had separated ourselves.

She just never saw her husband's faults, the way he ruled over others, the way he set all the tasks before people, then manipulated them into acting whether they wanted to or not. No, Jack and I agreed on that, we could never go to Aurora Mills.

Through all of this Keil said nothing, nodded his head as his wife pleaded his cause. Finally, "Louisa," he cautioned. "Sister Emma and Brother Jack would come if they could, but they are needed here. We are grateful for the hospitality they've shown us. You have Helena to help and others as well. We're fine."

I nodded to him, then hugged each of the women and watched with my shawl wrapped tightly around me in the clear, cold air as the colonists rode off through the trees following the river. Jack waved at them too. It would be at least four, maybe five days before they made it back to the relative comfort of their homes. They'd take respite in the cabins of strangers along the way. Had they accomplished what they'd come for? Had they meant to mourn, or lure us to Aurora? Maybe Karl Ruge or Barbara or the others had agreed to move. I hadn't even asked.

Their leaving left a longing. No more marrow or fatness, just a hunger. I'd liked having the house full of people. Jack hadn't barked as much and because of guests, I'd received two days without Jack here at all.

I turned to go back in when Jack closed the space between us in quick steps. He smelled of rye. *Did he hide it in the half barn?* "Things are going to be different now," he said. "No more of this pampering. You prepare meals for a dozen without complaint, yet with me you are always sick. Always whining. This will cease."

"You wanted me to serve our guests properly, didn't you? I was doing what you wanted. I had to do it in between being sick."

"You loved the little pearls they threw to you about how good things tasted and how skilled you are. You knew exactly what you were doing, winning them over so they'd try to lure you away from me, hide you away in Aurora Mills."

"Oh, Jack," I scoffed.

"It won't happen, Emma Giesy. Your mind may go away from me but you will never leave, at least not alive."

"Don't be melodramatic, Jack," I said.

He stopped me. He gripped with his hand, that wide palm squeezing my arm until if felt like no blood flowed through it. "You're hurting me," I said. My fingers tingled.

"Pain in your arm maybe could be just the beginning of your worries," he said. "It just maybe could be." He pushed me away then, and I stumbled but caught myself as he stormed into the cabin, shouting for Andy.

"You leave him alone," I said. I rushed after him, rubbing my arm. "Whatever you want done, I'll do it."

"Andy!" he shouted. "Get out here."

I tripped over the milk bucket. *"Ach!"*

Jack turned and, in a flash I didn't see coming because I stared at the milk spilled at my feet, he struck me. The back of his hand rocked my chin up through my teeth and into my eyes. I fell. That is all I remember.

27

Emma

You, You, You, Must Go

The voice began inside me when my eyes eased open to my new world. The words whispered over the broken place in my tooth, across my swollen lips. *You, you, you, must go. You, you, you, must go.*

It was nearly dark inside the cabin. I tried to make sense of things. Jack must have carried me to the bed. With the tip of my tongue, I felt the puffiness from the cut my tooth made. Andy sat at the foot of the bed, his back to me. I heard Kate and Christian chattering on the floor beside us, arguing over a toy. Christian stuttered, "That my-my-mine, Katie. My-my-mine." Shame washed over me, shame that I'd let this happen.

When I moved, Andy turned. I forced a smile. I brushed the chestnut strands out of his eyes. "Are you all right?" I asked him. He nodded. "Thank God for that," I said.

You, you, you must go. You, you, you must go.

My eyes closed. I'd been going my whole life, trying to make things happen, trying to push my way into a world I thought needed changing. Once I'd claimed a husband I loved, chose a wilderness to be with him. We'd survived a winter designed by the devil himself and lived to tell of it. We'd remained to build a home, a place I once called my own. Scripture promised "peaceable habitation, sure dwellings, quiet resting-places" and with Christian, I'd had that despite the trials. All was gone now. The song said I should go too.

I stared at the peeled-log ceiling. I wasn't capable of leaving. I had no-where to go.

Jack came in. Andy slipped to the far side of the bed. I almost felt him shiver. I sat up, kept myself from wincing as Jack knelt beside the bed. "I don't know what happened to me," he said. "I never meant to hurt you. I didn't." He pressed his head into my lap like a small boy. I didn't touch him. He lifted his head. "It's like I'm a firecracker that sizzles and snaps and then explodes. I promise to do better." He had tears in his eyes. "It was the whiskey, I think. It must have been. I've never struck a woman before, not ever."

"And the children?"

He shook his head. "*Nein*. I didn't do anything to harm the boy, did I, Andy?" Andy shook his head. "See. It will be better now. There were too many people around; too much going on. We just need to be here alone. It will be all right now." He patted my hand and I flinched. He stood then. "You get up now, Emma. See what I've done for you." He sounded cheery again as though all was forgotten. He helped me stand. The room spun, eventually settled. "I've made you a drawing," he said, nearly gleeful now. "Of us and all the children. You can make a wood frame for it when you feel up to it. Make those curlicues that Keil commented on. We'll be a good team. I draw; you frame. Look at it."

He pushed the paper into my hands. He'd made cartoonlike characters of us, like the drawings that accompanied little stories on the editorial pages of our German newspapers. He'd captured our essence as he saw us with slight exaggerations of a facial feature or behavior. He'd placed us outside with trees looming behind us and storm clouds shadowing. Kate stooped at the outside edge staring under a salal-berry bush. Next to her stood Andy with a lead rope on Opal. He petted it. Christian was drawn clinging to my skirts on the far side of me. Jack sketched me towering over him as he knelt in front, staring out into the wilderness, the rest of us a kind of semicircle around him. He put grotesque smiles on all our faces. He'd drawn a dark fence around us. While he looked vulnerable kneeling, he also blocked the fence opening. We'd have to clamber over him to get out.

It was a hideous drawing, more accurate than I wished. I had to change that picture.

———

After the New Year, we had a hard freeze. This had never happened in Willapa before, or so Sam Woodard reported at a Sunday gathering we attended late in January. Jack insisted we all go to both the New Year's gathering at the stockade and this late January event. I told him how tired I was and he said we could spend the night with Barbara then. When I protested, his nostrils flared and his eyes got that white around them and I said, "I'll go. We'll all go." Which we did. I was learning not to resist.

The men discussed how hard the ground had frozen and whether it would stay cold. The men had had to break the ice off the grass in addition to breaking the ice on the water troughs for the cows and mules to drink. Everything took much longer to do in the freeze, all the chores, and they commented on that. But it hadn't rained as much, and that was a gift, I thought.

I kept what was happening in our household to myself, not that the women questioned, but they might have seen the quick flinching of my children when someone reached out to hand them a cookie or might have wondered at the hollowness of my face. They looked the other way. But then I'd have denied any problems even if they'd asked. I had my stories: I wouldn't complain, not even explain.

We returned home, burned more wood, and still the house felt constantly drafty and cold. We walked as though on ice around the house. February's rains lasted the entire month with few sunbreaks. That's when Jack's temper roused itself again, and I wondered if his disposition might be mixed up with the weather. When it was cold but dry, he was happier; when it rained he found fault. That didn't explain his behavior in dry September, though. He was just an unpredictable man. He'd always been and I thought I could contain it. But I was so much weaker than I'd realized.

In March, my growing size repelled Jack; he blamed me for "eating so much that even affection between a husband and wife was impaired." I still had morning sickness and hardly ate a thing. I tried to explain about pregnancy, but he'd storm out of the cabin and be gone for hours. I savored the time without him, yet his absences scraped at my heart, knowing his return would bring pain of uncertainty.

He made lists of our errors. My list was the longest. My failure to patch up a pair of his pants adequately. My inability to know that he wouldn't want fish for dinner. That I spoiled the children, he said, turning my sons into rabbits scared of their shadows, feeding Kate into a "fat little pig."

I had never seen him hurt the children, physically, the way he'd struck me. And while he did aggress me again that month, it was in the smokehouse. He bent my fingers back getting me to admit fault for changing my mind about what we'd be eating without first getting his permission. He locked the smokehouse door, seeming to make sure the children didn't see him. Perhaps he knew that if the children witnessed his violence against me again, or if they ever tried to intervene and were hurt themselves, that then I would take a different tack through this storm. I would listen to that song: *You, you, you must go.* I wondered if I could.

I'd written to my parents, telling them of Jack's striking me and his sporadic behaviors that frightened us. I'd given the letter to Mary to mail. She'd taken it from my shaking hands, said nothing except she'd send it off. She wouldn't look me in the eye. I urged my parents to please come, that with them here, Jack would remain good, I felt sure of it. His bravado would be heightened and tempered by an audience, but he'd use words instead of fists to hurt us, and words we could endure if they were with us.

I heard nothing from them.

Jack made the trek to the Woodards' to pick up any mail, and he always returned empty-handed. I told myself they were on their way; I just didn't know it yet. It was a thread I hung on to.

The persistent cold weather went all the way to the coast, or so Karl Ruge said when he brought me a new almanac. He hadn't come by much since Jack and I married, and I missed his visits to my farm—our farm. My face had healed of any bruises that day and while my fingers swelled, I didn't think any were broken. There'd been no recent altercations with Jack, so I wasn't sure why Karl asked me if I was all right.

"I'm fine," I lied. His eyes wore concern. I picked up a piece of wood I carved, settled it against my burgeoning girth.

"We don't see you so much, so I just wonder." His wording made me think of Catherine and I smiled. "You smile," he said. "I guess I shouldn't worry. You're a newlywed still, *ja*?"

"I was smiling thinking about my sister. She's always 'wondering' about things. I haven't heard from her or Papa since well before I married Jack. I wonder how Lou is doing. She had a fall. But they don't write. So…" I shrugged. "Tell me what you hear about weather on the coast."

"There was a very high tide in February," he said. "Along with the freeze, the oyster beds… Well, ice formed over the oysters at low tide. Then the rising tide picked them up like sand dollars and floated them on to another's beds. Some even floated out to sea. Joe picked a good time to get us out of the business, by golly." *Another dream, gone. Did I ever think I might carry on the oystering on my own?* The sound of my wood scraping filled the silence. "You don't look well, Emma. Your eyes. That's why I ask."

"Just a woman's lot," I said as cheerily as I could. I wasn't about to discuss this troubling pregnancy with Karl nor mention the uncertainties of living with Jack. I worked with my drawknife, making another shelf to put in the loft, so the children would have a special place for their treasures of rocks and shells and pretty flowers pressed into books. I had yet to make a frame for Jack's drawing. He'd added that to my list of sins, tacked the drawing up along with several others that marred the back of the cabin. My finger stuck out at an odd angle. I stopped, folded my hands together as in prayer, resting them on my stomach. I felt the baby kick. "Do you have news of Missouri?"

"The war begins," he said. "Already Alabama and Georgia and Louisiana have joined those who remove themselves from the Union. They elected Jefferson Davis and Alexander Stephens as their president and vice president. Two presidents we have now! This is not good. There can be only one leader in a country." He took a draw on his long clay pipe. "Poor Lincoln. He has a bigger problem keeping people together than Wilhelm does, by golly."

"Maybe the people from Bethel will come out now. Maybe they'll hurry here to avoid fighting. Has Missouri seceded?"

"No. I hope you're right, Emma. It grieves me to see Wilhelm so tired in his efforts. They still have no church there, no school, either."

"I wonder what keeps you here instead of with your old friends at Aurora Mills," I said. He dropped his eyes. I thought the color on his neck and ears darkened.

"John has need of me here. School starts next month," he said. "I'll look forward to seeing Andy. Pretty soon your Christian will be old enough to come too, *ja*?"

"Kate's old enough now," I said.

"*Ja,* that's right." He hesitated, then said, "Well, we'll look for her then, too."

It would get her away from Jack's scowling. It was the first happy thought I'd had in weeks.

The days turned into themselves, and before I realized it, I was about to turn twenty-eight years old on the twenty-sixth of March. I had three beautiful children who needed me to help them remember that their father was a good, good man. I had another child on the way and a husband who was dangerous to me but appeared quite normal to those around us. He could make people laugh, and did; the contrasts frightened me all the more.

I rolled away from him the morning before my birthday and pulled my shawl on over my shoulders and lifted my belly from my thighs. This boy was larger than any of my other children. At least I assumed it was a he, since I'd gained such weight. I prepared a breakfast, then packed pancakes spread with thick butter and put several slices of smoked ham into a small bag. I thought of the chapter in the book of John where the disciples are fishing and see a fire on the shore, and then a man, who turns out to be Jesus, asks them to "come and dine." How I wished I could begin my day that way, being served and filled up. What a birthday that would be!

Jack expected food ready for him to lift up as he headed for the mill. Things were picking up there, and Jack showed surprising skill at repairing things, supporting his claim at "blacksmithing some" before coming west. I tried complimenting him on his abilities. He'd scoff, saying I couldn't manipulate him so easily.

The men began their spring routines that took them out of their cabins during the day, to the fields or the mill or the forests and away from the skirts and apron strings of their wives and *Kinder.* It was spring. I'd have the day without Jack.

I felt more hopeful in spring.

Jack slept as I waddled toward the half barn to milk the cows. I did the milking again, finding it a soothing thing to do each day. Routine had its way of bringing comfort. The smell of the warm milk made me ill, but I'd relieve my stomach and then return to finish the work, the cows looking bored with me as I pulled on their tails to help myself ease onto the stool again. I buried my head in the warmth of their udders, using their tails again to stand when I finished.

An eerie silence greeted me outside. The cows bellowed for no reason that I could see. I opened the gate so they could graze among the bushes and trees, but instead they ran together around the yard area, twisting their necks and tails up into the wind that had picked up. Swirls of leaves and needles blew about, driven from the east, which was unusual. There'd been no rain that morning yet, and now the sky had an odd greenish cast to it. Through the hole between the trees, I watched as the sky changed color and within seconds appeared black as charcoal. The goat bleated with her mournful cry. She shook her head, her little beard flapping as though she spoke to the wind. "I'll be back to milk you," I said, carrying the bucket to the house. That's when I felt the wind blast against me, pushing me forward as I reached the cabin.

"The wind's up," I told Jack as I came in, slamming the door behind me, which took more effort than it should have. "Listen to it."

We felt the house shake then with the violence. Through the window, I could see that trees leaned closer to the ground than I'd ever seen them, white oak leaves skittering through the air. Thunder rolled across us and then a lightening strike flashed and split Andy's cedar before our eyes.

"Andy. Kate. Christian. Get down here, now," I shouted. In Missouri, such a storm would drive us to the root cellar, but there was none here, nothing deep in the earth to offer protection. I just wanted them all close to me, huddled together. Christian cried and Jack told him to shut up, but I wanted to howl myself. My ears hurt. I held Christian and Kate, watched Andy who stood near the window staring at the storming rage outside.

"We-we be all right, Mama?" Christian asked.

"We will," I told him, sounding as confident as I could. I hoped the goat had taken shelter in the half barn, as the wind would just skitter her aloft.

Jack glowered. I screamed when I heard a loud crack, then saw a cascade of branches fall beside the house, their leaves darkening the window.

"What's wrong with you?" Jack said. "It's only a storm!" He stood up then and pulled open the door and plunged himself into the tempest. The rain and wind thundered through the open doorway sounding like a herd of horses.

"Jack! Get back here!"

But he stood against the elements, drenched within seconds, his arms outstretched, his head back, taking in the downpour, his hair whipping. He stumbled back, catching himself as leaves and boughs and branches brushed past him.

"Jack!" I left the children and made my way to the door. *Do I close it and let him stay out there as he wants, let what happens, happen to him? Or do I go out after him and try to bring him in?* I anchored myself to the door frame, my feet spread to the doorjambs. I reached my hand out. "Jack! Please! Come back in before you get hurt." I didn't dare let go of my hold, for the wind would surely knock me over. I called several more times, but he was a pugilist against the storm. There was nothing I could do to change his mind. I pulled myself back through the door. Andy helped me pull it shut.

"You took a bath with your clothes on, Mama," Kate said. I stood drenched before them.

"*Ja,*" I said. "And Jack's still taking his." I couldn't imagine what mood he'd be in when he came inside…if he came inside.

The storm subsided after a time into a drizzle, minus the blustering winds. A sunbreak followed behind. Jack entered as though he'd done nothing strange in standing out in a raging torrent. He looked almost…rested, the wild gaze gone from his eyes. He offered no explanation for not coming in when I called him, no comfort to the children. Such a contrast to Christian's tendering in a storm.

"Should be the last blow of the season," Jack said. He wiped his hand across his face, shook it of the rain. "School starts in April, right, Andy boy?" My son nodded.

"Kate gets to go too," Andy said. Kate smiled, nodding up and down. They were both quite recovered from the fear of the storm, already looking for the rainbow that followed.

"Something I decided out there in that little shower. Kate'll be needed when the baby comes. Just you," Jack said, pointing his finger at Andy. "Like before. I'll take you to school and leave you there at the Giesys. They'll like that."

"Mama?" Andy asked.

"Your mama agrees with me. She thinks that's just fine, don't you, Mama?" Water dripped off of his forehead. A puddle formed at his feet. *"Ja?"*

Is he crazy or just making me so?

"We'll talk about it later," I said. "I need to get some dry clothes on. You do too, Jack."

"No talking," he said. He grabbed my hand and pushed the wrist back. I saw Andy from the corner of my eye. His look…reflected Jack's, all dark and dangerous.

"I'll change and then head on over to the mill to see how it fared." Jack released my wrist. Behind the curtain, Jack stripped off the wet clothes, dressed, and left, grabbing the food sack as he walked out the door. His leaving was my sunbreak.

"I won't go without Kate and I won't stay there," Andy said. "You need me here."

"I want to go to school too. You said I could go, Mama."

"I'll talk to Jack. Whatever is decided will be the best for you. And I'll be fine."

"He doesn't listen to you. To nobody," Andy said. He kicked at the rocking chair, making it move without anyone in it.

"You don't have to worry. I—"

"I won't stay at *Oma's*," he screamed. "I won't." He opened and closed his fists at his side. It was a movement of his father's at his most frustrated. "I have to take care of you."

I pulled him into my arms. "And sometimes that means doing things you can't imagine can be helpful but in the end turn out to be. You have to trust me, Andy. It's best if we do what Jack says. Best for all of us. You have to stay at your *Oma*'s house." Kate started to protest. "No, Kate," I said. "You can't go to school just now. You," I swallowed, pointed at Andy, "must go."

"You-you-you must go, Andy," Christian said. I turned to my youngest son. Had I said those words out loud? Had he heard them before? No.

"I wish Papa was here." Andy sobbed the words into my shoulder.

"*Ja,* I wish it too." I stroked his back, swallowed my own tears. "But it is not to be. He didn't wish to leave us, but he did and so we must be wise, *ja*? We must make good decisions. Mama hasn't always done that, has she? *Ja,* well, she will do better."

Jack would return, but in what mood, who could say? He'd taken another step up that ladder of intensity by hurting me in front of the children. He was growing less cautious. He'd hurt the children next.

"Will you ask God to take care of us, Mama?" Kate asked.

I brushed the curls from her face. "I'll ask," I said. "Perhaps I'll even be heard."

28

Louisa

Even back in Bethel my husband sang her praises, as it was Helena who gave up the love of a good man because he would not join the colony. Wilhelm showed her as an example to the young people, how even without marriage one can be in service to the Lord. Maybe even be more in service without the distraction of a family. I heard him say that once, "without the distraction of a family." I don't think he meant it quite the way it sounds.

I would not ever say this to my husband, but sometimes I wondered about Helena's love affair with that bridge builder. Where had they ever met? Helena never left the colony and the bridge builder had no cause to purchase items from our colony store. His father built a famous bridge in Brooklyn and one wonders how Helena would have encountered such worldly folk. I should not judge.

Once I heard Emma Wagner—she wasn't married yet—say something of that sort too, that perhaps Helena exaggerated her sacrifice; or maybe that Helena was the rejected one and her story was a way of saving face. That Emma. So here we are, she and I thinking the same thing, again.

I was pleased to see how at home Emma made us feel on our journey north. Even Helena found no fault except in Emma's refusal to attend the memorial of Helena's father. But goodness, three little children, another on the way, a husband who was not the funny Jack that I remembered, rather one prone to melancholy and caprice—no wonder she wished a day at home. A wife and mother could understand Emma's wish even if Helena couldn't. She's much too quick to judge, that Helena. *Ach,* but so am I at times, so am I.

My husband raves about Helena's organizing the children and how she spoke to Karl Ruge, urging him to come to Aurora to teach them here. My husband thanked her profusely for her effort. I talked with Brother Karl too, but something holds him there in Willapa. Maybe he likes making his own choices without need to negotiate with my Wilhelm. Lord knows I'd like such an escape at times. To have to justify to my husband's satisfaction each thing I think, even if it's what we should have for dinner, is a tiring task. Warranted of course, as my Wilhelm needs much tending so he can give back to others. Even the slightest inconveniences that I can remedy, I wish to. Still, can there really be great fault between serving wilted lettuce with a vinegar dressing and one made with eggs and oil instead? Can it really matter whether the spoon-fork is lined up perfectly with the plate tin before one begins to eat? Does the food taste any less grand if the serving utensil sits a fingernail's width off from where he thinks it should? And where is it written that his is the card that trumps all others? *Ach,* I use gambling terms to describe my husband's wisdom. There is probably a sin there, and if my husband heard me say such things, he'd tell me to go deep to find it. I have no time. Maybe Helena does. A saint would, I suppose. There is still too much to do here every day and each day finds yet more undone. Surely God will understand if I fail to add one more trespass to my daily list.

Ah, I complain, I judge. I must not. Good things have happened in the midst of trials here. Helena has assumed the task of table preparation at our big house, and now the serving will be perfection. I can concentrate on gardening and helping with his herbs, being with my children, dying wool, writing letters back to Bethel urging others to come west. In any spare time, I can listen to the band rehearse while practicing my *Fraktur.* Is life so difficult that I should complain or use words such as *escape? Nein.* Life is good and could only be better if those from Bethel and Willapa would stop their stubborn ways and join us as intended all those years before. Perhaps we're closer to that end now that we've visited Willapa again. Maybe Emma and Big Jack will come. Maybe Barbara Giesy in her widowed state. After all, there's been a change for good: Helena came west, an act my husband says marks the start of the next migration. My husband is so pleased. I must be too. I'm sure that Helena is.

29

Emma

A Reason to Run Off

The unusual April frost along the Willapa felt fitting for the coldness of my life. I was bedridden at the middle of the month and most of May, grateful that Kate hadn't gone off to school with Andy. She was a fine helper for me and somehow knew how to scuttle out of Jack's way when he returned from the mill in a foul mood or when he sauntered in from the half barn whistling a tune. Kate reacted to him either way with caution, her eyes on me to see how to proceed. I hated that she wouldn't remember the love of her father, the safety and reliability that marked a good man. Instead she'd have this ebb and flow of an erratic stepfather to mark her memory. Maybe she'd never marry because of it, and who could blame her? Was that why some women chose the unmarried life? I'd never considered that before.

I knew my being in bed when he arrived home annoyed Jack, but I could not rise except to reach the slop jar. "Chamber pot" he called it, as though changing a name could make the thing different. The baby shifted and kicked and moved well, but it was the swelling I couldn't stand, literally, and so I was abed. My body bloated, my ankles, my fingers. My face puffed and my eyes sometimes stuck together, especially in the morning. I remembered my mother speaking of these things happening to pregnant women, and that bed rest was all that could be done except for drinking chamomile tea and steaming my face with the bouquet of herbs. Kate secured both for me until I ran out of tea and Jack refused to request more. He said I should just drink coffee like everyone else.

On weekends, Andy helped with the laundry and stayed out of Jack's way. During the week, Kate followed my directions carefully to make sure she served the bacon crisp as Jack insisted, the coffee sweet, and the whipped cream stiff enough to support a cinnamon stick. Christian, with his stutter ever increasing, huddled close to me whenever Big Jack stomped around.

I counted the days until the end of June when the baby was due and my life would return to some semblance of normalcy. *Ach!* My life had never been normal, not since I'd headed west with Christian. And I didn't want to return to the norm that was Jack. But I did need to stand, to hold my child, make a new plan and pray I had the power to complete it.

On the twenty-third of June, the baby made motions as though to arrive. Andy worked outside with Jack, cutting branches off the big cedar that had fallen in the March storm. At the first sharp pain in my back, I sent Kate out to tell Jack to send for Mary. I heard her shout as she headed out the door, "Andy, Mama's having that baby. She says to go get Aunt Mary." *Tell Jack,* I thought, but it was too late.

Andy ran inside. Jack followed him. "You women. You can wait until we're done here."

"I'll go," Andy said.

"You're always looking for a reason to run off. You stay and help."

"This isn't exactly running off, Jack," I said. A pain rose up and through me and I panted until it eased. "It might be sooner than you think. Please, just go get Mary."

"Please. Just go get Mary," Jack mocked.

I fell back onto the bed and closed my eyes. "Not now, Jack."

"Ach," he said. "I'll go then. Get this over with."

"Go finish up your work, Andy," I said. "Kate's here. Mary will be soon."

My oldest son moved at a snail's pace toward the door.

"Get out there!" Jack shouted at him. Andy slipped past him so the foot Jack kicked at him struck only air.

I felt the sweat on my brow, the rising of another pain. I pulled myself up onto my elbows. "Don't you hurt my son!"

Jack cursed me then, used words I've never heard a man say to any human being, only to mules or cows or hogs that didn't do what they wished. Kate's eyes were big as eggs and she put her hands to her ears. Jack hit the back of her head with his palm as she sucked her head into her narrow shoulders, moving out of his way as he pushed on by. Christian began to cry now next to me, and I shushed him, hoping to defend what I could.

Jack stomped outside. The goat bleated as she always did at a human's presence whether friend or foe. I heard him shout something to Andy that I couldn't understand. I hoped Andy didn't talk back. Jack's retort came from the direction of the trail to Mary's. Mary would come back with him and Jack would behave with her here. He'd show his cheerful side, the side that Mary expected. Sarah might believe me if I told her about my captivity, but I couldn't imagine any one of the Giesys giving any credit to my charges.

I was grateful when Mary arrived. We spent a long evening together as I panted and squeezed her hand to press against the pain. I heard myself saying as a rhythm to the arch, "You, you, you, you, you," but I silenced the end of it, kept "must go" to myself.

In the early hours while the children slept, I felt as though my insides tore in two. The warmth of my own blood seared like salt rubbed into an open wound. My second daughter arrived in the world.

"She's a big baby," Mary said. "She's torn you. I'll have to sew. It'll be painful."

"Let me see her first."

Mary laid her on my stomach while she tended to the cord. I'd decided to call her Louisa for our Prussian queen, but mostly for my sister. She could have been Kate's twin, the two looked so alike. She was the largest of all my children, and yet she weighed not more than eight pounds. Her heart-shaped face looked wrinkled and stressed from all the pushing and shoving, but she had blue eyes and a fluff of tiny dark curls covered her head like a cap. She didn't look a thing like Jack.

Mary's stitching hurt worse than the delivery, if that was possible. She used the needle from my chatelaine, moved it through a hot flame to sanitize it and then began to sew with a heavy thread. My baby's size and my great weight gain and lack of movement and that puffiness must all have added to the complications.

"Louisa?" Jack said when I introduced him later to his daughter. "No, we're not naming her for your sister. Didn't you say she fell and is strange now? Why would you name a child after someone not whole? No."

His words stung. My sister was whole and so was this child. "After Louisa Keil, then. Think of her name as honoring *Herr* Keil," I said, believing that might move him.

"*Nein.* If it has to be a girl rather than a boy you bear me, then I pick a solid name, a strong one. I pick Ida," he said. "Ida is what we'll call her. After my mother."

It was the first mention of Jack's real family he'd ever made.

Ida did have a good suck, and praises be I had milk to feed her. It seemed a wonder that after three children my fourth could take nourishment from me, a special though ironic gift. All the other children arrived as easy as otters slide the riverbanks but had been challenging to keep alive after that. Ida's pregnancy and delivery carried memories of complications, but in her taking her own breath, she gained weight and was a healthy child who made few demands. And I could fill her up. The smallest of blessings.

Jack paid little attention to Ida, wrinkled his nose at the smell of her soiled napkins. He couldn't use her so he ignored her, I thought.

In early July I told Jack I thought I should see a doctor. I knew from my own scent that I had a serious infection, and the pain grew worse. "Can you go get him for me, or will you help take us all there?" I dreaded riding a mule feeling as I did, but I didn't know if he'd believe me that I needed a doctor. "Maybe you could put me in the cart. I'm not sure I can ride."

"You want my help and then you want to tell me how to give it? You...woman," he said with such disgust in his voice that tears pooled in my eyes. My emotions were like a pot left boiling then cooled, then boiling again as though someone stoked the fire beneath it.

"You just want an excuse to get someone else to come here."

"I think the stitches are infected."

"Use your healing herbs, Emma Giesy. I've no time to run off and bring someone back for you for sympathy."

"Jack. I need someone. Send Andy, then."

"Stop being a burden on me, you and your children."

"Jack—"

"Will these demands never end?" He pressed his head between his hands. "These...these complaints that are in your head?"

"I'll go, Mama," Andy said. He ducked past Jack and headed toward the door, but Jack grabbed him and held him up with his arm. Jack was tall and strong and he lifted my son. While he dangled there, Jack struck him with his fist. My son yelped.

"You will do as you're told," he raged, then threw Andy against the door. I rose, shouted. He turned on me. "I'll break your cussed neck," he said. "Enough of this lying in bed." He began a tirade of cursing. Andy picked himself up and before Jack could reach him, my son shot through the door and ran toward the road.

"See what you've done?" Jack said as he headed out after Andy. "You did this!"

I prayed now.

I prayed that my son would know the little back ways to take through the trees, to be a silent as a mouse as he raced for help. I prayed that Jack would tire and return, be disgusted though his rage simmered. *Why does this have to be so hard?* I leaned back onto the bed. I was a little coin lost in the corner of a kitchen hearth, hoping to be picked up by someone safe and kind and loving. I'd once wanted to be the shiniest coin in the realm. Now, I just wanted to be found.

———

Jack returned, had not chased after my son. He ate, then left, and did not come back to the bed that night. This wasn't the first time he'd spent nights away. I was never sure where he went; I didn't care. The doctor arrived the next day. Andy was not with him. The doctor confirmed my suspicions and gave me packs to place across the stitches to try to pull out the infection.

"The stitching was well done," he said. "But there was infection there. It has gone…inside, *Frau* Giesy. It may affect your being able to conceive again if we aren't successful in treating it."

"I just want to be well enough to look after the four I have," I said.

"You have a good son there in Andy."

"He didn't come back with you."

The doctor didn't look at me, kept working. "He said he wanted to visit his grandmother. Fine lad. Very thoughtful."

And wise, I thought. *Very wise.*

Jack complained the following week about Andy's not being there to do his chores. I didn't try to defend my son, finding that my words only angered Jack more.

Later, I felt well enough to be up churning the milk for the first time in months. The day was hot and I waited until the evening to do it. I sat. Standing still caused pain. Ida slept and Jack stayed away late, a relief for us all. I finished the churning, then went to the half barn to bring in the chickens and check on Opal. I petted her back, ran her silky ears between my fingers as she nudged at my cane. I took short steps and breathed deeply. Kate had helped milk the cows and now played with her doll, convincing her younger brother that he was a dog. They laughed together like normal children. I leaned against the barn wall. If only it could be like this always, the children in peaceful habitations, secure dwelling places. At least Andy was safe. How ironic that I'd married Jack to keep my children with me and now my son's being with his grandmother was the better choice. I walked back into the house.

There sat Andy, Jack's muzzle loader laid across his knees.

My heart pounded. "What are you doing, Andy?"

"I'm waiting for Jack so he won't hurt anyone anymore."

You, you, you must go. You, you, you must go. Seeing my son sit there with a gun in his hands brought the words back. Andy had to go; so did we. If we didn't, Andy would do something that would grieve him for a lifetime. If Jack even knew he considered it, he'd harm the boy. I knew that too. Violence begat violence. I couldn't stay here any longer. I had to take my children and get out. I just didn't know how I'd do it.

"Andy, go back to your *Oma* and your uncle Martin, and stay there until I come to get you, all right?"

He shook his head. "I have to take care of you. He hurts people and he hurts you, and a papa isn't supposed to do that."

"I know. But you can't fix things by hurting Jack back. That isn't the way to do this. Your father would never want you to do it that way."

"Papa would want me to take care of you."

"And you have done such a fine job of it. You will, if you go now, before Jack comes home. Go stay with Martin."

"You won't come. It'll be like that other time."

"That's not true. I will come. See, I'm up using a cane now. Andy, give me Jack's gun. Please. You have to listen to me."

I'd let my son have too much say in our lives, depended on him too much, and now when I needed him to just be a child and listen, he resisted. "I'm still your mama, remember?"

He shook his head. "You're sick still."

Please, please, please. "I'm better. I've churned the milk and fed the chickens. Andy." I grabbed for the gun and had it in my hands before he could hold back. I was still stronger than he was despite my ailing. "Now go. You'll be safe at *Oma*'s. That's what matters. Please." He held his fists at his side, opening and closing them. I leaned into him then and hugged him to me. "You have to go," I whispered. "I'd die if Jack hurt you; you mean so much to me. It doesn't seem right, I know, but doing this, leaving, will be the greatest gift you can give right now. I'll make plans. I'll find a way. But first, you have to be safe."

I felt his shoulders sag, and then he straightened. "Should I take Christian with me?"

I hadn't thought of that. "*Ja*," I said. "That would be *gut*. Both of you, safe there." Then it would be easier for me to take Kate and Ida away from here while Jack was gone. I could collect the boys and then sail down the Willapa to the coast. Or maybe I could pick them up and go to Olympia or Steilacoom. And what then? I couldn't even stand for longer than ten minutes.

I started to cry but swallowed the tears. "Take Christian. I'll say that Karl came by and took him to visit you at his grandparents. Jack won't question that. You go. Christian," I called him in from outside. He ran with glee to Andy. "You boys be very quiet now. Andy is taking you to visit *Oma*, but you must stay out of Jack's way. He'll be coming back soon and you'll want to miss him on the trail. So you have to be quiet and very careful. It's a game," I told Christian. "No cheating. Just listen to your brother."

"Wh-what do I take?"

"Nothing," I said. "You both go. Now."

"Mama?" Kate asked. "Can I—"

"No." I hated that I put her at risk because she was a girl. "I'll need your help with Ida, and Jack would question why I let you go with Karl. We'll go there later."

My heart pounded as I put Jack's gun back on the pegs, then threw food into a bag for the boys. Andy took the bag over his shoulder, then reached for Christian's hand. Andy would be eight in October; Christian had just turned three. I hugged them both, then said, "Hurry. Stay away from Mary and Boshie's house, don't let them see you. Go straight to *Oma's*. Promise me." Andy nodded and I stifled a sob as I watched them walk bent over like little old men who'd already seen more than they should have.

My mind began to spill with possibilities. I'd wait until tomorrow, after Jack had left for the mill. Then I'd pack what we needed for the baby and forget the rest. I scanned the room. Leave everything here. And go…I still didn't know where, only that we had to leave this place and never return.

Sarah and Sam would take us in, but then Jack would direct his wrath at them, maybe Edwin. They might loan me some cash, though, enough for the ship's fare to…someplace. Maybe San Francisco, where we could get lost in the crowds. Maybe I could head back to Bethel, face my parents and beg their forgiveness. But I was so weak. Such long journeys would be too much, especially with four children in tow. Would it be better to wait for a month or so, until I was stronger? My eye caught Jack's gun. I remembered the look in Andy's eyes. He would kill Jack if given a chance. Jack wouldn't let them stay at Barbara's forever. He'd want Andy to work here. How ironic that having my son close to me could be the worst thing for him.

What would Jack expect when he came home to an empty house? That I'd gone to Sarah and Sam's. *So not there.* Maybe he'd think of Steilacoom, because I loved it there. *Not there.* Where do I go? Where, oh, where?

Aurora Mills.

The words stung like sand against my face. I tried to pitch the thought away but I couldn't. Go to Aurora Mills after all Keil had done to my life? I'd be admitting everything I'd done here was a mistake, was somehow wrong. I'd be failing Christian.

But of course I wasn't failing Christian. He wasn't here to fail. And he'd already forgiven Keil for that harsh winter those years past. Before he died he'd come to see Willapa as a part of Aurora Mills, as a part of the colony's growth here in the West, much as I hated that. Christian would be pleased I was heading there; maybe he was even pushing me in that direction, if a husband's spirit could do such a thing. But I couldn't; I just couldn't go there.

My brother wasn't there anymore. My face burned with the thought of having to ask for help. I could not find a way to live within the constraints of that colony; I could not!

But there was only one I could ask for asylum, one who might be strong enough to hold Jack in check. A rush of emotion heated my face. Should I leave Andy and Christian behind? Just for a time. I'd come back for them. I would. But once I was gone, would Jack take them, use them to compel me to return? We'd all have to go. To Portland. To San Francisco. It didn't matter where, just so long as we were far from here.

30

Emma

Attenuated Anguish

Once decided, my heart pounded with firm direction. Feed the baby. Prepare an evening meal. Act normal. Think. It felt good to be acting, to move past just huddling in fear, coughing up responses.

"Where's Christian?" Jack asked as we sat at the supper table. He'd arrived home, completed his usual chores, then come inside. His eyes looked red as though he hadn't slept well. I tried to remember how long he'd stayed up when he awakened in the night; couldn't remember when he'd come back to bed.

"Karl came by and picked him up," I lied. "He was visiting Martin and Barbara and thought we might want to go as well, to see Andy." Jack grunted. "But of course I told him I wasn't up to anything like that. I was sure Barbara would enjoy seeing both her grandsons and I didn't think you'd mind."

"People just come by and decide what to do with my children?" he said.

"I imagine he thought he was doing me a favor, taking a child off my hands with this little one so demanding."

"Her name is Ida. It means 'work and labor,' things children should learn at a young age," Jack said

"Does it?"

"You maybe could use her name."

"Yes, I could. And do." I served Jack his favorite, a cake with cocoa and honey and some of that coconut we occasionally got from the Sandwich Islands. He ate his fill, went outside, returned, dozed in his chair, then stood up with a start. "I'm going to bed. Keep your cleanup quiet."

He never even held his daughter. Instead, he snored while I stood over the hot water then sat at the table cleaning the dishes and watching him sleep. Later, I held Ida to me, feeding her, rocking her softly. Kate slept in the loft. I planned my future and what I'd take with me. Only eight years previous I'd made a similar sorting of what to take from Bethel to this new land.

The chatelaine Christian made me. I'd leave my drawing pencils. No room for those. The pearl necklace my mother sent me, the one I'd had Christian add the smaller Willapa pearl to. I'd pull it from its wrapping in the trunk after Jack left in the morning. Something of Christian's. His medal for marksmanship and my drawing of him. And the letter he'd carried from me. I pulled it from its hiding place and reread it. I'd once promised faithfully to support his work. Had that meant following Keil, or was Christian's real work about living out the Christian tenets of loving God and loving one another? Of late I'd done little of either. I never had reached out to the Shoal-water or Chehalis people in this region, even when they came by to trade their fish for my bread. I hadn't taught my children to trust in God but rather to look to me for all their needs, and then I'd failed them, kindling my own flames and burning away a path of faithfulness. The food I'd fed them had kept them alive but not living. Would going to Aurora Mills change that? Would going there be what Christian had wanted for us all along?

My mind froze with fatigue. I hoped it would thaw by morning.

That night, I lay down beside Jack for the last time. My movements didn't wake him. Hours later, when the moon was full in the window, I felt him rise from the bed while I pretended sleep. He dressed and went out. I hoped he'd come back, keep some little semblance of routine. Let him eat breakfast, get ready for work, leave. If this was one of his wandering-around nights, he might go straight to the mill and I wouldn't know for certain. I imagined how to adapt my plan, how long to wait before leaving if he never returned in the night. Was I "beginning to weave," hoping God would provide, or had I long ago used up God's thread and now weaved on my own?

I dozed, awoke to Jack shouting, then pulling a chair from the table where he sat. I rushed up to fix his meal, lightheaded. "I'll milk the cows for you," I said, preparing cakes for him. "If you want to get an earlier start to the mill."

"You're up to that now, are you?"

"I'll give a try," I said, making my voice light as a butterfly. I hated knowing those cows would be bellowing before evening, but I couldn't possibly take the time to milk them once Jack left. I couldn't use up what strength I had for that.

He grunted. "I'll see you this evening, then," he said, as he picked up the food bag I'd prepared while he ate.

I nodded agreement. What was one more lie?

As soon as he left I woke Kate, helped her dress, fed her, then told her to watch the trail. "If you see Jack coming back for some reason, you come and tell me. Don't wait to say hi to him, just come let me know." She nodded agreement, then headed out.

I'd taken what food Kate and I might need, one change of clothes, and then I looked for the pearls. They'd been wrapped in soft cloth and buried at the bottom of a trunk brought by Christian's parents for us when they came west. I pushed the latch and lifted the lid. They might be valuable enough to sell. Maybe it would buy our passage to…somewhere. Like taking a walk on a dark beach with a lantern to mark the path, I had just enough light for my next step but not yet a vision of where we'd end up. I folded my letter to Christian and put it in my reticule.

I felt a rush now, placing Ida in Christian's old baby board and wrapping her securely. She slept on the table while I went out to saddle Fritz. Another irony: my husband had access to a mule all the time for farming; now I'd use him to slip away. Kate came running when she saw me. "Nothing, Mama. Just the birds and those scamper rats."

"Ground squirrels," I said. "That's good. Now go inside and pick out your favorite toy. Just one. We're going on a trip."

Her eyes brightened. "To see Andy and Christian?"

"In part," I said.

I scanned the house. Only memories remained to be packed.

The act of saddling up took strength. I stopped to catch my breath. The infection continued to need treatment, but if I could stay well for the next few days, that was all I needed. Maybe we should just head east, follow the Cowlitz, leave the way Louisa and Keil had come and gone. But no, that would mean backtracking with the boys, and we might run into Jack coming home.

I returned to the house, fed Ida, who was crying, then put the baby board on my back and grabbed the food sack, which I placed over Fritz's neck. His tail flicked at flies. Kate carried her favorite soft doll. The cows bellowed and Opal bleated. "Sorry girls," I said, setting the cows and Opal loose. I hugged the goat, inhaled her earthy smell. "Good-bye." She bleated. At least they could graze. I hoped she wouldn't follow us. Then I grabbed Kate, lifted her up, and led the mule to a stump so I could mount. I felt a warm trickle on the inside of my thigh. *Blood.* It would just have to be. I couldn't stop to poultice it.

The mule trotted north along the trail. I looked back once, saw the goat trailing us. I turned the mule around. "Tie Opal back up," I told Kate. "Poor thing," I said. I couldn't afford the attention her presence would bring us.

When I looked back the second time, I saw only what Christian and I had done there together: the cabin, the half barn, the garden, that section of frivolous flowers. We'd made a life believing we followed God's plan. I turned away. I didn't know what would happen next and could only see a few hours in front of me, a small light in the dark, unveiling just what I needed next and no more. I'd have to trust God for the rest.

———

We approached Mary's house, Kate humming to make this a happy outing. Karl sat on the porch smoking his pipe. I waved but didn't stop the mule from its fast-paced walk.

"*Frau* Giesy," he stood, shouted to us. "Where are you off to this fine morning?"

"I thought I'd visit the children," I yelled back. "Have a good day."

"They're both at the Giesys then?" I waved and nodded. We kept riding. "Well, stop for some tea then. You've plenty of time."

"*Nein.* We need to be back before Jack gets home."

"*Ja,* by golly. You have a nice trip then," he called out. "Tell Henry and Martin hello for me."

"I will," I sang back over my shoulder. I held my arms to my stomach. My body ached all over.

We crossed Mill Creek. Jack worked upstream. There'd be sympathy galore for him once I was gone. Everyone would remind him of my willful ways and how difficult a wife I was and how fortunate he was to be rid of me. I could imagine how I'd add to the conversations at the stockade after I was gone. The mule plodded across the creek. I turned around now and then to see if anyone followed us. No one did. And I began to think I might be able to do this, I just might.

The Willapa ford came next. No need for the rowboat today. The mule splashed us across. Kate giggled at the wet splatter on her legs. On the far bank I slid down so I could nurse a hungry babe. "You stay close by, Kate," I said. I staked the mule so that it could rip at grass while I unwound Ida from her board. "Shh, *Liebchen,*" I said. She was my sweetheart now. I sang softly to her, felt the breeze against my breast. *The last time I'll see these trees,* I thought. I recorded last times, again.

When she was sated, I put Ida back in her board, then tried to stand. I felt dizzy, my knees as weak as *Spätzel.* I needed to eat. "Kate," I said. "Come help Mama walk to the mule." I looked around. "Kate?" Where had she gone? "Kate!"

"Here I am, Mama," she stepped out of the willows.

"Don't get out of my sight. Mama worries. She needs to see you all the time."

Kate's lower lip pooched out, but she came to me, helped steady me while I went to the mule. I opened the sack and gave Kate a biscuit and jerky, chewed a pancake myself. Kate and I drank from the canteen, then put the cork back. I lifted Ida. We were barely three miles from home and already I felt exhausted.

That's when I heard the sound.

"Hush, Kate. Someone's coming."

"Papa Jack?" Her voice quivered.

"I hope not."

There was no sense hiding. If it was Jack, I'd do my best to defend my story: we had chosen the day to visit. He'd take us back home. I'd try another day. Part of me almost wished it would happen that way, I was so tired. But I remembered seeing Andy's eyes as he held Jack's muzzle loader across his bony knees, and I knew there was no turning back even if it was Jack behind us on the trail.

It wasn't Jack, but Karl, who approached fast for an older man. "Karl," I said. I heard relief in my voice. "Did we drop something when we passed by?"

"No, by golly. I decide to take a visit to Martin's myself. You don't mind if I walk with you?"

"Not at all," I said. He'd slow us down but maybe his presence would give me cover if Jack appeared.

"Do you have business with Martin?" I asked Karl as we walked. We kept his slower pace. I tried not to let my fingers fidget.

"Maybe I'll see how the school is readied for the term. Talk to Martin about the latest news and whatnot." He walked in silence for a time. Then, "Maybe I'll take a trip out to the sea. Remember when we did that, you and me and Christian?"

"I do," I said.

"*Ja.* A long time ago that was. Christian's gone."

"Such a waste," I said.

"Joe's back in Bethel."

"It was a very long time ago."

We moved to the rhythm of Kate's humming. Inside my own head I heard the refrain of *You, you, you must go,* less driven now that we were on our way, but still like a drumbeat, like a husband's voice, encouraging. Maybe I should listen to that voice even if I wasn't sure of the outcome.

I took a chance. "I wonder if you might like to take the trip again," I said. "With the children and me."

"Oh, *ja,* that would be a good thing sometime."

"I mean…today," I said.

"Oh? Is that your plan then?"

I bristled. "What do you mean, 'my plan'?"

"You're not planning to come back home tonight, Emma Giesy. I knew you told a lie when you said that."

My mouth went dry.

"Why would you say that?"

"You have Fritz carrying a lot of food along for just an afternoon visit," he said. "A big pack for such a little time away from home."

"And if it were true that I wasn't planning to come home this evening—"

"I'd say it would be better if you went south on the Bay and then down the Wallacut. Jack won't think to look for you that way. He knows you don't like the ocean."

Karl knew! He knew about Jack's sporadic behavior. He knew we were in danger. He even knew about some of my demons.

I swallowed. "Will he know where we're headed?"

"*Ja*, to Aurora Mills. It's the only place left for you to go." He hesitated, then added, "But you don't have to go alone."

———

Aurora Mills. Keil. To go there was an admission of my need and failure, a silencing of my song. Yet it was what everyone else thought best for us. My parents were upset that I hadn't gone there with Keil in the first place. Jonathan thought I should have gone there after Christian died. Louisa Keil and Helena, Christian's sister, thought we should all come there to help relieve Keil's burdens. Maybe I had to lean on the wisdom of others in order to move me through my distorted world.

I can't go there.

"If it's so obvious, I should go to San Francisco, then. Or…" I sighed. I could smell the rot from my stitches. Going anywhere distant was a fantasy.

"Your husband recruited me," Karl reminded me. "I came to the colony as a way to be in service, to live my faith. When he went oystering, I promised your husband that whatever you needed would be provided. I didn't expect you to resist good gifts." He smiled. "You don't have to let Wilhelm Keil decide your life for you, Emma, even if you do accept his help. I am led by a faithful God, by golly. Not by Keil."

Was he suggesting that living in the colony didn't mean one must follow all Keil's teachings? I recalled a man in Bethel who'd operated a store in the middle of the town but never joined up.

"About Jack," I told Karl. "He's—"

"He spent long nights up and down at Boshie's. That's why Boshie provided a bed at the mill. He had a place for his drawings there," Karl said. "Strange drawings." He sped up to get in front as the trail narrowed, then walked beside Fritz again. He cleared his throat. "Jack hurts you. I didn't know how to help. Now I do."

"I...I annoy him, the children and I do. I think he struggles with how to live in a full house after staying alone at the mill."

"You're not leaving him because he's annoyed," Karl said.

I looked away. Shame bled through me. "I'm not a good wife, Karl. I am willful and wanting. But Jack...Andy...I have to get my children someplace safe. Jack, well Andy—"

"Aurora Mills. We'll keep you safe there if you let us."

"I have a pearl necklace. I can sell it, buy our way to San Francisco or Olympia."

"And then? With four little children? You will be like a widow, Emma, all over again but in the outside world, where people are not always friendly."

"They aren't always friendly inside this colony, either."

"Surrender, by golly. You are strong enough to accept the help of others, Emma. It does not mean your demise."

Tears of weariness slid down my cheeks. The visions of an artist's studio in Olympia rose before my eyes and faded. Those things would never be if I went to Aurora Mills. But Karl was right. My sons would be safe. I'd be safe. As much as Keil dominated the colonists, he was more like a band's conductor, using his wand to guide and direct but never to strike us. We women worked harder to express our music there, but we could. *We.* Was I still a colonist at heart?

We moved in silence then until reaching Barbara's home. This would be my last time here, too. I slid from the mule and stood for a time, just leaning against the animal, breathing in his scent of sweat. My whole body throbbed. My legs quivered with weakness. Ida made crying noises and I moved to pull her from my back. Karl assisted me. He grinned at the little wizened face that was my daughter. He would have made a fine father.

Andy ran out of the cabin. "You're here, you're here! I was afraid you wouldn't come. Or that Jack hurt you again."

"Shh, now. I'm fine," I said, holding him into my skirts.

"Let me help you," Barbara said. *Had she not heard Andy's words about Jack?* "You shouldn't be riding on a day like this. The boys do well here. There's no need for you to worry over them."

"She's taking us away," Andy said. He fairly sang the words. "We're going far away aren't we, Mama?"

"We may," I said. "I just need to rest now."

"Where are you going?" Barbara asked. "You surely didn't leave anything in Olympia you have to go back for."

I gave her a weak smile, motioned for the steps and sat down on them.

How can I possibly take these children and leave, moving fast enough to not be caught by Jack?

"I'll fix you something to eat," Barbara said.

Food. It solved everything for us Germans. Just feed the worry or problem and it would make it better. I shook my head. "No. We have to be going." I thought of the tides taking us out and wanting to be on a ship that went with it. I'd have to throw myself on the mercy of these people and ask them for money. Money to get away from them. Money to take my children to a place I could only hope was safer than where they were.

"You need to eat," Barbara insisted. *Is she stalling for time?*

"If you want to help, I need to go to Sarah and Sam's. If you'll watch Kate and the boys for a minute more."

She frowned.

Louisa shuffled outside with Christian following at her heels. He ran to me, patted my back. Maybe Louisa could travel with us.

"You'll be back right away?" Barbara asked.

I nodded. Karl frowned, but when I motioned to him, he assisted with my mounting the mule and handing Ida up to me. "I'll introduce her to Sam and Sarah. They haven't met her yet."

"I'll come too, Mama," Andy said.

"I'll be back," I said. "You wait here with Christian and Kate." I ignored my son's scowl as I pressed the reins to the mule's neck.

I rode the short distance to Sarah's and shouted for her. I didn't dare get off the mule for fear that I wouldn't have the strength to get back on. She opened her door to me, her own child on her hip. "Emma! Come in, come in."

I shook my head. "I've come to ask for money. I need money to buy fares to take me and the children away from here. I know I'm always thinking of myself, never was a good friend to you, and now I'm here being needy again."

"You can stay here, with us," she said. "Tell me what's going on."

"It wouldn't work. Jack would be here constantly demanding. I have to go away, far away. Someplace safe." I pulled the pearls from my reticule.

"Oh. Jack. Well, where will you go? Olympia? Portland?"

"Aurora Mills will keep my children safe," I said. I said it as though it was a truth.

"We'll get the fares for you," Sarah said. "It's a gift. I don't want your pearls and neither would Sam. Go back and get the children. The boat will leave before long. If you miss this one, you'll have to wait until morning."

I loved that she asked no more questions, just accepted my need. I headed back realizing she really hadn't met Ida. The sting of loss pricked my eyes. I couldn't afford to pay attention to it now. We were escaping. I'd deal with the difficulties of Keil when I reached him, but Karl was right: Keil needn't map out my life or my faith. I didn't want Jack to illustrate who I was, either. I needed to do that myself.

We were on our way. It was what I sang to myself as I headed the mule back. I sang it until I saw Jack, hands on his hips, a glare in his eyes, standing in the middle of Barbara's yard.

My heart pounded and the mule must have sensed it. Fritz started to dance around, bouncing Ida's board more. She whimpered. Not even a month old and she was being jousted around like a single egg in a basket.

"Well enough to ride, I see." Jack reached for the bridle and held the mule steady. Fritz sidestepped at Jack's abrupt movement.

"Did they not need you at the mill?" I asked as innocently as I could.

"I thought I should check on my sons, see if they were really here. Now I have the surprise of Ida as well."

Andy's eyes peeked from around the cabin's corner. "They're fine. You can go back to your work."

Martin stood beside his mother on the porch, and Karl had taken out his pipe and smoked as he stood on the other side of Jack. Were they my allies or allied against me? Had Karl gone to tell Jack before he caught up with us?

"*Ja,* everyone is well, Jack," Martin offered. "You go back to work and come later. Spend the night here. A little outing for you all. Emma travels to visit the doctor and stopped here. She'll go home with you tomorrow. Nothing more."

His voice soothed like one of his herbs, and I reasoned that he wasn't against me even though his words could be interpreted to express as much. "Come inside now. Mother will prepare food for you and you can go back to work."

Andy stood off to the side, watching. Jack hesitated, then let loose the bridle. He squeezed the calf of my leg with his wide hands. *A warning.* He walked into the house, and Martin looked at me before stepping in behind him. Was it a signal I should go? Stay? Would they keep him inside? Would he really just eat and go back to work? There wasn't time. The boat would leave. I signaled to Andy to come to me. "Go get Kate and Christian," I whispered to him. "Go. Now."

Karl shook his head at me as he saw Andy scramble around the back of the cabin. "It's too dangerous," he said, approaching me. He didn't look at me as he stroked the mule's neck. "You are too weak to start now and Jack is too close. Wait until morning. Come, I'll help you dismount."

"But—"

Jack came out of the house while Karl assisted me. He held a hunk of bread and cheese. "Be here when I get back later," Jack said. He held my gaze and it seemed to me he willed the opposite of his words; he willed me to go, to take my children and leave him before he did something that couldn't be taken back.

"Don't I always do what's best?" I said.

"*Ja,*" Jack said. "You're an obedient woman." With that he mounted his own mule and trotted off.

"Now," I told Karl when Jack was well out of sight.

"You take Ida and Kate and go," Martin said, coming out on the porch. "Leave the boys here."

"No! He'll come back and when I'm not here he'll blame Andy. Or worse, Andy will—"

"I won't let Jack hurt him or let Andy do anything rash. I promise you, Emma," Martin said. "The boys are my nephews. I only want the best for them. And for you. Go now while you can. You go to Aurora Mills. You trust me with your sons. Their presence here will buy you time."

"*Ja,* by golly, time is what you need, to get to safety and make a way for all your children," Karl said. "But help too. I'll go with you, Emma," Karl said.

"But you said to wait until morning."

"Martin's offer is sound. Leave the boys for him to bring later."

Were they all in this to take my sons away?

"We'll tell Jack you've gone for a visit to Aurora Mills," Martin said. "Maybe that you're hoping your parents are there by now. We'll suggest that you'll be back."

"He'll believe this if the boys are here," Barbara added. "He'll know you wouldn't stay away from them for long." She took my hand, the way she had the day she spent with me after Christian died, the day I'd once felt close to her. "That's what I'll tell him."

They would lie for me? Maybe they lie to me.

Would Andy ever forgive my leaving him again? Still, they were right. Jack wouldn't come after us if he saw the boys there. He'd be outraged and angry, but he'd expect my return and might not follow. Especially if he realized that Karl was along. Jack would expect Karl back for the school term. He'd expect me to come back with him.

The big unknown was whether I could trust Martin to do as he said, to bring the boys as soon as he could. He was a kind man, an uncle, the brother of my husband. Family. But he was a Giesy, as Jack was.

I had to trust them all and hope they were the calm in my storm.

"You'll prevent Jack from hurting the boys? And Andy…you'll keep him from, doing anything…foolish? You can't let Jack take them home with him."

"I promise this," Martin said. "Go now."

Andy rounded the corner with Christian in tow. Kate breathed hard, running to catch up. "We're going now, Mama?" It was Andy.

"*Ja*. But only Kate and the baby and me and Karl. Martin will bring you and Christian soon. He's promised."

"You can't go!"

"I have to, Andy." I reached for him. "Jack won't try to follow us if you're still here. He'll think I'll be back. Please. You can help by staying here with Christian and being quiet about Martin bringing you to Aurora Mills. Which he will."

Andy jerked from me. He stepped back, tears pooling and running down his hot face. He ran from me then, and while I wanted to pursue him, let him know he was not lost, I couldn't. The tide would not wait. Leaving now was our best chance.

"Comfort him, Martin," I said. Martin took Christian's hand. My youngest son twisted to see where Andy ran, turned back to stare at me. "I'll see you soon," I said. "Be good for *Oma* and Uncle Martin." Christian nodded. "When?" I asked Martin. "When will you bring them?"

"When the timing is right," he said.

It was as committal as he would get.

31

Emma

An Offer Tendered

I forced Andy's face from my mind. We rushed now. Martin loaned Karl a mule. We fast-trotted to the Woodards' wharf.

"Where are the boys?" Sarah asked as she helped me dismount, steadied me as I leaned against the mule, breathing hard. Kate rode with Karl and she stayed frozen on his mule.

"Martin's promised to bring them later," I said. "Oh, Sarah, pray that I can trust him. Pray that he won't hand them over to Jack." She held me and the gentle warmth of her arms brought the tears. "Pray. Please."

"I will, but your prayers are heard, too, Emma."

I wasn't so sure. I was returning to the colony I'd wanted most to avoid, leaving my sons behind. All I'd ever wanted to do was protect my children. Instead I'd made choices that put them in peril. That wasn't a path that led to answered prayers.

I pulled at my bonnet strings. "Maybe I should have taken my drawings to Olympia. Maybe I should have let the Willapa people take care of me without complaint, been grateful for what I had."

"If you can't accept the goodness your family offers now, how will you ever accept what God has to give? This is the first sketch," Sarah assured me, "of the new drawing you'll make." She held me by the shoulders, staring into my eyes. "What Karl gives, what Martin offers, those will keep you going for now."

She handed me the tickets. "And your help," I said. "Thank you. I'll pay you back, I will." I owed so many so much. I wondered if this was how Christian felt about repaying Keil. Debts mounted up inside the heart and mind. Maybe repaying Keil for our land was Christian's way of wiping the slate clean rather than an admission that he wanted to return to colony life under Keil's rule. Why hadn't I thought of that before?

Ida stirred in her board and I lifted her from the mule.

"We need to go, by golly," Karl said. He'd lifted Kate, dismounted, then taken the satchel from my mule's neck. All our earthly goods. Karl had brought nothing with him save the clothes on his back. But then, he trusted that he'd get whatever he needed at the Aurora colony store. Maybe one day I'd trust in that too.

Sarah kissed me good-bye and we walked as fast as I could to the mail boat, stepped up and in. We thanked the tide and the boatman's strong arms for oaring us away.

The sky loomed above us like a blue porcelain plate. No storms in the wind. Seagulls dipped and called. The oars sloshed against the Willapa River, and it seemed we ached away from the shore, hesitating, the craft resisting the boatman's efforts. Maybe hesitation marked all important changes, where the heart sensed that newness waited and took a last inspiring breath. The Willapa Hills watched our escape. I wished we could have gone once more to Christian's grave. I would have picked up the oyster shell painting as a reminder of how I didn't always see things at first glance, that I needed reflection to find true meaning. I wish I could have forgiven the old man whose furniture lured my husband to his death. No, it wasn't the furniture at all. Some things just happened to people. Christian had died caring for others. It was how he lived.

"Help me live to be a better, wiser mother," I whispered with a kiss to Ida's head. It was the only prayer now that mattered.

In Bruceport, Karl purchased fares for our journey south. Another debt owed him. The weather had shifted and dark clouds billowed up out over the sea. It was July and just threatened. I kept my eyes from the site where Christian had died. We took a wooden boat out to a waiting ship. Karl called it a tender, as I had heard before. But he explained, "A vessel attendant on another. It ferries supplies back and forth from ship to shore. The coal car behind an engine on a train is called a tender too."

"It serves something larger than itself," I said.

"*Ja*. It's a *gut* word."

"As you tender us to safety." As Martin tendered his offer to bring me my sons. "It's caring for another when we…when I…feel so fragile." I felt the tears press behind my eyes, blinked them away.

———

They put us in a small storeroom with one cot. I wasn't sure this ship took many passengers, but they'd agreed to take us. The room smelled of fish and lumber, ropes, and the sharp scent of pack rats. As soon as the children were tended, Karl said, "You rest now, Emma. I will watch the babies."

I didn't think I could sleep but I did. I dreamed then of a kitchen hearth with ten women dressed in white, their caps tied tight beneath their chins, all looking alike as they stood, five on each side of a long table piled high with food. Wonderful, steaming German food served on plates painted with mills and flowers and flying birds. Show towels hung on slender racks around the room. I wasn't sure how I could see the designs painted on the plates with so much food piled on top of them, but I did. Colorful, beautiful landscapes blessed by *Strudels* and cakes and sugar cookies. At the head of the table stood a man who looked familiar but I couldn't place him. It wasn't Christian or my father. His eyes looked dark, his eyebrows white and flying. *Where are the other men?* I wondered. The man at the head of the table gave a blessing to the food and bid the women to sit down. Chairs scraped against the wood floors. Their skirts swished and in seconds, they were seated, all except me. I couldn't move my chair! I struggled and pulled and felt my heart beating, working so hard. My children stood off to the side, waiting to come to the table, but I couldn't move the heavy chair or invite them to sit!

Then the man at the head of the table stood and called me by name and motioned me forward. How had he recognized me? We all looked alike in our uniforms of white. My heart pounded. I wiped my hands on my apron. I was being called before this dark-eyed man all because I couldn't get the chair to move!

But then this face, once fearful, turned friendly, his eyes warm molasses, not dark eggs of coal. He offered me his hand, reached out to me. "Come closer, Emma." He sounded welcoming. "You have nothing to fear." I wanted to surrender, to let him lead me forward, but I didn't know if I could trust him. I didn't know who he was. My father? Jack? Keil? "Come closer, Emma. Take this chair." He offered me a wooden chair large enough to hold me and my children, all of them. *"Komm und is,"* he said. *Come and dine.* I wrapped my arms around my children and we sat and ate at last, the children crying with joy.

I woke up with a start. "Ida?" I'd heard a soft cry. I looked around the small room.

"The *Kinder* are *gut,*" Karl said. "But I think your little one might be hungry. I can look after Kate but can't do what you can do for Ida." He smiled. He sat on the floor and played a game with strings, keeping Kate entertained. I lifted Ida from her board. So small. So tender. So easily crushed. She breathed deeply and returned to sleep now that I cradled her. Even without food she lay content just being in the comfort of my breast.

"I've asked for the ship's doctor to visit you later," Karl said. I nodded my thanks. Maybe the kindly man in the dream was Karl. But the man had been able to pull me from the others. He knew my name and didn't chastise me for my weakness. He understood that I couldn't make it to the table on my own.

I dozed after that, my baby heavy on my chest. I awoke when the doctor knocked on the door. He stepped over a coil of rope just inside the cabin and offered me a fresh poultice for my still seeping stitches. He and Karl discreetly left me to complete my ministrations. Later I fed Ida, grateful that I had what she needed, that we were not dependent on Opal or the kindness of strangers to keep her alive. We had enough food for the evening supper. Tomorrow would take care of itself.

With Kate in my lap, I asked Karl if the ship headed to the Wallacut River, if we'd have to portage to the Columbia or whether we'd head out to sea.

"I thought the way down the slough to the Wallacut might be too rough for you." It was the way Christian would have gone if he had lived. "We go to the ocean and sail south to Astoria. There we cross the bar and take another boat to Portland, and then ride the stage to Aurora Mills.

"If Jack comes overland could he beat us there?"

Karl looked thoughtful. "*Ja,* that is possible. It will take us a few days. We may need to rest in Portland. For you." *Unlike Jack, Karl doesn't think I pretend to be ill.* "Jack might go night and day and get there first."

"What will I have gained," I said, "if he meets us there?"

"You won't stand alone when you face him. But more, you'll have a safe place to stay when he leaves."

"I couldn't have done this without your help. Just getting in and out of the tender vessel took more effort than I imagined."

Karl shrugged. I thought the color on his face might have darkened, but the candlelight was dim in the small cabin. I wished, then, that I'd brought along Christian's lantern. It grieved me that I'd left it behind.

"*Ja,* by golly, you will be safe there. That will be an answered prayer."

I hadn't known Karl prayed about me or my family. He'd kept a watchful eye through the years and thank goodness it was friendly. "Christian's family never accepted me," I said. "So I tried to stay out of their way, not owe them any debt."

"*Ach,* Emma, you tell yourself a story there," Karl said. "You never waded in to their family. You always swam offshore, by yourself."

"And swam right into a shark named Jack," I said. "But doing things on our own—isn't that what we Germans are about? The strong don't need others."

"We all need tending," Karl said. "We are children in God's sight, and every good parent knows not to let their child stray too far from a father's love."

"Or a mother's," I said, though I'd let my children stray into Jack's life, bringing them harm. Through the closed door I could hear the water push against the ship's sides, a steady swishing rhythm taking us to Aurora Mills. "You're so kind to go with us, Karl," I said. "I am so grateful."

He shrugged. "I'm ready to stay. John will handle the instruction at Willapa and it's time there was a school at Aurora Mills. A church too. Wilhelm may need prodding about building the church." Karl grinned. "He still thinks he is in control of the colony, but I see how his grip slips and by golly, I think that's a good thing for us all."

"It's easy for you to say such things. As a man, Keil listens to you."

"It isn't Keil I'm trying to please," he said.

The words felt like a splash of cold water on my face. Who was I trying to please? Kate came to lie on the cot while I sat, her head in my lap. She snored a child's snore of contentment. The room smelled of fish and the old ropes that felt scratchy when I lifted them out of the way. "When you disagreed with Wilhelm and stayed in Willapa, that didn't change your confidence in the colony?"

"*Nein.* My confidence is in doing the Lord's work. It doesn't matter where I live to do that. Remember, Emma, in the Hebrew, *religion* means 'tying together again.' Sometimes Wilhelm's doctrine tied tight knots, but it's Christian love that binds. I look for God's threads to guide me, not Wilhelm's. You can do this too."

———

The journey gave me rested time to think, to grieve. When the image of Andy's despair at being left behind came to me, I spoke a prayer for him, that one day he'd understand. We sailed into Astoria, my stomach sickened from the rough bar crossing between ocean and river. Two mighty forces pushed against each other and I wondered if that was Keil and me. We stayed a day in the Oregon coastal town so I could rest and see another doctor. Then we took a smaller craft toward Portland. The costs of this journey grew, and I knew Sarah had not loaned us more than the first passage. Karl had provided the rest. I was in debt to him. Maybe I always would be. In debt to his kindness, to Mary's midwifery, to Sarah's understanding. I owed so much. People had kept us alive after Christian's death. I owed them too. Maybe I even owed Jack.

No. All Jack ever gave me was the oyster shell painting, and he'd taken that back. Well, he'd fathered Ida, but I felt nothing was due him for that.

The stage left Portland at eight o'clock on that early August morning, taking us through Oregon City. The stage road hugged black basaltic rocks to the east, followed the river at the west. Though the sky was cloudless, I heard a sound like thunder as we rounded a bend. Then I saw it. Mist rose up from nearly a quarter mile of horseshoe-shaped falls stretching across the Willamette River. Tons of water silvered its way over the ridge of rocks and plunged thirty feet to the depths below, rolling and surging, then cascading out toward the Columbia that separated us from Washington Territory. "It's where the Indians fish for salmon, by golly," Karl shouted above the noise. Docks stacked with wheat ready for shipment jutted out well below the falls. "It will drive industry too," Karl continued. "That chief factor of Hudson's Bay chose this site long ago. He knew. We're but a few miles now from Aurora Mills. It's a good place to settle, Emma." He smiled, and I thought he might take my hand in his and pat it. Instead he lifted Kate's little chin and directed her eyes. "A rainbow," Karl said. *"Ja?"* She nodded at the arc of color and light spinning over the waterfall. I saw her smile. She hadn't done much of that.

Maybe this *was* what I was supposed to do. Maybe when our minds and bodies are frayed, we have to do things that others think best, even when those things seem so contrary. In order to mend we allow others to light our paths back to safety, back to our place of belonging, into the folds of faith.

There were prairies here, more wide-open spaces, not unlike Missouri. The stage stopped and we waited for the tollman to come out and lift the gate. The driver shouted to get the man's attention but he didn't leave the tollhouse. We decided to walk across, as we were the only passengers and none waited on the other side. We carried little luggage, and I managed that while using my cane. For a moment I hesitated again, wondering if the tollman might be held hostage inside by Jack or if Jack would jump out at us partway up the hill. Would it always be thus, fears of the possibilities overtaking joyous potential? Only if I allowed it, I decided. I would force myself to think of the good that could be until such thinking was habit. It was what I controlled now, my thoughts.

The stage rolled through the open gate, and I balanced myself with my cane. Kate squatted to make mud pies along the riverbanks. It was a pleasant enough landscape with fir and white ash and cedar dotting the prairie. The air smelled fresh and sometimes when the wind lay, I thought I heard a band's music. We looked like a typical family of the time, especially during war, when the man of the family soldiered off somewhere and a grandfather became the support that a woman with children needed.

"What this place needs is an alert tollman, by golly," Karl said, as annoyed as I'd ever seen him be. A man came out of the small wood hut that housed him, stretched. He must have fallen asleep in the warmth. "Sorry," he said, putting his pail out for us to drop in our tolls.

"You missed six dollars to collect if you'd been awake for the stage," Karl told him.

"Not mine to earn or keep," he said, smiling. "He'll pay on his return."

The grassy trail followed a natural incline, taking us into the town I'd so dreaded. I knew it in my imagination. My son had been here, the only family member to see this place. Well, Jack had been here. I just hoped he wasn't here now.

"Are we there, Mama?" Kate asked. She slapped dirt from her hands.

"Almost," I said. I stopped to catch my breath and touched her head.

The sun warmed her dark curls. I shifted Ida on my shoulder, the weight of her a comfort.

"Look for the biggest house," Karl said. "That's Elim, or at least what Wilhelm is living in until they build him his big house one day."

Louisa had made it sound so glorious, but Aurora Mills wasn't much more than a few houses. Perhaps what gave someone the joy of home wasn't in the actual features of a place, the structures or even gardens, but in the people. Maybe that was why I'd convinced Christian to stay in the Willapa country with his family, our family. Then he died and all the relationships changed. Who I was as Christian Giesy's wife became the burden of Christian Giesy's widow. Worse, I didn't know who I was without him. Here, Louisa was surrounded by people who loved her and whom she loved back. No wonder she sang the town's praises.

We passed a single log house, then another with cut boards. Flowers grew at a window box. I wondered if the Wagonblast family that had walked their way across the continent with Keil and spent the winter with us had come here or had found lives outside the colony. *Perhaps they'll take me in.* I stopped, the compass needle spinning around toward new options.

"What is it, Emma?"

I started forward again. "I will trust and not be afraid," I said under my breath. "The Lord, the Lord is my song."

"From Isaiah," Karl Ruge said. "Think of this too, Emma Giesy: 'If we walk in the light, as he is in the light, we have fellowship one with another.' Like the disciples, we hold all in common. But we all have something to give; we share even what we fear as we walk in that light." I nodded. "*Ja*, by golly, that's what you must cling to now, sharing what you have and what you fear."

Beyond, hops fields would soon be ready for harvest. Small apple saplings grew amid stumps of trees. "I suppose Wilhelm still requires a tree be cut before breakfast," Karl said. "He's planted hickory trees, did I tell you this? Brought all the way from Bethel." He pointed then. "That's it." We walked up a grassy grade to a two-story house with a wide porch on both levels. My heart started to pound; I held back. Karl spoke: "This is the way. Walk thee in it."

"Knock and it shall be opened," I said, the old scriptures coming back to me like homing pigeons sent by someone I loved.

Before Karl could knock on the door it opened from the inside and there stood Louisa Keil, a smile on her face.

"I told Helena it was you!" she cried. "I said, 'Emma Giesy and Karl Ruge are walking up our path,' and she laughed. See who will laugh now! It's them!" she shouted back over her shoulder. "Come see, Husband. And little Kate too." She tried to squat, but her hip must have hurt. Still, Kate appeared to remember her from when they'd visited last year, because she didn't seem shy with Louisa.

"Can I have a cookie?" she asked. "I'm fairly hungry."

"*Ja*, sure. And who is this?" Louisa asked, as she steadied herself. She leaned over Ida's face.

"Ida," I said. "Jack's child."

"So fragile-looking, yet made such a long trip. You just come inside." She spoke the *j* so it sounded like *yust*. "My goodness, you must be weary. Are Jack and the boys behind?" She looked past me toward the trail.

"Jack isn't coming. I hope," I said.

"Ah," she said. Her words carried no judgment.

"You've left your husband?" Helena Giesy asked. " 'The Lord God of Israel hateth putting away.' " She quoted the Old Testament's Malachi.

"*Ja*, divorce He abhors, but more, He hates violence. It is in the same verse, Helena." I thought I caught Louisa smile as I turned to her. "The boys will come later, when Martin brings them."

"Then you are welcome to stay for as long as you like," she said, inviting us into the cool of the wide entry where a staircase rose to the second floor. She reached for Ida. "Helena, prepare food for our guests. God has led you here," she said to me. "That is all we need to know about the circumstances." She scowled at Helena, who hadn't moved yet. I hadn't noticed before Louisa's flying white eyebrows.

32

Emma

Prayers of Preparation

Within minutes of our untying our caps, Keil entered, filling the room. "Karl," he said, giving him a bear hug, slapping his back. "Always good to see you in Aurora. Look, girls," he motioned for his children, and four of them like stair steps stood beside him. "See who is here now. My old friend, Karl. Your teacher," he said. The children nodded politely, and then he dismissed them to one of the big rooms on either side of the entry. To Aurora he said, "Take Sister Emma's children with you when you go."

I hadn't been here five minutes and Keil, who had not even acknowledged my presence, already directed my children. "Kate can go, but Ida I'll keep with me."

"*Ja*, she's so young. Barely a month old she looks like," Louisa said.

Keil didn't seem to notice that she stood with me in defying him. "Get Kate some milk. And cookies," Louisa said, and Kate happily went with young Aurora, never looking back.

"So. You come to stay this time," Keil said. He spoke to Karl and it wasn't a question. "I cannot get those from Bethel to hurry along." I waited for Karl to reply as Keil motioned him into the side room. "You," Keil continued, turning to me, motioning me to follow. "Emma Giesy. Why are you here without the rest of your family?"

"I've come for…protection," I said. "From my husband. I'm no longer a widow, but I seek a widow's solace."

Those piercing dark eyes stared, ready to intimidate at a moment's notice. "I would not have let you marry Jack Giesy if you had sought permission, which you should have."

"I was never good at permission-seeking," I said.

"*Ja*. This I remember," he said. He raised his finger to the air. He grunted then crossed his arms over his broad chest. "Now you come seeking a widow's solace."

"As the colony protected women back in Bethel whether they were members or not. Whether they'd made wise choices placing them in need or not. Isn't that so? It was the Diamond Rule we tendered there, to make others' lives better than our own."

"Divorce we do not approve of."

"She quotes Malachi to us," Helena said. The tall woman had stepped into the room uninvited. I was pleased to see that Louisa had as well.

"Violence covering like a garment, the Lord does not approve of that either," I said. "Does God ask us simply to endure? Is this the Diamond Rule of the discipleship?"

I teetered at the top of a pyramid and could imagine Keil pushing me either way: to this colony and safety or back to the bed I'd made. I felt my face flush to be in such a precarious place, throwing myself at the mercy of the man I so despised. I decided then that if Keil would not receive us, I would get the boys and we would go to San Francisco, someplace far away, and we would make a path, God willing. But I'd never go back to Jack. I didn't belong with him.

"I won't need your protection for long," I offered. "I have a plan."

"*Ja*, you always did have that," Keil said.

"Women and children in need have always been safe with the colony," Karl said. "It is the Lord's most important directive to us. Is that not right, Wilhelm? Is that different here in Aurora Mills than it was back in Bethel?"

Keil placed his fingertips together in front of him, Karl's words causing him to pause.

"We offer protection for any who need it. Women, children, slaves. Does she need it?" He asked Karl.

He'd accept Karl's assessment but not mine. "I've seen enough of Jack's ways to be worried, by golly. Emma has no reason to come here otherwise. She gives up what she and Christian worked together for. She prays that Martin will bring her sons soon and that you will allow her to stay. Perhaps she can go somewhere else after that."

"Martin thinks about coming? To stay?" Louisa interjected.

"He would be a big help here," Helena said.

"As I've often said," Louisa added. "With your doctoring, my husband. You would have relief."

"Louisa, you mustn't—"

"It's true, Husband. Maybe more will come from Willapa now that Karl and Emma have. If we treat Emma as we should."

Keil sighed. "Oh, the weight of leadership." He looked at me. "Both of you speak truths. I know Jack. Something…happens to him at times." Keil looked away. "We saw it here. I thought it was the whiskey and prayed he would give it up."

"I speak another truth," I said.

"What is that, Sister Emma?" Keil said.

I swallowed hard, and my fingertips, crooked now from Jack's maltreatment, made tiny circles against the pads of my thumb. I had to be willing to accept the colony's help but also to assert my claim. "I ask for asylum then not as any widow but as the widow of the leader of the colony's scouts, as the wife of a man who did God's bidding and yours with a faithful heart. It is my due."

"You are a bold one, Sister Emma," Helena said. "After all that has happened."

"She only asks what a mother needs," Louisa said. "Even our Lord tells us to seek that."

"Christian would want you to do this, Wilhelm," Karl said. "Without asking, she deserves it. She is here asking. That is enough."

Keil clapped his hands. "You're right, Karl. You will stay here with us, in this *gross Haus* where we live and the bachelors live and where you can help Louisa and the girls with the cooking. You will give and receive in return. And our presence will offer the greatest protection for when Jack comes here. And I know he will."

"It will be like before when we all stayed together," Louisa said. Her voice was light, and she sounded like she planned an approved wedding. "Just like when we lived in the stockade together, only without the harsh winter this time."

"And without the husband who loved me," I said.

Louisa leaned in to me and patted my arm. "It has been four years, Sister Emma. Time to turn old griefs into tender stories."

In the days that followed, Keil couldn't have been more congenial to me. Maybe because I'd brought Karl with me. Maybe because we all awaited Martin's arrival with my boys, and Keil hoped he would convince Martin to remain, too. Maybe because I worked hard. Perhaps Louisa said good words about me and maybe Helena said nothing. I never complained, not once. Whatever the reason, he treated me as though I was a singular person, and I began to think I did deserve a life without threats, a safe dwelling place. Being here would never replace what Christian and I had built together in Willapa, but it would remind me always that God did provide and with that would come peace.

Helena led prayers in the morning before we began the day's cooking in the bottom floor of the house. I hadn't realized there were four stories when I'd arrived. It was a pleasant act, I found, starting the day with praise for life, thanking the hunters who provided the meat and those who tended the flour mill, hoping that harvest would go well. She asked that the food be prepared with love and then we'd begin, joined by other colony women, Louisa included.

Had the women done this back in Bethel? I couldn't remember. I'd lived in my family's home then, just a daughter helping my mother. We hadn't shared kitchens as we did here. We spoke a table grace but hadn't offered prayers for preparation. *Prayers for preparation.* That's how I began each morning now. I prayed that the boys would arrive soon, asked that Jack might never come. In the evening as we prepared to bed down, Keil spoke words to give us restful sleep. The bachelors and Keil's children all slept on the top floor, to which they'd go after the evening prayers. Keil and his wife slept on the first floor. Kate and I rolled out mats at the far side of the first floor in the kitchen area. I could see the moon rise through the window. I'd be able to hear anyone arriving on the porch. It was a short walk to the privy. How simple my needs were now. I'd be full every day if my sons were just here, if I was sure they were safe and that Andy had not returned to our home to get into Jack's way.

———

The time spent with the Keils gave me a new picture of Louisa. She did what she wanted, though mostly what she wanted was what Keil would approve of. Still, she influenced her husband and she lightened the tone for the workers, made little jokes. I'd always seen her as serious, somber even. Perhaps Helena's presence had rescued Louisa from having to be so stern. She liked words and their sounds and joked that my *Strudel* was as "fine as a frog's hair." When Keil's voice took on a frustrated tone, it was Louisa who calmed him and suggested who could assist, since he must be tired, so very tired, with all the burdens he carried. Once I thought she patronized with those words, but she meant them. She saw how he labored to make the colony operate and wanted to support him. It was how I'd served Christian once; I wished my wants were as generous and simple now.

One day Louisa surprised me by suggesting that I make a few drawings. "Why?" I asked.

"There's a harvest fair in October. Wilhelm says it will be the first-ever Oregon State Fair, and we can enter things that are judged. Paintings and needlework and dried fruits and baskets, even essays, words. And flowers."

"Women enter these things?"

"Last year there were several women who earned recognition. You draw lovely pictures. I've seen you do them for Kate. So then, go to the store and ask for drawing material."

"I doubt they'll have such a thing as pencils and whatnot."

"They'll get what you need. It's the common fund. Don't you remember?"

I remembered. "I'd always resented that practice," I told her. She raised an eyebrow. "It made me feel weak almost, that if I took something, then I'd always owe someone else. Or if I had nothing to give, then I was taking advantage of another. That's how I felt in Willapa after Christian died. It's why I tried so hard to do it on my own. Marrying Jack seemed like a good way to not be dependent on the Giesys. "

"*Ach*, Emma," she said. She patted my floured hand as I kneaded the dough. I added a little loaf sugar to sweeten it, something we didn't have in Willapa. I sat to do much of this work, still weak. "We put things into the common basket so it can be taken out. It's what love is. We all have things to give. The work we do that tends to others, that goes into the basket. What we grow for sale. Even our listening hearts, those are all a part of the fellowship of the common fund. It's not only money, Emma. There is always enough for everyone and all contribute. We put things in; we draw things out. Only God is enough."

"Andreas and Barbara wanted to raise my boys. They kept Andy there while he was at school. I didn't feel I could argue much since I was such a burden on everyone. That could happen here too."

"*Ach*, no. Here you are cooking. That is enough. You go now and get some drawing things when we finish here, *ja*? I insist."

I tried to imagine what I'd draw. The fields around Aurora Mills? The little house with the window box? The tollman asleep at his post? Would Keil approve of this frivolousness, a woman drawing pictures when she could otherwise be working?

"Will *Herr* Keil object?"

"He has his music. We have our needlework, show towels. Some men weave baskets and work with the looms, too, or they play in the band. These are practical, but they also lend beauty and lighten another's day. That is a contribution too."

"I suppose I could draw the girls," I said. "Aurora and Gloriunda, my Kate."

"Send one back to your parents. They'd like that. I'd like that. A drawing of my Aurora and Louisa and Amelia and Gloriunda."

"My parents do not write to me."

"Maybe they do but Jack intercepted their letters. They will write now to Aurora Mills and you can know you'll receive the letters. I still think they'll come here, and they won't have to make a detour to Willapa."

"Unless Martin fails to bring the boys."

"Did he say he'd bring them?" I nodded. "Then don't borrow trouble. Practice thinking good thoughts." She cocked her head as though she'd just said something out loud that surprised even herself.

I did go to the store and ask for paper and lead. I sketched eleven-year-old Aurora as she sat with Kate peeling an apple to eat. I drew my daughters, even Ida. I watched the other children as they played and saw the harvest of this colony, this place where people helped one another. There was a cost, yes, the little gripes and disappointments that flared up between people living close together. But the common bond of caring helped put the firebursts out. The heat diminished with familiarity and reminded me that in this living church, which is how I'd come to think of the people if not the colony, there were challenges, but none too big for God to turn around. Had I taken all the children and spent the time with Andreas and Barbara after Christian died, I might have been able to keep my home and my family together in Willapa. Instead I'd spoken vows with another and here I was, separated from the very children I'd hoped to always have with me. But no, I must not dwell on what was past. I had made the best decision I could then with no intention of making a poor choice. I'd done the best I could then; that's what I had to remember.

While I worked, I healed. I thought of that dream I'd had on the ship and decided it was a spiritual feast I'd been missing. I'd been trying so hard to get to the table but always doing it my own way. Someone strong sat at the head of the table. It wasn't Keil or Louisa or Karl. Most importantly, it wasn't me.

———

I hung wash on the line strung between two trees beside the washhouse. I heard a child's voice shouting, "Mama, Mama!" It wasn't Kate.

"Christian?" I turned toward the sound, and there my youngest son came running like a happy dog, his arms out and his legs swinging sideways as he tried to keep his balance with such uneven ground matched against his speed. I knelt as he approached, the cane dropping at my side. He knocked me over with his joy. "Christian, Christian, Christian, how good you look. How good you feel!"

"I took a bath. Martin made us."

"You were reluctant to take that bath. Tell her that," Martin said, as he caught up with Christian in the bundle of my arms.

"What's 'lucktent' mean, Mama?" Christian said, a small frown on his face.

"Unwilling," I said, kissing his sweet-smelling hair. "Mama can get reluctant, too, sometimes, avoiding things she doesn't want to face."

"Thank you, Martin," I continued. "For bringing him. Them." I wanted to ask if Jack had interfered at all, but I didn't want to upset Christian with such talk. I looked around. "Where's Andy?" I stood up. My heart skipped a beat. I couldn't see him.

"At the tollman's house. Karl's there, and Andy recognized him."

"Oh, good," I said. It was a sign that Andy could wait to see me. I felt a twinge of regret. He nursed a wound still open. I'd missed him more and needed to seek him out. "Take Christian inside to Keil's, will you, Martin? Kate's there and Ida. I'll go greet Andy, if I can."

I limped as I walked, thinking of what to say, of how I could explain why I'd left him behind again. Why I'd had to. I imagined Martin had told him some of it, but I wasn't sure how much Andy understood.

I sidestepped down the little knoll to the bridge. The stage already moved on up the road, having just brought Martin and my sons. Andy stood between Karl and the tollman, his hands on his hips as though the men spoke of harvest troubles or the price of wheat.

"Andy," I called to him. I was sure he heard me. Karl looked my way, said something to my son. "Andy." He turned to me then. "Come join me," I shouted. I walked closer, babbling as he stood, a solemn look on his face. "I'm so glad you came. I prayed that Martin would bring you. I missed you so." I knelt down. He looked through me, as though I were a stranger, someone he wasn't sure he'd met before. "Andy, I'm so sorry I had to leave you and had to make you wait. I'm so sorry. But you're here now. We're all together at last."

I don't know if it was the prayers I'd spoken daily since the day we'd arrived or if it was the prayers of preparation spoken by so many, but my oldest son did then walk toward me and put his arms around my neck. I pulled him to me, breathing in the sweetness of him, relishing his soft and tender skin, the clean smell of his neck as I kissed it. "It's a new beginning, Andy. We'll make our way here." He let me hold him and then he pushed away.

"You left us."

"I had to, Andy. It was the only way to trick Jack. I had to trick him so I could get here safely. And now you're here safely, too, so you see, it worked out." He stared. "Forgive me, Andy. Please. I should have done so many things differently and I'm sorry. I truly am."

He turned from me and walked away.

"Where are you going?" I asked. My heart thudded.

"To get something." At the tollman's house he lifted an object from a satchel. I recognized it and my throat caught in tightness. He carried the lantern that Christian had made the holder for; the one he'd held above us the last time we'd walked on the beach.

"Oh, Andy. You risked—"

"I went when I knew Jack wouldn't be home. It was Papa's. I carried it at his funeral, remember? I couldn't let Papa's light stay behind."

———

While I pulled weeds in the herb garden, Martin reported of Jack's return the day we'd left. He'd railed against me for changing my mind and heading off on "some fool trip to Aurora Mills," but he had calmed when he saw Andy and Christian still with my in-laws. I winced as Martin told the story, for it confirmed that I had used my sons to ward off the wrath of their stepfather. "But Henry and John, they both talked to him about how it might be good for you to go to Aurora with the girls. We reminded him that the children annoyed him and he agreed. We might have mentioned that he had the land to keep up; he owned that farm, so why not head home and farm it regardless of how long it took for you to return; we promised to keep the boys with us. Seemed to calm him," Martin said.

"Do you think he'll come here?" I asked. I could smell the woolly applemint when I brushed at its leaves in the late garden.

Martin squatted beside me. "*Ja*, he'll come here." He paused. "We should have spoken up when you said you planned to marry him. Most of us knew of his...ways."

"*Ja*, but I wouldn't have listened," I said. "So you can forgive yourself for that."

"Just let us help you when he comes."

As the grain harvest moved to a rush and the pumpkins were nearly ripe, we had fruit to turn into butter, vinegar to make. In late September when nights turned cooler and the mill race filled with confetti of colorful leaves, Louisa insisted that the portrait I'd drawn with colored pencils of Aurora should be entered in the state fair competition. I blushed.

"I like the one of the tollkeeper," Karl said. "You captured his sleepy look with his head against his chest while people wait for him to collect the toll. We could have the state contract for mail if we kept alert eyes, by golly. I think that man needs looking for another job."

"Well, then, enter both," Louisa said. "*Ja*. Enter them both."

So I did.

It felt like play as we walked around the fair grounds in October, looking at the harvest people brought as examples of their efforts. We ate our lunch, and the aroma of our warm potato salad and herbed sausages brought people our way, asking if we had any for sale. We had none but invited people to join us, and we laughed together over the food and the fair. At one booth I encountered the Wagonblast family. After hugs all around, I learned they'd gone from Willapa to Cathlamet, then down to Oregon City. They were practically neighbors!

In the booths showing crafts and wares, I lingered over the paintings and noted the name of one Nancy M. Thornton on several. One of her paintings already had a ribbon on it from the Benton County Fair, dated 1859. *Women were painting here that early,* I thought. The notation said she now taught in Oregon City at the Female School for Instruction of Young Ladies and Misses. Maybe I could take classes from her. Maybe my daughters could go there one day. And that took me to thoughts of my sons, who ran freely around the grounds, their little flat-top hats like lily pads in the sea of people. They would all go to school here. Andy would have a chance to be a doctor as he said he wished to be. He was still standoffish with me, but I prayed he'd warm again to his mother. Christian's stuttering had ceased since coming to Aurora Mills.

If only I'd done this before. If only I'd let Christian's family help me. No, I would stop such thoughts. I still had control over how I thought, and my meanderings must buoy me up, not hold me hostage.

After sunset, we rode back in a wagon, many of us from the colony gathered together on loose grass hay. Several sang, and the men had their brass instruments and a concertina they played now as we bounced along. The boys sat in a cluster of children. I shifted to find a better way to sit, grateful the stitches had at last healed. I held Ida in my arms. Kate had her head in my lap, already asleep, her fingers wrapped around a pale pink ribbon. The picture of Aurora had won an award. Not the top prize, but recognition just the same. A half dime came with the prize, the first real currency of my own I'd earned. I had it wrapped in the handkerchief that also held my pearls. My life was blessed.

It was dark when we reached Aurora Mills, and we carried sleepy children from the wagon. Aurora walked with Kate in hand and I had Ida in my arms. Both Christian and Andy slept on the grass hay of the wagon. I'd come back and fetch them later. I felt a lightness in my steps despite my fatigue. It almost felt like joy. Hope, that was it. I felt hope in my heart for the future I'd create here.

Helena opened the door, and Karl carried in some jars of vinegar that had also won ribbons and quarters to boot. Keil's "strongly medicinal" Oregon grape wine had won Keil a blue ribbon, which he held as he entered. Ida lay in the crook of my arm. Louisa brushed past me as Kate plopped down on the mat next to the door. "Let me light the lantern," she said. I moved Kate toward her own mat in the room on the other side and planned to return to get Christian when I heard Louisa exclaim, "Oh, you startled me!"

"I maybe could have done more than that," Jack said. "For keeping me from my *Kind*."

———

It doesn't take much to shatter a silky peace. I should have sensed that he was there, waiting for us. If I'd had any kind of motherly intuitiveness I'd have known, should have felt his glowering in the dark, menacing my children and my life. What a terrible thing I'd attracted into our lives with my willful ways.

"Now Jack," Keil said. "There's no reason to be upsetting."

"My wife and children defy me? That's reason to be more than upsetting. You've no right to harbor them"—he poked at Keil's chest—"as though they needed shelter in a storm."

"Every right in the world, Jack. We are Sister Giesy's family, and she's come to visit us." *Visit. Does he intend to send me back?* "Now just settle down. We are all tired. You bunk up there with the bachelors, and we can talk in the morning. It's been a long day. I imagine for you as well, *ja*."

We might have staved off the suffering and loss then but for Louisa's meant-for-cheering words: "Emma won a ribbon for her drawings," Louisa said. "See what a fine job she did penciling our Aurora?" She held the drawing up beside the lamp she'd lit.

"A perfect likeness," Helena agreed. She pushed the drawing toward Jack, who stood across from me.

Neither of them could have known how their praise of my work would enrage Jack. But I did.

Fearing he'd punch a hole through the drawing, I stepped in front of it.

"But it's not as fine a job as you might do, Jack," I said. "Jack's quite an artist himself." I turned toward Louisa.

Quick as a slap, Jack lunged across the space between us and swung to strike me with the back of his hand. The back of his hand cracked against the side of my face. I stumbled back, still holding Ida in my arms. "Come here, Wife!" It was just like him to cause pain then wonder why I resisted his commands.

Louisa cried out, *"Ach, nein,"* and I heard Kate scream as she ran toward me. I held Ida close to my chest but ducked my head over her, pushed Kate behind me to protect them both, knowing in a moment he would strike at me again. I hoped the boys remained asleep outside. Cajoling, capitulating, surrendering to such as Jack was not the answer. Neither was defiance. Maybe stating the obvious was.

I faced him. Something in my eyes must have reached him. His arm, midair, stopped. "It's over, Jack," I said. "You were right about our arrangement. Our loveless marriage never worked."

"You made a vow," he hissed.

"Not to let you destroy my life or the lives of my children. I made no vow about that. You go, Jack. You must go. I won't try to make a claim on the property that once belonged to me or ask you for help to raise your child. I've made my way here, and here I'll make my life."

He stepped closer, but I didn't back away. "Take Ida, Louisa," I said. She moved like an angel, whisking in then out of the scene of destruction. With her free arm she moved Kate before her.

Jack towered above me. "You—" He raised his fist again. *Let the blow come; my children are safe.* I closed my eyes. Waited.

"No, no, no, no, no! You will not do this, Jacob Giesy." It was Keil. He was slightly shorter than Jack, but his words held greater force. "This is the widow of a man whom I loved as a son, and you will harm her no more. You will go now. Now. Right now. You will return to Willapa or go wherever you wish, but you will not approach Sister Giesy again. We will protect her as a widow. Leave her be."

"She holds my child."

"Whom you paid no heed to when you struck at the child's mother." This from Karl, who had lit candles and the lamps to tint the room with light. "You might have hurt your daughter too."

"You too, Karl?" Jack said. He stood like a frightened animal now, cornered.

"No sympathy, Jack," Keil said. "The deed is done. Now go."

"Where are my sons?" he shouted then. I was sure Jack would strike Karl, but he didn't. Instead he glared at me, his face grotesque in the flickering light. "What have you done with those boys?"

"Take care of yourself, Jack," Helena told him. "Go now before you do something you will later regret." He acted as though he'd just become aware that Helena was even there. Her voice seemed to soothe him with its firmness.

"Those boys are in good hands," Keil said.

"There'll come a time, Emma Giesy," Jack said, "when you are not pampered by people you've bewitched. You'll not know when you're alone and then we'll see what maybe could happen."

We gave him the last word, and when no one responded, no one added fuel to his fire, his passion died. He lumbered out. I watched him while standing in the doorway, hoping that he wouldn't stop at the wagon where the boys slept. He headed toward the tollhouse and never saw Andy's head pop up from the grass hay, never saw Christian slide down on the opposite side of the wagon and watch their "Papa Jack" walk away before rushing up the steps of Elim and into my arms.

"You're shaking," Louisa said as she helped me to the chair. "Boys, help me get some water for your mama's face."

"Will he come back?" Andy asked.

"Don't borrow trouble," Louisa told them. "We'll see what happens in the morning."

Jack was nowhere around by morning. No one reported seeing him about, not near the furniture building nor at Rudy's sheep farm. The tollman said a big man had crossed in the night, his shoulders hunched up like "a fire-cracker ready to explode." He'd headed north, away from Aurora Mills. Away from us.

33

Emma

The Found Coin

I hardly slept, still wearing that fogginess of danger past without time to let peace massage my soul.

"We must build the church next," Helena noted in the morning as we cleaned up following the morning meal. "The prophet Haggai warns about building for ourselves before we build for God."

"My husband has been busy," Louisa defended. Then she added, "But if we had a church, I'd take you there, Emma, and we could just sit in the cool and thank God for your good fortune in arriving here, your children being safe. And you've earned recognition for your work, all in one month's time." She looked at the drawing of Aurora she'd hung on the wall.

"I have more than that to be grateful for," I told her. To Helena I posed, "Perhaps Brother Keil is right in having his home serve as a place of worship. It does double the work that way."

Louisa liked this idea. "*Ja*, that's right, Emma. A German efficiency. And maybe it gives the home a needed uplifting into the spiritual realm. A home, a hearth, surely God wants those to be central in our lives." She smiled, pleased with herself.

Helena's lips puckered as if gathered by threads. Like Keil, Helena didn't like to be disagreed with.

"I think I'll find a quiet place away today, though," I said. "That would be an advantage of a church building, finding quietness in the middle of a day."

Louisa smiled. Helena straightened her shoulders and began scrubbing potatoes.

The women gave me room to stretch after the tautness of Jack's visit, but I could see by Helena's rigid back and Louisa's grin that the communal threads that tied us together would also be stretched here. I would try not to break them, give each person room to save face.

I walked with the children across the open grasses just beginning to give up their brown to the greens of autumn rains. I looked back toward Keil's house as we walked, the soft October winds lifting the strings of my bonnet. Keil lived at the highest point of the village, but *he* wasn't the highest point. He had authority, yes, but not over our souls, not over our thoughts, not over our expressions of faith. In truth, he was an aging man who made mistakes too. I didn't need to seek his approval anymore, nor live in defiance of him.

I'd packed a lunch, and I spent the day with the children. When we returned, it was dusk. I lit the oil in Christian's lantern, thanking Andy again for bringing it. Then I knocked on the door of the private room the Keils occupied upstairs. "Emma," Louisa said. "Come in. You had a good afternoon, *ja?*"

"*Ja,*" I answered. "I wish to speak to *Herr* Keil, now. Is this possible?"

"Father Keil," she corrected.

I hesitated. "Brother Keil," I said. "I already have a father."

"*Ja,*" she said. "That makes sense. He works with his herbs." She pointed downstairs toward the room across from the kitchen. As I descended the steps, Andy saw me from the side room and nodded, but he didn't rush to me as he once would have. We had knots yet to tie, that was certain. I moved past him, carried the lantern down another flight, taking the shadows with me to where Keil worked. I was glad to be wearing leather soles instead of my wooden ones.

At the workshop, I waited amid the earthy smell of plants until Keil looked up. "Do you have a moment, Brother Keil?"

"Ah, Sister Emma. I recall occasions when you asked for my time. To seek permission for marriage if I remember well; then to convince me that letting you become a scout would be good for our colony. Of late, to seek refuge." He shook his head. "So many needs a woman has."

"*Ja.* But you also found refuge in my home," I said. "And I served you and yours, as my husband did. We gave what we had to give. My husband gave all he had, his very life, on behalf of another. Is this not the communal way?"

He returned to his mortar and pestle. "So, what is it you wish now?"

"I come to ask that the colony in Aurora Mills build me a house. As the widow of a colony leader, I seek a home for my sons and daughters to grow up in."

He stopped his work, laid the pestle down, brushed his hands against his wool vest and folded his hands over his wide chest. "Our house, where you stay, is insufficient for your many needs, Emma Giesy?"

"It is. This is not to insult your generosity. Not at all. I'll work here, cook and clean and wash and serve others, and those labors and my love in doing them will go into the common fund. But I wish my own home, my own place to teach my children and to raise them as their father would wish it. It's what I reach for from the abundant basket the colony is always speaking of."

"You'll be more vulnerable to Jack's antics should he return, living alone."

"I'll not let my life be only a reflection of what Jack might do to us," I said.

He was quiet a long time. If he refused, I'd already decided that in the spring I would take the children and leave. Maybe go to Oregon City, where they'd still be able to see their uncle Martin and I could still have them attend school with Karl. I could continue to work here and contribute and receive from the common fund, but I would find a way—sell my paintings or my pies—to put a roof over my children's heads.

"Well, I think that could be arranged then," Keil said.

"What?"

"We can arrange to have a house built for you, Emma Giesy. The Diamond Rule prevails. Or do you insist on building it with your own hands?" He chuckled.

"I could," I told him. "But no. I am more interested in what happens afterward, in making it a home."

———

"Here's my half dime," I told the shop tender at the colony store. It was late in the day, and shadows already covered the shelves of cloth and hats and newly cobbled shoes. Garlands of greens draped around the store and holly with red berries decorated harnesses for sale. The long pattern book of our feet lay on the shelf for the cobbler to use when we requested new shoes. Outside, a light snow fell. My shawl fell loose across my shoulders, though it was colder than normal. That's what everyone said, but I felt warmed in this communal store.

The shopkeeper had been the tollman, but Karl had moved into that role. The colony had the state contract for collecting tolls now. Still living in Keil's house with us all, Martin mixed up herbs to help ill people and had plans to go to medical school the following year. We hadn't heard anything from Jack since the day he left nearly two months before. Christmas ap-proached. They hadn't started on my house yet, but Keil had assured me that as the widow of Christian Giesy, I would have a home. When he'd an-nounced it, Helena grimaced and mumbled something again about how not building the church first invited trouble. Keil acted as though he hadn't heard.

I'd picked the house site, close to where the school would be built, not far from the Pudding River, so Andy and Kate wouldn't have to travel far. I knew what my view would be and in the spring, I'd have the home I wanted.

"I earned the money from a picture I drew," I told the shopkeeper as though he might care.

"Did you now? And what would you like in return?"

"Nothing. It's to go into the common fund, as cash against my ledger page. Later I'll need shoes for my sons and hair ribbons for my daughters. But I'm also going to have a home one day, just for me and my family, so I want to contribute."

I planned to make more drawings and to acquaint myself with that woman painter, Nancy Thornton. I had a plan for the next state fair as well, but so far I hadn't had the courage to bring that up with Brother Keil. It's how I thought of him now, like a brother rather than some sort of god who supposedly held all the answers. I'd taken one small step toward seeing Keil through different eyes. One small stitch in time, that's what I told Andy as we two tended our frayed threads too.

The shopkeeper opened the ledger book to my page, *Emma Giesy* written across the top. I took the small coin from my reticule and promptly dropped it. *"Ach, jammer!"* I said, as it rolled across the wooden floor and spun itself against a pickle barrel where it disappeared in the shadows. I heard it stop rolling.

It was all I had to give. I patted beneath the lip it had disappeared under. "It isn't much," I said. "But I earned it myself. Do you have a lantern I could hold to help me see?"

The shopkeeper complied and as he held the lamp high above me, I was reminded both of the woman of Luke searching for her lost coin and the walk along the Willapa beach Christian and I had taken that last night we had together. The lantern lit the way, and all else was darkness. We'd had enough light to take the next step. It was all we needed. Some days and nights, that was all the light there was.

I found the half dime and let out a little shout, then handed it to the shopkeeper. "I must call all my friends," I said. "I've found my lost coin."

He didn't seem to understand the biblical reference. *"Danke,"* he said and simply marked it in the book as *cash*. "That is our way, to have a generous spirit," he said then. "Your offering goes from 'yours' to 'ours' so now it belongs to 'us.' "

"So it does." I turned to go, as satisfied as if I'd just eaten a nourishing meal.

Epilogue

BETHEL, DECEMBER 1861

Dearest Sister Emma,

Herr *Keil writes that you are in Aurora Mills. Jonathan says you should have gone there when he asked you to, and Papa says it's good that you've come to your senses. But I fear it is not enough to bring us there anytime soon. Lou is not well now. She catches every little ailment and looks as frail as an old chicken. The men have trouble settling land issues, and Jonathan says he will not come back west for two or three more years until these things are worked out. I never know what "these things" are. The boys I know here are saying they will go to war and so girls my age will likely never marry. We'll be like Helena, only without even a proposal to decline.*

I have forgiven you for marrying Jack Giesy. It's better if I forgive you than to be angry with you always, for unforgiveness is the greatest sin. After all, we received forgiveness from our Lord, so what right have we to not give it back? Gift giving and receiving is the way of our lives, Papa says.

I'm glad your children are all there and I will be pleased to meet Ida someday. Mama does remind Papa that she has "family she's never even met." Papa sighs then. She tells him she needs to see her sister in the Deseret country, so maybe we'll come that far before I'm an old woman. Maybe I'll find a husband there. Or maybe we'll just keep coming west to find you. Pray that we do something sometime soon.

Have a blessed Christ Day, Sister. We will hang your etched eggs in your memory. Do you welcome the New Year with gladness? I just wonder.

Your loving sister, Kitty
(It's how I call myself now. There are too many Catherines in our family, don't you think? You're lucky there's only been one Emma. Papa says the rest of us are lucky that's true too.)

DISCUSSION QUESTIONS

1. This is a story about giving and receiving. Who gave up the most in this story? Who knew how to receive? Why are both capabilities important in our lives and in the life of a family?

2. This is also a story about community and individuals within a community having a voice and making choices. Could Emma have found a way to remain at Willapa and experience contentment there? What voice did Louisa have at Aurora Mills? Did either woman pass up opportunities to be heard more clearly?

3. Emma and Louisa both speak of the great longing, the *Sehnsucht*, that is within each of us. In the German language, the word implies something compelling, almost addictive, in the human spirit that drives us forward on a spiritual journey. What was Emma's great longing? Louisa's? Did these women achieve satisfaction in this second book of the series? Is there a relationship between human intimacy and such spiritual longing?

4. Give some examples of when Emma "began to weave" without waiting for God's thread. What were the consequences? Is it wise to "begin to weave" without knowing the outcome? Can we do otherwise? How do we live in ambivalence?

5. The author uses the metaphor of light throughout the book. Is having enough light for the next step really enough? What role does light play in Emma's discovery that finding meaning in life's tragedies requires reflection? Give some examples of Emma's reflective thinking. When might she have been more reflective? Would you describe Louisa as a reflective woman? What prevents us from being more reflective in our everyday lives?

6. How can we receive without feeling obligated? What qualities of obligation sometimes diminish gifts that others might give us? Why does that make it difficult to receive them?

7. Strength is often defined as self-sufficiency. How did Emma's strength reveal itself? What made it possible for her to ultimately accept the gifts of others?

8. Did Emma use her sons in order to get her own way? Discuss your opinion.

9. How much of Emma's feeling of isolation was self-imposed? How much was isolation related to the demands of the landscape? How much was a spiritual isolation or feeling of abandonment? Did you agree with how the author conveyed these qualities of isolation?

10. Did Emma make the correct choice at the close of the book? Have you ever had to make a choice where all options appeared poor? What helped you take the next step?

11. Molly Wolf in her book, *White China: Finding the Divine in the Everyday,* characterizes spirituality as milk and religion as the milk jug. Without the milk, the jug is dry and does not nourish, but without the jug the milk spills all over the table. What does this metaphor have to say about the Willapa community and the Aurora community's expression of religion and their spirituality?

12. Sometimes we stumble in our faith, and because of stress, loss, and challenges too great, we ache, moving away from what might give us strength. How did Emma stumble? Who or what brought her back to the source of her strength? What did she find she could trust? Are there times in your life that are reflected in Emma's journey?

An Interview with Author Jane Kirkpatrick

What was the impetus for the direction that this second book in the Change and Cherish Series took?

Emma's descendants, the Dr. David Wagner family of Portland, Oregon, were instrumental in researching the first book and in this one as well. About halfway through writing book one, *A Clearing in the Wild*, David shared a family story about a second marriage for Emma, to someone with the same last name as Emma's first husband. I trust family stories and believe they are remembered for a reason. At that point I'd seen no evidence of this second marriage (though I had known about Christian's death). We began a search of the historical record to see if the story could be documented. Irene Westwood, a volunteer at the Aurora Colony Historical Society (ACHS), located a divorce petition dated in 1891, thirty years after this novel ends. But it contained the seeds to help us understand many of Emma's earlier decisions. About the same time, we found a letter written by Emma dated 1862 indicating where she was then living. This confirmed some of her struggles and opened the door to exploring issues of independence and debt, giving and receiving, love and loss, community and the individual, and the role faith plays in lives filled with threads of wounding, grief, and love.

What was the religion of these colonists?

At signings and events, readers often ask that question, wondering if they were German Lutherans or derivatives of the Mennonites or some other tradition. While there were German Lutherans who participated and appeared to remain Lutheran (as we believe Karl Ruge did) and there was intermarriage among the Deseret Saints (Mormons), and people did associate with those in the Pennsylvania colonies (Phillipsburg and Harmony) and elsewhere, the majority of the colonists followed Dr. Keil's own brand of Christian theology. His views were unique, though based on the book of Acts in the New Testament about each giving what they had and receiving whatever they needed from a common fund. The colonists in this story had no formal liturgy, were not denominational in nature. They held church twice a month and did not celebrate traditional sacraments. They practiced their own religion.

Were there many other communal societies existing during that time, or were these colonists unique?
Many utopian communities formed during the early 1800s, some focused on "end times" while others sought the perfect blend of community and faith. Still others coming from the traditions of Thoreau and Emerson sought to form groups living close to nature. They hoped to dignify work and to have one's spiritual life a part of one's everyday life. They honored individual freedoms, and often women were treated more equally within these societies than in the culture at large. Interestingly, Keil did not require that one join the colony in order to live there. In fact, a story is told of the Bauer family, who left the colony after three years but kept their store open in Bethel and competed with the colony store!

Did the colonists in Willapa remain separate as Emma hoped, or did they continue their affiliation with the Aurorans and the Bethelites?
As much as I believe Emma wanted the Willapa group to be separate, there is strong evidence in the ledger books at Aurora and letters of colony members from Bethel that Keil attempted to keep the three groups under his wing as one flock. Aurora ledger pages show Karl buying school supplies for

Willapa; there is a page of credit at Aurora for Emma dated later on. Who bought what for whom revealed distinct affiliations among the colonists. While the land was in individual names at Willapa, there is evidence that the colony's common fund paid for the properties unless received by donation land claim. The property around Aurora and Bethel was primarily in Keil's name. The three groups retained unique features, and we know that well into the 1870s, colonists continued to migrate west. Some chose Willapa while others chose the Aurora community. Helena Giesy, for example, always kept her residence in Aurora once she left Bethel, but there were other Giesys whose descendants remain in Willapa today, who migrated after the Civil War. All those Giesys make for some interesting genealogical searching!

What values did all the colonists appear to hold most dear?

The Bethel-Willapa-Aurora colonists were known to be generous to their neighbors, to assist women and orphans whether a colony member or not, to work hard and be resourceful, to create fine crafts, and to uphold music as an important part of their worship and life. They really did believe in the Diamond Rule of making others' lives better than one's own, as directed by their Christian faith. I think that's what kept Keil from becoming a tyrant rather than someone who merely dominated. It was perhaps how Emma could make sense of her decisions as well. In Missouri, the colonists protected slaves, and according to letters, were generally sympathetic to the Union in the War Between the States. But they were not pacifists, as the Amana Society members were. One of Keil's nephews died in the Yakima Indian War, for example. Music was a major contributor to their interaction with the outside world as well as within the colonies. Recently, in the basement of what had been Martin Giesy's home in Aurora, original pieces of musical compositions were found. These are being restored and performed and recorded on CDs. More information about this can be read at the colony's Web site at www.auroracolonymuseum.com.

*Is the story about Keil berating a man for not having enough faith
to heal based on an actual account? What about his other somewhat
strange views?*

Keil did berate a Willapa family member back in Bethel for his lack of faith,
and it had dire consequences, as mentioned in this story. Keil also tried to
move the colony toward celibacy, though the reason for that is uncertain.
And he felt worship was something that could be integrated into everyday life
and thus did not need the prominence of liturgy and structure. He also held
women in less regard than men, from what I can determine. More than one
descendant claimed that Keil "took advantage of women" in the sense that he
had them work hard and discouraged marriage; and perhaps in other ways,
too, given the absolute power he could wield. Yet other descendants today tell
the story of his great egalitarianism and say that women in the colony had
opportunities to interact in the outside world in ways others might not have.
Women's roles in activities such as participating in the agricultural fairs,
building the hotel, dealing with railroad passengers, and so on suggest that
Keil's theology eventually slipped beneath his economic interests…but that's
for the rest of the story.

Did everyone get along as hoped for in a utopian world?

There is strong evidence of dissention among the colonists, though what they
presented to the outside world was a group of loving, supportive people. That's
not unlike most families (or even faith communities) where what we show to
others is not always what we reveal to our closest friends. As Patrick Harris,
curator at ACHS once noted, perhaps the colonists lived their ideals by what
they showed to the outside community through their generosity and their art.

*Were there really agricultural shows and competitions that early in
the West?*

Yes! And the colonists are remembered for their many talents in quilt making, furniture building, cooking, music composition and playing, and basket

making, among a variety of colony endeavors. (Many of these artifacts can be seen at the museum.) Festivals at Aurora and Bethel continue to celebrate their talents. Keil did win a ribbon in 1861 for his "strongly medicinal" wine. Painting classes were offered by Nancy Thornton. Despite the image of our ancestors working hard and long, they also apparently played often; the colony band was asked to perform for events in Butteville, Oregon City, Portland, and points farther away, though only men were permitted to play in the colony bands. They ate well!

How accurate is the tension you show between Emma's in-laws and the raising of her sons?

We do not know if the colony had a tradition of children being raised by uncles or grandparents upon the death of a father. But even children of prominent families from back East were often raised by uncles, even when their mothers remarried. Meriwether Lewis of the famous Lewis and Clark Expedition was raised by an uncle despite his mother's remarriage. The ledger information in Aurora and census records, as well as Emma's letter, suggests that sons were not always raised by their widowed mothers, and the records related to Emma and her two sons suggest conflicts over parental control.

On what information did you base Louisa Keil's point of view?

I wanted very much to show what was happening at Aurora while Emma was dealing with her own trials in Willapa. So I introduced Louisa. I'd actually given her a role in the first book, but after editorial discussions, took her out. But she remained a strong character for me and allowed a way for me to keep the tension between the two sites alive. There were no letters or diaries left by Louisa Keil. This is often the case with historical women. Articles about their husbands' building a bridge or even earning an award at an agricultural fair might be part of the historical record, but much of what women did is not. It was common for German Americans to order the almanacs and for women to make notations of how many eggs were collected on a certain day or how much rain might have fallen. Often these served as diaries. Upon their deaths, these almanac records of women's lives were seldom saved—a great loss, in my opinion. I based the everyday life of Louisa on other colony letters, some interviews in the historical record, and remembrances of descendants. But I believe Louisa Keil and Emma Giesy, both wives of prominent colony men, had more in common than they might have at first realized. I hope Louisa's point of view offers a glimpse into not only Dr. Keil and the development of the colony that we would otherwise not have had, but also another way that a woman might have lived with a distinctive man. Helena Giesy's entry into the story did occur about the time as I've portrayed. She was Christian's sister and carried considerable weight within the Aurora colony and is remembered today as "a saint." But saints are real people first, and I believed Helena acts as an antagonist for both Louisa and Emma, while creating vulnerability for these women as they seek to discover who they really are.

Who was Big Jack Giesy?

I wish I knew for certain! There is a Jacob Giesy living next door to Emma at Willapa in the 1860 census. Christian had a brother named Jacob, but he was not the right age to be Emma's "Big Jack" as she calls him in her letter. Jack was often the nickname for John, and there are many John Giesys, but none can be isolated as being Emma's husband. Speculation then moves in where facts cannot be captured.

Could Emma have remained and run the oyster operation or even gone to Olympia and lived on her own with her four children?

The choices a woman had in the 1860s were limited, but she did have choices, the most important being clear about what mattered to her and having the courage to act on that. Some women did operate in the oyster beds, but with children, they needed help from family members or friends. Emma would have had to accept the help of others, left her children with someone.

She might have sold her farm to use the money to hire help, but she was correct in knowing it would have been difficult to find a buyer, especially considering the economic uncertainty that coexisted with the war. Selling the property to other family members would likely not have gained her cash, but a ledger credit available to her only if she remained in the colony. Emma found herself dependent on the Willapa and Aurora colonies in ways she had not planned for. Whether she acted from grief, guilt, or stubbornness, or from courage, independence, or her *Sehnsucht*—her longing to be known while doing the best she could for her family—is the reader's decision. Being strong enough to accept help from others is a challenge for our own age of self-reliance. Finding community continues to be an important landscape of our souls. I hope Emma's journey of discovery offers insight into readers' journeys. I thank them for continuing to read about Emma and her story.

Join Jane for monthly memo updates on her writing life at www.jkbooks .com and learn when the third book in the series will be released and where she's speaking and signing. Jane is also available for speakerphone book-group presentations. Visit her Web site for additional information.

ACKNOWLEDGMENTS

C. S. Lewis once wrote of the German word *Sehnsucht,* referring to the longing or yearning of the human spirit. My German friends tell me the word carries weight, that such longing is almost an addiction, a compulsion. For me, *A Tendering in the Storm* is an interweaving of the *Sehnsucht* of one Emma Wagner Giesy, who lived in the nineteenth and twentieth centuries, and our own contemporary longings—to be known, to be loved, to find meaning despite life's trials. Through exploration of our longings, we are freed to live full, community-integrated lives and to discover how fortunate we are to have gifts enough to give away.

A great many people provided gifts to me in the researching and writing of this second book in the Change and Cherish Historical Series. Dr. David and Pat Wagner, descendants of Emma, provided access to family letters and photographs and artifacts, as well as the generosity of their home and a private tour of relevant Northwest-area sites. As with the first book, they willingly let me speculate about their ancestor and offered ideas of what might have motivated Emma's actions. Their discovery of a letter in Emma's hand was a delight to all of us, and her words turned us in a direction we might otherwise not have gone. David also read an early manuscript, and I am grateful for his suggestions and his encouragement of my telling this story.

The family of Dr. Jerry Giesy, descendants of one of Christian's brothers, shared copies of several colonists' "calling cards." It was a delight to discover Emma's card there, surrounded by pink flowers. The Bruce Giesy family donated a quilt of Emma's to the Society. Seeing her work helped inform her character. The Giesy's enthusiasm for my storytelling is greatly appreciated.

A great-granddaughter of Emma's, Louise Hankeson, and great-grandson Mike Truman provided information about the circumstances of Christian's death and the impact of that day on Emma throughout her life. I am grateful for their sharing.

Irene Westwood, a volunteer at the Aurora Colony Historical Society (ACHS), in Aurora, Oregon, became a valued ally and exemplary researcher. The information she located helped explain Emma's comments in her letter, clarified the family story, and set the stage for the decisions Emma later made. Irene is steadfast and asked the kinds of questions that make a novelist smile. There is no way to thank her enough.

Patrick Harris, curator at the ACHS, could not have been more helpful. He answered obscure questions (Did the bridge across the Pudding River wash out in the 1861–62 floods?), went through ledger books with me from the Keil and Company Store, tracked legal and land documents, and even gave me a walking tour of the Aurora National Historic District. He has a wonderful memory for colony names and descendants and like me, I think, finds great joy in discovery of some detail that will turn the story. He always greeted me with enthusiasm, as did all the staff and volunteers throughout the facilities of the colony. I am grateful to Patrick along with board members Norm Bauer and James Kopp, who read advance copies of the book, gave me insights about Aurora, took me on tours, and made helpful suggestions. Alan Guggenheim, former director of the Aurora Society, provided me with copies of architectural information and the news of Emma's interest in having a home of her own with the colony. John Holley, current executive director, continued to set the tone of access to the archives and the support of these stories, for which I'm grateful. The cadre of volunteers at the society is a gift not only to visitors but to my own research as well.

In Pacific County, Karla and Peter Nelson of Time Enough Books put me in touch with Dobby Wiegardt, a longtime oysterman who showed me a native Willapa oyster shell and talked about the oystering life, lending authenticity to this story. They also introduced me to Truman and Donna Rew, who offered their guesthouse (overlooking the Columbia River where it meets the Pacific) while I was in the area researching. Their generosity is greatly appreciated. The

Nelsons also hosted a grand launch at the Ilwaco Heritage Museum in Ilwaco, Washington, for the first book in the series, *A Clearing in the Wild,* and they've welcomed my husband and me and our wirehaired pointing griffon into their store with warmth. Their support, their reading of advance manuscripts, and their good humor could not have been more welcome. I thank them.

Bruce Weilepp, former director of the Pacific County Historical Society, and Sue Pattillo, board member, provided information and thoughtful speculation about how things were accomplished in the 1850–60s of this rain forest–like part of Washington State. Nancy Lloyd of Oysterville gave countless hours of creative research and speculation, offering a variety of suggestions, all of them valued. Board member Ken Karch sent me a CD of all the Pacific County Historical Society's journals, and it was in that search I discovered Christian had been a justice of the peace and a legislator. I am grateful!

Pacific County resident Marlene Martin and her daughter Joni Blake, and a cousin, Cameron Baker, descendants of another Giesy line, offered assistance to visit the Willapa cemetery and their ideas about what happened when. To all of these people I extend appreciation.

The Douthit family of western Oregon provided details about their ancestors (the Wagonblasts), and Oregonian Bernie Blum provided fascinating land-transaction information that provided insights about Emma's life. He included documents that gave me Emma's sister's nickname as well. A number of Keil descendants provided family stories that helped enrich Emma's journey.

The Oregon Historical Society and Oregon State Archives again provided valued documents.

Erhard and Elfi Gross provided valued reference on German words and usage but even more, made us at home with wonderful German cooking that Elfi is known for and that provided authenticity for Emma's interest in preparing fine German dishes.

Several descendants from Bethel contacted me after the release of the first book, including Lucille Bower, who continues to live in Bethel. Along with those from the Aurora colony and Willapa, and descendants from earlier colonies spread throughout the country, their stories became important threads in the weaving of this story.

I am especially grateful to the help of my editors: to Erin Healy and to Dudley Delffs of WaterBrook Press, a division of Random House, and to the team who supports me there in all departments, and to my agent, Joyce Hart, in Pittsburgh. I couldn't do this without them all.

My prayer team of Carol, Judy, Gabby, Susan, and Marilyn (posthumously), as well as many others who I know hold both Jerry and me in their hearts, make this storytelling seem like praying and thus a joy. Thank you. My friends Blair, Sandy, Kay, Barbie, the Carols, Susan, and my writing friends form my "colony," without whom I'd be as isolated as Emma was. Thanks for keeping me in your loop.

My family (extended and selected) and especially Jerry, have come to understand my quirks and timing, offered help in countless ways, and taught me to be a better recipient of God's good gifts. Thank you for knowing me and loving me anyway.

For whatever is authentic about this story, I give credit to the above people and others too numerous to mention; whatever errors exist are mine.

And finally, to readers who continue to honor me with your time, thank you. You make these men and women come alive to me through your letters and visits to my Web site, and through your kind words at signings and events. I hope you'll look for a continuation of Emma's story and the colony's journey in book three.

With gratitude,

Jane Kirkpatrick

Please visit Jane's Web site at www.jkbooks.com and enjoy her Monthly Memos of Encouragement. Write to her at 99997 Starvation Lane, Moro, Oregon, 97039.

Suggested Additional Resources

Allen, Douglas. *Shoalwater Willapa*. South Bend, WA: Snoose Peak Publishing, 2004.

Arndt, Karl J. R. *George Rapp's Harmony Society 1785–1847,* rev. ed. Cranbury, NJ: Associated University Presses, 1972.

Aurora Colony Historical Museum. *Oregon Music Project, Publication and Performance of Previously Lost Original Music Written by Members of the Aurora Colony Bands, Ensembles and Choral Groups between 1856 and 1883.* Unpublished manuscript, Aurora, OR: Aurora Colony Historical Museum, 2006.

———. *Emma Wakefield Memorial Herb Garden.* Aurora, OR: Old Aurora Colony Museum, n.d.

Barthel, Diane L. *Amana, From Pietist Sect to American Community.* Lincoln, NE: University of Nebraska Press, 1982.

Bek, William G. "The Community at Bethel, Missouri, and Its Offspring at Aurora, Oregon," pt. 1. *German-American Annals,* vol. 7, 1909.

———. "A German Communistic Society in Missouri." *Missouri Historical Review.* October 1908.

Blankenship, Russell. *And There Were Men.* New York: Alfred A. Knopf, 1942.

Buell, Hulda May Giesy. "The Giesy Family." *Pacific County Rural Library District,* memoir. Raymond, WA, 1953.

———. "The Giesy Family Cemetery." *The Sou'wester.* Pacific County Historical Society, vol. 21, no. 2, 1986.

Bush, L.L. "Oystering on Willapa Bay." *Willapa Harbor Pilot.* South Bend, WA, 1906.

Cross, Mary Bywater. *Treasures in the Trunk: Memories, Dreams, and Accomplishments of the Pioneer Women Who Traveled the Oregon Trail.* Nashville: Rutledge Hill Press, 1993.

Curtis, Joan, Alice Watson, and Bette Bradley, eds. *Town on the Sound, Stories of Steilacoom.* Steilacoom, WA: Steilacoom Historical Museum Association, 1988.

De Lespinasse, Cobie. *Second Eden. A Novel Based upon the Early Settlement of Oregon.* Boston. The Christopher Publishing House, 1951.

Dietrich, William. *Natural Grace: The Charm, Wonder and Lessons of Pacific Northwest Animals and Plants.* Seattle: University of Washington Press, 2003.

Dole, Philip. "Aurora Colony Architecture: Building in a Nineteenth-Century Cooperative Society." *Oregon Historical Quarterly,* vol. 92, no. 4, 1992.

Dole, Philip, and Judith Reese. "Aurora Colony Historic Resources Inventory." Unpublished manuscript funded by Oregon State Historic Preservation Office, in private collection at Aurora Colony Historical Museum.

Duke, David Nelson. "A Profile of Religion in the Bethel-Aurora Colonies." *Oregon Historical Quarterly,* vol. 92, no. 4, 1992.

Ficken, Robert E. *Washington Territory.* Pullman, WA: Washington State University Press, 2002.

Gordon, David G., Nancy Blanton, and Terry Nosho. *Heaven on the Half Shell, The Story of the Northwest's Love Affair with the Oyster.* Portland, OR: Washington Sea Grant Program and WestWinds Press, 2001.

Hendricks, Robert J. *Bethel and Aurora: An Experiment in Communism as Practical Christianity.* New York: The Press of the Pioneers, 1933.

Keil, William. "The Letters of Dr. William Keil." *The Sou'wester.* Pacific County Historical Society, vol. 28, no. 4, 1993.

Knapke, Luke B., ed. *Liwwät Böke: 1807–1882 Pioneer.* Minster, OH: The Minster Historical Society, 1987.

Lloyd, Nancy. *Willapa Bay and the Oysters.* Oysterville, WA: Oysterville Hand Print, 1999.

McDonald, Lucile. *Coast Country: A History of Southwest Washington.* Long View, WA: Midway Printery, 1989.

Nash, Tom, and Twilo Scofield. *The Well-Traveled Casket.* Eugene, OR: Meadowlark, 1999.

Nordhoff, Charles. *The Communistic Societies of the United States.* New York: Hillary House, 1960.

Olsen, Deborah M. "The *Schellenbaum:* A Communal Society's Symbol of Allegiance." *Oregon Historical Quarterly,* vol. 92, no. 4, 1992.

Simon, John E. "William Keil and Communist Colonies," *Oregon Historical Quarterly,* vol. 36, no. 2, 1935.

Snyder, Eugene Edmund. *Aurora, Their Last Utopia, Oregon's Christian Commune, 1856-1883.* Portland, OR: Binford and Mort, 1993.

Staehli, Alfred. *Old Aurora Colony Museum Architectural Conservation Assessment,* pt. 3. Aurora, OR: Kraus House, 2000.

Stanton, Coralie C. "The Aurora Colony Oregon." Thesis, Oregon State University, 1963, in the collection of Aurora Colony Historical Museum.

Strong, Charles Nelson. *Cathlamet on the Columbia.* Portland, OR: Holly Press, 1906.

Swan, James G. *The Northwest Coast or Three Years' Residence in Washington Territory.* New York: Harper and Brothers, 1857.

Swanson, Kimberly. " 'The Young People Became Restless': Marriage Patterns Before and After Dissolution of the Aurora Colony." *Oregon Historical Quarterly,* vol. 92, no. 4, 1992.

Weathers, Larry, ed. *The Sou'wester.* South Bend, WA: Pacific County Historical Society, 1967, 1970, 1972, 1974, 1979, 1986, 1989, 1993.

Will, Clark Moor. "An Omnivorous Collector Discovers Aurora!" *Marion County History, School Days I, 1971–1982,* vol. 13, Marion County Historical Society, 1979.

———. *The Sou'wester.* Several letters between descendant Will and Ruth Dixon. Raymond, WA: Pacific County Historical Society collection, May 29, 1967.

GLOSSARY OF GERMAN WORDS

Ach!	Oh no!
Ach, jammer!	an expression of frustration
auf Wiedersehen, or informally, *tschuess*	good-bye
Belsnickel	a traditional Christmas persona bringing gifts
Dreck	dirt or excrement
Dummkopf	dummy or stupid
Elend	misery
Frau	Mrs.
Fräulein	Miss
Fraktur	unique printing designs; a German calligraphy
gross Haus	large house
gut	good
Hasenpfeffer	rabbit or hare
Herr	Mr.
ja	yes, pronounced "ya"
Junge	boy
Kind	child
Kinder	children
Komm und is.	Come and dine.
Liebchen	darling or sweetheart
nein	no
Oma	grandmother

Opa	grandfather
Sehnsucht	a yearning or longing (of the human spirit) for something of meaning
Schellenbaum	A bell-like instrument known in English as the Turkish Crescent. Popular in the eighteenth and early nineteenth centuries, the large instrument combined music with a symbol of authority or standard of allegiance.
Scherenschnitte	German folk art; cutout paper pieces are glued together to create objects such as trees, flowers, animals, or decorative elements for certificates.
Spätzel	egg noodles
Tannenbaum	tree, especially at Christmastime